W9-AJQ-593

a FACE to DIE FOR

ALSO BY ANDREA KANE

FORENSIC INSTINCTS NOVELS:

THE GIRL WHO DISAPPEARED TWICE
THE LINE BETWEEN HERE AND GONE
THE STRANGER YOU KNOW
THE SILENCE THAT SPEAKS
THE MURDER THAT NEVER WAS

OTHER SUSPENSE THRILLERS:

RUN FOR YOUR LIFE
NO WAY OUT
SCENT OF DANGER
I'LL BE WATCHING YOU
WRONG PLACE, WRONG TIME
DARK ROOM
TWISTED
DRAWN IN BLOOD

ANDREA KANE

a FACE to DIE FOR

3 1489 00719 3251

ISBN-13: 978-1-68232-014-3

A FACE TO DIE FOR

Copyright © 2017 by Rainbow Connection Enterprises, Inc.

All right reserved. Except for use in any review, the reproduction or uti-
lization of this work in whole or in part in any form by any electronic,
mechanical or other means, now known or hereafter invented, including
xerography, photocopying and recording, or in any information storage
or retrieval system, is prohibited without prior written permission of the
publisher, Bonnie Meadow Publishing LLC, 16 Mount Bethel Road #777,
Warren, NJ 07059, USA.

This is a work of fiction. Names, characters, places and incidents are either the product of the author's imagination or are used fictitiously, and
any resemblance to actual persons, living or dead, business establishments,
events or locales is entirely coincidental.

For questions and comments about the quality of this book, please contact
us at CustomerService@bonniemeadowpublishing.com.

www.BonnieMeadowPublishing.com

Printed in USA

Publisher's Cataloging-in-Publication

Kane, Andrea, author.
  A face to die for / Andrea Kane.
  pages cm -- (A Forensic Instincts novel)
  LCCN 2017900386
  ISBN 978-1-68232-010-5
  ISBN 978-1-68232-014-3
  ISBN 978-1-68232-011-2
  ISBN 978-1-68232-012-9

  1. Doppelgängers--Fiction. 2. Mafia--United States--
Fiction. 3. Murder--Investigation--Fiction.
4. Thrillers (Fiction) 5. Detective and mystery fiction.
I. Title. II. Series: Kane, Andrea. Forensic Instincts
novel.

PS3561.A463F33 2017   813'.54
                QBI17-900043

To L.P., with heartfelt gratitude

PROLOGUE

Bay Ridge, Brooklyn, New York
March 1990

Anthony slid behind the wheel of his Ford Taurus and started it up, cranking up the heat the instant the engine turned over. It was friggin' freezing outside. Even in the five minutes it had taken him to walk the babysitter to her front door, the temperature outside felt like it had dropped ten degrees, and his car was an icebox.

Shivering, he zipped his parka up as far as it would go and gripped the steering wheel, maneuvering the car away from the curb. He'd finally shared an evening out with his wife. It should have eased the knot in his gut. After all, it had been the first time that he and Carla had left their infants with a sitter since the babies had been born a month ago. And Judy was the perfect babysitter—a good girl from a good family, one who studied rather than doing drugs and screwing horny guys.

Still, dinner had been strained.

Anthony had only picked at his manicotti, his favorite dish at Raimo's. His mind was far away, and acid kept building up in his stomach.

Carla couldn't stop worrying and talking about the babies. She'd checked her watch a dozen times, intermittently giving Anthony puzzled looks and asking if he was okay.

Each time she asked, he'd assure her that he was fine, just exhausted from work and midnight feedings.

As if to contradict his words, some new waiter had dropped a tray of dishes on the floor, and Anthony had nearly jumped out of his skin at the crash.

Carla rose, asking him to order her another drink and to get one for himself to calm his nerves. Giving in to her new-mother concerns, she went to the pay phone in the back to call Judy for an update. So far, so good, Judy had reported. But that didn't totally erase Carla's fretting. She tried her best to be bright and chatty, but the truth was that, as this point, she was ready to go. She'd fiddled with her napkin and sipped at her drink, making small talk and glancing at the door.

Getting the hell out of there had worked for Anthony. He was more than ready to be home with his family and not out in the open. He'd use his fatigue as an excuse. He had to continue keeping the inevitable from Carla, until he had no choice but to tell her. He'd soften the blow as best he could. But the important thing was that his family would be protected at all costs.

Now, the heat in his car roared to life, warming his body but doing nothing to extinguish his inner chill. He knew the rules. No transgression went unpunished.

Why the hell had he been so preoccupied with new fatherhood that he'd forgotten to make his collections from the designated list of construction foremen these past two weeks? That in itself was a huge black mark against him—one he'd be punished for. But the outcome of his stupidity opened the door to a far more lethal punishment. Someone else had been sent to handle his route, and his money. They would have collected and turned over twice the amount he'd been handing over. And that meant he'd better be able to explain the discrepancy—assuming he'd even be asked before he was killed.

Please God, let him have that chance. He was just on the verge of buying that gas station he'd been single-mindedly building his bank account for, just about to provide for his family's future.

And now this.

With shaking hands, Anthony switched on the radio, gritting his teeth as Madonna's voice blasted off the windows, followed by Michael Jackson's. He turned the dial until finally the soothing tones of Frank Sinatra's voice filled the car. Sinatra. Perfect. The Chairman of the Board's crooning was just the right medicine to ease his clawing anxiety.

He reached his street and turned down the line of small brick row houses, all identical in their flat lines, gated fronts, and tiny gardens. There was a certain comfort and peace about the sameness of it all; it made it feel like a neighborhood.

Would he ever feel that sense of comfort and peace again?

He pulled into his narrow driveway and spotted Carla standing at the front door with a broad smile, giving him a thumbs-up. That meant the infants had come through their first babysitting experience with flying colors.

He forced himself to smile back, but even as he did, his gaze swept the area around the house to see if he was alone. It appeared so. Quickly, he turned off the car and then made the frigid dash to his house.

He couldn't shut and lock the door behind him fast enough.

The soothing warmth from the heating system enveloped him when he stepped inside. Comfort in yet another form. He was home. Carla and the babies were safe. And for the moment, so was he.

With a wave of relief—however temporary—he let the tension in his body ease. He shrugged out of his jacket and hung it on the coatrack.

"You look happy," he teased Carla. "What's the final report?"

Carla's eyes twinkled. "They were perfect. Judy said they'd only woken up once for their bottles and a diaper change. Now they're sleeping like little angels."

"Good." Anthony looped an arm around his wife's shoulders and led her toward the living room. "How about a nightcap before bed—to celebrate the success of our first night out?"

"That sounds wonderful." Carla walked beside him, making a left into their comfortable living room.

They'd barely taken half a dozen steps when a tall masked man dressed in black rose from behind the large armchair, his .22 caliber pistol raised.

"Hello, Anthony."

Anthony knew that voice only too well, and it elicited the chilling knowledge that there was no way out. No threats. Just death. "Welcome home."

The man's finger tightened around the trigger.

"*No!*" Carla screamed.

She threw herself in front of her husband just as the pistol fired.

The bullet pierced her skull, and with a shattering cry, she crumpled to the floor.

"*Carla... no... Carla!*" Anthony shouted. He dropped to his knees beside his wife's lifeless body, grabbing her into his arms and openly weeping. "God forgive me. Oh, God forgive me."

He looked up in dazed anguish, just as a second shot was fired.

The bullet struck Anthony between the eyes. His head jerked backward, and he fell over his wife, dead.

Upstairs, the babies started to cry.

The gunman shoved his pistol back in his waistband. He knew the mob code like he knew his own name. No women. No children. *Omertà.*

A woman lay dead before him, the taunting evidence of a fuckup.

He took the steps two at a time.

Tucked in their cribs, the babies were still crying as their parents' killer entered the nursery and hovered over them.

Not even the nightlight could eradicate the darkness.

CHAPTER 1

Casey Woods' apartment, fourth floor Forensic Instincts brownstone
Tribeca, New York City
May 2017

The sun had long since made its bright yellow ascent, and the city streets were filled with commuters making their way to work. On the sidewalks, people hurried along, some in business attire talking on their cell phones, and some in athletic gear, striding to the beat of the music they were listening to on their iPhones.

Downstairs, in the professional hub of the brownstone, Forensic Instincts was gearing up for another busy day.

One by one, the team arrived, punching the key code into the Hirsch pad that allowed them entry. Inside, they each went to their work space, gathered up the necessary materials, and headed to the first-floor meeting room—the small, cozy space reserved for first-time interviews and subsequent meetings that required putting their clients at ease.

FBI Supervisory Special Agent Kyle "Hutch" Hutchinson heard the lower-level activity loud and clear.

He shifted onto his side in Casey's bed, wishing the workday would take a hiatus. But he also knew Casey would kill him if she were late to an appointment—*any* appointment, but most specifically a new-client interview.

"Sweetheart, it's time to wake up," he said.

His voice ruffled Casey's mane of red hair, now tousled and spread out across the pillows.

She mumbled an unintelligible protest and snuggled back under the covers.

A corner of Hutch's mouth lifted. "Come on, Case." He gave her a gentle shake.

Casey swatted his hand away. He'd kept her awake half the night, and her muscles were feeling it. "Tired," she murmured. "Need sleep."

A sated chuckle. "I'm sure you do. But I have to get to the FBI field office, and you have a new client meeting in forty-five minutes."

That did the trick.

Casey's eyes snapped open and she practically leapt out of bed. "Dammit," she said. "What happened to the alarm?"

Propping himself on one elbow, Hutch gave her his slow, sexy grin. "I might have accidentally turned it off."

Casey picked up a pillow and tossed it at him. "Just because you have an internal clock like the atomic clock at NIST doesn't mean we all do."

"Mine worked for both of us. I woke you when you needed to get going. Just one more perk of sleeping with me."

Casey's lips were twitching as she headed toward the bathroom. "You gave me enough perks last night. But for God's sake, Hutch, I'm the president of Forensic Instincts. We're interviewing a potential client. I need to set an example. Besides, I'm never late." She turned and gave him a warning look. "Don't even think of following me into the shower."

"I wouldn't dare." Hutch admired her nakedness until she'd disappeared from view. "But I will take a rain check," he called after her. "In the meantime, Hero needs a walk." Rising and pulling on his sweats and sneakers, Hutch made eye contact with the handsome red bloodhound who'd raised his head the minute he heard his name. "Come on, boy," Hutch said, giving him a hand signal—a signal that the former FBI human scent evidence dog instantly obeyed. "We've got time for a short walk, a quick breakfast, and then it's off to work for us both. You and Casey have to join the team downstairs, and I've got to shower and haul ass to Federal Plaza."

With a sharp bark of understanding, Hero snapped into active mode. He followed Hutch out of the bedroom and the apartment, hurrying down the three flights of stairs to the front door.

"Ah. You spent the night," Ryan McKay, the team's techno-genius, called out. "That explains our fearless leader's tardiness."

"It's eight twenty-two, your meeting's at nine, and fuck off," Hutch said good-naturedly. He clipped Hero's leash onto his collar. "Hero needs to take care of business. See you in a few."

Hutch rolled his eyes as he and Hero pounded the pavement. Ryan—who was the antithesis of every stereotype assigned to an IT-guy—was already preparing to needle Casey about this. Well, Casey would put him in his place in a New York minute. Poor Ryan still had trouble realizing that, no matter how tight a family they all were, Casey was Forensic Instincts' leader.

Fifteen minutes later, Hutch and Hero returned to the upstairs apartment. Casey was already showered, dressed in a light blue silk blouse and white slacks, and munching on a protein bar as she scanned her notes.

"Hi," she said, glancing up. "I've got to get downstairs. Can you feed Hero?"

Hutch nodded. "I'm willing to pay penance for turning off the alarm. I'll make Hero's food, shower while he's eating, and then deliver him to the first-floor conference room."

"Thanks. Just text me when you're coming down. One of us will step out and get him."

"Right. Client confidentiality. Got it." Hutch walked over, tilted Casey's chin up with his forefinger, and gave her a quick kiss. "I'll call you."

"You'd better." She smiled, turning and descending the steps. "Have a good day."

"Yeah, you, too. Oh, and be ready to cut Ryan off at the knees. He's in top form today."

"Thanks for the warning."

* * *

The FI team was gathered around the meeting room, sipping their coffee and chatting. The entire room was warm and inviting, from the soft cream walls to the clusters of buttery leather caramel tub chairs and matching sofas. The sideboard— with its JURA Professional coffee station and built-in fridge and wine cooler—was a rich cherry wood, as was its matching coffee table.

Casey walked in with a wave of her hand and headed for her usual tub chair, positioned directly across from the doorway, where she could watch the client from entry to departure and interpret his or her body language throughout the meeting.

"Good morning, Casey," greeted a computerized voice that seemed to emanate from every part of the room. "I've programmed the appropriate video and audio configuration for your meeting. It's available in the usual way."

"Thank you, Yoda." Even though Casey was still in awe of Ryan's omniscient artificial intelligence system, she'd actively started thinking of it as a team member—one who was almost as human as the rest of them.

"Will there be anything else?" Yoda inquired as Casey put her folder and iPad Pro on the side table to the right of her chair. "Otherwise, I'll be on standby."

"Standby is fine, Yoda." Casey went over to make herself a cup of coffee. "Hey, guys," she said, returning to her chair. "We've got a few minutes to discuss the prospective client, and a few minutes to redistribute responsibilities, given our reduced staff."

Casey was referring to the fact that her right-hand man, Marc Devereaux, former Navy SEAL and former FBI Behavioral Analysis Unit agent, was on his honeymoon. And Patrick Lynch, retired FBI special agent and security specialist was with his wife, Adele, at their daughter's college graduation in Virginia.

So the team was down to five, counting Hero.

"Both Marc and Patrick have said they're available if necessary," Casey continued. "But it won't be necessary. We'll handle whatever's thrown at us. They deserve this time away."

"Given their reasons for being away, I'd opt for Marc's scenario any day of the week," Ryan said, leaning back in his chair and interlacing his fingers behind his head. "Two weeks in Aruba trumps two weeks in Virginia and DC. Not that I believe for a minute that Marc and Madeline are spending much time on the beach." One dark eyebrow rose. "Which reminds me, boss…"

"Don't even think of going there." Casey shot him down before he'd even gotten started. "You won't like my reaction."

"Gotcha." Ryan had the good sense to look sheepish. That was rarely the case. His ego matched his genius, at least when it came to his strategic skills and hacking abilities. But the rest? He gave little credence to his magnetic Black Irish looks and well-muscled body, the former being a happenstance of birth and the latter being a product of his gym rat tendencies. And frankly, though he had a healthy sexual appetite, women who stared longingly at him and looked ready to jump his bones irked the shit out of him.

He preferred a challenge.

At that thought, his gaze shifted to the willowy blonde sitting two chairs away. Talk about polar opposites. Claire Hedgleigh, or Claire-voyant as Ryan called her just to piss her off, was his one-eighty. He was all about facts and strategic thinking. She was all about auras and insights and whatever the hell claircognizants or psychics—or whatever you called them—used as their core database. He couldn't argue with Claire's success ratio, not that that made him a believer. What he also couldn't argue with was the way she fired him up—on all fronts—in a way that no one ever had. It was more than a little unsettling.

The object of his thoughts spoke up. "If what Brianna Mullen said on the phone is true, then this is a dangerous, predatory situation." Claire tucked a wisp of blonde hair behind her ear, looking at Casey and opening the dialogue about their potential client. "I realize that stalking is far from uncommon, but what she's describing is dark and obsessive, with the potential for physical harm."

Casey nodded. "Let's just remember that we don't have all the facts yet. Brianna gave us only pieces of information."

"That's because she was hysterical."

"I know. But she didn't even give us the name of her stalker. Does she know him? It sure sounded like she did. Is he an ex? A grad school classmate? Or is he a stranger? I want to hear her full story in person." Casey took a sip of coffee. "That's the only way we can make a judgement about whether or not she's reading the situation clearly, and how serious the risks are."

"Can I stay for the whole meeting?" Emma Stirling interrupted.

As always, Emma's enthusiasm made Casey smile. At twenty-two, Emma was the team's newest and youngest member. But what she lacked in years, she made up for in life experience. She'd been orphaned when she was young and had been in and out of foster care for years, often living on the streets. She'd survived because she'd used her cunning mind—together with the fact that she looked like an innocent Alice in Wonderland—to hone her pickpocketing skills until she rivaled the Artful Dodger.

That life had grown old.

She'd joined FI, reformed and eager, and her street smarts had already proved her an invaluable team member. Not to mention, she had guts. She'd been instrumental in solving FI's last case, putting her own life at risk to do it.

Emma had more than proven her loyalty. She'd joined FI as the receptionist. But she'd turned into so much more.

"Of course you're staying," Casey replied. "Just do your thing out front when the doorbell rings, and then join Ms. Mullen when you show her in."

"Cool." Emma grinned, immensely pleased with Casey's response. "As long as I'm part of the investigative team, I don't mind getting coffee, managing schedules, and answering telephones and doors."

"Nice to know, since that's what you were hired to do," Ryan said with teasing sarcasm. He had a lot of respect for Emma. The kid was a firecracker.

"I got a promotion, remember?" she shot back.

"Would you let us forget?" Now Claire was laughing.

Casey met Emma's gaze. "Correction: you didn't *get* a promotion. You *earned* one. We're proud of you. Now do as good a job on this case as you did on the last one—without scaring us to death this time."

"Will do," Emma said, a shadow of memory crossing her face. But just as quickly, it was gone. That nightmare was over. She was healing with time—and the support of her teammates.

Casey glanced around. "We all got electronic copies of Brianna Mullen's deep bio, courtesy of Ryan. Questions?"

Claire, Ryan, and Emma shook their heads.

"This is comprehensive, as always." Casey scanned the documents on her iPad Pro, opening each one using the Box app. She'd already read them through three times. Ryan turned up information that few others could—not unless they knew how and where to look and were willing to go the route of the less-than-legal.

First came the easy stuff.

Brianna Mullen.

Age: twenty-seven.

Height: five-foot-seven.

Weight: one hundred thirty pounds.

Race: African-American.

Background: grew up on Manhattan's Upper West Side.

Current living arrangements: a studio apartment on Waverly Place near Washington Square Park. (Note: For past three days, has been staying with Lina Brando, her best friend, at her one-bedroom apartment on West Eighth Street.)

Occupation: full-time graduate student at NYU Stern Business School, studying for her MBA in marketing. GPA: 4.0.

Current Employment: During school year, works twenty hours a week at the Starbucks on Fourth Street, about a block away from Stern Business School. Currently (summer months), working full-time at Zolmer Advertising, Inc. (See next section: prior employment).

Prior employment: 2011-2016 (full-time)—Zolmer Advertising, Inc., Madison Avenue, New York. Jobs held: Media Associate, (2013-2016), Junior Media Associate, (2011-2013), focusing on clients' digital, mobile, and social media marketing programs.

Then after a list of Brianna's online and social accounts came the more probing stuff.

Personal life: Dated infrequently and discerningly. Studied religiously. Had a small nucleus of close friends (list appended as Schedule A), all of whom helped her start an anonymous GoFundMe page for female stalking victims. A portion of the donations helped her pay Forensic Instincts' fee. No arrests. No drinking. No drugs. No falling-out with family. Mother a pediatrician; father an investment banker—both affluent enough and willing enough to pay for Brianna's tuition and a good chunk of her living costs. The rest, Brianna paid, including all personal expenses.

Actions taken re stalking threat: three visits to the NYPD Sixth Precinct to report incidents. None of the attempts yielded any results other than three filed complaints.

"She's scared enough to be staying with her best friend, rather than at her own place," Casey noted aloud. "Also, given the support she's getting on her GoFundMe page, it's clear that, while the police might not believe her, her friends do. That speaks to her character and her social circle. Or, if the stalker is someone they know, his lack of character. Or both."

Claire nodded. "She seems to be a fine young woman, a hard worker with a supportive bunch of friends and family, and no known vices or offenses."

"No unknown ones, either," Ryan responded with an emphatic glare. "Deep bio means deep bio. If she'd gotten drunk and thrown up even once, that data would be in those searches."

"Of course it would." Claire rolled her eyes. "My apologies, Mr. Peabody."

Ryan's glare disappeared, replaced by a huge grin. "The ultimate genius straight from *Rocky and Bullwinkle*. Great analogy. Thanks for the compliment."

"I didn't mean it as one."

"True. In that case, the idea of accepting your apology hangs in the balance."

"My heart breaks."

Casey was about to intervene, when the thermal and proximity sensors registered a heat source at the front door.

"Ms. Brianna Mullen has arrived," Yoda announced. "Body temperature elevated. Respiration rate high. No weapons detected."

"I'm on my way, Yoda." Emma sprang to her feet and hurried down the hall.

She returned a minute later with their client at her side and Hero at her heels.

CHAPTER 2

Brianna Mullen was a striking young woman with high cheekbones, a long mane of curly black hair, and wide dark eyes. Beneath those dark eyes were even darker circles, and inside their depths was sheer terror.

So much for her misreading the threat. This girl was genuinely traumatized.

"Hi, Ms. Mullen—or may I call you Brianna?" Casey rose and extended her hand. "I'm Casey Woods, president of Forensic Instincts."

"Yes, call me Brianna," the girl said in a quiet voice, shaking Casey's proffered hand. "It's such a relief to meet you."

Casey introduced the rest of the team and then gestured toward the chair they reserved for clients. "Have a seat. Can we get you anything—coffee, tea, water?"

"No thank you." Brianna sat down. She crossed her legs—rigidly, so as to still their trembling—and placed tightly interlaced fingers in her lap.

Leaning forward before retaking her seat, Casey handed Brianna some paperwork. "That's our contract. Please take your time and review it before you sign."

As if on autopilot, Brianna took the papers, barely scanning them before placing them on the floor beside her purse. "They're fine. Do I pay you now?"

"First, let's talk. Do we have your permission to videotape this meeting? If we don't come to a mutual agreement today, we'll delete the recording and it will be wiped from our database."

Alarm flashed across Brianna's face. "You *have to* take my case. I have nowhere else to go. Please," she begged. "I'm being stalked by a psycho who's taking steps toward hurting me—or worse. I'm not paranoid," she added, gazing around the room with the realization that she sounded as if she were exactly that. "I don't have many hard facts. But I do have *some*—along with strong feelings and instincts." She turned her gaze to Claire. "I heard that you're a psychic. That has to mean that you trust in things you just *know* but can't prove. I'm appealing to that now. Please don't turn me down."

A flash of compassion crossed Claire's face. She hated that Forensic Instincts had become so successful that they'd captured the media's attention. Less anonymity. More revelations. Much had been made about her claircognizance—the metaphysical sense of clear knowing—although she'd stayed as far out of the limelight as possible. Still, her gift was publicized enough for potential clients to be aware of it and to seize the feeling of hope it provided.

That part sucked. But right now her every instinct was screaming that Brianna's fears were as real as her desperation. And Claire just couldn't ignore that.

"I'm open to what you have to say," she finally replied, balancing her answer so as to calm Brianna without sealing the deal on their services. "I can see how distraught you are."

Brianna was fumbling in her purse, her attention now turned back to Casey. "I have enough money to make an initial payment. Tell me your total fee and I'll take a second job to pay the full amount. I'll take a semester off if I need to. And if I can't pull that off, I'll go to my parents... I didn't tell them anything because I didn't want them to go crazy with worry... But if I have to..."

"Stop." Casey held up her palm. "We're not turning you away. We just want to get all your facts—and your feelings—before we make this a fait accompli. As for our fee, it's negotiable depending on the financial well-being of our client. So put that concern aside. We'll work something out."

Brianna visibly relaxed. "Thank you. And, yes, you're free to videotape our meeting."

"Good. Yoda?" Casey summoned him.

"Yes, Casey," the computerized voice responded. "Shall I turn on the video-recording devices now?"

"Please."

Brianna was looking around, as startled as all their clients were when they first "met" Yoda.

"Our virtual team member," Casey explained briefly. "Now let's get started."

"Okay." Brianna sucked in her breath. "As I told you on the phone, I'm a grad student at Stern. I just completed my first year. The professor who taught my marketing class this spring was Dr. Thomas Hanover." She visibly shuddered at the mention of his name. "A little over a month before the semester ended, he started making sexual advances toward me—first subtle, then overt."

"Can you be more specific about subtle versus overt?" Casey asked.

A nod. "He'd brush up against me or lean over my shoulder to look at my computer screen while his gaze was pinned to my breasts. It made my skin crawl. But I kept telling myself I was imagining it."

Brianna stopped to swallow back tears. "Then one day he asked me to come see him about my work during office hours. I made sure it was daytime and that the building was full. Not that it mattered. He didn't touch me at all. He didn't even blackmail me with a bad grade. He simply said he wanted me and that he knew the feelings were mutual. He flat out stated that we should act on those feelings, immediately but discreetly—not only to protect his job but his family. He has a wife and two young kids. His eyes were flat and empty when he told me that. It's like his family was information, not people. I can't explain it. But it was eerie. And as for his plans for me—they weren't a request. They were an order. One that was repeated three times after that."

"He propositioned you four times?" Ryan asked.

"Yes. His office was the first time. Then, twice in empty classrooms, where I was the last to leave and he obviously followed me. And once right outside the ladies' room in an empty corridor. Each time his tone was rougher, and the look in his eyes was scarier than the time before. Especially when I turned him down. The last time his teeth were clenched, and I swear there was a vein pulsing at his forehead. He looked so crazy that I was braced for him to grab me."

"But he didn't," Casey said. "He wanted to keep it at his word versus yours. Any physical assault would have given you tangible evidence to share with the police and probably generate some interest on their part. What happened next?"

Brianna's fingers tightened in her lap. "He stopped asking me to come to his office or 'accidentally' running into me. Instead, he confined things to our classroom, which in some ways was more terrifying. I felt like a trapped animal. He kept making eye contact with me during class—constant, threatening eye contact. He wanted me to know he wouldn't stop. I just didn't know what he planned to do next, or when. But I was afraid. I made sure not to be alone on campus. I walked in crowds, especially at night. I kept to well-lit areas."

She swallowed. "That wasn't enough. Twice I saw him standing on the campus grounds staring at me. He wasn't anywhere near his office or the quad where his classes are held. But he was in the exact path I took every day at that time. He was standing still as a statue, hands in his pockets, fixing his hostile gaze on me. It was no accident."

"No, it wasn't," Casey agreed. "It was purposeful, a communication that he was taking this fixation outside of class."

"That's when I went to the police for the first time."

"And they blew you off," Claire supplied. "An upstanding professor, an overly imaginative student—there was no basis for an investigation."

"Exactly. They took my complaint, then bluntly told me there was nothing they could do for me without evidence of a physical assault." Brianna ran a nervous hand through her hair. "The next time I saw him was outside the Starbucks where I work when school's in session. I was making drinks. I looked up and he was standing right outside the front windows, his gaze on me. Only me. He was waiting for me to look up and see him. When I did, he gave me an evil smile and then walked away."

"He was escalating," Casey said. "First, his advances were confined—from the classroom to his office to school corridors. Then, his advances turned stalker-ish—outside the school buildings, yet still on the grounds. And finally, he abandoned the confines of the school entirely and stalked you at your workplace."

"Three times," Brianna clarified. "The first two were at Starbucks. The last was after classes had ended and I was at Zolmer Advertising—that's my summer job."

"Shit," Ryan muttered. "He went all the way over to Madison Avenue to watch you? This guy is on a mission."

"It didn't stop there," Brianna said. "I started feeling as if I were being followed, not only to and from work but everywhere. The feeling was real. I know it. Several times, I thought I caught a glimpse of him in the crowd, but then he'd vanish. The scariest moment was when I spotted him outside my apartment building. I know it was him. But I couldn't convince the police."

"That's when you filed the second police report," Casey clarified.

"Yes. And it was just as pointless." Tears slid down Brianna's cheeks. "These last two weeks have been the worst. I started getting hang-up calls on my cell phone. The numbers are blocked, and when I answer, I hear raspy breathing on the other end, followed by a click. No voice. No message. Nothing. But on the days of the calls, I get a little gift left at my door, no note, no return address."

"What kind of gifts?" Claire asked.

"The kind that only someone who knows me well could send. A snow globe of the English countryside—I visited England twice and fell in love with the beauty of its shires. A hook rug kit with a ferret at the center—I love ferrets and have one for a pet. I also love rug-hooking. It relaxes me. And a book of poetry by Emily Dickinson, my favorite poet."

Brianna dashed away her tears. "That pushed me over the edge. I packed some things, left my apartment, and moved in with my best friend, Lina. She was with me the night I *know* he was standing outside my apartment. And she went with me when I filed my third police report, right after the book came. The officers were nice. But I still couldn't give them any real evidence. No threats had been made. No notes had been left with the gifts."

"I doubt the police were blowing you off," Casey said. "They simply don't have the manpower to investigate these situations."

"Maybe, but I don't think they were really concerned or taking it all that seriously. They gently suggested that the offender might be a determined ex-boyfriend." Brianna's chin came up. "But I know it's not. And I pray you do, too."

Casey had long since made up her mind. Brianna had had her at the physical description of Dr. Hanover's flat, empty eyes—a psychopath's eyes. Nonetheless, she silently looked at her teammates for their reactions. If there was anything but unanimous agreement, then Brianna would have to wait in the reception area while the differences were hammered out.

Ryan's and Claire's nods were instant and almost indiscernible. Emma's was more emphatic, as she had yet to learn the subtleties of the job.

Regardless, a decision had been reached.

"We believe you." Casey gestured toward the documents, still sitting on the floor alongside Brianna's purse. "Let's sign the papers. Consider yourself our client."

CHAPTER 3

Plaza Hotel
Fifth Avenue
New York City, New York

Gia Russo loved her job, despite the fact that most brides-to-be were crazy.

She'd known what she was letting herself in for when she joined the team at Shimmering Weddings, an exclusive company that catered to the über-rich bride. Gia's clients would have over-the-top demands. But they'd also have super-deep pockets, which meant the sky was the limit. And Gia couldn't resist the opportunity to allow her creativity free reign.

She was a damned good wedding planner, as her growing client list, reputation, and resulting income could attest to. She was requested more than all the other planners at the company combined. And she wasn't good at just the organizing and the multitasking. She excelled at managing her clients—socialites who wanted it all and who wanted it now.

That didn't mean it was easy. Sometimes she was at her wits' end. But the pluses far outweighed the minuses.

This afternoon had been a definite minus.

She'd spent the past two hours in the Plaza's gilded, crystal-chandeliered grand ballroom having a high-maintenance tête-à-tête with Bridezilla Melanie Waverton and her helicopter mother, Leanora. The formidable duo were determined to complete the Cinderella-themed wedding—to be held here in a week—by having the groom, a.k.a. Prince Charming, ride up to the altar on a white horse, while Melanie and her parents would arrive in a pumpkin-shaped, horse-drawn carriage that carried them to meet the bridegroom.

All they imagined was the sheer romance and extravagance of it all.

All Gia imagined—not counting the gazillion health and safety code violations and the hotel's refusal to accommodate them—were the horses breaking free, knocking guests off their chairs, pausing only to defecate on the polished wooden floors.

The magnificently planned wedding would become a freak show.

Biting her tongue, Gia had just strolled with her clients through the Plaza's gilded, crystal-chandeliered ballroom, smiling and using all her skill to convince the ladies that there was a much more memorable and breath-catching way of accomplishing their goal—a way that would keep all eyes on the bride and groom, showcasing them like Hollywood celebrities.

Seeing Melanie's eyes light up, Gia had let her mind fly and her mouth ad lib. The bride and her parents would make their grand entrance escorted by two authentically dressed groomsmen. Prior to their grand appearance, the ring bearer—Melanie's eight-year-old cousin—would walk down the aisle carrying the prearranged royal-purple velvet cushion. Only now, it would brandish a glass replica of the bride's custom-made Louboutin-styled crystal shoes, inside of which would be the gold and diamond wedding bands. He'd present them to the groom in a flourish, and the entire room would ooh and ahh.

As for the groom, Gia would arrange to add dashing, thematic touches to his tuxedo: a gold jacquard sash and, on each shoulder, a regal ornamental shoulder piece called an epaulet. Gold cufflinks would simulate the prince's gold cuffs, all of which would create the imperial look of Prince Charming.

The incomparable total package would result in their domination of social media platforms for weeks.

Goal accomplished.

Gia had wrapped up the meeting by promising her clients that she'd handle all the details and be in touch with them tomorrow. Bidding them good-bye—at least until the next text or phone call—she'd promptly retired to the hotel's Champagne Bar, where she treated herself to a glass of wine and some downtime.

Sipping her Chardonnay, Gia had pointedly ignored the admiring glance of the Brooks Brothers-looking guy at the opposite end of the bar. She was in no mood for a pickup. She felt as if she'd just run a marathon. Three straight days of these last-minute, over-the-top meetings was a lot, even for her. But it was almost June. And, no matter how you sliced it, the romantic wish to be a June bride was still very much alive.

She'd handled just one uncomplicated wedding this past month—surprising, given that it began with a phone call from a frantic bride whose event was less than a month away. But the planning had gone off like clockwork. Plus, it had bound together two gracious, truly-in-love people, Marc and Madeline Devereaux. They'd been a delight to work with. Madeline's mother? Not so much. She'd been the reason for the last-minute SOS. But Gia had gotten her under control. And she'd truly relished being instrumental in making Marc and Madeline's day the joyous one they wanted.

But now she had other, not-so-easy brides to deal with.

Setting down her glass, Gia left the bar and the hotel. She headed down Fifth Avenue, zigzagging her way through the crowd of pedestrians who were either striding professionals, window-shopping consumers, or ambling tourists who seemed oblivious to the fact that they were about to be mowed down by the commuters who were determined to get out of the city before rush hour got worse.

Gia was one of those commuters. She scanned the traffic-crammed street, walking to the curb and simultaneously raising her arm to hail a taxi. She wasn't up for the subway today. Nor for the marathon walk. She'd grab a cab to Grand Central Terminal, where she'd hop a train to her suburban townhouse in Rye.

She'd made eye contact with one driver who began veering his way through pre-rush-hour traffic in her direction, when a breathless female voice beside her said, "Danielle! What are you doing in the Big Apple? Is there some kind of veterinary conference going on? Or do you have another interview at that prestigious animal clinic? And I love your hair! Did you get extensions? Did you have it done here?"

Startled, Gia turned around. The woman was about her age—late twenties—with wispy bangs, a Midwest twang, and smiling eyes. The rest of her was swallowed up by the slew of Bergdorf Goodman bags she carried. She'd obviously done some serious shopping.

"Pardon me?" Gia replied.

"It's me—Sarah." The young woman lowered her bags to the curb, letting Gia see all of her, as if that would reveal her identity. "Sorry. I just took a week's vacation and promised myself all the wonders of the Big Apple, including a spa day, theater tickets, and shopping, shopping, shopping. I fly home on Monday. Do you have time for a drink or dinner, or are you tied up in animal-speak all weekend?"

Gia shook her head in confusion. "I'm so sorry. You have me confused with someone else."

Sarah's brows arched. "Very funny."

"I'm not being funny. I have no idea who Danielle is, but I'm not her." Gia frowned as her taxi pulled away.

"I don't understand." Sarah was peering at her closely, inspecting every feature. "I've known Dani for twelve years. And you're the spitting image of her—except for your hair." A pause. "And your accent. Kind of like a New Yorker, but not."

"New York suburbs by way of Montana." Gia smiled faintly. This Sarah was nice and clearly puzzled by the mistaken identity. But she herself was beat. She wanted to go home, grab some Chinese, and be a couch potato. She had three weddings this weekend—two tomorrow and one on Sunday. She needed to soak in a hot tub and zone out.

"How weird." Sarah pulled out her cell phone and quickly scrolled through some photos. "Here," she said, holding out the phone. "That's Dani and me at our ten-year high school reunion. It was taken just last week."

Politely, Gia took the phone and glanced down at the picture. There were two young women posing at a catering hall, raising their glasses to the camera. Sarah and… Gia's eyes widened as she focused on the other girl, and she almost dropped the phone. Small as the photo was, the smiling girl with short dark hair—rather than her own stylishly highlighted shoulder-length cut—was a dead ringer for her.

"Wow." She held the phone closer, turning it horizontally and stretching the picture to make "Danielle's" face larger and clearer. It was uncanny. The woman even had the same dimple in her right cheek. And the shape of her eyes… the curve of her mouth… The resemblance was startling and kind of creepy.

"No wonder you didn't believe me when I said I wasn't her." Gia couldn't stop staring at the phone. Her curiosity was beyond piqued. "Danielle what? From where? And you said she's a veterinarian?"

"Yes." For a moment, Sarah looked uneasy about giving out information on her friend. Then she seemed to realize the extenuating circumstances, as well as the general nature of Gia's questions. Plus, as a veterinarian, Danielle's photo and bio would be posted on the practice's website. So anonymity wasn't exactly an issue. "It's Danielle Murano, and she's a vet in Minneapolis."

"You're good friends?"

A nod. "We met at a sweet-sixteen party. We've been close ever since—close enough that it's ridiculous for me to mix her up with someone else." She shook her head, utterly baffled. "But you could be twins."

"Yeah . . ." Gia reluctantly handed Sarah back her phone. "My name's Gia Russo," she said, extending her hand to shake Sarah's. It was time to reciprocate the info sharing. Poor Sarah had the right to know the specs on her friend's double—if for no other reason than to laugh about it over drinks. "I'm a wedding planner here in the tri-state area. And you were right about my accent. I didn't always live here. I spent my childhood in Bozeman, Montana."

"A wedding planner?" Sarah looked intrigued as she met Gia's handshake. "That must be quite a job in this area. Oh, and I'm Sarah Rosner."

"Hi, Sarah." Gia grinned. "And if you mean, is my job rewarding but overwhelming, the answer is yes."

Before Sarah could reply, she was jostled by two women in business suits, who blew by her and nearly knocked her down. She regained her balance, gazing ruefully after them. "I'm not used to this. Minneapolis is hectic, but nothing like New York. Plus, I kind of think we've outworn our Fifth Avenue welcome."

Gia nodded. "Yeah, no surprise."

"You look exhausted, or I'd suggest we grab a drink."

"Normally, I'd love to." Gia was frank. "But it's a Friday in May. I have two weddings tomorrow and a wedding on Sunday, not to mention a dozen texts to answer and a venue to scout out in between. All the brides are, understandably, frantic. I really need to get home, do some work, and collapse." She dug in her purse and gave Sarah a business card. "Here's my contact information—just in case your friend wants to laugh over the coincidence."

"Can I take a picture of you?" Sarah asked.

"Sure." Gia waited until Sarah had taken a couple of cell-phone shots. "Now I really have to get going. It was a pleasure to meet you."

"You, too. I'll pass along your info and picture to Dani."

"Good. Take care." Gia turned and headed for the subway station. So much for a taxi. The streets were fast becoming gridlocked.

She could sense Sarah staring after her until the crowd swallowed her up.

CHAPTER 4

It was just before noon the next morning when Casey walked down Waverly Place and passed under the awning that read "Joe's." She stepped inside the coffee shop and inhaled appreciatively. The decor might be as plain as a fast-food restaurant, but the wonderful smells of just-brewed coffee and mouthwatering baked goods drew the patrons' attention where it belonged.

Besides, she wasn't here for the food. She was here for the meeting.

She glanced around, searching for the person who matched the photo Brianna had showed them on her iPhone. Nope. Not here yet. Not really a surprise. Casey was early. And very few students did the early thing. That's why Casey had chosen noon rather than her preferred breakfast meeting, which wouldn't have broken up her workday. But a Saturday morning in academia-land meant sleeping till eleven—and then rolling over and zonking out until three. Casey remembered it well.

She bought a latte and a chocolate croissant and scanned the room. The side to her left was filled with little tables that were one on top of the other, all of them packed with university students. The other side was quieter, with several larger tables set wider apart for those who wanted to work while they ate.

Focusing on that section, Casey was relieved to spot an empty table right up front, next to the radiator and flush up against the glass storefront. Her and Lina's only company would be the guy at the next table, who was pounding away on his keyboard, so absorbed in what he was doing that Casey doubted he knew there was a world around him.

Casey claimed the table before someone else could. She settled herself, placing her carefully wrapped croissant and latte on the wooden tabletop and her handbag on the empty chair beside her.

Reflexively, she checked her cell phone. No missed texts or calls. No important emails, just junk. Which hopefully meant that Lina was on her way.

Sipping her latte, Casey gazed up and down the street. A light stream of pedestrian traffic and an even lighter stream of cars. Brick buildings all in a row. And lots and lots of bicycles, some with riders and many more chained up along the sidewalk.

Somehow—based on Brianna's iPhone photo—Casey didn't visualize Lina as a bike rider. So she kept her scrutiny on the pedestrians. She wanted to spot Lina as soon as she arrived.

Sure enough, at twelve ten, a young woman with straight, shiny, almost-waist-length dark hair hurried to the front door and stepped into Joe's. Casey had time for a quick assessment, which only confirmed what she'd noted in the photo Brianna had shown them. Lina was one put-together girl. She wore expensive, trendy clothes—a black silky rag & bone top and designer AG Jeans—and sunglasses that were worthy of Rodeo Drive. When she pulled them off to scan the coffee shop, Casey could see that her makeup was impeccably applied and that her nails were professionally manicured.

Definitely not a poor girl.

"Lina?" Casey stood, beckoning her over.

Lina walked over to the table. "Hi. You must be Casey."

"I am indeed." Casey shook her hand. "I really appreciate you meeting me. Why don't you get coffee and one of these unbelievable chocolate croissants and then we can talk."

Lina smiled, one of those face-lighting smiles that was pure sunshine. "How did you know my weakness? And they are unbelievable. I'll be right back." She reached into her Louis Vuitton handbag and pulled out a ten-dollar bill, then leaned across the table to drop her bag alongside Casey's.

"Could you watch this for me?" she asked.

"Sure."

"Great, thanks." Lina turned and walked over to the counter.

Casey eyed the handbag. It was the real deal, not a fake. It cost almost two thousand dollars. And the casual way Lina handled it—this girl was used to money. Her family must be loaded. That explained how she could afford a one-bedroom apartment located at the university's doorstep.

A few minutes later, Lina returned to the table carrying a replica of Casey's order.

"I love their lattes," she said, taking her seat. "And as for their croissants, I'd be an elephant if I ate here more often. I limit myself to once a month."

"Smart move." Casey took her first bite. "M-m-m, this is decadent."

"Told you so." Lina bit into her own pastry, then put it down, used a napkin to wipe her fingers, and picked up her latte. "I'm glad Brianna took my advice and came to you. Forensic Instincts has a great reputation. And Brianna is really losing it—not that I blame her. Even I'm getting more and more freaked out by this psycho-stalker, and I'm not his target."

Casey set down her cup. She liked the fact that this girl seemed to cut straight to the chase, no bullshit. "Do you mind if I tape this conversation?" she asked. "It'll make it easier to focus on what you're saying, rather than my being distracted by note-taking." *Not to mention it will give me the ability to watch your face and read your body language.*

"Sure," Lina agreed at once. She waited while Casey scrolled to the right app on her iPhone, placed the phone on the table, and pressed the record icon.

"All set." Casey continued to sip her latte, keeping her body relaxed and her actions casual. No point in freaking out the poor girl. To a novice, these recorded meetings could feel like a police interrogation. "Let's start by keeping our voices low and not using any real names, not while we're in public. Refer to the man in question as Joe. That name is used in here every five seconds, given where we are. So no one will be looking up to see who Joe is and why he's being discussed. As for your friend..." Casey avoided using Brianna's name again. "... she'll be Anne."

"Good point." Lina nodded. "Okay. Tell me what you want to know. *Anne* is my best friend. Anything I can do to help her, I will."

"Loyal friends are hard to come by," Casey replied. "Anne is fortunate to have you. And, please remember, no matter how probing my questions might seem, we're all on the same side. I just need your take on things, partly because it will be less biased than Anne's and partly because I want to know what you saw firsthand rather than what Anne told you."

"Shoot."

First came establishing credibility. That's where Casey's behavioral analysis skills and gut instincts came in. The combination would tell her a lot about Brianna's best friend. Was she as much of a straight shooter as she appeared to be? Or was she an exaggerator? A half-truth teller? An evader? How much could they call upon her during this investigation? Was she reliable? Shrewd? As loyal to Brianna as she appeared to be? And how much face-to-face knowledge did she have or could she acquire?

Time to start the process of finding out.

"You and Anne met in an economics class?" Casey asked.

"The first week of our first semester," Lina replied. "We hit it off right away."

Casey digested that and then went on to get a better insight into what made Lina tick. "I know that Anne went the corporate route in between her BS and her MBA. What about you?"

Lina's grin was rueful. "When I graduated from FIT, I wasn't sure how I wanted to apply my education. I've always had a business head. My mom owns a boutique in SoHo. She suggested I come on as her buyer. That really appealed to me. So I dived right in. Ultimately, I decided I wanted to go into product development and marketing at a luxury brand—you know, like LVMH—so I applied to Stern and got in. I'll be getting my MBA in marketing with a specialization in luxury marketing."

Casey's brows rose. "That sounds impressive."

"I doubt it'll be impressive when I'm working sixteen-hour days," Lina replied dryly. "But hopefully I'll love it enough not to mind."

"That's how it is with me. My career is much more than a job. It's a huge part of who I am. Sometimes it sucks me dry. But it's worth every drop of lost sleep." Casey took another bite of her croissant and a sip of her latte and then returned to the matter at hand. "So you and Anne became fast friends. That's great. And clearly you built trust. Also great. When her problems with *Joe* began, did she immediately confide in you or did she keep it to herself for a while?"

"She didn't wait a second. She ran straight to me from the first time that prick came on to her. She was totally freaked out. I was furious. If it had been up to me, I would have gone to the dean—after I kicked *Joe* in the balls. But I'm a hothead. Anne knew better. We had nothing concrete to report. And that bastard knew it."

"Do you know him personally?"

"I wasn't registered in any of his classes, if that's what you mean. But he's pretty brilliant when it comes to marketing. He sometimes gave extra workshops, which were open to the entire student body. I attended a bunch of those. And he showed up at school functions, so I've seen him outside the classroom, too. I hear that he's teaching a digital marketing course this summer to the part-time MBA students. All in all, I certainly know who he is. Then again, most of the female grad students do."

The disdainful note in Lina's last sentence wasn't lost on Casey. "Are you implying he has a reputation for this kind of behavior?"

"Let's put it this way. His reputation is based only on rumors—but there are way too many of them to be bogus. No woman has actually come forward, probably for the same reasons Anne hasn't. But hey, where there's smoke, there's fire."

"How much fire? Has there ever been any talk about rape?"

"Not that I've heard. Besides, he's too smart to flush his career down the toilet from an accusation like that."

Mentally, Casey had to agree. "Anything consensual?" she asked.

"Again, not from what I've heard. But I doubt a student would publicize her affair with a professor. So who knows?"

"Does he seem to have a type he focuses on?"

Lina shrugged. "Pretty. Guileless. Other than that, he's an equal opportunity perv."

No surprise there. Ryan's research had shown much the same pattern—or lack thereof.

"Okay, give me a rundown on what Anne told you—from the come-ons to the gift deliveries."

The story Lina relayed was totally in line with what Brianna had said—only less emotional. That was exactly the tenor Casey was hoping to establish. Now she could build on it and move on. "Now tell me what things you actually *saw*, not the things Anne told you."

Lina didn't look surprised. She was a bright girl. She knew where this was headed. "I saw the gifts," she replied. "I was with Anne a few of the times she discovered them on her doorstep. I was also with her when she got those creepy phone calls—all breathing and hanging threats, no words spoken. But what you really want to know is, did I see Joe that night outside her apartment building. And the answer is yes."

Casey's brow furrowed. There was a note of absolute certainty in Lina's voice that puzzled her. "You sound as if you're positive the man you saw was Joe. Did you actually see his face? Make out his features?"

"Neither. It was dark. And we weren't close enough to distinguish facial details."

"Then how can you be sure it was Joe?"

Lina looked Casey straight in the eye. "Part of the reason I'm such a good buyer is because I'm a very visual person. Just as I know the lines and styles of clothing, I know the lines of the human body. I can make out body types, stances, and distinct gestures."

Casey processed that. Lina wasn't a behaviorist. This was a reach, one she couldn't blindly buy into.

"Let's say that's possible," she said. "Wouldn't it only work if you've had the opportunity to thoroughly study someone? You just told me you've only seen Joe at a podium in a crowded auditorium, or occasionally around campus."

"Until all this went down with Anne that was true. But since then I've watched him like a hawk. Trust me, I can pick him out in the dark, even from a short distance." Lina counted off on her fingers, supplying Casey with the proof she needed. "He's tall and lean, but he has a bit of a gut. He plants his feet apart but leans slightly to the right. He paces back and forth, and he keeps his left arm folded across his chest. He smokes—which the guy outside Anne's apartment was doing—and he holds his cigarette in his right hand. Everyone who smokes has a specific style—his is taking slow, long drags and then exhaling in an upward stream, almost like a rhythm. And he's very neat about disposing of his cigarette butts. He grinds them under his heel and then picks them up and tosses them in the trash. I guess that, besides being a perv, he's an environmentalist."

Casey did a mental double take. She was surprised and more than a little impressed. This was no spoiled little rich girl. This was one damned smart woman. "Maybe you should come work for us."

Lina laughed. "Doubtful. That's where my talents end. I can't pick up on people's thoughts or their emotions. Just their physical stuff."

"Just the same, you make one hell of a good witness. The information you supplied will really help. I hope we can continue to count on you, especially since Anne is staying at your place."

"Yeah, she and Bandit moved in earlier this week. Anne's a pleasure; Bandit not so much."

Casey felt her lips twitch. "I assume Bandit is the pet ferret."

"Destructo-pet," Lina corrected, rolling her eyes. "He pretends to be cute and cuddly. Meanwhile, he's taken a liking to my Burberry cashmere scarf. It's become his toy of choice. I doubt it'll be part of my winter wardrobe next year."

"Maybe he'll pay for a new one," Casey suggested, mirth dancing in her eyes.

"I wouldn't hold my breath."

With a hearty laugh, Casey rose, extending her hand again and shaking Lina's. "Meeting you was a pleasure. I have your number. I'll be in touch."

Lina met Casey's handshake. "Please do," she said, her expression growing troubled. "I'm sure I'm not saying anything that you and your team haven't already thought of, but the fact that Joe is going to such great lengths to continue stalking Anne is really scary. Bad enough that he did it during the school year when they interacted several times a week. But now? When she's not taking summer classes and she's working on the Upper East Side? This is serious, Casey. Anne is in real danger."

CHAPTER 5

Thank God that Gia's last über-wedding that weekend was a Sunday afternoon wedding at a Westchester County country club in Armonk. That meant the festivities were over by seven rather than midnight, not to mention it was only a twenty-minute drive from the club to her townhouse.

It was a rare event for Gia to be home, in her sweats, and curled up on her living room sofa, eating a Lean Cuisine and watching *Dancing with the Stars* on her DVR, before nine p.m.

This weekend had been a killer. The sound system at Saturday afternoon's wedding had gone on the fritz. The maid of honor in Saturday night's wedding had gone MIA ten minutes before show time. And at today's wedding, the hem of a bridesmaid's dress had gotten caught and mangled in a golf cart.

Gia to the rescue. She'd paged her sound tech, who was on retainer and at the wedding. He'd found the electronic glitch pronto and fixed it minutes before the procession began. Saturday night's maid of honor had been located—and swiftly extricated—by Gia, where she'd been hooking up in the coat closet with the groom's cousin. And Sunday afternoon's dress had required some quick work on Gia's part—a shearing scissors, a tube of Krazy Glue, and a patch of material taken from the gown's underside to cover the visible damage. Then came a quick steam, and the dress looked as good as new. Potential crisis averted.

Gia tackled each disaster with adrenaline-induced intensity. She didn't stop to think, just acted totally on autopilot. She held on to that intensity, carrying it from event to event. And at last, when the final task had been completed—and her final bill had been paid—she could crash.

Tonight was crash night.

She polished off her Lean Cuisine and glass of Pinot Grigio and then treated herself to a whopping bowl of Ben and Jerry's Chunky Monkey ice cream. She deserved it. She'd go to the gym tomorrow morning and work it off, before heading into the office and turning in her reports and checks to Ashlyn Cushing, the owner of Shimmering Weddings. Ashlyn was a tough but fair boss, with a pencil-thin figure and the natural blonde beauty of a California Miss America contestant, despite having just turned forty-five. She made no secret about the fact that she considered Gia to be her star employee—uniquely talented and with a brilliant future ahead of her. She'd even privately hinted about someday giving Gia a small piece of the company.

Gia wasn't foolish enough to tell Ashlyn that she had plans of her own—using this experience to someday open her own wedding planning business.

Someday was a way off. Tonight, she was too exhausted to even think about her dream.

She contemplated taking a hot bath and wondered if she had the strength to walk upstairs to the master bathroom. Ultimately, her body aches won out over her fatigue, and she took her replenished glass of wine and headed up to turn on the faucets. She hadn't paid extra for the Jacuzzi; it had just come with her townhouse model. But, damn, did she thank heaven for it, time and time again.

After stripping off her clothes, she pinned her hair on top of her head, grabbed a bottle of body wash, and paused to place her glass of wine and her cell phone on the bathtub ledge. Pain-in-the-ass cell phone. She wished she were one of those lucky people who could survive without having it as an appendage. She wasn't. It was partly her job and partly her OCD tendencies, but she had to stay connected twenty-four seven.

With a sigh, she climbed into the tub, leaned back, and let the jet sprays do their job. The body wash could wait a few minutes. All she wanted was to soak in her steamy tension-cure. She shut her eyes, cracking them open once in a while to reach for her glass and take a small sip of wine. Otherwise, she just languished, wondering if there was such a thing as a Jacuzzi-potato.

She was about to start the getting-clean process when her phone went *br-r-r-ing*. It wasn't the text *bing* or the email buzz, and it definitely wasn't the repeated vibrating of an incoming call. Every one of Gia's functions had a separate and distinct sound. This musical tone was assigned to Facebook—either a message or a comment.

Normally, Gia would find that an ignorable annoyance. But after a weekend like this one, she could use the diversion. She hadn't been plugged in to social media all weekend long. Time to see what was going on with her Facebook friends and to kick back and catch up on announcements, recipes, and plain old gossip.

She dried her hands on the towel she'd strewn over the side of the tub. Then she picked up the phone, raising her knees and stretching the towel across them as a kind of lap desk to cradle the cell and keep it from dropping into the water—every cell phone fanatic's worst nightmare.

She tapped the Facebook icon. A slew of notifications greeted her, along with the private message that had just signaled its arrival. Curious, she opened it.

Her eyebrows arched when she saw who it was from.

Hi, Gia, Danielle Murano wrote. *I hope you don't mind me contacting you, but when Sarah told me what happened and showed me your photo, I couldn't believe it. I didn't want to do something intrusive like call or email you, or something lame like send you a friend request, so I'm messaging you. Actually, I'm not even sure what to say, except that I couldn't resist reaching out to someone who looked so much like me. Kindred spirits maybe?* ☺ *If you're as intrigued as I am, give me a shout. Dani*

Gia had almost forgotten about her Friday afternoon meet-up with Sarah Rosner and the bizarre coincidence that conversation had yielded. At the time, Gia had considered contacting Danielle Murano herself, but then wedding-planner mania had ensued, and all else had been forgotten. So Danielle—Dani—had beaten her to the punch. It was kind of cool that she'd been so proactive about following up. A do-it-now person. Something Gia could definitely relate to.

She pressed reply and typed:

Hi, Dani. I'm glad you contacted me. If it hadn't been such a crazy weekend, I would have done the same right after I left Sarah. How weird is this whole thing? I think we should friend each other, just for fun, and then keep messaging. I'd love to know more about you; I know you're a veterinarian and that you live in Minneapolis. And you know that I'm a wedding planner and that I live near Manhattan. Let's see what else we have in common besides our looks: tastes, interests, etc. It should be a great diversion for us both. Share as little or as much as you want to. Hope to hear from you soon, Gia.

Gia pressed send.

Offices of Forensic Instincts
Tribeca, New York

Emma was sitting at her desk, her brow furrowed as she tried to absorb everything Ryan was explaining to her. But how could she when her brain was fried *and* on weekend mode? It was ten o'clock on a Sunday night. She should be out with her friends or home watching something cool on Netflix. Instead, here she was, having to process Ryan's plan for her role in solving Brianna Mullen's case.

"Emma, are you listening to me?" Ryan was leaning over her shoulder, looking really pissed. And Emma guessed he had reason to be.

"Sorry," she said, feeling especially guilty because she really did want to help Brianna. "My mind wandered. But, yes, I'm listening."

"Good. Consider this a training ground. You want to be a full FI investigator. I'm teaching you to be one. So look, listen, and learn." He pointed at the intricate map of NYU he'd created. It featured a zoomed-in area of buildings that was the Stern School of Business— classrooms as well as professors' offices, all of which included typed names of the various buildings.

"Oh, God." Emma blanched at the intricacy staring back at her.

"I know it looks overwhelming, but it's not," Ryan replied.

"That's easy for you to say. You're a genius."

"You don't have to be a genius to memorize this. I know NYU is a city unto itself, but the Stern grad school isn't big. There are only eight hundred full-time MBA students covering this small section of buildings near Washington Square. And you're registered for the summer session for part-timers, which means five hundred students, tops. Forget the student housing; you're not living there. Forget the undergrads; you're not going to be one of them. And forget the full-time Stern grad students; they're not allowed to use summer courses toward their degrees. It'll just be a small group in a limited environment. Stick to the area I sectioned off."

Ryan traced that area with his pencil. "Your class will be held here." He circled a building. Then, he shifted his pencil point. "And this is where you'll find Hanover's office." Again, he shifted his pencil, circling a second building, just a short distance from the first. "Second floor. Three doors down to the left of the staircase. That's where I need you to be, several times a day. Check out traffic patterns—times of day when the halls are crowded, when Hanover's in his office, that kind of stuff."

"So I'm just going to stand there like a plant? Repeatedly? No self-respecting pickpocket does that. Someone's going to spot me."

"Uh-uh." Ryan shook his head. "You give the world entirely too much credit. Even Brianna didn't remember exactly how many doors down Hanover's office is when I asked her. She said she just kind of headed down the hall until she found it. People don't notice things. Not unless it's in their faces, which you won't be. You'll wear different clothes each day. Change the way you wear your hair. Stand in a different place in the hallway. No one will be paying attention to their surroundings except you. And you'll have this to back up your efforts."

He held up a pair of what looked to be small diamond studs.

"Earrings?" Emma blinked. Unable to help herself, she reached over and snatched them, "I get diamonds as a bribe? Wow, I..." She paused, studying the stones. "Wait. These are cubic zirconia. Cheap substitutes." She shot Ryan a dirty look. "Are we taking a page out of the Ryan McKay book of seduction? You give women fake diamonds they think are real and they hop into bed with you? Boy, I'm glad this is a business bribe and that I know my real jewels from my fakes."

Ryan was clearly not amused. "They're not a bribe, they're an investigative tool. To do what you get paid for. As for my sex life, that's off-limits to you, brat."

Emma stuck her tongue out at him.

"Now, do you want to stop acting like a two-year-old and listen to me?" he asked.

A grudging nod. "Yeah, go ahead."

Ryan took the studs from Emma, indicating their centers. "I planted mini cameras in each of these. They'll take a video of everything you're seeing. I purposely picked earrings because they're pretty close to eye level and completely inconspicuous. So the visuals between the cameras and your reports will be similar."

"Cool." Emma's interest was, once again, piqued. "Okay, so I'm using these to cruise the halls and get a handle on when the traffic around there is light—and when Hanover is least apt to be in his office. What else?"

"You're a brand-new student and you're pretty. Good combo. Go up to Hanover and request a meeting with him to explain some material you don't understand in his class. I want you inside that office—just once. Your job is to locate items of Hanover's that can be used to make scent pads for Hero."

"And what do we do with those scent pads?"

"For starters, we let Hero tell us if Hanover left those gifts for Brianna. We'll also have him sniff outside her apartment to see if Hanover has recently been there. Most of all, we have him memorize Hanover's scent. Because logic tells us that the psycho's pursuit of Brianna will soon become more tactile."

"You mean he'll stop the gifts and just attack her?" Emma looked horrified.

"It won't get that far," Ryan assured her. "Our security team would intervene in a heartbeat. But if he so much as touches her, he'll leave his scent behind, and Hero will recognize it. Between that and the accompanying report filed by our security guys, there'd be enough to capture the NYPD's attention."

"Okay." Emma still looked a little green, but she nodded. "I'll get into Hanover's office and pick out the right items."

"And if he comes on to you, just sidestep it," Ryan said, intentionally lightening the mood. "That means no kicking him in the balls."

Emma responded with a smile. "Gee, you take all the fun out of things." As she spoke, she glanced back down at Ryan's diagrams and her eyebrows knit. "Ryan, all this is very well planned. But if this is a limited summer school program, how do we know that Hanover is even teaching? He could be taking the summer months off."

"Nope. I checked it out. He's teaching one consumer behavior course and one digital marketing course. The first is on Monday and Wednesday nights and the second is on Saturdays. You'll be registered in the Monday-Wednesday consumer behavior course—sizing people up is your forte. You'd drown in digital marketing. But that doesn't mean you won't be hanging around campus on Saturday mornings. Hanover will be there. And so will you. Go to the library, get something to eat, whatever. Just time it all with Hanover's schedule and his comings and goings. We're covering all bases, trying to predict all his actions—including those that involve stalking Brianna. She may not be taking summer classes, but that clearly hasn't lessened his obsession with her. Plus, he's a sexual predator whose targets are his students. NYU is his hunting ground. He'll be hanging around campus even when he's not teaching."

Groaning, Emma dropped her head onto her folded arms. "The Saturday part's fine. But as for the rest, do I have to remind you that I barely got through high school? No college. No interest in the classroom. No academic experience. And consumer behavior? I was a pickpocket. I sized up those consumers so I could steal from them. So, fine, you'll get me into the class. But I'll be tossed out on day one. I don't know shit."

"Ah, but Kate Lowe does."

"Who the hell is…?" Emma's question died on her lips, and her head came up as Ryan placed some documents on the desk: a driver's license, credit card, college transcript, and student ID—all in the name of Kate Lowe—and all authentic, right down to the photos of Emma on the driver's license and student ID.

"Meet your better half," he said.

Emma picked up each item, studying them and shaking her head. "This is great," she said dryly. "I now have a new name, a college degree, and a 4.0 GPA. Enter Kate Lowe. That's fine. I can pull off any alias, no problem. But what happens the first time I'm asked to participate in something I don't have the first clue about?"

Ryan grinned. "That what earbuds are for. As of today, you'll do some speed-reading—I got you some good equivalents of Cliffs notes so you'll know the basics. The rest I'll feed to you during class on a need-to-speak basis. Not to worry. Like you said, I'm a genius. And whatever I don't know, Casey will. You'll be fine."

"Why do I doubt that?"

"Emma." Ryan was clearly trying to be patient. "You only have to do this for two weeks, tops. That's four classes. Maybe less, depending on how quickly our plan moves. You already missed the first week, so coming off as being a bit lost is to be expected. Just use that sharp con-artist mind of yours to pull this off. Go into Hanover's classroom all enthusiastic about his class and eager to understand more. Play to his ego."

"That part's a piece of cake. I'll be your grad school Barbie and your Bond girl all rolled into one. Not to worry."

"Good. In the meantime, Casey and Claire are coiled and ready to strike. Once you give us the info we need, they'll break into Hanover's office, get their hands on the personal items you've located, and make scent pads for Hero. They'll do it right there in Hanover's office so they can return the items to their proper places without him ever missing them."

Emma grinned. "They're stealing Marc's job. He's our breaking-and-entering guy. He'll be so pissed."

"I doubt that. Not when he's in Aruba with his new wife. Besides, he's the one who taught Casey how to pick a lock. He'll be proud."

"Okay, so in a nutshell, I'm stalking the stalker."

"You got it. The more frequently touched items will yield the best results."

Once again, Emma's brow furrowed. "Knowing you, this is probably a stupid question. You said I'll be registered for the Consumer Behavior course. Have you already enrolled me? Or do I have to do something?"

"You're all set. The admissions office knows that the reason you're coming in late is because you just moved here from San Francisco, after graduating from Stanford." With that, Ryan slapped a few pages in front of her. "Here's your full bio. Know it like the inside of your hand."

"That I can do." Emma glanced at the fact sheets and then slid the pages into her tote bag. "I'll print a few extra copies of this before I go home."

"Good idea. And just so you know, I also put the bio on your laptop and your iPad if you need to access the details without reaching for paper. Just do everything very stealthily."

"Stealth is what pickpockets do best."

"Just one more sheet of hard copy, also installed on your laptop and iPad." Ryan placed a page in front of Emma titled: *Dr. Thomas Hanover*. It had a full-color photo and comprehensive bio. "Here's our target. So you have a basic rundown and visual."

Emma picked up the page and studied it. "Not bad-looking for a middle-aged guy with a dated goatee and creepy eyes." She skimmed the data. "Solid credentials. Too bad they don't list psychopath in the background description."

"They tend to be unaware of those personality traits," Ryan returned dryly.

"Yeah, well, we're not." Emma added the new sheet of paper to the others in her tote bag, thinking about how much memorization and reading she had to do. She'd cram as best she could, be prepared to start in as little as a week. Ryan wasn't the patient type and time was of the essence. Plus, she knew the extreme measures he was taking were, in part, a test of her abilities. Well, she intended to pass that test with flying colors.

"When do I officially begin my charade?" she asked.

"Wednesday."

Emma's jaw dropped. "*This* Wednesday? Are you crazy? That gives me three days to get all my shit together."

"Yup." Ryan reached over to an end table, picked up some books, and plopped them down on Emma's desk, adding to the pile of stuff she'd be taking with her. "Here are your 'Cliffs notes.'"

For the first time, Emma was slapped in the face by the enormity of what she had to do, and a wave of something she rarely felt swept through her—self-doubt. "Ryan," she said quietly. "This is too much. I don't think I can pull it off."

"And I know you can." Ryan didn't look the slightest bit ruffled by her insecurity. "Tonight you'll be a wreck. By three a.m., you'll be giving tentative glances at the material. By breakfast, you'll be reading. And in a couple of days, you'll be your cocky self, armed and ready for battle."

"Ya think?"

"I know." Ryan produced another tote bag and shoved all Emma's goodies inside. "Your ego is as over-the-top as mine. Now go home and do your thing, Kate."

CHAPTER 6

Nine fifteen on Monday morning, Gia blew through the double glass doors of the private office building in White Plains. Her heels clicked on the parquet floor, and she shot a wave at Marsha Comstock, the flawlessly made-up middle-aged receptionist who sat behind the mahogany desk and screened people as they arrived.

Marsha waved back. "Busy weekend?" she asked.

"Three weddings and a hot bath," Gia replied, heading toward the double set of elevators.

A smile curved Marsha's glossy lips. "At least you got the bath."

Grinning, Gia stepped into the elevator and pressed two. She should feel guilty. She should be taking the stairs. But after the vigorous workout she'd just completed at the gym, her entire body was screaming for comfort. So the elevator it was.

She emerged on the second floor, the entirety of which belonged to Shimmering Weddings. The moment a pampered bridal client stepped out of the elevator, she was enveloped in a plush waiting room that Ashlyn herself had designed—one that looked more like the living room of a Victorian mansion than a reception area. Polished oak floors. A warm rose and gold décor. Four club chairs, upholstered in rose brocade, situated in pairs around a gilded coffee table, with end tables flanking them. All curved around a fireplace that remained lit from the onset of the day until the last person left the office.

Directly over the fireplace hung an intricately designed gilded mirror—one that was worthy of Snow White herself—that reflected back the beauty of the room and made it seem twice the size. The walls were the palest of pink, the front desk was the color of rose quartz with rivulets of gold ribboned through it, and vases of fresh flowers were arranged on all the tabletops. Along with the flowers, there were bridal magazines and photo albums of recent Shimmering Weddings events—all there to be viewed while the bride awaited her personal wedding planner.

The pièce de résistance was the gracefully hung gold and crystal chandelier, whose dozens of tiny light bulbs cast a diffused, shimmery glow throughout the room. The employees all joked that the lighting was what had given Shimmering Weddings its name.

"Hi, Gia." Laurel Sweeney's musical voice greeted Gia as she approached the desk. Laurel was a head-turner—an unapologized-for requirement of Ashlyn's for all her employees—with rounded curves, huge blue eyes, and a smile that could melt a Greenland iceberg. She was the ultimate definition of a Southern belle, in her late thirties, with tawny blonde hair arranged on top of her head in a sleek chignon. She graced the front desk, greeting each bride as if she were the only person on earth, and she did it with an honest, natural charm that made her efforts all the more appealing. She had an equally warm and generous heart, and Gia was crazy about her.

"Hey, Laurel." She approached the desk, greeting her colleague with the open, non-business side of her that she carefully meted out. Wedding planning was a cutthroat business, and despite the pleasant comradery the office employees shared, each one was ambitiously battling her way to the top. Gia's high level of success and overt approval by the boss represented the ultimate threat. So, friendly or not, Gia kept a thin wall of self-protection up between herself and the other four wedding planners in the group.

Laurel was different—and not only because she wasn't a competitor but because she was a sweetheart.

"You look stunning, as always," Laurel was saying. Gia was dressed in an ivory and black silk sheath dress and black sling-backs, with small gold hoop earrings and a matching bracelet. She was a firm believer that you had to look successful to be successful.

"Thanks, but it's all a façade." Gia's expression was rueful. "I feel like a squashed tomato." She leaned forward, speaking in a conspiratorial whisper. "I had to unwrap the maid of honor's legs from around the groom's cousin's hips at Saturday night's affair."

"No." Laurel's blue eyes went wide with shock. "Right there at the wedding?"

"In the coat closet. Minutes before the ceremony started. They were doing a full-court press."

"Oh my." Laurel pressed her palms to her face. "I can't imagine how you handled that."

"Not in a friendly manner," Gia replied. "I was ripping pissed. Once they had their clothes back in place, I had seven minutes to fix the maid of honor's gown, hair, you-name-it and get her in the procession line. Not a fun time."

"You're amazing. I would have run to the ladies' room and cried."

"That's because you *are* a lady. This girl was *not*." Gia waved away the memory. "Tell me about your weekend. I'd rather discuss something cheerful."

Laurel laughed. "Well, mine was indeed saner than yours. Lots of sunning and gardening. I brought in strawberries from my fruit garden. Be sure to have some. They're sinful."

"Thank you." Gia sighed. "Sunning. Relaxing. That sounds like heaven. Ah, well… I'll savor your strawberries and live vicariously through you." Another more exaggerated sigh. "Since I have no life."

Laurel rolled her eyes. "Now you cut that out, because you're not fooling anyone. You love your job. You thrive on solving your weekend debacles. And you could have any mouth-watering gentleman you wanted if you took the time to notice them. They certainly notice you."

"I'll bear that in mind." Chuckling, Gia turned and began walking down the hall to the semicircle of offices in the rear. "Is she in?" It was a rhetorical question. Her boss was always in. She worked even more obsessive hours than Gia.

"She's in, she's alone, and she's waiting for you like a sentry at the gates," Laurel called after her. "So you're good to go."

"Thanks." No surprise there. Ashlyn could smell money a mile away. And this week Gia had delivered a bundle of last-minute, super-lucrative extras.

She rounded the bend, waved at her counterparts as she passed their offices, and paused outside the enormous corner office with the gold plate that read: ASHLYN CUSHING, PRESIDENT.

Gia put her ear against the closed door and listened attentively. Good. No ongoing phone calls.

She gave a brief knock. "It's me, Ash."

"Come on in."

After turning the door handle, Gia stepped into the massive office that, despite its warm rose coloring and obvious personal touches, was Ashlyn's business domain. Her sweeping cherry desk was the size of Rhode Island, its matching swivel chair was a decadent suede, and all the file cabinets and occasional tables were made of cherry identical to that of the desk, all hand-crafted, and all of which cost a small fortune. Her computer system was state-of-the-art. Its components were the only items on her pristine desk, other than a canister of pens, a few writing tablets, and a stack of current client files perched on the right-hand corner.

As for the personal touches, they consisted of pricy paintings hanging on the walls and equally pricy sculptures on the side tables, in addition to intricate crystal pieces on her window ledge—all collected during various trips abroad. That was as personal as it got. There were no family photos or sentimental items, because Ashlyn was single, married to her career.

Now, wearing a chic midnight blue Armani suit, Ashlyn smoothed a blonde hair into place and sat back in her reclining suede chair—or her throne, as the planners liked to call it. She interlaced her fingers on the desk, tilted back her chin, and gazed expectantly at Gia.

"Good morning. I'm glad you're here. I could use some good news—I've been doing billing and paying vendors all weekend and I have two major client meetings later today, neither of which I expect to be cakewalks."

"Do you know one that is?" Gia asked.

"No." The two women shared a smile of understanding.

"Well, hopefully this will make your morning brighter." Gia plucked out final tallies on this weekend's weddings and placed them in front of her boss. "I think this constitutes good news."

Ashlyn glanced down, and a triumphant smile curved her lips as she skimmed the totals at the bottom, silently adding them up. "It certainly does." She looked up, giving Gia a proud nod of approval. "You've outdone yourself. Brava." One pale brow rose. "How bad was it?"

"Electrical outage, mangled bridesmaid's gown, and coitus interruptus. A day in the life."

Ashlyn burst out laughing. "I don't even want to know the details. I might not hold down my cup of Laurel's strawberries."

"Probably not," Gia agreed. She placed the final reports on Ashlyn's desk. "Besides the checks, what's important are the rave reviews our clients gave us. We'll be getting three definite and two probable referrals. All from clients who have assured me that price is not an object. In fact..." Gia glanced at her watch. "Potential bridal client number one will be arriving at ten thirty for our first meeting. She's bringing her mother, her future mother-in-law, and her sister."

"Then I'll let you go to your office and prep." Ashlyn rose and walked around the desk to give Gia's hands an unexpected squeeze. "You really are a wonderful asset. I see a big promotion on the horizon—and not too far in the future if you keep up this track record."

"Thank you, Ashlyn. That means a lot." Gia squeezed her hands back, once again feeling that tinge of guilt. Ashlyn was a great boss, but the junior partnership she was alluding to was not what Gia had in mind for her future.

She left Ashlyn's office and headed down the hall to her own home base—a small, cozier copy of Ashlyn's office, with the addition of a half-dozen family photos and an upholstered rose and gold lounger. Gia adored that lounger. It doubled as a stylish sitting area for her clients and an I-desperately-need-to-take-a-break relaxation spot for her when the day was spinning out of control. Now, she shut her door and blew by the lounger, heading for her desk and her upcoming meeting.

She'd just begun glancing through her notes when her cell phone rang. She glanced down at the caller ID and smiled.

"Hi, Mom," she answered.

"Am I interrupting a meeting? Or maybe a circus?" Maria Russo's voice was tinged with humor.

Gia chuckled. "No, the wildness is temporarily over. And I don't have a client meeting for an hour. So what's up? Are you and Dad okay?"

"The usual. Dad is working too hard, running from New Rochelle to the Bronx and back since he doesn't fully trust anyone to manage the delis without him, and I'm working too hard taking care of his billing and collecting."

Nick Russo owned two small Italian delis, where you could get anything from a hot or cold sandwich to a full takeout meal—cooked to order from scratch—to homemade desserts that would make your mouth water. And Maria was not only the baker, she was the accountant. They had a few great cooks and sandwich makers, but, like Gia, her parents were control freaks.

As a result, the Russos were far from rich, but they were doing okay, particularly for this lousy economy. They lived in a modest house in New Rochelle—a house they'd bought twenty years ago after leaving Bozeman to move back east. Talk about a bad fit. The Russos were about as well-suited for life in Montana as they were for life on the moon. But Gia had been adopted after an endless wait, and her parents were off-the-charts protective. Her mother had read that Montana was a much healthier environment for a child to grow up in. Thus, the move.

They'd hated the West from the start. Far from the city they loved and, more importantly, from the extended family they loved, they'd lasted eight years in Bozeman before relocating back home.

Gia had no problem adapting. Even though she'd really liked the open space and cold air of Montana, she loved New York more. Her parents often took her to the City to see the sights, and the pulse of the Big Apple gave her a rush of excitement even then. Plus, she was surrounded by doting relatives—eight aunts and uncles and twelve cousins, which made the situation the best of the best.

Even now that she was on her own, she'd stayed close to home. Her parents' house was about a twenty-minute drive from Gia's place in Rye, and Gia went there at least twice a week for dinner or to hang out and watch a weeknight Yankee game.

She understood that her parents would have wanted a big family. But it wasn't meant to be. Gia was their miracle. So they'd poured all their love into her. And she'd blossomed from that love.

Given how close they all were, Gia knew her mother and father to a tee. And right now, there was an undercurrent to her mother's voice that Gia picked up on right away.

"Okay, Mom, what is it?" she asked. "You didn't just call to say hi. You sound like a kid who's asking for an extra portion of ice cream and is nervous about what her mother would say."

"That would be you, Gia, not me," her mother retorted good-naturedly. "Ice cream was always first on your list. Did you think I didn't notice the spoon marks in the part-used gallons—the ones you tried to smooth over?"

Gia flinched. All these years, she really thought she'd pulled one over on her mother with that one. "Guilty as charged."

"Same here."

"Meaning?"

"Meaning I have a favor to ask of you."

"Shoot."

Maria sighed. "Uncle Frank's sixty-fifth birthday is coming up next month. Aunt Silvia wants to do something special, not just a backyard barbecue. Your name came up, and she was wondering if you might have any suggestions."

Gia burst out laughing. "Translated: Could I please come up with the most awesome birthday theme ever and then pick the place, take care of the arrangements, and pull off the whole celebration sometime in the next few months."

"July ninth," Maria clarified. "I think it's a Sunday. But it's also Frank's lucky date, whatever that means. Silvia wants to have it then."

"Even better. I now have six weeks to make our entire family happy with as little infighting as possible."

"I'm sorry, sweetie. I know you're swamped. If you can't, you can't."

"Of course I can." Gia was wildly racking her brain, trying to figure out when she was going to get the time to scope out venues and hire top-of-the-line vendors on such short notice. But this was her family. She'd find a way. She only prayed she didn't have a Sunday afternoon event that day. But if she did, she'd work her uncle's party around it.

An idea flashed through her mind, and she locked it in as a winner. Uncle Frank was an avid boat lover. He spent two weekends each summer visiting Mystic, Connecticut, to see all the magnificent historic ships. And he spent the rest of the summer weekends sitting on a beach on the ocean side of New Rochelle, viewing sleek yachts leaving from the marina.

Perfect. Uncle Frank would feel like a king if he celebrated his sixty-fifth on a lavish private yacht filled with family and friends. Gia could organize that with a few targeted phone calls. She had business relationships with more than one private yacht company, and they had vessels ready for just this type of event. Time to call in a favor.

Gia smiled with satisfaction. She'd make the necessary phone calls right after her morning client meeting ended.

Which reminded her...

"Mom, I have to go now. I've got a pile of notes to review before my first bride comes in. But I've got an hour or two in between appointments, and I've also got an idea. I'll get right on it. Tell Aunt Silvia that we'll give Uncle Frank the celebration of a lifetime."

Her mother's sigh of relief was audible. "Thank you so much, sweetheart. I don't know how I would have told Aunt Silvia no."

"Me, either. Let's be frank. She would have ripped you a new one. So, let's keep that from happening. Love you."

Gia hung up, quickly entering the date into her iPhone calendar, even as she scanned the day for conflicts. She had the Pollman wedding at seven o'clock that evening at the Westchester Country Club. She couldn't have planned that one better. New Rochelle to Rye. One afternoon event, one evening event. Now she could work the times of the two parties so they rolled smoothly from one to the other, rather than clashing and causing wild pandemonium. Gia wouldn't let her parents down. But she also couldn't let her clients down.

Of course, she could send Liz to the Pollman affair in her place. Liz Watts, another planner at Shimmering, had her own clients, but she also assisted Gia at many events where one planner, no matter how proficient, wasn't enough. She was quite good in her own right and would soon be a confident, in-demand wedding planner who rivalled the rest of the staff. Still, assisting at an affair wasn't the same thing as running the show. And if there was some major complication, which there almost always was, well, that would be on Gia's shoulders.

Besides, even if things went smoothly, the fact was that the Pollmans had been referred to Gia, they were attached to Gia, and they expected Gia to run their wedding. And frankly, Gia couldn't blame them. It was way too late in the game to send in a pinch hitter.

So she'd book the yacht from twelve to five. That would leave her ample time to give hugs all around and ease from one event to the other. Her mother would explain that Gia had to run to another job. She'd listen to the grumbling about how Gia worked too hard and should think about settling down with a husband and kids. And her mother would know just what to say to smooth things over.

A husband and kids would be nice. Someday. When she had a chance to breathe.

CHAPTER 7

Twin Cities Animal Clinic
Minneapolis, Minnesota

"Dr. Dani?"

Jessie Long, the practice's newest and most enthusiastic vet tech, popped her head into the examining room where Dr. Danielle Murano was fiddling with the buttons on her white lab coat while reading over the file for her next appointment.

"Hmmm?" Dani murmured.

"Beaker's owner, Mrs. Simpson, is on the phone. She's stuck at work, but she's freaking out about the amount of blood Beaker had on his feathers when she brought him in. She's been on the Internet all day, reading about how small a bird's blood volume is and how serious it can be when they lose too much of it—even a parrot of Beaker's size. I calmed her down, but she wants to talk to you. I know you're backed up, so I can tell her again how well he's doing, unless you want to take the call?"

Dani looked up, her attention now fully locked on what Jessie was saying. She understood how anxious Maura Simpson was. Beaker was her feathered baby, and she adored him. Dani would take a million owners like that over the ones who didn't care. Restoring good health to her patients was number one in her book. Bringing joy and relief to their owners played a close second.

Fortunately, Beaker's injury—a blood feather—had been an easy fix, despite how bad it had looked and the fact that there could have been complications. Dani had used a hemostat to pull out the broken, bleeding feather, applied a little pressure to the area, and Beaker had responded beautifully.

"Is Beaker still behaving normally—eating, drinking, and *not* picking at his feathers?" she asked Jessie. "I checked on him earlier, but I was in surgery for hours and I've been swamped with patients since then, so I haven't had a chance to get back to the recovery room again."

Jessie's head bobbed up and down, visible pleasure on her face. "He's not picking at his feathers, so I don't think an Elizabethan collar will be necessary. As for eating and drinking, he's doing both. He's also crazy about the new food you switched him to. I guess he doesn't realize he's getting healthy by eating great-tasting meals. I wish it worked that way for me." A rueful glance at her hips.

"Tell me about it," Dani commiserated.

Jessie's brows rose. "You're kidding, right? You're probably a size two."

"Dr. Dani, your four-thirty appointment is here," the receptionist's voice echoed from the intercom into the examining room.

"Give me five minutes, Rosa," Dani responded. She placed down the file and headed for the door. "If I'm thin, it's because I never have time to eat," she told Jessie. "If I did, the pounds would fly on, trust me." She paused in the doorway. "I'll take the call. Beaker will be ready to go home when Mrs. Simpson arrives. I'll give her follow-up instructions then." A hint of a grin. "He doesn't like being contained. My index finger can attest to that."

Jessie laughed. "Yeah, he's quite a character."

"And he knows it," Dani added. She looked over her shoulder at the examining table. "Could you please set up the room for me so I'm ready for Gomer?" she asked, referring to the guinea pig who was her next patient. "I'll grab the phone and be back in five."

* * *

Two hours and six patients later, Dani was still making phone calls at her desk—some return calls and some calls checking in on her recent patients. Thankfully, it was a good day. No bad news to report and no bad news received.

At long last, she pressed end for the final time that workday and let her head sag back against the headrest of her chair, stretching her legs out in front of her.

Damn, she was tired. Her hours were insane, usually seven to seven, with surgery taking up the middle chunk of the day. And she was on call every third weekend, as well. It was pretty draining. But it was even more rewarding. And given the professional competition out there, she felt lucky. She was getting the chance to do what she loved in one of Minnesota's best veterinary practices.

She'd been hired two years ago, right after graduating with honors from the University of Wisconsin–Madison, having earned her DVM. The staff and the partners were great, the animals they treated ran the gamut from dogs and cats to turtles and iguanas and everything in between, which was giving her a broad spectrum of experience, particularly surgical, which was her passion. Plus, she was less than an hour away from home, so she could drop in on her mom and dad—and get a home-cooked meal—whenever she wanted to.

In an uncharacteristically impulsive move, she'd recently applied to—and miraculously been interviewed by—Metropolitan Animal Clinic, a renowned veterinary hospital in Manhattan, New York. She'd been drawn to the opportunity because of the clinic's emphasis on cutting-edge surgical procedures. But she was still on the fence about the whole thing. The next step would be a working interview, where she could be observed in action—and that would place her one step closer to making a decision she doubted she wanted to make. It was an amazing opportunity, but it would mean uprooting her whole life. And truth be told, she was becoming more and more reluctant to do that.

No, instinct told her she'd be staying right here, which was just fine with her. Life was good. Not to mention that her social life was looking up. She'd run into her college boyfriend, Gabe Hayward, at a regional veterinary conference. He'd been an animal science major, she'd been pre-vet. They'd broken up for the usual reasons college kids did—to find themselves and their paths in life. She'd heard from friends that he'd gone on to be a vet tech. At the recent conference, she'd learned that he'd expanded his interests and his education and was now a physical therapist for animals—a skyrocketing field. He was still as bright and as hot as she recalled.

That said, she'd learned a lot from him over dinner—about cold laser therapy for animals with arthritis, about water treadmill therapy, about the use of ultrasound. And after dinner, she'd also learned that the chemistry between them was still very much there. The snag was that he lived and practiced in Cleveland, so their renewed relationship thus far had been limited to the few heated nights at the convention, a quick overnight just this week, and a bunch of phone calls and texts. *Definitely* not what the doctor ordered.

Still, as was evidenced by their recent "quickie," it was only a two-hour plane flight separating them. The subject of one of them flying over to see the other on their next mutual weekend off had come up in their last round of text messages. If they could make that happen, Dani's love life—or at least her sex life—would be on the upswing.

And speaking of interesting new people in her life…

Dani picked up her iPhone again, this time migrating to her photos. She scrolled down until she found the picture Sarah had taken of Gia Russo. She'd looked at it a dozen times, and the resemblance never failed to startle her. It was like looking in the mirror and seeing a far more sophisticated version of herself, with a more stylish haircut and some expertly applied makeup. Clearly, a New York girl. But all that was topical. The shape of their faces, their features, even their dimples—they were identical.

Was that conceivable? Obviously, it was. Maybe the concept of a doppelgänger wasn't so sci-fi-y, after all.

Chatting with Gia was a lot more fun than doing Sudoku puzzles on her iPhone to relax.

Time for another Facebook message.

Angelina's apartment
West Eighth Street

Lina opened her front door, smiling when she saw Casey and her lovely, refined blonde companion standing there. "Hi." She gestured for them to come inside, and her gaze shifted from Casey to her colleague. "You must be Claire." Lina extended her hand. "It's great to meet you."

"Likewise," Claire replied, returning Lina's handshake and immediately getting warm vibes from her, as well as from her surroundings. Oak floors. Fuzzy white love seat and butterfly chairs. Bright aqua and hot pink accents, from the throw pillows to the curtains to the wall of picture frames that held an array of family photos. Everything was bold, funky, and eye-catching—just the way Casey had described Lina. "Thank you for seeing us," Claire added politely.

"Are you kidding?" Lina shut the door behind them. "I couldn't wait. A real psychic..." She stopped herself. "Claircognizant," she corrected, "in my living room? I was thrilled when Casey called and asked if you could try picking up vibes here. Brianna should be home in a minute. She ran out to buy something for Bandit's cage—not that it isn't already a ferret condo."

Claire's lips twitched. There was something instantly likeable about Angelina Brando. She was open, intelligent, and just plain real, despite the fact that her Dolce & Gabbana sundress had to have cost over a thousand dollars.

"I made herbal tea and bought shortbread cookies from a health food store. I hope that's okay?" Lina glanced quizzically at Claire.

"For claircognizants, you mean?" Claire couldn't resist teasing her. "Seriously, that was very kind of you. And, yes, I drink herbal tea nonstop and I could eat a whole tray of shortbread cookies on my own. So I appreciate you thinking of me."

Lina beamed. "I set things up at the coffee table. Brianna has been sleeping on the fluff-couch, as we call it, and a lot of her personal things are out here." A roll of her eyes as a small racket ensued from a cage sitting atop the end table. "Including Bandit. He'll be happy to throw wood pellets at you if you're interested."

Claire's brow furrowed, and she walked over to the large metal cage, where Bandit was currently snaking his way through a plastic play tube. She watched him reach the bottom and then snuggle into a plush scarf, blinking at her in curiosity.

"That scarf…" Claire murmured.

"Yes, it's a Burberry and, yes, it's cashmere," Lina supplied with a sheepish look. "I turned out to be a bigger softie than I thought. Bandit was so attached to the thing that I finally gave it to him as a nesting present."

Claire shook her head. "That's not what I meant. What was there before, until recently?"

"You mean Bandit's former nesting home? Brianna's NYU T-shirt."

"Gray? With purple and black lettering and an insignia that's partly worn away?"

"That's the one." Lina looked über-impressed. "Bandit's claws did the damage. Wow. You really are good."

Claire was lost in thought. "Brianna frequently wore it on campus when she went running—until Bandit inherited it a month ago. So it actually moved from her personal space to her academic space and back. Does she still have it?"

Lina glanced around. "It's here somewhere. Brianna will find it in a minute. She'd never part with that shirt. She reclaimed it after Bandit went upscale. The only thing is, the T-shirt's been washed a bunch of times since then. Is that okay?"

"Hopefully, yes," Claire replied. "What I need goes a lot deeper than the washing machine and dryer."

A key turned in the lock, and Brianna walked into the apartment, carrying a small brown bag and giving everyone an apologetic look. "I'm so sorry I'm late. The gourmet pet store finally got in the higher-protein food I've been waiting to give Bandit. If I'd waited, it would have been gone." She gave Casey a tentative look. "I hope you're not upset that I went out alone. Normally, I stick with Lina or other friends. But the pet store is just a few blocks away. And it is daytime."

"No problem," Casey replied. "And not because I'm happy with your decision. But I knew you were safe. The day after we took your case, I assigned a security guy to you: John Nickels, one of our best."

Brianna blinked. "I never saw anyone."

"That's the idea. I'll introduce you to John before we leave."

"I… Thank you." Brianna sounded as taken aback as she did grateful.

"This is serious stuff, Brianna," Casey reminded her. "We don't want to give Hanover any opportunities to get close to you. We've got eyes on him, too."

Brianna shivered. "You're right. I'm sorry. I'll try to make Mr. Nickels' job easier by sticking to the rules."

"Wise idea."

"Have you been here long?"

"Five minutes," Casey assured her. "You didn't miss anything. Go ahead and feed Bandit while we settle in. But first, do you remember where you put your NYU T-shirt? The one Bandit used to sleep in before the scarf took over?"

"Sure." Brianna put down the bag and headed across the living room to a small suitcase—one of two that sat open in the corner. Neatly, she moved a few articles of clothing and pulled out the shirt. "Here it is. A little worse for wear but still functional." She handed Casey the shirt, giving her a questioning look. "Why do you need it?"

Casey let Claire reiterate what she'd just told Lina.

"That's amazing. Feel free to examine it all you want."

Claire took the shirt and walked over to the corner where Brianna's suitcases were. There, she sank down to the floor and settled in cross-legged. "I want as much proximity to your things as possible," she explained. "Now all I need is a little quiet. Not silence," she added, a smile tugging at her lips as she heard Bandit dashing around at the sight of his new food. "Just minimal soft conversation."

"You got it," Lina said.

Claire lay the T-shirt across her lap, then shut her eyes, moving her fingers lightly over the material. Instantly, she got an image of Brianna running. At first, it was recreational jogging, pacing along as she cleared her head and strengthened her body.

Abruptly, it changed, and Claire's fingers stilled where they were. Brianna was no longer exercising. She was fleeing, running away, her chest pounding, no longer with exertion but with fear. In the shadows stood a man. Tall. Lean. Smoking a cigarette. First watching, then striding straight in Brianna's direction. Coming after her. Closer. Closer. Not a threat, a reality.

The man was evil. And he was closing in fast.

Claire's eyes fluttered open. She realized she was tightly gripping the T-shirt.

And she was clutching it right where Brianna's heart would be.

CHAPTER 8

It was Wednesday, and the world's conventional workweek was half way gone. To Gia, that meant that the crux of *her* work week—Friday and its weekend frenzy—were just around the corner. She had two more days of scheduled meetings and venue scouting before the onslaught of weddings and rehearsal dinners began.

She had to be crazy to thrive on this. But thrive she did.

She was shrugging into her blazer, ready to head out of the office for a final run-through with the electrical engineer who'd be handling her Friday night wedding, when the Facebook Messenger tone on her iPhone binged.

She finished wriggling her right arm into its sleeve and picked up her cell. Given the communications with her newfound lookalike, she no longer ignored that particular *bing*. The two of them had messaged back and forth a bunch of times since Sunday, and Gia was starting to really look forward to hearing from her new Facebook pal. Dani was warm and witty, and while their worlds were very different in some ways, they were very much alike in others. They both had demanding careers and warm, loving families, plus a riot of who-could-top-whom storytelling.

Yup. The message was from Dani.

Hey, Doppelgänger. I was thinking about you and wondering if your day was turning out to be as exhausting as mine. Then I re-

*membered that you deal with humans—brides, no less (are they hu-
man?)—while I deal with animals (they're better than humans). So,
any way you look at it, your exhaustion trumps mine. Surgery on a
bullfrog versus pulling apart two humping people? No contest.*

Gia began to laugh. Dani not only had a great sense of humor,
she told it like it was. Very Midwest refreshing. If Gia were as frank
as she, she'd be out of a job in a New York minute.

She scrolled down, and the next paragraph surprised her.

*I've been working without a break for two years now, and my
boss just kindly informed me that I need to take several mental health
days off. As it so happens, I met an old flame at a recent veterinary
conference, who, just my bad luck, lives in Cleveland. I thought I'd fly
there for a day (and a night ☺) and then maybe continue on to New
York. I know you're crushed with work, but I'd LOVE to meet you.
What do you say? It'll be midweek next week, so it won't interfere with
your "wedding weekends." Can you swing it? Just let me know and I'll
start packing. ☺*

Gia felt a surge of anticipation. This would be Dani's first real
trip to New York, since the only other time she'd been here was for
a day-long job interview. It would also be their first chance to meet,
hang out, and get to know each other. How exciting was that? Gia
would swing it, no matter what she had to move around to make it
happen.

Quickly, she replied to the message.

*Hey back. I'd be thrilled to have you here, and to introduce you to the
really-not-so-scary Big Apple. The people are mostly great, and their pets
are the best-dressed ever. I envy their wardrobes, and so will you. Most of
all, I'd love to have the chance to get to know each other and to talk in person. I feel as if it's been months rather than less than a week since we first
connected. Just send me your itinerary when you have it; I'll even pick
you up at the airport. And since my look-alike couldn't be anything but
trustworthy, you'll be staying with me, so don't bother booking a hotel. ☺*

Not two minutes after Gia hit send, her cell phone binged again.

Great, thanks! I'm calling Gabe now to see if Cleveland is a go. Right from there, I'm coming to New York. I'll be booking my flights on-line ASAP. I'll send you my whole itinerary tonight. In the meantime, you can start planning our nonstop talk 'n tour. Later!

Later, Gia messaged back with a grin.

Still smiling, she slipped her iPhone into her handbag. Another week and she'd be meeting her look-alike. That would be a blast. And given that Dani seemed to have as much energy and stamina as she did, Gia would make it a whirlwind two days, crammed with all the City had to offer, leaving lots of talk time.

She'd plan it all out tonight.

5:30 p.m.

He blew off his mound of paperwork and came straight home. Without so much as a trip to the bathroom, he headed to his computer to do what he was being paid to do. Good money. Good cause. Great perks. He had full control of Danielle's video camera and microphone. He had a front-row seat to her life, and right about now, he'd love some playtime, hopefully watching her strip down to that lacy bra and thong of hers. But movie time would have to come later.

Quickly, he logged on to Danielle's computer and downloaded the information captured by his spyware. The keystroke logger reported everything she typed.

The data popped up. He scanned the screen.

Shit. A message with an itinerary—an itinerary that led straight to New York.

He grabbed his burner phone and made the necessary call.

Todt Hill, Staten Island

"Get ready for takeoff," Lina told Brianna in a teasing voice. Her father had sent a driver and a Town Car to pick the two of them up at the St. George Ferry Terminal. The first few minutes of travel had been uneventful. But the fun part was about to begin.

"Takeoff?" Brianna's forehead creased in question. She'd never had occasion to visit Staten Island, but when Lina had invited her to dinner at her family home, Brianna had jumped at the reprieve. She was still shaky from Monday's meeting with Claire and Casey. Claire had all but told her that the vibes she was picking up off the T-shirt meant things were about to get much, much worse. She and Casey had even taken a few more personal items of hers with them when they left. And reassurances or not, Brianna was a basket case.

She felt a little guilty about going to Lina's parents' when she'd been putting off seeing her own. The problem was that, much as she adored her mom and dad, the next visit she had with them was going to be intense and emotional. She owed them an explanation. She was a lousy liar, and they also had the right to know. But meeting Lina's folks would come without that burden. It would, hopefully, be an evening of relaxed conversation and home-cooking—just what Brianna needed.

She was about to reiterate her question about takeoff when the road ahead provided her answer.

The driver downshifted, and the Town Car began climbing up the steepest incline Brianna had ever seen in New York City. The initial part of ascent was flanked by condos, apartments, and a school playground. But as they climbed higher, the scenery changed. Magnificent homes and estates began to appear, many of them gated, most of them boasting ornate statues and exquisite lawns.

Brianna blinked. "This is where you grew up?" she asked Lina in astonishment. She'd known Lina was wealthy, and she'd expected her to have lived in some exclusive area, but these houses looked like castles.

"Isn't it cool?" Lina grinned, staring out the window, clearly immune to the grandeur and more intrigued by the natural landscape.

"Todt Hill is the highest natural point in the five boroughs, four hundred ten feet above sea level, and made entirely out of rock." She turned to give Brianna a mischievous look. "When I was a kid, I used to dream of sledding down the full length of the hill. Talk about the fearlessness of youth. I once made the mistake of mentioning that dream to my parents. They took a sled off my Christmas list—permanently."

"Do you blame them?" Brianna asked.

"Nope. But it was still a great dream." Lina pointed to a pair of iron gates at the end of a cul-de-sac. "That's home."

"Oh my God." Brianna just stared. "Lina, why didn't you prepare me for this? I'm wearing jeans, for heaven's sake."

"So am I. And there's nothing to prepare you for. We're rich. So what? My parents are awesome. You'll love them, and they'll love you. I talk about you all the time."

"I wish you'd done the same with me about them." Brianna was trying not to feel intimidated. "I know your dad's a state assemblyman and a lawyer, and that your mom owns a Soho boutique that you worked in between college and grad school. I've got an investment banker and a pediatrician as parents. They make lots of money. But this?" She waved her arm. "We're almost at the gates. Give me a twenty-second crash course in what I'm missing and what I'm about to face. Please."

"Sure." Lina was puzzled but amenable. "Like you said, you already know the basics. As for our wealth, before my dad went into politics, he was already a defense attorney. His legal practice made a fortune. His investments made even more. Now, he's lightened his client load considerably. He's concentrating all his efforts and a good chunk of his money on his campaign."

"What campaign?"

Lina blinked. "I didn't tell you? He's running for US House of Representatives. The primaries are in a few weeks. He'll sweep those. He got a ton more signatures than necessary to file for candidacy.

And his platform is great. He's all about improving America's digital infrastructure. He's so passionate about it that it's infectious. He's hoping to get an endorsement from a powerful former congresswoman. I know he'll get it. Just like I know in my gut that he'll win in the general election. How awesome is that?"

Brianna released her breath in a hiss. "Wow. That's pretty amazing. I can't believe you never mentioned this."

"I really thought I did." Lina waved the topic away. "As proud as I am, that's not what tonight is about. Tonight is about my incredible parents meeting my incredible best friend. Okay?"

"I guess. I'm just a lot more nervous than I was before. It's just me, my jeans, and a black forest cake." Brianna gestured at the white bakery box on her lap.

"Don't underestimate chocolate." Lina's eyes twinkled. "You'll win my dad over with that cake alone. And don't be nervous. This is going to be great." She sat up as the iron gates swung open. "Pay no attention to the size of the house. It's big, but it's filled with love."

Big wasn't exactly the word that the Brandos' house conjured up in Brianna's mind. *Ginormous* would be more fitting. The trees looked like manicured sculptures, and the sculptures looked like something out of an architectural magazine. Huge. Ornate. Extravagant.

And then there was the house or the manor or the mansion or whatever you called something that was probably close to seven thousand square feet of stone with twin columns, a double staircase, and a row of chiseled shrubbery stretching from end to end.

The driver pulled around the circular driveway and stopped directly across from the entranceway.

"Thanks, Eddie." Lina was already out of the car, waiting for Brianna to join her.

Just as Brianna climbed out and slammed the car door shut, the front door opened, and a petite woman of about forty-five with short, fashionably styled dark hair and a radiant smile stepped outside and walked down the stone steps. Brianna was thankful to see that she was also wearing jeans and a print silk blouse that was very boutique-y.

"Hi, sweetheart," she greeted Lina with a tight hug. She then turned that same enveloping smile on Brianna, who was approaching them. "You must be Brianna. Finally. Lina talks about you nonstop. I'm Donna, Lina's mom." Forgoing protocol, she wrapped Brianna in a welcoming hug.

"It's such a pleasure to meet you, Mrs. Brando." Brianna found herself returning the hug. It was easy to see where Lina got her warmth and exuberance. "And thank you so much for inviting me." She eased back and held out the cake, which Lina's mother graciously accepted.

"How lovely. Thank you. And, please—call me Donna. Otherwise, I feel old. Lina and I have been trying to arrange this get-together for weeks now." Donna rolled her eyes. "But everyone's schedule is so crazy."

"Well, we're here now," Lina announced. "My favorite people finally get to meet. Where's Dad?"

"Finishing up a call in his study," Donna replied. She scooted down to the kitchen with the bakery box, and then returned, gesturing for the girls to follow her. "Let's go in and relax in the family room. The living room's way too formal. Dinner should be ready in about a half hour."

She led them through a pillared marble foyer with a crystal chandelier and two symmetrical circular staircases leading upstairs. Then she turned down a corridor, past a formal dining room and a massive kitchen that was all cherrywood and marble countertops, and walked into a surprisingly normal-sized family room. Brianna didn't know much about furniture, but she recognized the Queen Anne period pieces that defined the room. Everything was done in a rich, classic walnut. Two curved sofas, upholstered in gold and burgundy, a wingback chair, a coffee table—filled with photos of Lina—a liquor and china cabinet and a fireplace, alight and ready to welcome guests. The end tables held miniature statuettes, and the walls were filled with still-life art.

Lina's mother had been right. Despite its expensive décor, this room felt surprisingly cozy.

"Please, sit." Donna gestured at one of the sofas. "What can I get you girls to drink?" A twinkle. "I'd go for wine if I were you. My mixed-drink-making skills are severely lacking. So unless you want your liquor straight up or you want to wait for Joseph to come in, I'd highly recommend the wine. We have a fabulous new Sauvignon Blanc. We loved it so much that we bought a dozen cases of it. I doubt they'll be staying in the wine cellar for long."

"That sounds wonderful," Brianna said, settling herself on the upholstered sofa cushion. "Thank you."

"Ditto for me," Lina inserted. "Can I help?"

"Not necessary, sweetie. I'm here." A masculine voice came from the doorway, accompanied by the appearance of a man whose lord-of-the-manor demeanor identified him as Joseph Brando. He strode over to the liquor cabinet and kissed his wife's cheek before taking down four wineglasses, uncorking the wine bottle, and pouring. "I'll do the honors. Lina, I'd ask you to make the introductions, but none are necessary." He shot a warm glance in Brianna's direction. "Hi, Brianna. It's great to finally meet you."

"It's a pleasure to meet you, Assemblyman—"

"Joseph," he cut her off to say. "Please. This is our home. And here, I'm a husband and a father—my favorite roles." He handed Brianna her wine, giving her a broad, welcoming smile.

As she studied Joseph Brando, the first word that popped into Brianna's mind was *powerhouse*. Even in the casual attire of a golf shirt and khakis, Lina's dad emanated a take-charge energy that screamed leader. He was tall, more charismatic than handsome, with sharp features, thick black hair and brows, and probing eyes that seemed to take in the entire room with one glance. He had the solid build of someone who had daily workout sessions—probably at five a.m. so as not to cut into the business day.

No surprise that this guy was running for US Congress, and that he'd probably win. He was a unique combination of dynamic and charming. A born politician.

"Please, let's relax and chat a bit," he said now, waiting for all the ladies to get comfortable before lowering himself into the club chair. He raised one dark brow in his wife's direction. "You did say that dinner wouldn't be for a while, right? I don't want to be the cause of it burning."

Donna smiled. "No worries, darling. We've got a solid twenty minutes before I have to serve. By all means, let's talk. I feel as if we already know Brianna. But it will be lovely to get to know her in person, rather than via our talkative daughter." She winked at Lina, who grinned back.

"There's not much to tell." Brianna found herself wondering just how much Lina had shared with them about the nightmare involving Dr. Hanover. Probably not much, since the two of them totally respected each other's privacy. Still, she was very much an open book, she was close with her family, and she was protective of Brianna. No doubt she'd implied that Brianna was going through something upsetting enough to warrant a warm family dinner.

"Lina says your parents live locally," Donna said.

Brianna's parents. A safe topic if ever there was one.

She nodded. "They live on the Upper West Side. My mom's a pediatrician and my dad's an investment banker. They both work incredibly long hours, so it's a real juggling act for us to get together. But we're a close family, so we manage." A surge of guilt shot through her. The truth was that she'd been the obstacle of late. She'd have to rectify that, and soon. She missed them, and they needed to know what was going on.

"You're an only child, like Lina?"

"Yes." Brianna smiled. "I don't think their schedules would allow time for another child. But that doesn't matter. Selfishly, I've always enjoyed being the only one. This way, I never had to battle for attention."

"Amen to that," Lina said. "I'm a brat. I want all my parents' time and energy focused on me, whenever it isn't taken up by political campaigns and agendas for a better future."

Joseph gave her an indulgent grin.

"Dad, I filled Brianna in about your congressional campaign," Lina supplied.

Her father's smiled broadened, and he leaned forward in his seat, rolling his wine goblet between his palms. "I'm glad. Actually, I have some good news on that front."

"I knew it!" Lina exclaimed. "That phone call you were on. You were talking to Uncle Neil, weren't you? You got the endorsement you were counting on!" A quick pivot toward Brianna. "Neil Donato is my dad's campaign manager. He's also a partner at Dad's law firm. I've known him my whole life. He's awesome." She gazed back at her father. "Am I right about your good news?"

"You are indeed. Neil told me that Hailey Sorensen is giving me her official endorsement. We'll be holding a televised press conference tomorrow for her to announce her endorsement to the public and to the media."

He filled in the details for Brianna. "Hailey and I go way back. She served as a House representative for three consecutive terms. Like me, she's always been a strong advocate for technology and improving the digital infrastructure of our country. So our paths have crossed numerous times. Now, she's a technology lobbyist based in DC. She's strongly regarded, both by the government and by big businesses. An endorsement from her will carry a lot of weight."

He barely heard Brianna's congratulations over the shrieks of excitement that came from Lina and her mother as they leapt up and ran to him. He rose quickly to his feet.

"Oh, sweetheart, that's wonderful." Donna hugged him, closely followed by Lina, who launched herself at her father so hard that Brianna was afraid his glass would shatter.

"Daddy, you're going to Washington!" Lina shrieked. "I knew it!"

Joseph hugged his wife and daughter back, giving Lina an indulgent smile. "Let's not get ahead of ourselves, honey. There are still almost five months till the election and a lot of ground to cover."

"Neil must have been elated," Donna said.

"He sounded psyched. This is a huge boost for our campaign." Abruptly, he cleared his throat, giving Brianna an apologetic look. "And here I promised you I was husband and dad in my home. I'm sorry about the interruption and the timing. From now on, I'm all yours."

"Please don't apologize," Brianna said. "Your news is wonderful. I'm honored that I was here to share in the joy." She glanced at Lina, smiling fondly as she watched her friend calm down enough to sit.

Donna had already taken her seat, crossing her legs and turning her full attention on Brianna. "Let's talk about you. Tell us about your plans once you've completed your MBA."

The next fifteen minutes were filled with easy, light conversation. So was dinner, although Brianna did wonder if an additional eight guests were expected, given the amount of food.

Donna Brando made a killer lasagna, one that filled half the length of the dining room table. Between that, the caprese salad, and the to-die-for garlic bread, Brianna thought she might burst—although she still found room for a chocolate-covered cannoli, a tiny sliver of the black forest cake she'd brought, and a cappuccino.

Finally, she sat back in her seat, taking a deep breath and exhaling slowly. "I don't remember the last time I was this full," she admitted. "But everything was so delicious that I couldn't seem to turn away seconds and, in some cases, thirds. You're an amazing cook, Donna. I can't thank you enough for having me over tonight."

"It was our pleasure," Lina's mom replied, visibly pleased that Brianna had enjoyed herself. "I'll pack you a doggie bag to take home with you."

Lina turned to her friend. "Just to prepare you, in our house, a doggie bag means enough food for a pack of Huskies."

Laughter bubbled up in Brianna's throat. "Now why doesn't that surprise me?"

"It's so good to hear you laugh," Lina said quietly. "Lately, there hasn't been much cause for it."

Silence hung in the air, a silence that was broken by Donna clearing her throat.

She set down her coffee cup, clearly about to approach her next topic with caution. "Lina mentioned something about you going through a difficult time—one that involved a level of danger, or I'd never even bring it up. I know you've been staying at her apartment this week. If I'm intruding, please tell me. But we'd like to help if we can."

Brianna was touched by the offer—and surprised by the realization that she wanted to fill Lina's parents in. Maybe it was because she was vulnerable. Maybe it was because they were so much like Lina—warm and caring—and making her feel like part of their family tonight. Or maybe it was because the urge to share was too strong to ignore.

"I'm being stalked," she heard herself say. "Not just stalked but closed in on. The situation is out of hand." She proceeded to tell them everything, concluding with her hiring Forensic Instincts to ensure her safety and to stop Dr. Hanover.

"My God." Donna's eyes were filled with worry. "I had no idea… You poor thing. Why don't you stay here with us? I realize the commute would be lengthy, but our security system is far superior to Lina's."

"That's a very kind offer," Brianna replied gratefully. "And I thank you. But I feel a lot less alone since I've been bunking at Lina's. Between her and my other friends, I make sure there's always someone with me. And Forensic Instincts assigned a security guard to me. Dr. Hanover won't get past him." She gave a tiny shiver. "I just wish this were over and he was in jail, where he belongs. He's a sick man."

Joseph's brows were drawn and his head was inclined as he processed Brianna's every word. "I've certainly heard of Forensic Instincts," he said. "They've solved some high-profile cases. Their reputation is stellar." He paused. "Still, even the best investigative firm has just so much man power to go around. I have quite a few contacts, including some in law enforcement, some in private investigating, and some at NYU. I'd be happy to make a few phone calls—to give Forensic Instincts a little help."

"That's a great idea!" Lina turned to Brianna. "Dad knows everyone. He's got a ton of political supporters and zillions of contacts from his years practicing law."

"I…" Brianna was feeling more than a little overwhelmed. "I really appreciate your kindness. But I just hired Forensic Instincts and I don't want to offend them by implying I doubt their abilities. Maybe if things aren't going well…"

"I understand," Joseph replied immediately. "I didn't mean to bombard you. I'm just not liking what I'm hearing. This Hanover guy sounds like a psychopath. But I understand you're already on overload. So stick with Forensic Instincts for now. Just know that my offer stands if you change your mind." A pause. "Also, I'm sure they're expensive. I'd be happy to contribute to their fee—make it a loan if you'd prefer."

"Once again, I thank you." Brianna met his gaze, hers filled with gratitude. "But so far, I'm okay. And I'm sure my parents will help out if I'm not."

"They don't know, do they?" Donna asked.

"No." Brianna sighed. "I've been protecting them like crazy. I know how freaked out this will make them. But things have escalated to the point where I have no choice. I'll go over there this weekend and fill them in."

"Do that. Trust me. No matter how much it upsets them, they'll want to know." Donna's expression was nostalgic and tears glistened on her lashes. "Parents don't stop loving and worrying about their children once they've grown up. *You* may feel like an adult, but to your mom and dad, you'll always be their baby. That's how we feel about Lina."

"Come on, Mom, don't get all mushy," Lina said, squirming a bit. "It's embarrassing."

"I think it's wonderful," Brianna said, unused to such open displays of emotion, yet deeply touched by this one. "I also think your mom is right. My parents will take this hard. But they'd be devastated if I didn't tell them. They'll want to be a part of things, to do everything in their power to help."

"And if they need backup, we're here," Joseph reminded her. "I know we just met tonight, but you're Lina's best friend, you're a fine young woman, and you're now part of our family. Whatever you need, all you have to do is ask."

CHAPTER 9

As much as Emma loved playing Spy vs. Spy with her cool earrings, it took her just till the end of the week to figure out the traffic pattern on the hall where Hanover's office was.

No surprise, daytime was a disaster. There was a ton of traffic—both students and faculty—setting up meetings, holding office hours, and chatting in the halls about coursework. After five o'clock wasn't great, either, since professors seemed to show up then to collect material to take home.

Surprisingly, nighttime was also busy, but for a different reason. The custodial staff was all there, doing their thing both inside the offices and up and down the hallways. It took Emma one trip to size that one up, hiding in the shadows so she wouldn't be seen.

So there were no weekday or weeknight opportunities for Casey and Claire to do their thing.

Hands down, the overall best shot they'd have was Sunday morning. Everyone was either at church or sleeping in, and the halls were deadly quiet. The biggest problem here was that the buildings were locked tight on Sundays. Which would necessitate Emma "borrowing" a faculty member's ID card to enable Casey and Claire to swipe their way in. No sweat on that front. Emma might be a retired pickpocket, but she was a damned good one.

Not so much on the grad student front; Emma was barely holding her own in Dr. Hanover's course.

There were two things working in her favor. First, the arrogant bastard loved to pontificate and to hear his own voice, which immediately cut down on the need for Emma's participation. And second, she had Casey, Ryan, and her earbuds. Whenever Hanover did shoot a question at Emma and her mind registered a total blank, either Ryan or Casey filled in that blank. That was a godsend since Hanover was like a shark smelling blood. He knew that Emma was struggling. So he threw a disproportionate number of questions that required complicated analyses in her direction.

The miserable shit had no idea that he was feeding right into Emma's plan—a plan that was aided by the fact that, despite Hanover's desire to humiliate her, he'd been eyeing her, subtly giving her the once-over every few minutes.

Three sessions were enough for her to go for it.

Right after Wednesday evening's class, Emma walked up to Hanover's desk and, with feigned nervousness, admitted that she was struggling with the coursework.

"That's quite clear, Miss Lowe," he'd replied in an icy tone.

Emma wanted to smack that smug look off his face. Instead she stayed on track. "I was hoping I could set up a meeting with you—at your convenience, of course—to help me catch up. I'm afraid I'm not up to your course expectations."

"Correct." His bold stare strayed up and down her body, after which he nodded. "Very well." He checked his electronic schedule, then began packing up his briefcase. "I teach on Saturday mornings. I have an opening during my office hours this Saturday at noon. Be there."

"Oh, yes, I will." No hesitation on Emma's part, although she was beginning to regret her promise to Ryan about no balls kicking. "I really appreciate it. I'll be there."

"Make sure you're prompt." With that, he strode out of the room.

"Prick," Emma muttered under her breath.

"Emma," Casey cautioned in her ear. "Cool it and keep doing your job. You're almost there. With any luck, you can drop the course next week."

"Can I drop Hanover on his head? Or better yet, on his dick? Hopefully, a good fall would snap it off."

Casey couldn't choke back her laughter. "Not to worry. I'm sure his fellow prisoners will be happy to oblige. Keep focusing on the end goal. Brianna will be safe, and Hanover will be behind bars."

"You're right." Emma gathered up her things. "I'm getting something to eat. I'm starving. I'll go to one of the local hangouts and check out the hot guys. Looking at eye candy will cheer me up. So will to morrow, when I'll go buy a new outfit for my Saturday meeting."

"Nothing too revealing," Casey cautioned her. She was still protective of Emma after the outcome of her femme fatale role in their last case. "Just something... nice."

Emma well understood Casey's concern. "Not to worry, boss. I promise to stay away from stuff that makes me look like I've been poured into it. All I need is something that will capture the scumbag's attention—like a short skirt and a top that shows a little cleavage."

"Not too much cleavage."

"Yes, boss." Emma grinned. "Why don't you come shopping with me? It'll make you feel better and it'll be fun. I'll even buy you lunch. Hey, it's all going on the FI credit card. So the sky's the limit."

"Good night, Emma."

"Is it a date?"

Casey found herself grinning again. "Yeah, it's a date."

* * *

At precisely twelve noon on Saturday, Emma stood in front of Hanover's office door. She ran her fingers through her hair, simultaneously inspecting her appearance. A pale blue V-neck top and a matching flair skirt that showed just enough leg, along with heels that were high enough to draw attention to her exposed skin. A tote bag rather than a backpack. Definitely a soft, feminine package.

"Ready for action," she muttered to Casey and Ryan.

"Piece of cake, Kate," Ryan replied in her ear. "Just find some target items and then get the hell out of there."

"Believe me, I'm not planning on hanging around."

She switched into Kate mode and knocked.

"Yes?" Hanover's cold response could have iced over the hallway.

Pasting a nervous expression on her face, Emma slowly opened the door, pausing before taking a step inside. "Dr. Hanover?" The jerk was sitting behind his desk, wearing a sports coat and dress shirt, sitting as regally as if he were a king on his throne, and writing notes on students' papers as if he were issuing edicts. "I'm here for our appointment."

He put down his work and turned his stare on Emma, swiftly eyeing her from head to toe—lingering a second or two on her breasts—in a way that made her want to take a shower.

"Come in and shut the door," he said. "Standing there like a terrified child won't get you a passing grade."

Yeah, but unzipping your fly and taking care of you will, Emma thought with an internal shudder of revulsion.

She walked into the room, closed the door, and immediately began to scan the place for items that were potential candidates for Hero's scent pads.

It was the typical boring educator's office. Dull off-white walls. Heavy, ugly bookshelves filled with textbooks and other assorted course-related crap. A coatrack with a tweed sports jacket hanging from it. Unimpressive steel file cabinets. A matching steel desk with computer equipment that was archaic enough to make Ryan roll his eyes in disgust. No family photos. No personal touches.

No surprise.

The books and the computer keyboard had promise. Those would definitely be things that had Hanover's scent on them. And the sports jacket—Emma had a few questions about that. But not just yet.

She sat down across from Hanover, placing her tote bag on the floor and leaning over to search for a pad and pen, using that time to scrutinize the office more closely. There was a gym bag that had been carelessly tossed in the far right corner. The bag was unzipped, so Emma could see the sneakers and towel inside.

Great find.

"Are we going to get down to business or are you going to spend the time digging in your bag and shaking in your shoes?" Hanover demanded.

Good, Emma thought. *The scumbag assumes I'm rummaging around because I'm nervous.*

"I apologize," she said, sitting up and arranging her writing material on her lap. "I'm not used to feeling so unprepared, either in a class or in a meeting with one of my professors."

Hanover sat back in his chair, steepling his fingers under his chin. "Have you had many meetings with professors? Am I to assume that means you were struggling in their classes, too?"

Emma bit her lip. "Actually, no to both questions. I've always been considered to be an excellent student. Maybe the bar is set much higher at Stern—"

"Or maybe it's set much higher in my classes," Hanover finished for her. "That's quite probable, Miss Lowe. I'm a perfectionist. I expect the same from my students." He slid open his narrow desk drawer to retrieve a pen.

Emma leaned slightly forward to see as much of the drawer contents as she could, fully aware that Hanover thought she was offering him a closer look at her breasts.

A comb, she mentally catalogued as she spied it. *And the pen that he took out. Two more items for Casey to use.*

One more clothing item. Just in case he decides to take the gym bag home.

That brought Emma's thoughts back to the sports jacket. Why did he have it here when he was already wearing an equally serviceable jacket? She had a strong hunch—one it was time to pursue.

The dialogue she was going for would require a delicate segue. But she had to pull it off so she'd know if the jacket would be an available option for Casey. And if her hunch paid off, it would be.

With that, Emma's curious gaze slid to the coatrack, and her eyes flickered over the sports coat—once, then twice.

"Miss Lowe?" As expected, Hanover intercepted her look. "Are you seeking my help or assessing my wardrobe?"

Emma's tongue slid anxiously over her lips. "Both. I do want your guidance, and I'm willing to work hard to meet your requirements—any of them." She crossed one shapely leg over the other, exposing a bit more thigh. "I'm also admiring your sports coat—I was thinking of getting something like that for my brother. He's going on his first round of job interviews."

A slew of points for her. To begin with, Hanover had homed right in on her body language. His eyes were glittering, and he probably had a hard-on already. Also, he was visibly flattered that she'd considered his jacket—which was as bland as uncooked rice—fitting for a much younger man.

Slowly, he rose from behind his desk.

"I think we can work something out to bring up your grade," he said, circling her chair and watching her reaction. "It would require extra hours spent in my office."

"Of course." Emma nodded, forcing a flush to stain her cheeks.

Hanover's lips curled. "I want to make sure we're on the same page, Miss Lowe," he qualified. "Our work will require discretion and a locked door. Am I making myself clear?"

"Crystal clear, sir." Emma folded and unfolded her hands in her lap. "When did you want to have these meetings? I assume that early mornings are out."

One brow rose. "And why would you assume that?"

Emma pointed at his gym bag. "You're clearly a runner. I wouldn't want to interfere with your running time."

"That's very considerate of you," Hanover replied. "However, early mornings are often ideal. It's quiet, there are no classes or office hours to interfere, nor are there any nosy custodians to bother us. It's true I run in the mornings, but that's before dawn. I can shower and come directly here." He waved his arm at the file cabinet. "I keep an extra set of clothes in there, plus an extra jacket like the one you were admiring for just this purpose. You need only to show up—with your class material, of course—and leave the rest to me. And for the record, I like skirts and dresses very much." He looked at her with grave, empty eyes. "I'm less fond of undergarments."

I'm sure you are, you perv, Emma thought. But she could barely contain her triumph. A whole drawer of clothing, along with a permanently hung jacket. Talk about hitting pay dirt.

Mission accomplished. Time to bid adieu to Dr. Scumbag.

Smiling shyly, Emma rose from her chair. "When will we be having our first meeting?"

He stopped in front of her, twisting a strand of blonde hair around his finger. "Monday morning. I'm not teaching till your evening class. I have midday office hours. And I'll be running at dawn. So be here at six thirty."

"I will." Emma extricated her tendril of hair, squeezing his hand as she did. "I look forward to acing your class."

Office of Forensic Instincts
Tribeca, New York

Perched on the edge of the desk in Ryan's lair, Casey pulled out her earbuds and turned to him. "We've got to move now or Emma will be on her back in Hanover's office come Monday."

"Agreed." Ryan looked as worried as Casey. "We can make this happen tomorrow. Remember, Emma said that Sunday mornings are the best break-in times."

"Yes. And Claire and I will be there right after dawn. Once that's done, get Emma out of that class. I don't care how you make it happen. Just do it. She's been through enough trauma playing roles like this. I'm not putting her in danger again."

"No arguments." Ryan interlaced his fingers and locked his hands behind his head. "I'll have Kate send Hanover an email. Since those can be monitored, she'll keep it short, sweet, and nondescript. She'll just say that she's freaking out because she can't handle what's required of her. She'll tell him she's dropping the class, withdrawing from the program, and heading back home. As long as Kate doesn't implicate Hanover in writing, he won't even blink. His primary target is Brianna, anyway. Kate was just a sideshow."

"And the administrative arrangements?"

"Piece of cake. Don't worry. Kate will be extricated ASAP. I'll take care of the red tape tomorrow morning, as soon as you give me the go-ahead."

"On Sunday? No one will be at their desks."

"They don't need to be. I'll do it all electronically. Relax, boss. Everything will be wrapped up before Emma's predawn meeting on Monday. You and Claire just get your canine vacuum and its accoutrements, and do your thing. Leave the techno-stuff to me."

"I always do."

CHAPTER 10

It was a little after nine, with a late May nighttime just settling over the city, when Brianna let herself into Lina's apartment.

Immediately, Lina jumped off the sofa, scrutinizing her friend's weary expression.

"How did things go with your parents?" she asked. "Was your security guy there the whole time? Did you get any inkling that that asshole was following you?"

"Emotional, yes, and no," Brianna replied, smiling in spite of her exhaustion. The past few hours had been draining. A dose of Lina's bursting energy was just what the doctor ordered. "Mr. Nickels drove me to my parents' apartment and walked me to the door. He met me in the hall when I called him afterwards and drove me back here. I'm sure he's right outside your place now. Believe me, I was safe. And, no, I didn't see any sign of Hanover. I guess that's a blessing."

Lina chewed her lip, watching her friend. "And your parents? Are they okay?"

"Of course not. They're worried sick. They're also upset with me for not coming to them sooner. And they're right. I dumped the whole situation on your parents earlier this week, but I kept my own parents in the dark."

"You were protecting them."

"I know that, but it was stupid. I needed their support. Now I have it. They asked if they could speak with Casey. Obviously, I said yes. I left a message on Casey's phone, giving FI permission to talk to them. And I'll be reporting in to my folks daily like a teenager. But that's fine with me. Truthfully, at this point I'm grateful for everyone's support. I'm so on edge that I feel like I'm coming apart at the seams."

"I know," Lina said softly. "And I'm so sorry. But I know Forensic Instincts will get the bastard. Just hang on." She gave Brianna a hug.

"Thanks." Brianna dashed tears off her face. Crossing the room, she went to her neatly stacked pile of clothes, pulling out a tired T-shirt and jeans and quickly changing out of the blouse and slacks she'd worn to her parents'. She frowned as she hung them up on the makeshift clothing rod she and Lina had set up. "I need to pick up more things from my apartment. I've been washing and wearing the same outfits all week."

"No problem." Lina, the reigning queen of fashion, nodded vigorously in understanding. "Why don't we grab a cup of coffee and head over there? We'll buy a cup for Mr. Nickels, too. He'll walk us to and from your apartment. You can get whatever you need."

"Sounds good."

* * *

Brianna knew something was wrong the minute she stepped inside her apartment and switched on the light.

She couldn't explain why. The place looked just the way she'd left it. And the front door had been locked. But she had the creepiest feeling—one she couldn't shake.

"Something's not right," she told Lina, glancing around the living room.

"What do you mean?" Lina asked.

"I don't know." She peeked into the kitchen and then headed for the bedroom.

She flipped on the light switch, took one step inside, and let out a shrill cry. "Oh no! *No!*"

Her lingerie drawer was yanked open. Her bras and thongs were tossed about in total disarray. There was a tangled trail of underwear leading from the dresser to the bed. The toiletries on her dresser had been shifted around, and her perfume bottle was open, the cap sitting purposefully beside the naked-looking atomizer.

And there, in the center of a visibly mussed bed, were a dozen white roses, with one red rose in the center. The whole arrangement was snuggled in white tissue paper, with a lacy bra wrapped around the stems.

The scene was Brianna's worst nightmare.

"Oh my God," Lina said from behind her. She grabbed Brianna's hand and tugged. "We can't go in there. He might still be inside. We've got to get Mr. Nickels."

Brianna was shaking so badly she couldn't answer. She was frozen in place, reeling from the terrifying invasion of her space, her life.

"Brianna—come on!" Lina dragged her friend out of the apartment, where they crashed into John Nickels in the hallway.

"What is it?" he demanded, already reaching for the gun inside his shoulder holster.

Lina blurted out what they'd found.

"Both of you stay out here," Nickels ordered.

Pushing the door open with his foot, he crept inside, pistol raised. Slowly and methodically, he checked each room. When he was sure no one was in the apartment, he holstered his weapon and whipped out his cell phone. In rapid fire, he snapped a series of photos, sending them right off to Casey. Then he returned to the front hall. "Come in," he instructed the girls. "But stay just inside the apartment. Don't touch anything, not even the door handle. This is a crime scene."

"We won't." Gently, Lina guided Brianna back inside. "We'll stand right here until the police arrive."

"I didn't call the police," John told them quietly. "I'm about to call Casey. She might want to handle things differently."

"I…" Lina's eyes widened. "Okay."

"He touched my things. He was on my bed," Brianna whispered. "I think I'm going to be sick."

"Well, you can't be," Lina said, trying to snap Brianna out of her hysteria by using humor. "There's no receptacle to be sick in. We can't touch the trash can or the toilet. So pull it together and forget the idea of throwing up."

Brianna managed a wan smile. "Thanks, Li."

"Hey, it's as much for me as it is for you. When someone near me vomits, I immediately begin doing the same. And I happen to like the outfit I'm wearing."

John was about to punch in a number when his cell phone rang. He glanced at the caller ID, although he knew full well who it was.

"I was giving you a minute for the photos to go through," he answered without prelude. "So I'm assuming you got them." A nod. "Yes, Brianna and Lina are both fine. Shaken but fine. They're right here with me."

A long pause as he listened to Casey's instructions.

"How long?" he asked. A pause. "Then that's what we'll do. But I think it's about as far as we can push it. Okay, done."

He pressed the red phone button to end the call.

"We're going to have to wait about an hour or so," he said, turning to Brianna and Lina. "Then, we'll call the police." He cleared his throat. "We'll have to amend our story—specifically the time we arrived. I'll go over the script with you after I turn off the lights."

"We're standing here in the dark for an hour?" Lina asked.

"Unfortunately, yes."

"Why?" Brianna was re-centering herself, forcing herself to think straight. "Why aren't you calling the police right away?"

John pursed his lips, clearly deciding how much to say.

"Given this much evidence, the NYPD would step in and take over the entire case. Casey doesn't want that—not until she has the evidence she needs to turn over to them. She's getting it now." John gazed from one girl to the other. "Trust her."

"We do," Brianna said at once.

"Yes, we do," Lina echoed.

"Good." He reached past them to turn off the front hall light. "I'll go take care of the bedroom light." He took a step in that direction.

"This plan of Casey's—it falls outside the lines, doesn't it?" Lina blurted out.

John didn't reply.

"Whatever it is, let's give her the time to do it," Brianna answered for him. "That's why we hired her."

* * *

After rushing down the four flights of stairs at the FI brownstone, Casey burst into Ryan's lair. He looked up from his computer, surprised at her uncustomary dramatic entrance. But seeing her expression, his eyes narrowed.

"What's wrong?" he asked, swiveling his chair around.

"Where's Claire?" Casey's gaze took in the entire room. "Is she with you? Please say yes."

"She just left to buy a box of herbal tea."

"Call her. Get her back here. Now."

Ryan asked no questions. He just did as he was told.

Not three minutes later, Claire appeared in the doorway. She looked embarrassed. "Ryan and I were just…"

"This isn't about the two of you. That's none of my business. It's about Brianna." Casey explained everything John had told her, showing the photos to both of her teammates.

"Shit," Ryan breathed. "Where the hell was the security detail watching Hanover? How did he get into Brianna's apartment without being seen?"

"I don't know," Casey replied. "Somehow he got by them. We'll figure out what went wrong later. Right now, our focus is on Brianna."

Claire had paled. "This reached the crisis level much faster than we expected."

"And we have to rectify that." Casey was in military mode. "Claire, you and I have to break into Hanover's office now. As in right now. Whether or not it's a good time. We need those scent pads, and we need Hero to confirm Hanover's presence in Brianna's apartment. John's waiting an hour before calling the cops. That's as far as we can push it. After that, they'll have to be alerted."

"And we'll lose control of the whole case," Ryan finished for her. He began rummaging around on his desk, finally producing a faculty ID card, which he gave to Casey. "Emma charmed this out of some semi-retired professor's pocket. It'll get you in the building." He rose and went over to a shelf. "Here." He tossed two NYU T-shirts and two pair of jeans at them. "These were down here for safekeeping. You'll just be wearing them tonight instead of tomorrow." He turned his back. "Get dressed."

Both women pulled off their work clothes and donned the T-shirts and jeans Ryan had thrown them. They'd planned their attire. They had to look like any other grad students.

"I'll get the equipment," Casey said. "Then we're gone."

CHAPTER 11

NYU Stern Business School
Faculty wing

The ID card Emma had ripped off worked like a charm. Forty minutes after Casey spoke with John Nickels, she and Claire had swiped their way into the building, dashed up the stairs, and were poised on the second-floor landing.

Casey balanced the large duffle bag she'd slung over her shoulder as Claire turned on her iPhone flashlight and peeked around the corner at the top of the stairs.

"Clear," she muttered.

They headed down the deserted hallway and stopped in front of Hanover's office.

Casey gave another quick glance from side to side and then pulled two pair of latex gloves out of her jeans pocket. She handed a pair to Claire, and they both yanked them on. Then, Casey set down the duffel bag that held all the tools she needed. "Let's see if I can do Marc proud," she murmured. "Shine your light on the lock."

Claire leaned over and complied.

With that, Casey unzipped the bag and pulled out a torque wrench and a pick. Concentrating, she followed through on what she'd seen Marc do a dozen times, and the process he'd explained to her while he was doing it.

She inserted the flat end of the wrench first, exerting just enough pressure to the L-shaped top of the tool, which was serving as a lever. Now came the delicate part. She inserted the pick and ever-so-carefully tapped each pin out of the way. There was a slight click, followed by a subtle movement of the cylinder as the torque wrench acted as a substitute key.

It turned the entire cylinder and disengaged the lock.

They were in.

"Obi-Wan has taught me well," Casey whispered. She sounded more than a little proud.

Claire's lips curved. "I can't wait to goad him about how much better and faster a job you do." With that, she pushed open the door, and all banter vanished.

They slipped inside and shut the door behind them.

"Don't take the chance of turning on the overhead," Casey said. "I brought two low-light flashlights in my duffel. We'll use those and our iPhones."

Claire nodded, and the two women went straight to work. Gloves in place, Claire swiftly retrieved each of the items Emma had reported on, all of which were there, even the gym bag.

She pulled a towel out of the gym bag, held it for a minute, and gave a shudder of disgust. "Dark energy. A twisted sexual mind. And sick images of him violating Brianna."

"See if you can focus on where he is. Hopefully far away from Brianna's apartment. I don't want him anywhere near there when we bring Hero over. But he's a psychopath. If he knows Brianna's home—even armed with security—he'll hang around to see the results of his handiwork and to congratulate himself. If need be, I'll check in with our security detail and get his location—after I rip them a new one for screwing up. And if he's outside Brianna's place, Ryan will arrange a diversion."

Claire nodded, sitting down and continuing to grip the towel. "Let me see what I can pick up on. The vibes from this gross rag are strong."

Casey knelt down, opened the duffel bag wide, and removed the STD-100 scent transfer unit—or canine vacuum, as Ryan called it—along with the necessary jars, sterile scent recovery pads, alcohol wipes, and Ziplocs. She knew the drill like the back of her hand. Set up the vacuum. Put the pads in place. Put the personal articles on the pads. Vacuum for thirty seconds—more than enough time for the pads to collect the crucial smells and then be stored in jars.

Pack up her gear, grab Claire, and get the hell out of here.

She was halfway through her task when Claire's voice interrupted her. "Hanover is pacing around outside Brianna's building. He knows she's being guarded and that he's being watched. Those facts are actually exciting his sick mind. So's the fact that he managed to elude security long enough to violate her space."

"No surprise." Casey turned off the vac for a minute. "Okay, there's got to be a back entrance to the apartment. Call John and tell him to be ready to run down and unlock it. Next, call Ryan and tell him to get Hero in the van and to speed to Brianna's. Hero can do his thing in the back alley. Then he'll execute inside." She turned the vac back on. "Give me five more minutes. Then we'll put everything back in place. We were never here."

* * *

Emma and Ryan came speeding around back of Brianna's building and double-parked. Ryan leashed Hero up and led him out of the van. The trained bloodhound was already on high alert, somehow aware that he was about to be called upon to fulfill his role on the team.

"Thanks for calling and telling me what was going down," Emma said as she jumped out of the van. "Most of all, thanks for letting me come. I've never seen Hero at work. I can't wait."

As she spoke, Casey and Claire appeared, rushing down the dark stretch to avoid detection.

"Hanover's around here somewhere," Casey said, dropping her duffel to the ground. "We've got to work fast. It's your show, Hero." She gave his ears a quick scratch as she unzipped the bag.

Hero spotted the familiar scent transfer unit, and he sat, his stare fixed on Casey as she squatted down and began to remove jars from the duffel bag. "I'm glad you're here, Emma," she added. "You deserve to be. We got everything. It was all exactly where you pointed us. Great work."

"He didn't take any of his personal stuff home?" Emma asked.

"Nope. But now he can do whatever he wants with it. It's served its purpose."

"And so has grad school. Emma's about to be done with it." Ryan's jaw set. "I'll set things in motion as soon as we get back."

"My official get-out-of-jail-free card," Emma said. "Thanks." She watched what Casey was doing. "I get it. Those pads have Hanover's smells on them. Hero's going to match them with the stuff in Brianna's apartment."

"Yup." Casey was already opening the first jar.

"By the way," Claire informed Ryan with a twinkle. "According to Casey, she got into that office five seconds faster than Marc would have."

"And *I'm* the arrogant one?" Ryan teased. A sudden grin lit his face. "Damn, it will be great to rub Marc's nose in that."

"Stand in line," Claire retorted. "I was Casey's wingman. It's my honor to go first."

"You always do, Claire--voyant." Ryan gave her a wink.

"Cut it, Ryan," Casey ordered. "This isn't the time. Hero has to concentrate." She opened a jar and offered it to the bloodhound. "Go on, boy. Take a whiff."

Hero went into action, thoroughly sniffing the jars containing every pad Casey had made. That done, he sat down again, looking straight into his owner's eyes, letting her know he was ready.

"Let's go." Casey scrambled to her feet.

Claire tried the door while Casey packed up. "It's unlocked. Bless John."

They were all inside the building, up the stairs, and at Brianna's door in minutes. John ensured it was them and then let them in.

"Thank God," Brianna breathed, sagging with relief when she saw them. "I'm not sure I could have stood here doing nothing much longer."

"I'm pretty freaked out, too," Lina confessed.

"We're down to the home stretch." Casey was holding Hero's leash, unsurprised that he was staring in the direction of Brianna's bedroom, tugging and whining to get going. "Hang tight a minute or two." She turned on her flashlight and allowed Hero to pull her where he wanted to go.

The minute they crossed the bedroom's threshold, Hero became a whirlwind of motion. He walked back and forth alongside the line of scattered undergarments, giving a sharp bark as he did. He looked up at the dresser top and sat down, signaling Casey with his body language that Hanover's smells were on it. Most importantly, he raced up to the bed, put his front paws on the comforter, and gave several sharp, meaningful barks before resuming a sitting position on the rug.

"Good boy." Casey produced a few pieces of Hero's favorite beef jerky. "Excellent work."

They returned to the others, who were watching them with anxious expressions.

"Brianna, call the police," Casey instructed. "Hanover's scent is everywhere, most importantly on your bed and on your intimates. We've got him."

Brianna's hands were shaking as she took out her iPhone. "Mr. Nickels told me that, when I call the police, I should tweak my arrival time a half hour or so. That's no problem. But what do I say about how we got Hanover's personal items?"

"You say nothing. That's our job. You just make the call and report the break-in."

Nodding, Brianna complied, dialing 9-1-1. "Now what?" she asked when she'd supplied the necessary information and hung up.

"Now we wait. When the police come, you report exactly what you found when you got here. After that, you let us do the talking. The cops know you filed three complaints against Hanover and that there wasn't enough proof to warrant follow-up. That'll explain why you hired us. It'll also explain why we've been watching Hanover and how we got his scent off a sports towel he left on the ground during his morning run."

"A white lie," Lina murmured.

"A necessary one," Casey replied. "Out in the open means fair game—*and* admissible. Believe me, the NYPD isn't going to grill us. They want this scumbag off the streets as much as we do. They'll be delighted with what we're handing them. Just stick to the basics. Any elaborations will come from us."

"Will they arrest Hanover right away?" Brianna asked.

"They'll bring him in for questioning and ask for a DNA sample. In the meantime, Crime Scene will be here, packing up everything so they can do a full DNA analysis. They'll find Hanover's genetic calling card all over your personal things. That'll be more than enough to charge him."

"And then the floodgates will open," Ryan added. "Once we give them a list of the other women Hanover has sexually harassed, the cops will talk to them and, hopefully, convince a few to testify at Hanover's trial. But that'll just be the icing on the cake. We already have what we need to get him locked up. He'll be behind bars and you'll be free."

"Thank you." Brianna's eyes filled with tears. "You're amazing. I can't begin to tell you…"

"You don't have to." Casey squeezed her arm. "Now let's get this wrapped up."

CHAPTER 12

Dani boarded the plane and stowed her carry-on under her seat. She was still smiling as she settled in and fastened her seat belt.

The two days and one sleepless night with Gabe had been… wow. She hadn't expected things to burn quite that hot—hotter than at the convention, even hotter than when they were in college. It had taken her aback, as had her level of stamina. Evidently, being a workaholic meant that you stored up your carnal needs until you were sex starved, so that when you let loose, you became a wild woman.

In between lovemaking sessions, she and Gabe had talked. They'd always been strong on the communication front. And now, they had more in common than they had before, being in complementary fields. They'd shared war stories as they sipped on wine and nibbled on cheese. They'd also taken a tender stroll down memory lane, alternately laughing and falling silent, pondering the past with nostalgia. Different choices might have meant a different future, but that's what life was all about. They'd been kids. They'd gone in different directions. But this was the here and now, and it was pretty damn wonderful. From this point, they'd see how things played out.

All in all, a most satisfactory visit to Cleveland.

Physical exhaustion was finally making itself known, and Dani sank back in her window seat for a catnap. The direct flight from Cleveland to New York City's LaGuardia Airport was quick—less than an hour and a half—and she'd be landing just before six. She planned to use every minute of that time to recoup her energy for part two of her mini-vacation. Her time with Gabe had been great. But she felt an equal amount of anticipation about the next lap of her trip.

She couldn't wait to meet Gia.

Despite her marathon hours with Gabe, Dani had managed a rapid-fire back-and-forth message exchange with Gia. Everything was set. Gia had managed to lighten her schedule to just a few meetings, during which time Dani would explore Manhattan on her own. The rest of the time, they'd see the sights and get to know each other, which, given the fun they shared in their messages, would be a blast. They'd even gotten silly about the whole thing, each collecting a series of childhood photos to show to the other, since they were dying to see if there had always been such a strong resemblance.

Just as Dani had little time for romantic ties, she had little time to form close friendships. Her career simply didn't allow for it. Sarah was her dearest friend—they'd been tight since high school—but that was about it, other than her family. So, the rapport she had begun to establish with Gia meant a great deal to her.

And she knew in her gut that Gia felt the same way.

* * *

Gia walked into the terminal at LaGuardia early, at five thirty, just in case the "on time" status showing on the airline's web page turned out to be wrong. Airline schedules were about as accurate as meteorologists. And Gia didn't want Dani standing around waiting.

Weaving her way through the crowds, Gia realized how much she was looking forward to these next few days. True, she was in desperate need of a self-imposed break. But that wasn't what was driving her. The real reason for her anticipation was that she was dying to meet Dani. She had to find out if the uncanny way they'd hit it off had any link to them being dead ringers for each other.

Situating herself as close as she could—just on the other side of the passenger screening lines—Gia gave another quick check of the airport's data screen. "On time," Dani's flight still read. That meant a half hour to go. Perfect. Gia leaned against the wall and began scanning her emails to pass the time.

* * *

Thirty-five minutes later, Dani's flight arrival was displayed on the screen. Gia snapped to attention. She was surprised to find that her heart was racing—an odd reality, considering how cool she always was when dealing with emotionally charged situations. But somehow this was different. She couldn't put her finger on it. But she had the weirdest feeling that this meeting was going to have a powerful impact on both Dani and her.

No time to ponder that thought. The girl who walked down the exit ramp, scanning the throngs of people, was a mirror reflection of Gia. Having the advantage of focusing on Dani first, before she was spotted, Gia did a sharp double take, catching her breath and just staring. Facebook photos were one thing. Up-close-and-personal was another. Different hair, different clothes, but, hell, talk about identical. This was downright surreal.

She snaked her way forward, waving as she did. "Dani!"

She knew the second Dani saw her. Her eyes widened, and a flash of stunned awareness shot across her face. Studying Gia with amazement, she gripped the handle of her rolling carry-on, pulling it along as she made her way over.

The two girls stared at each other for a long minute and then spontaneously hugged, laughing as they did.

"I can't believe this," Gia said, taking a step back and scrutinizing Dani from head to toe. "I think I'm in shock."

"I almost passed out when I saw you," Dani admitted in return.

A middle-aged woman who'd been one of Dani's fellow passengers on the flight from Cleveland walked by them and paused. "What a lovely reunion," she said, smiling. "How long has it been since you've seen each other?"

They both stood there, uncertain what to say.

"Ages," Gia finally supplied. "We have so much to catch up on." She was trying to be as tactful as possible without bluntly asking the woman to go away.

Fortunately, Gia's attempt was successful, and the woman took the hint graciously. "I won't keep you. From what I've read, it's difficult for identical twins to be apart for long. Have fun." With another smile, she hurried off.

"Identical twins." Gia shook her head as she spoke. For a complete stranger to jump to that conclusion? It spoke volumes about the way things appeared. "I knew we looked alike, but seeing you in person…"

"It's bizarre," Dani finished for her. She opened her mouth to say more and then flinched as a man in a business suit blew by, his suitcase whacking her as he did.

"Sorry," he muttered, never breaking stride.

As Dani rubbed her elbow, Gia rolled her eyes at the man. "Well, welcome to New York," she intoned. "Let's get out of here. We'll go back to my place so you can change and unwind. The rest is completely your call. We can race around like thoroughbreds, or we can hang out like couch potatoes. I'm up for either."

"The first part sounds great," Dani replied. "Going back to your place for a while. I need to catch my breath. Also, we'll have some time in the car to talk. I'd like that before we start making our to-do plans."

"Perfect. Let's go."

* * *

A pair of eyes watched intently. The information he'd received had been accurate. There was nothing good about what was happening.

He followed the two girls, walking at a leisurely pace.

He wasn't worried about losing them. He knew what car Gia drove, where she was parked at the airport, and where she lived.

He'd be where he needed to be and do what he needed to do.

This get-together would be brief—and hopefully bloodless.

Offices of Forensic Instincts
Main conference room

"Last night was a slam dunk. What an adrenaline rush." Ryan was perched on the windowsill, looking out over the New York skyline as the last filaments of sunlight caressed it. "The rush that comes from solving a case never gets old, especially when it means putting a scumbag behind bars." He tipped back his head and took a swallow of his beer, as usual opting out of FI's traditional case-ending glass of champagne. Screw the cache. Blue Moon trumped Veuve Clicquot every time.

"We still have a ton of follow-up," Casey reminded him. She was sitting at the head of the conference room table typing notes into her MacBook Pro while savoring her glass of champagne. "Although everything's proceeding nicely. Hanover was taken in for questioning, CSI is doing its job, and the wheels of justice will soon be turning."

"And Hero is a hero once again." Claire set down her flute on the floor beside the beanbag chair she was sitting on and began stroking the top of the bloodhound's head. "You're brilliant, you're loving, and you're warm-hearted. You're even gorgeous. Who could ask for a more fitting hero?"

Clearly, Hero liked the praise and the stroking, because he gave a contented grunt and rolled over to have his belly scratched.

"Hey, I'm all those things," Ryan piped up. "Do I get that kind of attention, too?"

Claire bit back a smile as she looked at him. "No. You're also arrogant and exasperating. Hero's neither. You lose."

"The jury's out on that one," Ryan muttered. But he wisely kept any further comments to himself. Another innuendo and he'd be taking a cold shower tonight—something he had no intention of doing.

Emma ignored them both, drinking her champagne with a mixture of satisfaction and happiness. "Seeing the relief on Brianna's face made going back to school and sucking up to that pig worth it." A quick glance at Casey. "I know I was being trained and tested. What's the verdict?"

Casey stopped typing to give Emma a thumbs-up. "You were great. I'm really proud of you, Emma. You've come a long way in a short time. I'll be counting on you more and more from this point on."

Emma's whole face lit up. "No more tests?"

"I didn't say that," Casey replied with total candor. "I test all of you at different points. It keeps everyone on their toes. And before you ask, yes, I test myself. Every day in every way. I'll never take my leadership role at FI for granted. You guys deserve the best because you are the best. And if you ever remind me that I said that, I'll deny every word and cut your salaries."

"Yes, boss." Emma zipped her fingers across her mouth in a my-lips-are-sealed gesture.

"I really like Brianna and Lina," Claire said. "They're great girls."

"So do I," Casey agreed. "And the feeling is mutual. They both asked if we could still hang out together—socially, since the investigation is now in the hands of the NYPD. Successful case, new friends. It's a win-win all around." She raised her flute. "Here's to another coup for FI."

They all raised their glasses, or, in Ryan's case, his beer bottle.

"Time to choose our next case," Emma said. "We've got a stack on my desk. I scanned them all. Nothing urgent. Some more interesting than others."

"We'll pass them around for review tomorrow," Casey replied. "Tonight is time to celebrate and unwind. Also, Marc and Patrick are due back this week. So we'll all jump into something new together."

"Cool." Emma polished off her champagne. "Whatever we choose, I hope it'll be as high-octane as this past case."

Casey's brows arched. "Be careful what you wish for."

Gia's townhouse
Rye, New York

"Wow." Dani perched her carry-on in the hallway and walked through Gia's combo living/family room. "This place makes mine look like a cardboard box."

Gia smiled, glancing around the modern layout with a happy, grateful expression. The townhouse wasn't huge. But it was open and airy, which made it look larger than it was. That was one of the reasons Gia had fallen in love with it.

"I got lucky," she replied. "The previous owner was transferred to Seattle. She needed to get out fast, so she took a low bid—mine. I'd just earned a hefty bonus, and my income qualified me for a decent-sized mortgage. It all came together at once. So here I am. And I've gotten spoiled. I really love this place."

"I don't blame you." There wasn't a shred of jealousy in Dani's voice, only admiration. "I guess I don't need to ask if there's enough room for me to sleep. I was going to offer to take the couch."

"No need. There's a guest room upstairs. I already made it up for you. Did you want to rest?" It was hard for Gia to hide the disappointment from her tone.

"No way." Dani shook her head. "All I want is a quick shower and a change of clothes. I've got to set up my laptop to catch up on a couple of case files, since my pet patients are being handled by an associate while I'm away. Then we can go out." She wrinkled her nose in a way Gia recognized as something she always did when she was thoughtful. "Would you mind very much if we stay local tonight and do Manhattan tomorrow? I'm kind of feeling the past few days."

"Not a problem. We'll go low-key tonight and all out tomorrow."

Excitement flickered across Dani's face. "Is the Big Apple really awesome? All I've seen of it is an airport, a postage stamp of a hotel room, an Uber, and the inside of a veterinary clinic."

Gia nodded. "The city is a world unto itself. It gets in your blood and pulses through you until it's got you hooked. If you're up for it, we could catch a train in earlier and do some shopping. Then we could go to a club or a restaurant or even a Broadway show if you're willing to take whatever tickets are available. Your call."

"Yes to the shopping. Then let's do dinner and a club." Dani sounded like a kid in a candy store. "I want to do all the nauseatingly tourist things that first-timers do. Fifth Avenue. Times Square. The Empire State Building. Dinner somewhere that native New Yorkers roll their eyes about and call a tourist trap. Oh, and I want to drink and dance at the trendiest club you know."

Gia was laughing. "Forget the afternoon train. We'd better leave right after breakfast to get all that in."

"Do you mind?"

"Are you kidding? I'll love it. I'll get the chance to see the city for the first time all over again. What could be better than that?" Gia's eyes danced. "Besides, our meeting is a celebration. Let's do it in style."

CHAPTER 13

The Pub
Rye, New York

The Pub was Rye's local watering hole, noisy, rustic, and complete with a jukebox, a dartboard, and great beer and food. Given this was a weeknight, the place was only three-quarters packed, and Gia and Dani were seated and served without a wait.

"This is exactly what I needed tonight," Dani declared a little while later, munching on a personal pizza and watching a group of college kids wearing SUNY Purchase T-shirts playing darts while they tossed back their beers.

"Yeah, the Pub is our go-to place." Gia took a bite of her bacon cheeseburger, wondering if Dani would be willing to go with her to the gym before they headed off to the city tomorrow. A whopping burger with fries and beer, leading into a full day of stuffing her face in Manhattan would tip the scale, and not in Gia's favor. It would also make her next gym visit grueling. She'd be a slug, rather than being primed to get the adrenaline rush necessary to kick-start her workday.

"What are you thinking?" Dani asked.

Gia tilted her head hopefully. "Do you like working out?"

"Yes, if I ever have a breathing minute to do it. I'm on call a lot. And I go into the clinic early. So there's no gym time. I make up for it by running a few miles every morning. Why?"

"Because I'm kind of obsessive about my time at the gym. Would you mind going with me, just for an hour, really early tomorrow? That would give us plenty of time to shower, get dressed, and head off to the city. Or would you rather sleep in?"

Dani grimaced. "I'm not sleeping in. We've only got two days together. Resting doesn't factor into that. How about a spin class? I haven't done one of those in ages."

"Great. That calls for another beer."

Gia glanced around for their waiter, who was somewhere lost in the crowd. Instead, she caught the eye of the bartender—a nice-looking blond guy about their age, who was hanging out behind the bar, mopping the countertop, in a rare free moment. Gia signaled to him that they just wanted two beers on tap. He snapped off a salute, siphoned their drinks, and walked over, setting down their glasses.

"Sorry, Gia, I think your waiter ran out for a cigarette break…" His words trailed off, and his startled gaze darted from one of them to the other.

"Gia?" he asked tentatively, focusing on the girl who'd flagged him down. "That's you, right?" He eyed her longer hair, obviously using that as an identification marker. "You have a twin?" This time he stared at Dani. "Wow, identical honeys!"

Both girls grinned.

"Even the same smile," he noted.

"Yes, Jay, it's me," Gia said. "And I hate to disappoint you, but we're not twins—just friends. This is Danielle."

"It's nice to meet you, Jay," Dani replied.

"Friends my ass." Jay was practically drooling as he ogled them, one by one. "Danielle. So you're the twin. Different hair. Different accent. Dead ringers. Why the secrecy?"

"No secrecy," Dani assured him. "Just fact."

"You live in the Midwest?" the bartender asked her. "I went to college there. I recognize the twang. I'm not just a bartender," he hastened to explain, clearly eager to impress. "I do this for extra cash. I'm in finance."

"Good to know." Dani was having a hard time not laughing out loud. "And, yes, I do live in the Midwest—shrewd observation."

"I go back a lot to visit friends. Give me your number before you leave. I've tried to pry Gia's out of her a couple of times, but no luck. Maybe you'll be easier on a guy's ego? We could have dinner, either while you're in town or when I'm in your neck of the woods. No strings."

Fortunately, Dani didn't have time to answer. Another patron called out for Jay, and reluctantly, he turned away. "Gotta go. But I'll be back to get your number and to hear your deep, dark secret. Whatever your reason is for this pretend-to-be-friends thing, I'll tell you now, it won't work. Identical twins are identical twins. But nice try." He winked and headed off.

"You have a new fan," Gia commented, taking a swallow of her beer. "Do you think Gabe would mind?"

Dani's lips twitched. "I think Gabe's feeling pretty secure right about now. But at least I have a gentle way to let Jay down. There's nothing like the words 'I have a boyfriend' to pour cold water on another guy's hopes." Her brows knit quizzically. "What about you? In your messages, you said you don't date much—too overwhelming a career. I can relate. Until I ran into Gabe again, I was practically a nun. Not a healthy lifestyle balance."

"You're right." Gia gave a rueful sigh. "I hear about it from my parents on a weekly basis. I do actually date—at least once in a while—but so far I haven't met Prince Charming. Also, remember that most of the guys I meet are about to be married themselves—to other women. Kind of limits the future of the relationship."

"I see your point." Dani paused, her finger tracing the rim of her glass. Clearly, her thoughts had taken a different turn. "I also see Jay's. Not about a date, about us. We do look exactly alike. Unfortunately, I don't have a genetic lineage to trace. I was adopted."

"What?" Gia did a double take. "So was I."

A long moment of silence hung between them.

"We can't be twins," Gia said finally, her mind working through the details. "Believe me, I'm an only child. My parents tried for years to have a baby. If they'd had a chance to adopt two, they'd have grabbed it with both hands."

Dani nodded. "So we're each an only child. We're also the same age. Facebook says your birthday is January twelfth. Mine's Valentine's Day."

"Different birthdays. Still, is it possible we share some blood ties—cousins or even half sisters, maybe? Our biological father could have been spreading the wealth around."

"Great. Two simultaneously pregnant women, both of whom he dumped. Nice guy. If that's what happened, I'm glad I never met him."

"Do you know anything about your biological parents?"

"Nope. Closed adoption. No contact and no knowledge."

"Same here." Dani blew out her breath. "I can't believe we're having this conversation."

"How could we not? Since the moment I saw you, my mind's been racing from one possibility to the next."

"Mine, too." Dani gestured at Gia's shoulder bag. "Do you have those baby pictures with you? I brought mine."

"So did I."

They both dug around in their purses. Dani pulled out a small but full photo album. She shoved the album across the table to Gia. "That about covers my life, newborn through high school, with a smattering of college and vet school." She smiled fondly. "My folks are big on capturing the moment—every moment."

"I hear you." Gia produced her own album, which was more neatly organized but equally thick. "I had to pull out the baby bathtub and changing table shots. Way too embarrassing."

The girls shared a laugh.

Fifteen minutes later, they weren't laughing or even exchanging lighthearted chatter. They were soberly comparing photo albums, staring at pictures that were eerily similar to each other. The girls in those photos—whether as babies, toddlers, young girls, teens, or adults—were almost identical, not just in appearance but in facial expressions, unconscious hand gestures and body motions, everything down to the space between their two front teeth that had required braces to fix.

Gia broke the silence, her voice shaky: "I'm starting to freak out."

Dani nodded, white-faced, as she continued to compare two photos of two little girls in Brownie uniforms, smiling their pre-orthodontic smiles. Finally, she placed the pictures on the table and interlaced her fingers in front of her. "There's no point in trying to explain this away. Whatever ties we have are real. The question is, what are we going to do about it?"

"I'm a get-it-done-now person, Dani." Gia was a wreck, but she held Dani's gaze as she spoke. "I vote for a DNA test. We can Google the closest testing center and go there tomorrow. I don't know how long the results take to come back or—"

"That's what the Internet's for." Dani was already using the browser on her cell phone, entering key words into Google. "Where's White Plains?" she asked. "Or New Rochelle? They both have testing centers."

"I grew up in New Rochelle," Gia replied. "My whole family still lives there. So that location is out. We'll do White Plains. It's closer anyway—just ten minutes away. What time do they open?"

"Wait." Dani held up her hand as she scanned the information. "It says you need an appointment and a doctor's prescription." She frowned. "We don't have either. It shows places you can order DNA test kits from, but that will take time. Apparently, even drugstores carry them now, but you still need medical authorization. More time. More hassle."

"I don't want to wait."

"Neither do I." Dani continued scrolling down on her phone. Abruptly, she stopped. "There's a place in Manhattan that has a doctor on site to issue the prescription. One-stop shopping for DNA testing. But we still need an appointment."

"What time do they open?"

"Nine a.m."

"We'll be there at eight forty-five. We'll tell them the truth—that you're only in town for a day. We'll appeal to them on every level possible. We'll offer to pay them extra if we have to. I do this kind of thing for a living. I'll find a way to make it happen." Gia's voice had steadied. She was all bulldozer now, ready to take on the world and win. "We'll get this ball rolling first thing tomorrow."

"Agreed." Dani looked equally resolute. "And while we're at it, let's have them do the whole gamut of testing—from distant genetic ties to a much closer link, like siblings." A long pause. "Or twins. No matter how impossible it seems—Gia, I need to know for sure."

"So do I." There was no hesitation on Gia's part. "I assume it's the same one-time mouth swab. If it's multiple swabs, then fine. Either way, the lab does the rest. It'll come down to how extensive and costly the testing is. And regardless of the price, it's worth it. So we'll check every box on the form."

"I'm in. Whatever it costs, it costs." Dani took a gulp of beer—one that would do nothing except quench her thirst. "I'm not discussing this with my parents," she stated flatly. "Not until we have results and not unless those results confirm we're related. I don't want to upset them that way."

Again, Gia nodded. "My parents would fall to pieces if they even set eyes on you, much less knowing our plan. I'll go to them *if* and only *if* there's something for us to discuss." She polished off her own beer and then tossed her napkin on the table, leaving half her burger untouched. "Sorry. I've kind of lost my appetite."

"So have I." Dani pushed aside her pizza. "Why don't we call it a night?"

Seeing the expression on Dani's face, Gia felt a pang of regret. They'd planned two days of fun and bonding, and instead they were dealing with a sober, life-altering matter.

"Dani." Gia's innate calming skills kicked in. "We'll take the test. But whatever our answers are, we won't know them for days, after which, we'll deal with whatever we have to. In the meantime, let's not waste this mini-vacation of yours. Let's walk out of that testing center, take a deep breath, and go do all the things we talked about— from the shopping and sightseeing to dinner and a club. And let's do it like carefree kids."

Gia's words put a smile back on Dani's face. "You're *good*, Ms. Wedding Planner. I feel better already. So, you're on. We'll take care of business and then give the Big Apple and our credit cards a run for their money."

* * *

The man pulled his baseball cap down low on his forehead as he watched them leave the Pub, climb into Gia's car, and drive away. He turned over his ignition and followed at a respectable distance. Seeing where they were headed, he made his phone call.

"Dinner's over and they're heading back to her apartment," he reported. "Tonight's a bad idea. Suburb is way too quiet. That means too many nosy neighbors vying to be Good Samaritans on TV news. Tomorrow, they'll be in the city, swallowed up by the crowds and urban indifference. I'll take care of it then."

CHAPTER 14

Doing the DNA tests had taken far less time than Gia's convincing the center to accommodate them without an appointment.

Ultimately, the technician at the center had caved. Between Dani's appeal that she was returning to Minneapolis tomorrow and Gia's pointing out that they could have had three DNA tests done in the amount of time they were pleading their case, the technician had sought approval and gotten it.

After presenting several forms of personal ID, filling out a gazillion forms, and finally getting the necessary doctor's prescription for the multiple tests being run, Gia and Dani had gotten their cheeks swabbed. The technician explained to them that notification containing the results would be accessible by email and by phone using the file number assigned to them along with a secure password. So there'd be no problem accessing the results confidentially from two different cities. And since Gia and Dani had opted for express delivery, they'd have their answers two to three days from now.

After leaving the testing center, it took Gia and Dani awhile to recapture their enthusiasm over the day ahead. But two lattes and a Fifth Avenue shopping spree later, they were in a poorer but far happier state of mind and ready to embrace the city.

They were oblivious to the man watching every step they took.

Green Lawn Cemetery
Brooklyn, New York

It was hard to believe this was Brooklyn, he thought, just as he did each time he visited the mausoleum. The city felt far away, like it was a separate world, far removed from the plush green hills and utter sense of peace that surrounded him. Silence, broken only by the occasional chirp of a bird, made it easy to focus on where he was and why.

He knelt down at the foot of the marble crypt bearing a plaque that read:

Angelo Colone
July 1962 – March 2017

"Hey, Angelo," he whispered.

He placed the flower arrangement against the cold stone wall. He bowed his head, tears seeping from his eyes. He stayed that way a long time, feeling the same deep sense of loss, coupled with the surreal sense that this was all a bad dream, that any minute now, Angelo would walk up behind him, slap the back of his head, and tell him to stop crying like a baby.

That wasn't going to happen.

He sat back on his heels and wiped his eyes with the backs of his hands.

"I still can't believe you're gone," he said. "You always had my back—always." He swallowed hard. "But you wouldn't have stood for this crying shit. You'd tell me to be strong, to be the man you taught me to be."

He pictured Angelo as he'd last seen him—on his death bed, weak and still, his breathing shallow as death drew near. Powerful Angelo, barely there and yet still a presence. He'd called him over, whispered something in his ear.

Only Angelo could have made him smile through his tears.

With that vivid memory, he reached into his pocket and pulled out a silver dollar, turning it over in unsteady hands. "I still can't get over that, for all these years, you knew I'd stolen your lucky coin and you never said a word. I thought I'd really put one over on you. Then, as you were slipping away, when you told me to keep the coin but to never forget that you were always smarter than me... I..." He squeezed his eyes shut again. "I fucked up, Angelo. I created a big problem. You and I both know it. And now, with you gone, I've got to fix this myself. And I will. You have my word."

A lonely silence was his only reply.

Le Bernardin
155 West Fifty-First Street, Manhattan

"Wow." Dani couldn't stop looking around. She'd certainly heard of Le Bernardin. It was a top-ten NYC restaurant. Its prix fixe dinner cost a small fortune. But she'd gladly charge it and pay it off on her credit card. The dining room was magnificent. It had been recently remodeled, and the traditional French aura had been replaced with a trendier look, probably to attract a younger crowd. From the large triptych of storm-tossed waves hanging on the wall adjacent to their table to the intricate panels of latticework on either side of the painting to the awesome shimmery metal and bamboo window treatments—Dani was hooked. Her mouth was already watering for the red snapper she'd read was one of the chef's specialties.

"Guess I made the right choice," Gia teased, watching Dani's fascinated scrutiny of the restaurant.

"Ya think?" Dani tore her eyes off the painting to meet Gia's amused gaze. "Standing at the top of the Empire State Building was the best," she declared. "Seeing *Hamilton*—I don't how your contact managed to get tickets when the show is booked for months—that was the best. Strolling all over Central Park was the best. Well, this is definitely up there with all those bests."

"I'm so glad—about all the bests."

"I'll say it again, you're an A-plus event planner. You even arranged for our shopping bags to be held at the Crowne Plaza Hotel so we can party now and pick up later. Remind me to call you when I get married."

Gia laughed. "Will do."

"How did you pull this off?" Dani asked, curious and enthralled at once. "I might not be a New Yorker, but I've done my research. Le Bernardin books a full month in advance. Yet here we are."

Gia's eyes twinkled. "I've done a number of weddings here." She pointed upward. "At Bernardin's Les Salons, just one floor up. The room is stunning—all etched glass, floor-to-ceiling windows. They host elegant, small affairs. So when I explained the last-minute circumstances, the maître d' was kind enough to accommodate us. Thankfully it's a weeknight, or we would have been SOL." She shot Dani an apologetic look. "There's a small catch. I'm handling a fall wedding here, and the planning stages are heating up. The chef wants a word with me after dinner. Quid pro quo. I'm sorry. It'll be quick, I promise."

"No problem," Dani assured her. "It's a beautiful night. While you have your meeting, I'll stroll down to Rockefeller Center. Google Maps told me it's a four-minute walk. I'll hang out there and wait for you."

"Perfect." Gia waited as the uniformed waiter placed a glass of white wine in front of each of them.

"I'll be back shortly with your appetizers," he said before politely vanishing.

The moment he left, Dani leaned forward, her eyes still filled with an endearing childlike excitement. "What club are we going to? My feet are about to fall off, but I don't care."

"You wanted trendy? Well, we'll pick a place where the rich, famous, and beautiful people hang out—and where we can get in without a reservation. My professional ties won't help us. Anyway, we'll find somewhere we can dance and people watch."

"I'll do a Google search while I wait for you. And if I fall in love with Rockefeller Center, I'm coming back here in December to see the tree, the display of angels, and to go ice skating." Dani rolled her eyes in self-admonishment. "I sound like a ten-year-old, huh?"

"You sound like a first-time visitor to the most dynamic city in the world," Gia replied. "That's how it should be. Now let's savor a meal to die for and then work it off on the dance floor."

* * *

Dani strolled past Radio City Music Hall, soaking in the lights, the noise, and even the crowds. She was sure that those same crowds would be annoying as hell during the morning commute. But tonight they were part of a vibrant city, and she was loving every minute of her walk. The pedestrian arcade leading to Rockefeller Center was just ahead, and it would be pleasant not having to deal with traffic but just to be a gawking tourist.

She never saw him coming.

In a flash, her purse was yanked violently from her arm, the strap snapping under the strain. She was shoved—hard enough for her to topple forward onto the sidewalk. Dazed, she forced her head around in time to see what looked to be a teenage boy wearing a black hoodie taking off like a bat out of hell, pushing his way through the crowd and vanishing into the night.

A few people stopped beside her, helping her to her feet and asking if she was all right.

Reflexively, Dani glanced down at herself, shaking like a leaf as she did. Physically, she seemed fine. Her slacks were torn, and she was covered with dirt and grit from the spalled concrete. And, yeah, her hands were scraped, bleeding a little and throbbing from where she'd hit the ground. But none of that was severe. Her nerves, on the other hand… She was so rattled she could barely focus.

"I… I guess," she replied, vaguely aware that, seeing she was basically fine, the bystanders were now dispersing and heading on their way. "I'm just…" She had no idea who she was talking to.

"Do you need me to call the police?" a female voice asked. "I'm guessing your cell phone is gone with your bag."

Dani turned to see a college-aged girl in jeans and a T-shirt squatting down beside her. She looked sympathetic but not particularly surprised. She was the only person still hanging around the scene.

"You're clearly from out of town," the girl explained. "Nobody but a tourist leaves her purse swinging freely on her arm. And nobody strolls around staring at Rockefeller Center like they're about to start taking pictures. You're a walking target."

"I suppose." Slowly, Dani was starting to collect herself. "And, yes, I'd appreciate if you'd call the police. Also, one more call—to the friend I came into Manhattan with. She's just a few blocks away at a meeting."

"Sure. No problem." The girl took out her phone. "I'm Michelle, by the way. And I wish I could say I'd be your witness, but all I saw was a teenage kid in a black hoodie blow through the crowd with your bag. I'll gladly tell that to the cops, but all they can do is check trash cans for your empty purse. That kid is long gone, and so is anything of value you were carrying."

"I'm Danielle, and yeah, I know." Dani rubbed her arms, cold despite the fact that it was a warm night in early June. She was probably overreacting, but she'd never been mugged before. Not only was the experience miserable but she'd now lost all her cash, her credit cards, her cell phone… the whole thing sucked.

The girl, Michelle, was kind enough to stay with her until the police showed up. Two minutes later, Gia came bursting onto the scene, visibly thrown by what she'd been told on the phone.

"Are you okay?" she asked, gripping Dani's forearms and eyeing her torn clothes and bleeding palms.

"Fine." The trembling in Dani's voice said that she was anything but. "I just want to answer the policeman's questions, futile as they might be, and get out of here. I have to cancel my credit cards, change my passwords, and God knows what else."

"Excuse me, miss?" A middle-aged man made his way over, holding up her tattered purse. "I saw a kid drop this in the trash two blocks down. I was here when he grabbed it. I doubt there's much left of value inside, but I assumed you'd want it."

Dani took it on autopilot. "Thank you so much." A hint of a smile. "The muggers in New York City are outnumbered by the kind people. I appreciate you retrieving this and bringing it to me."

"No problem." He turned as the cop asked him a couple of questions, all of which he answered with the same ambiguity as Michelle had.

With Dani's property having been returned and a report containing what flimsy details there were in his possession, the cop was ready to call it a night. He told Dani he'd contact her if he learned anything and then got in his squad car and drove away.

Dani muttered a thank you, but the truth was, she was barely listening. Something was off. Her purse was still zipped and it weighed too much to be half-empty.

She unzipped it and began fumbling inside, her puzzlement increasing as she pulled out one object after another. "My wallet's still here," she said in amazement. She went quickly through it. "So is my cash and all my credit cards. They don't even look touched. And my cell phone is here, too. I don't get it."

Gia peered over her shoulder. "There's nothing missing?"

Dani rummaged around again and was about to shake her head when she froze.

"What is it?" Gia demanded.

Slowly, Dani's head came up and there was a freaked-out expression on her face. "The little photo album," she said. "It's gone. Gia, it's the only thing missing."

"Are you sure?" Now Gia was going through Dani's purse. "Maybe the album fell to the bottom. Or maybe it fell out while he was running away?"

"It's not there. I went through every nook and cranny of this thing. And it couldn't have fallen out. The bag was zipped. He had to have unzipped it, taken what he wanted, and re-zipped it before he tossed the bag away. There's no other explanation I can think of."

By now, Gia had paled. "Who would want pictures of you as a child?"

"I don't know. But they obviously wanted them badly enough to mug for them." Dani raked a hand through her hair. "I don't feel great."

Gia took out her phone and fired up the Uber app. "Car service," she explained, seeing the questioning look on Dani's face. "Neither of us is up for a long walk and a train ride. Given what's happened, a car service is the best alternative. We'll swing by and get our packages from the hotel, then head back to my place."

* * *

An hour later, Gia turned the lock of her townhouse door and let the two of them into her apartment. They'd barely spoken during the drive home. Both of them were exhausted, creeped out, and in a bit of shock. They'd checked Dani's purse a few more times, each time confirming what they already knew—that the photo album, and *only* the photo album, was gone. They'd even checked Gia's purse to see if it had gotten mixed into Gia's things, but only her album was there.

Maybe the plan had been to steal Gia's photos, too.

Maybe the opportunity just hadn't presented itself.

It was a reach, but it was a scary one—one that wasn't out of the realm of reality. Did someone *else* actually have an interest in their physical likenesses?

The thought was weighing on both their minds as they made their way into Gia's living room.

"I'll get you some Neosporin and a bunch of Band-Aids," Gia said, tossing aside her purse and shopping bags and eyeing Dani's knees. "You need to treat your cuts before they become infected."

Dani shook her head. "Thanks, but I'd rather take a shower first. Then I'll treat them. I'm dirty, achy, and tired."

There was something in the sound of her voice, and Gia gazed at her, knowing the answer even as she asked the question. "You're flying back early."

Slowly, Dani blew out a breath. "I'm going to try to get my flight changed from tomorrow night to tomorrow morning. It might sound juvenile, but I'm a total mess, not as much from the mugging as from what was taken. I have a feeling you and I will be talking far into the night. After that... I don't feel much like partying or sightseeing anymore. I need some time alone just to chill before I go back to work the following day. Are you okay with that?"

"Of course. I'm pretty much a mess myself. I doubt I'll be doing anything productive tomorrow, either. But, yeah, we have to talk about this, explore it from every angle. Something's off. We know that. What we don't know is why."

With only a terse nod, Dani went off to take her shower.

* * *

The plan had worked.

The girl used her cell phone and switched her plane tickets to a morning flight. That meant she was scared shitless. She'd be out of New York and back in Minneapolis where she belonged.

Major threat averted—at least one end of it.

Now it was time to take care of the other end.

CHAPTER 15

Gia drove Dani to the airport and walked her to the check-in point.

"Safe flight," she said, fiercely hugging her friend good-bye. "Message me later. Whether or not we're related, we have a strong connection. I don't want to lose that."

"We won't." Dani hugged her back. "I'll touch base after I've had some recoup time, probably tonight."

"Perfect."

From the airport, Gia drove directly to the gym, where she worked out for two hours like an animal in the hopes of diminishing her anxiety.

The workout left her exhausted, panting, and still unnerved.

She sank down on a bench after her cooldown, a towel draped around her sweat-drenched neck as she breathed deeply in and out.

Dani had been right—neither of them had gotten any sleep last night. They'd discussed the missing photo album ad nauseam and gotten no closer to a solid theory for why it had been stolen or the lengths the thief had gone to in order to steal it.

"He either didn't have the opportunity to grab yours or one album was enough," Dani had said. "But enough for what?"

"I keep drawing a blank," Gia had replied. "Someone was either trying to scare you or get his hands on something we don't realize matters."

"What would that be? A picture of me in my bassinette? There's nothing valuable in that album, Gia. I didn't keep anything tucked inside it, either—like a safety deposit box key or anything else you see on crime shows. It was just a bunch of photos."

"I know."

They'd played devil's advocate all night, trying out different, far-fetched scenarios and coming up with nothing.

But Gia wasn't letting it go. No matter what the reason, Dani's photo album had been worth something to someone. She just had to figure out the why and the who.

She rose from the bench, debating whether to take a shower here or just go home and take a longer, hotter shower there. She was way too drained to set up client meetings, and everyone at the agency assumed she was taking today off to spend time with her friend. Which meant she didn't have to do the split-second-shower-and-put-on-business-attire thing, the way she usually did. Given that, maybe she'd just go home, shower, and try to chill out.

She'd just packed up her gym bag when her cell phone rang.

Glancing down at the caller ID, she was surprised to see it was from Mrs. Kaye, her neighbor from the townhouse next door.

"Hi, Mildred, what's up?" she answered.

"Gia, I know you're probably working, but you need to come home right away," the elderly woman said, her voice high and thin.

A tight knot formed in Gia's gut. "Why? What's wrong?"

"I just got home from the supermarket, and I heard the shrill sounds of your smoke alarm. I also smelled smoke coming from inside the house. I used the key you gave me and let myself in." Mildred was talking a mile a minute, and she paused to catch her breath, then rushed on. "The candle you left burning on your mantel had toppled over. It must have happened just before I got there, because only the photos on the mantel top were burning. I threw a bucket of water on the flames, and it seemed to do the trick. But

I was so frightened. I ran outside and called the fire department. They're here now, looking around."

Gia was already running to her car. "I'm ten minutes away. I'll be right there."

* * *

There was a fire truck parked outside Gia's townhouse unit when she arrived.

After slamming her car door shut, Gia raced up to the front door, which was ajar, sounds of activity coming from within. Nearby, Mildred was pacing around, wringing her hands. Gia could smell traces of smoke as she approached her neighbor.

"Thank you for all you did. You saved my house." Gia gave Mildred's hand a quick squeeze. "We'll talk after. Let me see what the firefighters have to say."

She'd barely taken a step when a solidly built man in full firefighter gear strode outside.

"I'm Gia Russo, the townhouse owner," she said without preamble. "How bad is the damage?"

The firefighter yanked off his helmet and dragged a forearm across his sweating brow. He scowled at Gia.

"You're very lucky you have such an attentive neighbor," he told her bluntly. "A few minutes later and your whole house would have been engulfed by flames. It's a good thing she came home when she did. She did our job for us. The fire's out. All that's left is residual smoke and a pile of burnt picture frames. The pictures inside them are dust. And the photo album that was closest to the candle is burned to a crisp. What were you thinking, going out and leaving a lit candle sitting there?"

"I didn't leave any candle, lit or otherwise," Gia shot back. "I don't have a candle on my mantel or anywhere else in my living room."

"Right." The guy clearly thought she was lying. "Well, then, someone bought you a present you don't remember and lit it for you. Because the thing was definitely there, definitely lit, and definitely the cause of the fire."

Gia wanted to rip him a new one. But she held her tongue. She might sound aggressive, but the truth was, she was one step away from breaking. She had fewer answers than this bruiser did and a hell of a lot more terrifying questions. Plus, given the circumstances, if their places were swapped, she wouldn't believe her denials, either. And maybe it was time she stopped issuing them. If the police were called in, this would become an open investigation. Gia had a different avenue in mind, one that was both private and secure.

"Look," she said, this time with forced calm. "I don't want to argue. If there was a candle there, I don't remember it. When I left the house, I was sure everything was properly turned off. If I was wrong, I apologize. I truly appreciate everything you did."

That seemed to mollify him. "Well, it's over now. Just don't ever repeat the mistake."

"I won't." She swallowed her irritation. "May I go inside now?"

"Yeah. We opened all the windows, so the smell of smoke should clear out fast. We deactivated the smoke detector, so once the house is clear of smoke, make sure the battery is in place and the thing is working right. Don't do any cleanup for a while; the mantel's still pretty hot. But otherwise, you're good to go."

As he spoke, the second firefighter emerged. He was younger and a little less gruff than his partner.

"Hi," he greeted Gia. "This your place?"

Mutely, she nodded.

"Well, it's in good shape. Fire's completely out. No major damage. Just remember that candles should be extinguished before you leave the house."

It was all Gia could do not to scream and remain calm. "Your partner already cautioned me about that," she replied. "I won't make the same mistake again."

The firefighters drove away, Gia thanked Mildred profusely, insisted on taking her out to lunch soon, and promised to come over for a cup of tea—just not right now. Right now, she needed to go inside and reassure herself that her home was intact.

Fortunately, Mildred understood. Exhausted from the events of the past hour, she admitted that she needed a nap, then went off to take one.

Gia waited until she was sure she was alone. Then she squatted down at her own front door, scrutinizing the lock. There was no sign of tampering. Then again, she hadn't thrown the deadbolt when she left, and a basic lock was easy enough to pick. Was that what had happened? Or had the intruder come through a window? Those, Gia rarely locked. Then there were her sliding glass doors off the dining room—she couldn't remember if she'd flipped the lock on those. Her neighborhood was so safe and so densely packed with townhouse units that Gia was pretty lax about this stuff. Obviously, too lax.

In any case, someone had gotten inside. The facts were the facts. A candle that didn't exist had appeared in her home and nearly burnt it to the ground. Someone had planted it there and set the scene. He wanted that photo album destroyed and he was ensuring that it was.

But why not just take it? Why go to all the trouble of setting a fire and incurring all the risks that might come with it?

There was only one answer Gia could come up with.

They wanted to scare the shit out of her. Just the way they had with Dani. There was no denying what was staring her in the face: someone wanted to keep the two of them apart.

Why?

Straightening, Gia glanced at her watch. Dani would just be landing. As soon as she checked out her home, Gia would send her a text and ask her to call the second she stepped off the plane.

A warm June cross breeze greeted Gia when she walked inside the house—a reminder that all her windows were open, diffusing the acrid smell of smoke still permeating the place.

She gazed around, taking in all the downstairs rooms. Other than the cluttered debris on her living room mantel, everything looked so untouched, so *normal*—when, in fact, nothing could be farther from the truth.

With her customary do-it-now attitude, Gia crossed over and scanned the mantel, remembering not to touch anything as she did. There were traces of candlewax alongside a clutter of burnt picture frames and the singed photos inside them.

Most important was the totally destroyed photo album that lay closest to the trail of wax. Gia could still make out frayed pieces of the album cover. But the contents were reduced to a pile of ashes.

Trying to keep it together, Gia took out her phone and sent a brief, pointed message to Dani: *Call me the second you get this. It's urgent.*

* * *

Dani rolled her carry-on down the exit ramp and into the waiting area. As always, she stopped there to check her texts and emails for anything urgent. She wasn't expecting anything.

She was wrong.

Every hair on her body stood up when she read Gia's message. She yanked her luggage to the nearest chair, sat down, and called.

"Thank God," Gia answered. "I don't think I could have dealt with this alone much longer."

Dani's panic intensified. Gia was freaked out in a way Dani had never imagined her to be. This was going to be bad.

"What happened?" she demanded. "Are you all right?"

"Listen to me." Gia had had enough time to realize that communicating with Dani this way was unsafe. She'd also had enough time to do something about it at her end. Time for Dani to do the same. "I need you to find a place in the airport that sells disposable phones. Buy two. Then call me back on one of them, but not on my regular cell. Call me at the number I'm texting you now."

"Gia, you're scaring me."

"Just do it—please."

"Done." The line went dead.

Gia tossed down one of the disposable phones she'd run out and gotten and began pacing. She didn't stop until that phone rang, this time with an unknown number showing in the caller ID.

"Hello?" Gia answered tentatively.

"It's me."

"Good." Gia wished she could stop shaking. "Now we're going to exchange phone numbers—not the one you're calling me on or the one I'm answering on. The other two—the ones we haven't used yet. After that, we're going to toss these phones and talk to each other only on the unused ones."

This time Dani didn't ask questions. She just gave Gina the number. Gia did the same.

"I'll call you now," she told Dani.

Dani answered before the first ring had completed. "What happened?" she demanded.

Gia blew through the story as quickly and accurately as she could, omitting none of the details. By the time she was done, Dani was gripping her phone so tightly her knuckles were white.

"This is surreal," she managed, bile rising in her throat. "A nightmare. Are you sure you're not hurt?"

"I'm fine. But I realized that whoever's doing this knows when we're together and what we have planned. That means they must somehow be intercepting our calls and texts. We can't take the chance of using our regular phones with each other."

"So from now on, it's these. I get it." Dani sucked in her breath. "How do we figure this whole sick thing out?"

"Without putting ourselves in danger, you mean?" Gia asked. "Whoever's doing this is obviously willing to go to extreme lengths to have us forget we ever met and to abandon poking around in our roots. If we ignore their warnings, who knows what they're capable of doing?"

Dani gritted her teeth. "I just wish I understood how our trying to figure out if we're biologically related would threaten them." Abruptly, a thought struck her. "Gia, the one thing they clearly don't know about is the DNA testing we had done. We never discussed that on the phone, through our Facebook messaging, or anywhere. Plus, if they did know, they wouldn't be wasting their time burning up photo albums. They'd be trying to intercept those test results. Look-alike baby pictures versus DNA? Not even close."

"You're right. And they won't be intercepting anything. The minute we hang up, I'll call the lab, make them aware that others might want to get their hands on our test results, and inquire about their security policies. That will probably piss them off, but it'll raise the red flags we need."

"That's a smart precautionary step."

"Yes, but probably unnecessary. Your logic makes sense. Given the tactics they're using to scare us off, I doubt they have a clue that we've gone for absolute proof."

"Which brings us back to, what do we do? Our lives could very well be in big-time jeopardy."

"I know." Gia had already thought this one through. "The test results aren't due for a couple of days. So let's let the bad guys think they've won. Let them think we bought these phones because we're scared rabbits. We'll each stay in our own neck of the woods, go about our usual routines. Their fears will die down. Meanwhile, we'll wait for the test results. Once we have them, along with the answers both our instincts are screaming they'll provide, I know the perfect pros to go to for help."

"Who?" Dani demanded.

"Forensic Instincts—a private investigative firm in Manhattan. Very avant-garde and very proactive, even in the absence of legal evidence."

"Which we have none of," Dani realized aloud. "Are you sure we can trust them?"

"I'm sure. They have a well-earned reputation as being the best. And that's not just hearsay, although they're in the media often enough. I know one of their team members, Marc Devcreaux. I handled his wedding a few weeks ago. He was a Navy SEAL and an FBI agent before joining Forensic Instincts. He's a great guy, but formidable as hell. If I didn't like him so much and see how devoted he was to his fiancée, I would have been scared to death. Trust me, a criminal wouldn't want to meet him in a dark alley."

"Okay, you've convinced me. So you have an in. I hope it's enough to get them to help us."

"There's only one way to find out."

CHAPTER 16

Offices of Forensic Instincts
Two days later

"I'm bored," Emma muttered aloud.

She'd just vetted the last of the new potential cases on her desk, written up her recommendations, and slapped the paperwork on her pile. She had to bring these in to Casey and the team to evaluate. She knew Casey wouldn't be inspired by any of them. They'd already accepted and solved one case on the original pile. The president of a staffing firm had convinced them that his company's database was being hacked and money being siphoned out of its accounts. It turned out—no surprise—to be an internal crime, conducted by a disgruntled and computer-savvy employee. Some discreet questioning by Casey and some techno-magic by Ryan, and FI had cracked the case in one business day.

Other than that, the only case of interest had been a request for Casey's consultation services from the NYPD. They were interrogating an assault-and-battery suspect and asked for Casey's expertise in body language analysis to help determine the suspect's guilt and to move toward getting a confession. She'd helped. They'd gotten their confession. Case closed.

No other cases had whetted their appetites.

These new ones wouldn't, either.

"Boring, boring, boring," Emma repeated, flipping through the paperwork and talking to no one in particular.

Someone in particular answered her.

"Your assessment reflects judgment, which is an inappropriate response, Emma," Yoda announced. "The full team must review the potential cases. Decisions will be based on the cumulative responses."

"Yes, Yoda, I know the drill." Emma rolled her eyes. "But I also know Casey. None of these cases is going to make the cut." She pushed back her chair. "But fear not. I'm following the rules. I'm bringing the paperwork upstairs right now for group evaluation." She leaned forward and pressed the all-call intercom button. "Time to gather in the main conference room for full review of potential cases."

The team was filing into the conference room when Emma walked in. Casey was seated at the head of the table, flanked by two familiar faces that Emma had missed.

"Marc! Patrick! When did you get back? How did you slip by my desk?" she asked in excitement. These two men were very special to her. Each had saved her life in different ways. She wouldn't be here if it weren't for their skill and loyalty. And she'd never forget it. Never.

"Hey, Emma." Marc's fingers were linked behind his head, and he looked tan, well-rested, and very much at peace. "We came in at the crack of dawn. Casey's been bringing us up to speed."

"You look awesome," Emma told him. "Marriage agrees with you."

"Yup." For an instant, Casey's hard-core right-hand man softened. "I'm one happy camper." The softness vanished, and Marc's usual hard-core presence returned. "It seems that Patrick and I missed a great case. I'm ready for another one."

"Well, I doubt you're about to get it from this sludge," Emma replied, placing the paperwork on the table in front of Casey and turning to the distinguished man with salt-and-pepper hair sitting to her right. "Patrick, welcome home." She gave him a big hug. "How were the graduation and the vacation?"

Patrick Lynch—retired FBI agent and FI's security expert—gave Emma a fond smile. "My daughter has become a young woman. Watching her, I realize she's almost your age. I can't believe it. But Adele and I were bursting with pride when she went up and accepted her diploma. And the family vacation was just what we all needed. But it's good to be back. I missed the action—not to mention the security lapse that allowed that psychopath to get into Brianna's apartment. You can be sure something like that will *never* happen again."

"We missed you, too." Claire was already settling herself at the table, armed with a cup of herbal tea. "By the way, Marc, you and Maddy took off before I could tell you how beautiful the wedding was."

"Thanks, but I can't take any credit for that. Maddy and her mother did all the initial planning, and that lifesaver of a wedding planner pulled it all together."

"Well, it was awesome," Emma said.

"Not as awesome as the honeymoon, I bet." Ryan grinned as he brought over his coffee and pulled out his chair.

Marc arched a brow. "I obviously wasn't away *that* long, Ryan. You haven't aged a day."

"And so it resumes." Casey gave an exaggerated sigh. "It's official. You're home. How did we survive without you and Ryan busting each other's chops?"

"My guess? Very nicely." Patrick chuckled.

"Yeah, but this is much less boring—unlike those potential cases." Emma gestured at the paperwork sitting in front of Casey. "I could barely keep my eyes open reading through those. I took Hero on two runs in the park just to wake up my brain."

Casey reached for the pile. "I got it, Emma. Loud and clear. You don't like any of them. Please give the rest of us a chance to weigh in."

"Oh, Marc?" Before they got started, Claire had something to say. She was a woman with a mission. "You should know that Casey's lock-picking skills are amazing. She's quicker and with a lighter touch than you."

"Oh, snap." Emma brightened.

"Really?" Marc's face wore its customary unreadable expression. "Casey told me you two broke into Hanover's office. Looks like I'm one hell of a teacher."

"Not to worry," Casey assured him. "I might pick a great lock, but I don't have your nerves of steel. I'll leave the breaking and entering to you." She began passing case requests around the table. "Let's dive in."

Rye, New York

Gia logged into the secure mailbox provided to her by the DNA testing center, unsure whether or not she would find the results today. Two days was the minimum. The doctor had said it might take up to three, plus Gia was more than aware that no medical results were posted before nine a.m. Still, she was losing her mind. Dani was equally on edge. So, she had to give in to the urge to look.

She logged in and then nearly bolted out of her chair, her heart racing a mile a minute. The notification stared back at her. *DNA testing results: Gia Russo and Danielle Murano.*

This was it. The answers she and Dani had been holding their breath for. And now that they were here, she was scared to death. What she was about to read would, quite possibly, change her life forever.

Her hands trembled on the keyboard. Her index finger was poised to open the file, but she didn't—*couldn't*—do it. She realized she was being irrational, but she felt as if she were standing at the edge of a high diving board with no choice but to take that last step and plunge.

She didn't want to take that plunge alone.

Gia glanced at the time on her laptop. Seven ten a.m. Six ten in Minneapolis. She hadn't admitted it to herself, but she knew this was the reason she hadn't gone to the gym this morning. She had to be at her computer, just in case. In her gut she knew Dani felt the same way. So maybe she hadn't taken a crack-of-dawn run and headed off to the animal clinic. In which case they could do this together.

On that thought, Gia picked up her disposable cell phone. She and Dani had talked a bunch of times each day, sometimes to reinforce their connection, sometimes to share their tension, and sometimes to talk. And now—it felt imperative that they share this experience.

She called Dani's disposable phone number.

"Hi." Dani answered on the first ring, her voice already fraught with tension—doubtless from the moment she'd seen Gia's number on her Caller ID. "Are they in?"

"They're in. Are you home?"

"Yes. I couldn't go out—just in case. But I was trying to hold off—at least till business hours—so I wasn't disappointed again." A pause. "Did you look?"

"I wanted to. But somehow I needed for us to do this together."

"Let me log in." A few clicks and Dani blew out a breath. "I'm there."

Gia swallowed, hard. "Ready?"

"Ready."

"Okay, go."

They opened the file simultaneously.

On each of their computers, the PDF appeared. A one-page document, consisting of the lab's bold letterhead and a two-column results summary of all the tests run.

The right-hand side of the page consisted of rows of data markers—codes followed by long numbers that were indecipherable to both Dani and Gia.

It didn't matter.

The left-hand side, much more succinct, had two sections—the top labelled *conclusions* and the bottom labelled *statistics*.

The conclusions were a two-paragraph explanation of the findings and the numerical likelihoods of each genetic connection the girls had been tested for. It held the longer-version answers they sought. But it was the brief statistics section below it that told them all they needed to know in one short phrase:

Monozygotic twins 99.9%.

"Oh my God," Dani whispered.

Gia couldn't even speak. She just kept staring at those two words—*monozygotic twins*—torn between shock at seeing them in print and a bone-deep awareness that both she and Dani had known the truth since the day they met.

They were identical twins.

"Gia?" Dani managed.

"I'm here. I… Dani…" She began to weep.

Dani was already crying. "We both knew. Somehow we felt the truth. But actually seeing it in writing… I just don't understand. Our birthdays. Our parents clearly not knowing the truth. How could this have happened? And why?"

"I don't know." Gia dashed the tears from her cheeks. "But someone out there *does* know and is clearly threatened by the truth leaking out. He's used some pretty extreme scare tactics to keep us apart."

"The mugging… the fire…" Dani's wheels were also turning. "He probably thinks he's won. Except for one thing. He doesn't know we took a DNA test and that we know we're twins. Not yet. But if he has a way of finding out—that ups the ante. Scaring us might not be enough."

"But we can't leave this alone. We need resolution."

"And to feel safe again."

A chilling silence hung in the air.

"Who was that investigative team you mentioned?" Dani broke the silence to ask.

"Forensic Instincts." Gia had been thinking along the same lines. "I wanted to call them sooner. But I felt like such an idiot, giving them nothing but speculation. But now... staring at these DNA results... I'll call them as soon as we hang up. The minute they can squeeze me in, I'll go."

"*We'll* go," Dani qualified. "I'm running over to the clinic right now and tending to my urgent patients. Then, I'm explaining to my boss that I have a family emergency and will need a short leave of absence. I'll do it without pay if need be. My colleagues are great; they'll pull together and fill the gap while I'm gone. I'll take the earliest flight I can." A pause. "But I need to talk to my parents first."

"Don't." Gia felt like an ungrateful bitch as she spoke. Her parents? Her wonderful parents? Never. But still... Her eyes welled up again. "You have no idea how much I want to go to my parents. But we can't."

"Why not? You can't possibly think they were part of something illegal?" Dani asked incredulously.

"Illegal? Of course not. But, Dani, my parents—and I'm sure yours—desperately wanted a child. Emotions that intense sometimes trump reason. Actively doing something illegal and looking the other way are two very different things. We've never been in their position. We can't imagine what they were going through or what a blessing it was to find out their prayers could be answered."

"I hear you," Dani said softly.

"No matter how much we love our parents, we can't screw things up by tipping our hand. We have to leave it to Forensic Instincts to find out if our folks can tell them *anything*, even the most minor detail, surrounding our births that would explain this."

"You're right. They're the professionals. We're not, plus we're too emotionally involved." Dani's sigh was pained. "But I feel like the worst, most ungrateful, and most deceitful daughter on earth."

"So do I. But we have to do it this way. For all we know, an interrogation by us could put them in danger."

"I never thought of that." Dani's resolve strengthened. "Call Forensic Instincts. I'll catch the first flight out I conceivably can. As soon as I have my itinerary, I'll call you with it."

"Wait," Gia said. "Before you log off your laptop, print a copy of the results. I'm doing the same. I'm also copying the file onto my flash drive. We need backup copies, and Forensic Instincts needs concrete documentation."

"I'm printing as we speak," Dani replied. "I'm also grabbing my flash drive. We should have two sets of everything."

"You're right." Gia's hand was shaking as she pressed the print button. "We don't know what's going to happen next. We need to be prepared."

* * *

DNA test results?

When the hell had they taken that test? During their day in Manhattan? How had his employer missed seeing them stop at a fucking DNA testing center? It didn't matter now, not when the results were glaring at him from her computer screen.

Shit. Shit. Shit.

He threw the wireless mouse against the wall, shattering it into pieces. If she knew, then the other one—Gia—did, too. It would explain the flight reservations Danielle was making now. An afternoon flight back to New York. The fire and the mugging had been wasted efforts. Now that they knew the truth, nothing would keep them apart.

Which meant that threats would no longer be enough.

CHAPTER 17

Emma was relieved when the phone rang. She'd spent the past hour emailing prospective clients, telling them the team would not be taking on their cases, and recommending easy fixes for their problems—like installing a new lock when an ex kept letting himself back into your apartment. Boring.

Whoever was calling had to be more interesting than this—hopefully.

"Forensic Instincts," Emma said into the phone.

"Hello, my name is Gia Russo." The woman at the other end had a direct approach and more than a little anxiety in her voice. "I'd like to speak to Marc Devereaux right away. It's urgent."

Emma's antennae went up. This was already intriguing. It was rare that someone, other than Madeline, called and asked specifically for Marc. He wasn't exactly the nurturing type.

"May I ask what this is in reference to?" Emma inquired.

"Is he in?" Gia Russo responded, this time more forcefully.

Emma's brows rose. "I'll check. But I'll need the reason for your call."

"He knows me. Just give him my name and tell him it's imperative that I speak to him now. I don't mean to be rude, but time is of the essence."

Emma's instincts told her this was legit. "Hold on, please."

She pressed the hold button that shut off the outside world and used FI's internal system instead. She could have dashed up the two flights of stairs to where Marc was doubtless ensconced in the corner office on the third floor, where he always did his solo work. But this way was faster, and Gia Russo sounded close to frantic.

Emma tapped the button labeled *Marc*.

"What's up, Emma?" Marc sounded a little bored with what he was reading.

Well, maybe his professional life was about to take an upswing.

"There's a woman on the phone who's desperate to speak with you. As in right now. She sounds like she's coming apart at the seams. Her name is Gia Russo. Do you know her?"

"She was Maddy's and my wedding planner." There was definite surprise and puzzlement in Marc's voice. "She's also a bulldozer. Gia doesn't come apart at the seams."

"Well, she does now. She says it's urgent and she'll speak only with you. That's all I've got."

"Put her through."

Marc closed the document he'd been reading and placed his iPad on the desk in front of him. His phone gave one *bing*, signifying that his caller was there.

"Gia?" he answered.

"Oh, Marc, thank God," she breathed. "I was afraid your receptionist would blow me off."

"What's going on?" Marc had to admit that Emma hadn't been exaggerating. Frantic Gia was one he had never heard.

"It's too long to go into on the phone. Suffice it to say, my sister's life and my life are in danger. We need to meet with you, hire you, like, *yesterday*. I know Forensic Instincts has a long waiting list of potential clients. And *you* know that I have just as long a waiting list for my services. I'm calling in the favor you offered when I bailed you out at the eleventh hour. My sister is flying in this afternoon. When's the earliest you can see us?"

Marc had a million questions. But instinct and experience told him that now was not the time. For Gia to be pushing this hard, it had to be bad. And grilling her on the phone would be wasting precious minutes.

"Hang on. I'll see what I can do." He pressed *T and his cell phone number. Immediately, he answered his now-vibrating phone and simultaneously put Gia on hold. He left the room, opting to talk to Casey in person. He loped up the single flight of stairs that separated them and knocked on the conference room door. "Casey, it's me."

"Come on in," came her reply.

He strode in and shut the door behind him. "Remember my wedding planner, Gia Russo?"

Casey's arched her brows. "Only what you told me. From your description, she was a get-it-done wizard with an iPhone and an earpiece."

"She's on the phone. She's a wreck. According to her, she and her sister are both in life-threatening danger. They want to see us ASAP." Marc met Casey's gaze. "This one's for real, Casey. Gia's not the type to freak out. Can we skip the preliminaries and see them late today? Her sister's flying in this afternoon in order to be here."

Studying Marc's expression, Casey didn't hesitate. Marc's instincts rivalled hers. If he said it was for real, then it was for real. "Find out when she lands, then set a time. I'll alert the team."

"I owe you one."

Marc got Gia back on the line and got the details, wondering all along what could have so badly shaken the strong young woman he knew.

LaGuardia Airport

This time, the greeting between Gia and Dani was a very different one than the last. It had been days—and a lifetime—since then.

The instant Dani stepped into the arrival area, she and Gia rushed toward each other, hugging tightly as soon as they could. There was a newly formed bond between them, and a sense of belonging. But both those precious things were marred by an underlying profusion of fear.

"This was the longest flight of my life," Dani said in a shaky whisper. "My emotions are all over the place. I have a twin, and I can't get over the joy of that. I have a million questions, all of which have me tied up in knots. And someone is trying to hurt us—or worse—and I can't wrap my mind around that, either."

"I know." Gia stepped back and squeezed Dani's hands, surveying her once again with that awed surreal feeling. Her twin. She had a twin. "I'm thrilled and I'm lost and I'm terrified all at once. But that's why you're here and we're together—to get the help and the answers we need."

"You said Forensic Instincts is expecting us," Dani responded. "I know next to nothing about them, except what I saw online."

"I'm not an expert, either," Gia replied. "But I did ask Marc some questions when I was handling his and Madeline's wedding. I'll tell you what I know in the car. Let's get going." She seized the handle of Dani's carry-on. "I assume you brought more luggage than this?"

"Since I have no idea how long I'll be staying, yes," Dani replied. "One suitcase and a garment bag."

Gia nodded. "We'll go straight to baggage claim, yank your stuff off the carousel, and carry it to the car ourselves. We have no time to deal with carts or porters. Marc's team is staying late for us. I don't want to keep them waiting."

"I don't want to keep *any* of us waiting."

Office of Forensic Instincts
First-floor meeting room

The team took their coffee mugs and settled in, either on one of the leather tub chairs or on one of the twin matching couches situated between them. Hero stretched out on the area rug alongside Casey's center-stage chair.

This was the same meeting room the team had used to interview Brianna Mullen. It was unintimidating and meant to put nervous clients at ease. In contrast, the main conference room was ideal for keeping more complex and ambiguous clients awed and a bit on edge as they were being closely interviewed.

The choice of which room was used during a first-time client meeting was Casey's. She seemed always to make the right call. And as she'd determined re their meeting with Brianna, this time she was equally certain that the team's interview with Gia Russo and her sister belonged right here.

"Gia Russo didn't give you any information other than the fact that she and her sister are in danger?" Patrick asked Marc, perching on the edge of a sofa cushion and taking a belt of coffee.

"Nope." Marc shook his head. "But my gut tells me it's bad. The Gia I worked with was a force to be reckoned with. She's a bulldozer, running over anyone and everyone if the sweet-talking doesn't work first. That wasn't the woman I spoke to on the phone. Whatever's going on, it's not imaginary or exaggerated."

"Yeah, she sounded that way to me, too," Emma said. "She couldn't get me to put Marc on the phone fast enough. I know the sound of desperation—that was it."

Claire frowned. "It's strange. I never met Gia at the wedding."

"That's not strange," Marc replied. "Gia's philosophy is that a good wedding planner's job is to make everything perfect while staying invisible. Kind of like a puppeteer who pulls the strings but remains out of sight."

"She sure pulled that one off," Ryan commented. "Not only didn't I see her, I'm still not sure what a wedding planner does. But whatever it is, I guess she did it right, because the wedding was way cool."

Casey was watching Claire. "That's not what you meant when you said it was strange, is it?"

"No." Claire's frown deepened. "I'm getting an aura of shock and confusion mixed with a sense of discovery. And danger—a strong surrounding force of it. What's strange is, I'm getting all this having never made contact with either of these two women, or even with a person or an object close to them. I don't think that's ever happened to me before."

"That is weird," Ryan said. "I don't get how this works. Does that mean you expect to have a stronger-than-usual connection once you've met them?"

Claire's shoulders lifted in a shrug. "I have no idea."

"It looks like we've already made progress on a case we have yet to officially accept," Casey noted.

"They really need our help, Casey," Claire told her.

"Between what you, Marc, and Emma have each said, I don't doubt it." Casey glanced at her watch. "They should be here any minute, based on the ETA Gia gave Marc when she called from the road. Given the circumstances, I think Marc, not Emma, should be the one who greets them at the door. There's an element of trust Gia already feels for Marc. Let's use it. I'll go out behind him, wait a minute or two, and then round the corner and introduce myself. I'm hoping that realizing the president of FI is on board will give them an added sense of security."

As if on cue, the doorbell sounded.

"Gia Russo and her sister have arrived," Yoda announced. "I apologize for the omission, Casey, but you didn't provide me with Ms. Russo's sister's name."

"We don't have it yet, Yoda." Marc was already headed for the door. "But we're about to."

* * *

Marc opened the door, his mouth already open to greet Gia.

It snapped shut as he looked from one of the girls to the other.

"Gia?" he guessed, his startled gaze settling on the longer-haired girl.

"Yes, Marc, it's me." Gia shook his hand. "And this is my sister, Danielle Murano."

"It's nice to meet you, Marc." Dani also shook his hand. "Thank you for seeing us with virtually no notice."

"Ms. Gia Russo and Ms. Danielle Murano have arrived." Yoda's voice echoed through the townhouse as he corrected his omission at once.

Both girls jumped.

"Not to worry," Marc assured them. "That's Yoda, our artificial intelligence system." He didn't wait for their response. "Gia, you didn't mention that you and your sister were identical twins."

"Monozygotic twins," Yoda clarified. "Definition being that a single egg was fertilized to form one zygote, which then divided into two separate embryos."

"Got it, Yoda." Marc was cutting this off before Yoda gave them a full genetics lesson. "I can take it from here."

"Certainly, Marc. I'll complete preparations for the meeting."

Gia blinked. "That's not an AI system. That's the Wizard of Oz. Who designed him?"

"That would be Ryan McKay, FI's technology magician. He was at my wedding, along with the entire team." Marc turned to Dani, silently getting a read on her. "Welcome to the Big Apple. You're from the Midwest. I recognize the twang."

A hint of a smile touched Dani's lips. "Actually, I speak normally. It's everyone here who has the twang—New Yoik-uhs to the core." Her smile faded. "But you're right. I'm from Minneapolis. That's why it took me so long to fly in. I'm sure you'd rather be home with your new wife, having dinner, than meeting with us."

"No worries. I can manage both." From somewhere behind him, Marc sensed Casey's presence—and yet, she was making no move to join them. He wondered what her motives were and finally decided she was giving him a little more time to help the girls relax. That wasn't Casey's usual style, but he'd go with it.

He continued to make comfortable introductory conversation with the girls.

* * *

Casey was reeling with stunned awareness.

She'd walked out two full minutes ago, ready to join Marc and their new clients. She'd reached the corner and was about to turn into the hallway. Instead, she'd come to a dead halt, staring at the girls Marc was speaking with.

Lina. It was Lina. Times two.

CHAPTER 18

What the hell was going on?

Casey was still gaping. Mentally, she kicked herself. There was no time to process what she was seeing. She had to alert the team before someone—probably Emma—made a huge faux pas.

Reversing her steps, she ran down to the office where everyone was waiting. She burst in and shut the door behind her, leaning back against it. Everyone's head shot up in surprise. Even Hero snapped into ready mode.

"We have an issue," Casey informed them. "And we need to deal with it in the next thirty seconds."

"What's wrong?" Patrick asked, taken aback by the shaky tone of Casey's voice and the shocked expression on her face.

"Gia Russo and her sister, Danielle Murano, are identical twins." Casey paused. "Well, not twins."

"Which is it?" Ryan demanded. "Twins or not twins? Either way, why is it a problem?"

"Because they're each a mirror image of Lina Brando." A quick glance around at the members of the team who had yet to meet Lina—sans Marc, who would have to hear this later. "Patrick, you and Marc were briefed on the Brianna Mullen case, and, Ryan, you were part of the investigation, so you all know who Lina is."

"They're a mirror image of her?" Emma had jerked up in her chair. She'd met Lina last Sunday when she'd joined Casey and Claire for their last-minute brunch with her. They'd hit it off instantly. "Are you saying…?"

"Triplets," Claire finished for her. "Yes. They're triplets. And none of them have any idea."

"Shit." Emma looked like a rocket about to go off. "I don't understand how—"

"Let Casey talk," Ryan instructed her. "Our thirty seconds are up. What do you want us to do, boss?"

Casey didn't hesitate. "Don't show our hand. Don't give them the slightest clue that a third sister even exists. We don't know what we're dealing with yet. Bringing Lina into the mix is out of the question now. I need each of you to do a flawless acting job."

"Done," Ryan replied.

Patrick nodded. Like Ryan, he'd be on board even if he didn't have the distinct advantage of having never met Lina. The same would apply to Marc once he knew.

Claire shook off her faraway gaze and resumed her usual calm demeanor. "This is the absolute right thing to do, so, yes."

"Emma?" Casey prodded, turning to face her. "Are you up for this, or should you sit this one out?"

"I'm fine," Emma surprised her by saying. "I'm a full team member now. And you know I'm a hell of an actress. So count me in. No Lina."

"And no shocked expressions when they walk in," Casey pressed. "Just the usual procedure of our team greeting new clients. Agreed?"

"Agreed."

"Good." Casey opened the door. "I'm going out there to introduce myself and to bring Gia and Danielle in."

* * *

"Ah, just who we were waiting for," Marc said as Casey walked into the entranceway. "I told Gia and Danielle that you were on your way."

"And I'm sorry I was detained," Casey said smoothly. "I had an important call I had to take." She extended her hand to each girl. "I'm Casey Woods, president of Forensic Instincts." Her brows drew together. "And you have me at a disadvantage. Which of you is Gia and which of you is Danielle?"

The girls clarified, each one shaking Casey's hand and thanking her for seeing them. As Casey had hoped, her presence and supportive attitude seemed to take their anxiety down a notch. It helped even more when she told Gia that Marc's wedding had been incredible and that she was obviously a planning genius.

"It helped that I was working with such a terrific couple," Gia replied. "It's not usually that easy."

"I bet." Casey was leading them down the hall to the meeting room. Small talk was over. It was time to switch gears. "Marc filled us in on the sketchy details you told him. He felt strongly about seeing you tonight, and I trust his instincts. My team and I are ready to hear your entire story."

"Thank you," Danielle said earnestly. "We're pretty freaked out." She pursed her lips in a gesture that screamed Lina.

Casey was having enough trouble tamping down her reaction. She prayed the team could pull it off. Whatever the triplet tie was, they had to figure it out before Gia and Danielle did.

Pushing the half-open door wide, Casey led the girls in. She watched the team's faces as she made the necessary introductions, and she was incredibly proud of them. Not a flicker of awareness was demonstrated, not even from Emma. Bravo, Casey thought to herself as she gestured for their new clients to have a seat.

Without realizing it, Dani helped diffuse any lingering tension.

"What an exquisite bloodhound." She gazed at Hero and then at Casey, her brows lifted in question. "May I?"

"By all means." Casey gestured for her to approach Hero, a slight smile curving her lips. "You might be sorry. He's a shameless beggar and attention seeker."

"I'll take my chances," Dani replied, also smiling. She walked over to Hero, squatted down, and offered him her hand to sniff. "I read about you, Hero. But you're far more handsome than your photo."

Hero took a few whiffs of her hand, then wagged his tail and rewarded Dani with an enthusiastic lick and a hopeful look.

"No problem, boy," she murmured, fumbling around in her purse until she pulled out a small bag of dog treats. "Here you go." She offered him one.

Hero needed no second invitation. He snatched the treat and began to noisily chomp on it.

"You carry those around with you?" Ryan asked, astonished.

"Yup. I've got cat treats, too. I'd rather give them a healthy, organic snack than see them eating processed food or, worse, food that could potentially make them ill. That's the veterinarian in me talking."

"Well, you just became Hero's favorite client." Ryan chuckled as he watched Hero lick up the last crumb and then give Dani another hopeful look.

"Nope. One to a customer, no matter how charming." Dani stroked his head. Then, she rose, leaving Hero to his water bowl and walking over to take her seat. "That's also the veterinarian in me."

"Now that you've fed Hero, let us do the same for you," Emma piped up. "We've got great coffee, espresso, latte, and awesome snickerdoodle cookies. What's your pleasure?"

"A latte would be wonderful." Gia inclined her head in a way that was totally a Lina gesture. "The cookies sound delicious, but my stomach is in knots."

"I understand," Emma replied sympathetically. She turned her questioning gaze on Dani. "Danielle?"

"I think I'll just have some bottled water if it's convenient," Dani responded. "The last thing I need is more caffeine. I'm already a bundle of nerves. And please call me Dani. Everyone does."

"Dani it is." Emma walked over to the JURA and made the latte like a true barista. "Sugar?"

"Just some Splenda if you have it," Gia replied.

"We have everything. We're coffee fanatics." Emma plucked two packets of Splenda, pulled a bottle of water out of the mini-fridge, and brought everything over.

"Thank you," they each said.

"Now let's talk." Casey set down her own mug. "According to Marc, your lives are in danger. Start at the beginning and provide as many details as you can."

Dani and Gia each contributed to laying out the full story for the FI team—from the day Sarah Rosner had mistaken Gia for Dani right up to the mugging, the fire, and the DNA results.

"We also bought burner phones," Gia concluded. "For them to know so much about Dani's and my plans, they must have hacked our phones and our Facebook accounts. So that's one hole we did try to plug up."

The entire team listened and took notes, most of them typing directly into their iPads. Given how quickly and nervously the sisters were speaking, everyone let them talk without interruption. Questions would come later.

"I think that's everything," Dani said at last.

With that, Casey set aside her iPad Pro and studied the two girls—as she had been throughout their whole explanation. Her own expression was pensive—for more reasons than Gia and Dani could possibly know. "No wonder you're both so rattled."

Gia frowned at what she perceived as a reserved note in Casey's voice. "Please don't say you think the mugging and the fire were coincidences. Or that you doubt the fact that they're tied to Dani and me finding each other."

"I definitely was not going to say either one of those things," Casey assured her. "I was just processing all the facts. Normally, the team and I interrupt with questions, but in this case, we wanted to hear the whole story from beginning to end."

"And?"

Casey glanced around the room and got the unanimous show of imperceptible nods she was waiting for.

"And we'll be taking on your case immediately. The attempts to frighten you off were pretty extreme. That implies that this situation is rapidly escalating. Whoever's after you is already desperate, and that's presumably without knowing you took a DNA test or that you've gotten the results."

"Which means that once he or she has all the facts, your lives will be in even greater danger," Marc said.

"That ship might have already sailed." Ryan's expression was grim. "If your phone calls, texts, and Facebook messaging have all been compromised, my guess is that your computers have been, too."

Gia shot straight up in her seat. "So they know about the DNA test results?"

"I'd say yes."

"Oh, God." Gia instinctively reached for Dani's hand. "Then our lives might really be on the line."

"Nothing's going to happen to you," Marc assured them. "Our job is to make sure of that. We'll keep you safe *and* we'll solve the case. Trust us."

The two girls nodded wordlessly.

Ryan continued, speaking as gently as he could. "I want you both to use your personal laptops only for work emails, Google searches, innocuous posts on Facebook and tweets on Twitter—everything you do on a daily basis. Omit anything that relates to the two of you, your fears and suspicions, and this investigation."

"A smokescreen," Dani murmured.

"Exactly. If you stop using your laptops altogether, they'll get suspicious. Let them think you're trying to go on with your lives."

"Then what do we use for the case-related emails, Google searches, and research?" Gia asked.

"I'll give each of you a Raspberry Pi. It's a full computer about the size of a pack of cigarettes. I've added a few goodies to the Linux operating system and added a Tor browser. Even the Chinese wouldn't be able to get in without me knowing about it. Plug it into a TV, a mouse and keyboard, and voilà. I always keep a few of these on hand—complete with accessories—just in case. Take them back to Gia's place. Reserve them for case-related research and communication."

"We'll do everything you say." Dani looked as if she'd been run over by a steamroller. "But tell me, how do we fight some nameless, faceless person who's been determined to keep us apart since birth, and who clearly has ominous motives for doing so?"

"*You* don't," Casey replied. "*We* do."

"How?"

"First, by figuring out the *why*. As you said, what's the motivation behind this whole scenario?" Thoughtfully, Casey tapped her finger against her mug. "Have either of you spoken to your adoptive parents?"

"No." Gia shook her head. "We wanted to. We both have close relationships with our parents. Because of that, we were afraid our love for them might turn this discussion into an emotional fiasco. Dani and I agreed that it would be best if you handled it. You're pros. We're not."

"That was a smart move," Marc replied. "We'll ask different questions than you would and with more objectivity and training." He penned more notes in the thick spiral binder he'd been using during the interview. Marc's process was to handwrite his notes and then enter the data, with additional comments and questions, into his laptop immediately after the clients left.

"Are your original birth certificates available?" Ryan asked.

"No. The adoptions were closed. The birth records are sealed—for both of us," Gia said.

"And neither of you knows the name of the agency or the attorney who handled your adoption?"

Both girls shook their heads.

"Then I've got my work cut out for me. There's no time for lawyers or petitions. I've got to get into the New York City Department of Health's records so I can manage a do-it-yourself unsealing of the birth certificates. I need to know your actual birthdate, birth hospital, and the names of your biological parents—or at least your biological mother if she listed your father as unnamed."

Claire had been quiet up until now. And she had that aura-seeking expression on her face. "Do you have any personal childhood toys, dolls, etc. that you were particularly attached to?" she now asked. "If so, I'd like to have those."

Gia and Dani turned to stare at her in that awed way Claire was all too used to. "You're the clairvoyant member of the group," Dani said.

"Claircognizant, but yes." Claire gave them a faint smile. "You've done your homework."

"Gia brought me up to speed. Between living in New York and knowing Marc, she had a head start on me. But I caught up. I Googled Forensic Instincts after we talked."

"We're going to help you," Claire said in response. "I'm hoping that by holding your personal childhood things, I can pick up something that might help me do so." She tucked a wisp of blonde hair behind her ear, giving each of the girls a gentle look. "I realize this has taken a backseat to the chaos in your lives, but congratulations on finding each other. You've discovered a precious connection—an identical sister. That kind of bond is unique."

"Thank you." Gia turned to smile at Dani. "We're certainly learning more about that connection every day."

Patrick cleared his throat. "I handle the necessary security for all our clients. Clearly, your situation warrants some level of protection. I'm not trying to frighten you. But the warnings you received involved physical harm. And if Ryan is right and our target already knows that you have proof you're identical twins, he'll escalate his attempts—especially once he determines you've hired us. I'd like to put you both under security watch."

"What exactly does that mean?" Dani asked.

"First of all, how long do you plan to stay in New York?" Casey inquired. "Because ideally I'd like you here until this case is solved so we can better keep an eye on you."

"I took a two-week break for a family emergency. So I'm not going anywhere." Dani frowned. "In which case, how will I get you the things you need?"

"Easy," Ryan replied. "You'll give us your apartment key. We'll put together a list of what we need, and you'll tell us where we can find them. One, probably two of us will be flying to Minneapolis to talk to your parents. We'll stop at your place and collect the necessary items."

"Do you both have passports?" Casey asked. "Because that's one of the things we'll need. Also your adoptive birth certificates."

"I have both at home," Gia replied.

"Me, too." Dani nodded. "I'll tell you where they are so you can add them to the list."

"Good. In the meantime, what county were you each born in?" Casey omitted the word *presumably*.

"New York. Manhattan."

"Same here."

"That's a good start."

Patrick interrupted to answer their question about the security angle of things. "For now, I won't do anything drastic to disrupt your lives. No in-home surveillance. Just a couple of my guys alternating their watch on Gia's place and a couple of others who'll follow each of you when you go out. I'll introduce all of them to you. After that, you won't even know they're around. But you'll be able to reach them at the touch of an iPhone button, even though they'll probably beat you to the punch."

"Oh." More and more, Dani was realizing the magnitude of what they were facing. "Under the circumstances, I think that will make us both feel better."

"I hope so," Patrick replied. "Because it means cooperation on your part, including supplying me with a list of your schedules and where you plan to be when. Dani, I realize you don't have a regular routine in New York. We'll have to sit down and figure something out. And it goes without saying, there'll be rules about both your activities. No stupid risks. No taking off without giving my guys a heads-up. And no discussing any part of this with anyone, not friends, co-workers, no one. Are we clear on that?"

Both girls nodded.

"Good." Patrick studied their faces and was satisfied with what he saw. "Then let's get the necessary information from you so we can start doing our jobs."

The next hour was filled with every scrap of information that Dani and Gia could provide on the assaults—including photos of the fire that Gia had taken, in addition to the DNA testing process, the security measures provided by the DNA testing center—which Ryan would follow up on anyway—and the best way to approach their parents. Dani wrote up a list of everything Claire and Ryan needed, each for their own purposes, and sketched out a floor plan indicating where each item could be found.

"Gia, I want to talk to your mom and dad tomorrow," Casey said. "I'll call first, tell them who we are, and say we have some questions about a case we're working on. There's no point in scaring them off by revealing the whole truth on the phone. When is the best time to reach them?"

"Call them tonight and make arrangements," Gia replied, worry written all over her face. "They're up with the sun. And they'll see you before they leave for work if you can get to their place by eight." A pause. "Please don't freak them out. Ask what you need to, but please be gentle. This is going to tear them up. Maybe I should be there."

Casey was already shaking her head. "That will throw things into emotional chaos. Trust me, Gia. I'll handle the situation, including making sure they know why you left this in our hands. My expertise is in reading people. I'll only push as far as I can, and I'll make sure to ask my questions with respect and care. They'll be shocked and on emotional overload, but once I tell them how much you love them and that you'll be coming by tomorrow night—with Dani, just so you can introduce her to them and bring her into your circle— they'll be okay. Also, Claire will be accompanying me to the meeting. She has an innate way of calming people, and she'll soften the meeting and the outcome. Everything will be fine."

Gia had been listening intently, although she still looked concerned. "Will you call me the minute you're finished and fill me in on everything?"

"Absolutely."

"What about my parents?" Dani asked. "Which of you is going to talk to them, and when?"

"I'll go," Patrick said immediately. "I'll take the first available flight to Minneapolis, tonight if possible. I'm a parent, too, and my kids are in their twenties. I feel for what your folks will be going through. I'll ease them through it." He turned to Marc. "You come with me. You can take care of things at Dani's apartment while I'm meeting with her parents. That will cut down on our time away."

"Done." Marc nodded. "We'll undoubtedly have to make at least one other trip there. But first things first. Let's call Dani's parents now and try to catch a night flight out." He glanced at his watch. "Seven o'clock. We're pushing it."

The glowing lights that arced across the wall—and the voice that accompanied them—told the team that an answer was near.

"Sun Country has a nonstop flight tonight that departs at nine o'clock from JFK and lands in Minneapolis at 11:11 p.m. central time," Yoda supplied. "The aircraft is a Boeing seven-thirty-seven. Five coach seats are still available—seats nineteen A and B, seats twenty-four B and C, and seat twenty-five F."

"Good," Casey replied. "Book two tickets right away, Yoda."

"And the return date and time?"

"Late tomorrow evening," Casey supplied. "That will give Patrick flexibility to talk to Dani's parents at a time that's most convenient for them, Marc time to collect everything we need, and more than enough time to get them back home in one day."

"Very good, Casey." There was a moment or two of silence. "Task completed," Yoda returned to announce. "Seats nineteen A and B are now Marc and Patrick's. Confirmation and boarding passes should be added to the Passbook on their iPhones any moment now. A car service will be arriving in fifteen minutes in order for them to leave immediately. Arriving one hour prior to takeoff is advised."

Patrick and Marc were already on their feet, simultaneously taking the written material Dani had provided and checking their cell phones. All the necessary confirmation and boarding information was there. And their carry-on bags were packed and ready; each member of the FI team kept an emergency bag at the office just for situations like this.

"You all set?" Marc asked, stuffing the notes from this meeting into his case, where they'd be ready to be transcribed into his iPad.

"Yup. Let's grab our bags and wait outside for our car. We'll call our wives and Dani's parents from the road." Patrick turned to Dani. "We'll keep you posted every step of the way." His voice gentled. "Don't worry."

"What about your security team?" Gia asked. "When will they start?"

"Immediately. I'll call and finalize their posts during our drive to the airport. I'll arrange for John Nickels, one of my most experienced men, to come to the brownstone ASAP. The whole team knows him, so they can make the introductions. That way, you'll feel more comfortable going with him when he walks you to your car. He'll follow right behind you in his car. Don't worry about losing him; you won't. Just drive normally and leave the rest to John. As for the other three men, I'll text you photos and basic specs so you'll have all the info you need. Wherever you are is where they'll be. Oh, and Dani, until we figure out your daily routine, either stay inside Gia's condo or accompany her wherever she goes."

"I will," Dani replied.

As he finished packing up his case, Marc leveled a steady gaze at Casey. "I'll call in," was all he said before he and Patrick left the room.

Casey heard Marc's message loud and clear. The team needed to talk, but not while Gia and Dani were there. The elephant in the room could only be addressed when the FI team was alone.

And that wouldn't be until John whisked their clients out of there.

CHAPTER 19

Thankfully, John arrived twenty minutes later. He introduced himself, chatting a bit with the team and with Gia and Dani, making sure to put the two girls at ease.

Catching Casey's eye, he nodded almost imperceptibly. Patrick had filled him in. "Okay, ladies, let's head up to Rye," he said to Gia and Dani. "You've had a long day. Time to rest."

Gia turned to Casey. "You'll call and tell us when you're seeing our parents?"

"The minute we make the arrangements, we'll reach out to you," Casey replied. "Expect tomorrow to be an emotional day. But it will also be day one in our information gathering." Seeing the defensive look flash in both girls' eyes, she clarified. "I wasn't implying guilt on their parts. It's always possible that an innocent person unconsciously knows something. It can only help us if that's the case."

That did the trick. Gia and Dani thanked them, took their Raspberry Pis, and left with John.

The team waited.

* * *

"All parties have left the building," Yoda informed them a few moments later. "Privacy is ensured. A team meeting can commence."

Casey picked up her iPhone, pausing to look at Emma. "You hid your reactions and kept it together. I'm proud of you." She pressed Marc's number and tapped on the speaker button while it rang.

"They left?" Marc asked without preamble.

"Yes. You're on speaker."

"We've got you on our earbuds now," Patrick replied.

Marc had fired up Ryan's custom-made app, which muted the iPhone speaker and patched in any of FI's earbuds within Bluetooth range.

Instant team audio conferencing.

"We shut the partition between us and the driver," Patrick continued. "He's listening to music. We can talk freely. I filled Marc in on the missing piece of this bizarre puzzle."

"Lina." Emma blew out a long breath, as if she'd been holding it for hours. "I can't believe it. I sat here and watched it, but I still can't believe it."

"It must be pretty hard for you to absorb," Patrick said. "Casey, you're absolutely sure?"

"I'm sure. They're triplets."

"I'm sure, as well," Claire said quietly. "Now I know why I had such a strong pull toward Gia and Dani even before they arrived. Lina. She's the third piece of the puzzle, and the one I already knew."

"Gia's and Dani's body language, their gestures, even their intonations—I heard and saw Lina more times than I can count," Casey said.

"Even the light-up-the-room smile," Claire added. "They all have it."

"What Gia and Dani *don't* have is any idea that Lina exists." Ryan's intense tone and expression indicated that his thoughts were rapidly transforming into strategies. "And neither of them knew each other existed until a few weeks ago. Obviously, their adoptive birth certificates were doctored, since they each believe they have different birth dates."

"I wonder if their parents knew about that doctoring," Casey murmured. "The results had to be genuine or the government never would have issued the girls passports."

"Right," Ryan replied, typing some notes to himself into his iPad. "Which means the job was professionally done, with or without their parents' knowledge. I'm leading with that assumption. But figuring out who did the doctoring isn't first up on the to-do list. First up is ferreting out the original birth certificates. I'll have to hack into the New York City Department of Health's records. No sweat."

"Patrick and I will push the Russos and the Muranos," Casey said. "Hopefully the information they give us will be consistent and just a small part of what they tell us. We have to find out if they're on the up-and-up."

"I've already spoken to Dani's parents," Patrick said from the other end of the phone connection. "The Muranos were very puzzled as to what case we were investigating that spanned all the way from New York to Minneapolis, but they agreed to see me tomorrow morning at nine o'clock their time."

"I'll call Gia's folks the instant we hang up," Casey said. "But putting all our heads together and getting on the same page takes priority."

"Yeah," Marc agreed. "And clearly this one runs deep."

"Can we address a key component here?" Emma blurted out. "What are we going to do about Lina? Tell her? Tell them? They're identical triplets. Don't they have the right to know that?"

"Yes—but not yet." Casey had clearly thought this one through. "Gia and Dani are in danger. It's possible that Lina's ignorance of the truth is the only thing keeping her safe. We have to figure out who's doing this and why. Until we have some handle on what's going on, we can't drop a bomb like this on them—or Lina."

"Casey is right," Claire said. "We have too many facts to assimilate before we say something that might increase the risk." Her gaze grew misty. "Whatever's going on is like a minefield we have to cross. Years of lies and deceit. Darkness and death. Terrible danger. There's so much buzz in my head right now I can't absorb it all, much less break it down. But we have to move forward with what we've got, not add Lina to the mix. That will come, but not until it's time."

"So we're not talking to Lina's parents?" Emma asked.

"Eventually," Casey replied. "We'll need their help in keeping their daughter safe. And, yes, they have the right to know what's going on. But not until we're ready to add Lina to the equation."

"Lina's not in danger right now," Claire stated. "She doesn't know about her sisters and they don't know about her. Still," she added thoughtfully, "I do think we should touch base with her again, just in case."

"I was about to suggest the same thing," Casey concurred.

"But you just said…" Emma looked confused.

"I said let's keep this investigation contained for the time being. Let's start with the Muranos and the Russos, plus getting the personal items we need from Dani's apartment. I said we should keep this situation from Lina for the time being. I didn't say we shouldn't keep an eye on her to see where her head is and to make sure she's blissfully ignorant of what's going on and that she hasn't received even the slightest threat to her well-being."

"And how do we do that?" Emma asked.

"That's where you come in." Casey's lips curved as she watched Emma snap to attention, her eyes bright with curiosity. "Tomorrow you're going to be a busy girl. First, I need you to keep Dani and Gia engaged and in check. Give them a call first thing in the morning and tell them you're on your way to Rye along with breakfast for all of you. They'll be on edge waiting to hear from me so they can rush over to the Russos'. Put them at ease. You're the most social person I know. Use that ability. Maybe you'll learn a tidbit or two, or maybe you'll just keep them distracted so they don't fall apart."

"Okay, consider it done," Emma responded. "What about Lina?"

"Lina is part two of your social agenda. Touch base with her. Find a way to meet her later in the day, for drinks or to hang out at her place and talk. You two had no problems monopolizing the conversation at brunch the other day. Claire and I could barely get a word in edgewise. So do a repeat performance. Talk clothes, shoes, guys—whatever you want. Just get a feel for what's going on in her life and see if there's anything we should worry about."

"No problem." Emma grinned. "I love this part of my job."

"I never would have guessed," Casey replied dryly. "But Emma…"

"I won't mention anyone to anyone," Emma finished for her. "Not a word about Lina to Gia and Dani, and not a word about them to Lina. I promise."

"Good." Casey was convinced. "So we're all in sync? Claire and I will check in after we talk to the Russos and give Gia a brief heads-up. Patrick will do the same after he talks to the Muranos and gives Dani a call. No details, just some bare-bones facts, quick reassurances, and a promise to discuss everything as soon as you get home. Agreed?"

"Yup," Marc said at the other end of the phone. "That'll give the team a chance to get our stories straight and filter what we need to before Gia and Dani show up at our doorstep the minute we get back from the airport."

"Exactly. Then that's it for now." Casey glanced at her watch. "I want to call Gia's parents before it gets too late. Safe flight, guys."

CHAPTER 20

Just before seven a.m., Casey watched the house numbers ascend as she drove the FI van up the block. It was a quiet street in suburban New Rochelle, lined with split-level homes, the driveways filled with cars, bicycles, and an occasional tricycle or scooter. A few cars were pulling out, presumably to head off for work. There was something homey and personal about the area, a kind of *Donna Reed Show* sense of family and security.

A peaceful security that Casey and Claire were about to disrupt.

"There." Claire pointed at a white shingled house with gray shutters and a sweeping maple tree out front. "That's number fifty-five."

Nodding, Casey pulled over and parked along the curb. She turned off the ignition and took a deep breath. "This is going to be difficult."

"I know. I'm already feeling a sense of irrevocable change and pain," Claire replied. "The Russos are a close family. They're going to be badly thrown, especially since we're catching them totally off guard. They have no idea that the case we're here to discuss with them involves Gia and her... *situation*."

Casey stared at the house, trying to compose herself as best she could. "Remember, let's steer clear of the heavy-duty danger and stick to the secret twin angle. Plus, no mention whatsoever of Lina."

"Of course," Claire replied, acknowledging what she already knew. She and Casey had talked through their strategy—the dos and don'ts of what to say during this interview—right after Casey had spoken with Maria Russo and set things up. Still, Claire understood why Casey was now repeating herself. She needed to focus on the aspects of this meeting that she could control. The rest was out of her hands and would be have to be dealt with on the fly. Not optimal for a control freak. But Casey was Casey. No matter how things played out, she'd handle it all like the pro that she was.

"Let's go," she said now, unbuckling her seat belt and glancing over at Claire. "You okay?"

Claire gave her an encouraging smile. "Yes. And so are you."

Casey didn't even pretend not to know what Claire meant. When it came to picking up on other people's vibes, Claire rarely guessed. She knew.

They both got out of the van and made their way up the walk, climbing the three stone steps to the front door and ringing the bell.

A mid-fiftyish woman, dark-haired and petite, wearing a black and white shirt, black slacks, and a curious expression, opened the door. "Ms. Woods?" she asked.

"Yes, and you must be Mrs. Russo." Casey shook her hand and gave her a warm smile. "This is my associate, Claire Hedgleigh." She waited while the two women exchanged greetings. "We very much appreciate you agreeing to meet with us."

"Of course." Maria Russo opened the door wide and gestured for them to come in. "You have us very curious, but if there's some way we can help an important investigation of some kind, we want to. The only thing is, we can't make this longer than an hour. Nick and I own two delis. He needs to run them and I need to supervise the preparation of the hot food for lunch."

That explained the seven-a.m. meeting time.

"No problem," Casey assured her. "We'll be out before eight."

Maria nodded. "Nick's in the living room. I brewed some coffee and put out a plate of my homemade biscotti." There was professional pride in her voice.

"That sounds wonderful," Claire replied, rewarded with a beaming smile.

They walked through the hallway, the walls filled with family photos, the furnishings well-worn but lovingly arranged. The living room was wood-paneled with an upholstered sofa and love seat, two wing-backed chairs, and a coffee table containing a steaming pot of coffee and a large plate of biscotti.

A man nearing sixty with graying hair and a bit of a belly protruding over his belt rose from one of the chairs. "Hi," he greeted them. "I'm Nick Russo." He waited while his wife made the introductions. "Please"—he gestured at the sofa—"have a seat."

A few minutes of pouring and fussing commenced, until the Russos were convinced that Casey and Claire were all settled and had the proper refreshments.

Perched at the edge of his chair, Nick got straight to the point. "So what's this about? What kind of case are you working and how does our neighborhood factor into it?"

Casey set down her cup and saucer, meeting Nick's gaze directly. "This has nothing to do with your neighborhood, Mr. Russo. This has to do with your daughter."

Maria nearly leapt from her seat. "Gia? Oh, God, is something wrong?"

"Not in the way you mean," Casey answered quickly. "Gia's fine. We're just helping her with a personal matter."

Maria crossed herself furiously. "I knew something was wrong. She's been so evasive. And she hasn't been here all week. See, Nick, I told you something was wrong!"

Nick gave his wife a tight nod, his own expression rife with worry. "What personal matter?" he asked Casey.

"Her birth. What can you tell us about it?"

Maria hesitated for a second and then turned up her palms in a gesture of non-comprehension. "Do you mean the fact that she's adopted? Gia's known that since she was a child."

Honesty and elusiveness all at once.

"Tell us about the adoption." Clearly, Claire sensed the same mixed message as Casey did, because she was leading the conversation in a specific direction. "Was Gia born in New Rochelle?"

"No, she was born in Manhattan."

"And who handled the adoption?"

At that, Maria lowered her gaze, fidgeting on the love seat.

"Why are you asking?" Nick demanded. "It was a legal adoption. We have the papers to prove it. And I don't understand why Gia isn't asking us these questions herself. We've always been honest with her. She's the center of our lives. Why is she turning to private investigators to ask these questions? And how do we know for sure that she did?"

Casey was ready for that challenge. "We have a letter in her handwriting asking you to talk to us." She passed it across the table to Nick. "As you can see, she's waiting to speak to you herself. She loves you. She's worried about you. She just felt it would be better and less emotional if we handled the initial conversation."

Nick read the letter thoroughly. Then, he nodded. "Okay, go ahead. Ask your questions."

"We need to know the details of the adoption." Casey wasn't mincing words. Not once she sensed the Russos were holding something back. "Was it handled by an agency? If so, which one?"

The Russos exchanged a nervous glance. "It was a private adoption," Maria said. "No agency, at least not that we know of. A lawyer handled everything."

"What was that lawyer's name? We'd like to speak with him."

Maria looked like a bird that wanted to take flight. "His name was Constantin Farro."

"Can you spell that for me please?" Casey waited for Maria to do so and quickly scribbled down the name. She'd have Ryan run it ASAP, along with every detail about the man that he could find.

"Can you describe him?" Casey asked.

"Average height and weight," Nick replied. "Curly brown hair. Light eyes, maybe blue. A pointy nose. I don't know what else to say. It was twenty-seven years ago. He showed us his credentials. He had a lot of experience with adoptions."

"That's very helpful." Casey jotted that down.

"We followed all the legal steps he explained to us." Maria was unraveling. "I don't understand why this is coming up now."

"You wanted a child very badly," Claire said with gentle certainty. "You'd tried every agency you could find. The waiting list was unbearable. This was your opportunity. So you didn't look too deeply. You just accepted the blessing that was being handed to you."

Maria stared at Claire through her tears. "Exactly. How did you know?"

There was no need to go into Claire's abilities. "I didn't know," she replied. "But it wasn't a reach. As long as you had legal adoption papers, you didn't care who did what to make it happen." Claire took a purposeful bite of biscotti and smiled at the flavor. "The only thing I don't understand is how you found this lawyer."

"We didn't," Nick admitted. "He found us. Apparently he had business relationships with some of the adoption agencies we'd applied to—business that allowed him access to their files. He saw from the reams of paperwork we filled out time and time again how desperate we were. So when Gia was due to arrive, he spoke to the birth mother and approached us. As you just said, we weren't about to look a gift horse in the mouth. Besides the legalities, we had a few rules to follow. We promised to do so. In return, Gia was ours."

"Rules?" Casey's antennae went up. "What rules?"

"We had to be part of a close-knit Italian family. We had to move to an area of the country where people were kinder and the air was clean. Bozeman, Montana, was suggested to us. We agreed to move there. We didn't care where we lived if we could adopt Gia. It was required that we live in Bozeman until Gia was at least of kindergarten age. We were prohibited from moving to New York City or Minneapolis, where the birth father lived at various points in time. We asked about New Rochelle since our entire extended family lives here. It was approved for a later move because it was only a suburb of New York City. But like I said, we had to stay in Bozeman until Gia was in elementary school."

"Does Gia know all this?"

Nick fiddled with his coffee cup. "We never went into these specifics, no. All Gia needed to know was the most important truth— that she was wanted and loved more than any child ever could be. That has never changed." He met Casey's gaze, his brows drawn in question. "Now that we've shared more details with you than we ever have with anyone else, it's time you told us what this is about. We talked to you for Gia's sake. Is there some loophole in the adoption we don't know about? Because Gia is ours. She always will be."

Despite all the information Claire and she had acquired, Casey felt sick at what she was about to do to the Russos.

"I don't doubt how much you love Gia," she said. "Neither does she. But there's definitely an inconsistency, with her date of birth and the facts you were given. We're not sure how deep this deception goes or who orchestrated it—or why. But it's fact, not conjecture, and it's illegal."

Maria's lips quivered. "How do you know that?"

There were no easy words to use. So Casey just told them as gently as she could. "Because Gia has an identical twin." No mention of the word *triplet*. "They've been DNA-tested and there's no room for error. Plus, given what you just told us, someone is trying to keep them apart. Her twin was also adopted and was raised in Minneapolis—one of the places you were forbidden to live."

Both the Russos recoiled in shock, their faces turning sheet white. If ever there was a doubt that they'd been kept in the dark about Dani's and Lina's existence, that possibility was annihilated by their reaction.

"Dear God," Maria whispered, pressing her palms to her cheeks. "A twin? How can that be? It was just Gia. We would have been told if…"

She broke down and started to sob.

Nick rose, walking over to stand beside his wife. He placed his hand on her shoulder in a show of comfort. But his hand was shaking violently as he held her. "The birth records are sealed. All we have are the reissued ones, with Gia's adoptive birth certificate naming us as her parents. We don't know anything more."

"We realize that," Claire replied. "But the girls have met and have been talking. According to them, their birthdays are a month apart. Which means those are the dates you were given, which would make the idea of an identical twin an impossibility. There might have been other tampering done on the sealed birth records. Someone went to a great deal of trouble to hide the truth."

"Why? *Why*?" Nick's eyes glistened with tears.

"That's what we're trying to find out," Claire said softly. She was almost as pale as the Russos, and her voice quavered as she spoke. "I'm so sorry."

"Mr. Russo," Casey pressed gently, "were you at the hospital when Gia was born?"

He shook his head. "We were told the biological mother wanted some time alone with the baby she was about to give up. Plus, Gia was a preemie. She had to stay in the hospital until her lungs were fully developed. She was brought to our home three weeks later."

"By the attorney," Casey said.

"Yes."

"Gia's… twin," Maria stumbled over the word. "What's her name?"

"Danielle Murano," Casey replied. "She's here visiting now, and she's staying at Gia's townhouse. Gia is going to come by soon—to your house or your deli, that's up to you. She wants to talk. And she was hoping to bring Dani to dinner tonight so you can meet her."

"Of course." Maria's head bobbed up and down emphatically. "Do they really look exactly alike?" A hard swallow. "I want to prepare myself."

"They're identical." Claire knew that this was her territory. "But you're Gia's parents. I'm sure you'll see and sense differences that we don't. Mannerisms and obviously speaking voices. As we told you, Danielle is from Minneapolis." She paused. "Do you have any questions for us, or should we leave now so you can talk to Gia?"

"We need to talk to *our daughter*," Nick said.

"Do you have a business card so that we can be a part of this process?" Maria asked.

"Of course." Casey rose and gave them each a card. "Call us anytime. Our job is to help Gia find her answers. Excluding her parents is the last thing we want to do." She went on, treading carefully. "Are the adoption papers here or in a safety deposit box?"

"They're here. We keep them in our home safe," Nick replied. "Why? Do you need to see them?"

"I'd like to take photos of them, if I may. The information there might help us in our investigation."

"I'll get them now." He left the room, returning moments later with a large envelope marked: *Gia*. "Here," he said, handing it to Casey.

Swiftly, Casey removed the documents and whipped out her iPhone, taking photos of each page. "Thank you, Mr. Russo." She handed the envelope back to him. "We truly appreciate your cooperation. We'll be on our way now so that you can talk to Gia."

Claire had already risen to her feet. Her gaze met Maria's. "Gia loves you very much," she said softly. "She's desperate to protect you. She knows what a shock this is. She was equally shocked. So never doubt her feelings for you, nor the fact that she regards you and only you as her parents."

"Thank you, Ms. Hedgleigh," Maria whispered.

"It's the truth. Remember that when you talk to her."

CHAPTER 21

"That went as well as could be expected," Claire said the minute they climbed into the van.

Casey nodded, looking a lot less stressed than she had before their meeting with the Russos. "Thanks for picking up the conversation at all the right times."

Claire gave her a small smile. "That's what I'm here for."

"In addition to softening the blow, you also helped me get a decent amount of information. Let's run with it. I'll email these photos to Ryan. But before I do, I want to call Gia now."

"They were telling the truth."

"I know." Casey pulled away from the curb and pressed the touchpad numbers as she drove. The Bluetooth would put them on speakerphone.

"Hello?" Gia had obviously pounced on her burn phone the minute it gave its first chirp.

"It's me," Casey said. She could hear Dani's and Emma's voices in the background—voices that stilled the minute Gia started to speak. "Claire and I just left your parents' house."

"How did they take it?"

"With emotion and strength." Casey laid out the bare-bones bullet points of the meeting, holding off on informational details so Gia's parents could have first crack at sharing them with their daughter—and so the FI team could weave their stories together before having a choreographed discussion with the girls. "They have a lot to tell you. Once they do, and once Patrick has reached out to Dani after his meeting with her parents, you and the FI team will get together and field any questions you have—probably tomorrow, given your plans for today and tonight. But you need to call them now. They're good people and good parents who've been thrown for a loop. They're waiting on pins and needles—to see you and later to meet Dani."

"I'll call them right away." Gia's voice was strung tight, and she was clearly struggling with a question. "Is there anything I should be prepared for?" she finally blurted out.

"Not in the way you mean." Casey read between the lines, understanding fully what Gia was terrified to ask. "They had no knowledge of Dani's existence or of any illegalities. All they wanted was their daughter. That hasn't changed."

"Thank you," Gia said, her relief coming through loud and clear. "I'll go call them."

The minute Casey ended that conversation, she called Ryan.

"Hey, boss, how did it go?" he answered.

"Difficult but productive." Casey handed her cell phone to Claire as she continued to speak on Bluetooth. "I'm driving back to the office now, so I'll bring you up to speed there. In the meantime, Claire is about to email you Gia's adoption papers. It was a closed adoption. The Russos confirmed that, to their knowledge, Gia was born in Manhattan. Constantin Farro was the attorney who handled the adoption. That's C-O-N-S-T-A-N-T-I-N F-A-R-R-O. Both those facts should give you a leg up. Start digging."

Ryan whistled. "Nice job, ladies. I'll get on it ASAP."

"Any word from Patrick or Marc?"

"Not yet. And not a surprise. It's barely eight o'clock in Minneapolis. Their meeting with the Muranos isn't scheduled until nine o'clock central, ten o'clock our time. I'll text you if anything changes and they call in. Otherwise, let's see what I can accomplish in the next hour while you two brave rush hour."

* * *

Tactfully, Emma excused herself from Gia's living room. Gia and Dani needed a few moments together, and Gia needed privacy to call her parents.

It was the perfect time for Emma to make her own phone call.

She walked to the rear of the townhouse, eased open the sliding glass door, and stepped out onto the patio, making sure to close the slider behind her.

Pulling out her iPhone, she scanned her contact info and tapped the necessary name.

"Hello?" Lina sounded a little sleepy.

"Hi, Lina. It's Emma. Did I wake you?"

"Emma!" All the fatigue vanished from Lina's voice. "It's so good to hear from you!"

"I left you a message last night. Didn't you get it?"

"What? Oh, no, I'm so sorry. I was doing some work for my independent study. I researched until I couldn't keep my eyes open. Then I crawled into bed and collapsed. I never checked my messages."

"No problem," Emma said. "I've been thinking about you, and I decided to see if you had any time today or tonight to get together and catch up. Drinks, dinner, whatever works for you."

"I'd love that!" Bubbly Lina was back in full force. "Why don't you come over to my place? We'll order in and have a girls' night."

Emma couldn't contain her grin. People told her *she* was exuberant? Lina was like a burst of colorful fireworks. "Sounds great. What time?"

"Does six thirty work?"

"I'll be there," Emma replied. "With a bottle of red and a bottle of white, so we're covered no matter what food we order."

"Perfect. See you then."

Emma considered calling Casey with an update but decided to wait. Gia would be rushing off any minute to see her parents, after which she had a bunch of clients she needed to see before tonight's dinner. And that would leave Dani here alone, anxiously waiting for a call from Patrick. Emma's heart went out to her. She'd keep her company—and, in doing so, maybe gain more insight into Dani and her childhood that could help FI's investigation.

Offices of Forensic Instincts

"I didn't think we'd ever see home base again," Casey muttered, grateful to see a parking spot right across from the brownstone. After a two-plus hours' drive from New Rochelle, most of it spent in bumper-to-bumper rush-hour traffic, she was practically leaping out of her seat. Relinquishing control was not something Casey did willingly.

"Me, either." Claire stretched in her seat. She had a lot more patience than Casey did, and even she was on edge. "We should have taken the train."

"In retrospect, you're right. I thought driving was the better choice. Never again. I can't believe that all those commuters do this every day. I'd implode." Casey turned off the ignition, simultaneously unbuckling her seat belt and reaching for the door handle. "Let's see what Ryan's accomplished."

The instant Ryan heard Yoda announce Casey's and Claire's arrival, he loped up the stairs from his lair, Hero at his heels.

"Hey, when you called in to say there was traffic, I didn't think you meant a standstill."

"Yeah, well, things went from bad to worse," Casey said, tossing down her handbag and squatting to scratch Hero's ears. "So let's not waste time discussing lousy roadwork and obnoxious drivers." She rose. "What's happening here?"

Ryan heard the impatient tone loud and clear. "I did some digging and have preliminary results. Where do you want to talk?"

"Main conference room." No surprise there. That was Casey's favorite place to work. "Claire and I will head up there right after we hit the ladies' room. You go grab your notes. In the meantime, I'll try to calm down. I might even drink a cup of Claire's herbal tea and do some deep breathing—that's how revved up I am."

"Gotcha, boss." Ryan gave her a sympathetic nod. "Be there in a few minutes." He retraced his steps, hurrying back down to his lair.

They'd just settled themselves around the expansive oval table, Hero lying beside Casey's chair, notes spread across the table, tablets poised and ready, when Casey's cell phone rang.

She glanced at the number, then pressed the answer button, followed by the speaker button, and placed her phone on the table. "Hi, Emma."

"Hi." Emma's voice was tentative. "Is it a good time? Today is such a crazy day."

"It's fine. I'm at the office with Claire and Ryan. I just put you on speaker. What've you got for us?"

Emma heard Casey's tone and got right down to business. "Gia wept on the phone with her parents before she took off to see them. Dani was a basket case waiting for Patrick to call, which hopefully will be soon. I hung out to keep her company for a while. Then, she got a call from her veterinary practice, so I excused myself and left." Emma sighed. "I probed for as many childhood memories as I could without sounding like I was interrogating her. I have no idea if any of what I learned is significant, but I'm on my way back to the office and you'll tell me. Oh, and I'm going to Lina's place at six thirty for a girls' night."

"Sounds like a good day's work," Casey said. "And you talked to Lina out of earshot?"

"Yes. I went out on the patio when Gia and Dani were talking privately and Gia was preparing herself to talk to her parents. I don't think they even noticed I was gone. All cool."

"Nice job," Casey praised.

"Thanks. I'll be back soon. I'm hopping on the train now."

"At least *you* were smart enough to take it," Casey muttered under her breath. Then, in a normal voice, she said, "See you here," and disconnected the call. Immediately, she turned to Ryan. "We'll fill you in on all the details of our meeting with the Russos when Marc and Patrick call in. There's no point in repeating the story twice. Instead, you tell us what you found."

"It's more of what I *didn't* find," Ryan replied.

"Nothing in the New York County Clerk's office?"

"That part's underway. I hacked in, zeroed in on closed adoptions from January to February of twenty-seven years ago, and am slowly isolating the ones that could even remotely fit the bill. We should have an answer soon."

"Great." Casey frowned. "More waiting."

"You said that something you *didn't* find was important," Claire interrupted to ask. "What was it?"

"Constantin Farro. The man doesn't seem to exist. And believe me, I've hacked into every related database, from national birth and death records to the American Bar Association. I traced the name—spelled three different ways, in case the Russos remembered wrong—all the way back to thirty years ago. Zip. Which tells me that whoever the lawyer was who handled the adoption—assuming he even was a lawyer—used a fake name. If that's not a warning bell that this whole adoption process was illegal, I don't know what is."

"Anything else?"

"Yeah. While I was waiting for the County Clerk results, I poked around a little into Lina's life, just in case there was something of interest we should know. As it turns out, I didn't have to get past page one of a Google search to start the process."

Casey's brows rose. "Why would a grad student generate that level of interest?"

"Because Lina's father, Joseph Brando, is a New York City assemblyman who's running for the US House of Representatives. The primaries are next week. The predictions are that he's a shoo-in to win, both the primary and the general election."

Awareness dawned in Casey's eyes. "That's why the name Brando seemed familiar. I thought it was because I associated it with Marlon Brando. But now, I realize I must have read something about the upcoming elections that mentioned his name. What did the articles say about Lina?"

"The basics, plus a bunch of family stuff that I need to review. There were a few great photos with her father. She's quoted as saying she's ready to jump in with both feet to support her father's campaign. From what I've already read, it's clear that she and her folks are close. I'm going to turn my attention to Joseph. It can't hurt to be armed with knowledge before we decide to contact him. He's a powerful man and needs to be approached with care."

"Absolutely." Casey nodded. "Anything we learn will ease our way into that conversation. The timing is good. Lina's parents will be consumed with the upcoming primaries. We'll call them the following week. I'm hoping by then we'll have more data at our disposal."

"Count on it."

Casey's cell phone rang again, and once again, she glanced down at the number. "It's Patrick." She repeated the process that she had when Emma called, placing her iPhone on the table, speaker button engaged.

"Hi, Patrick. You've got me, Claire, and Ryan. Is Marc with you?"

"Yup," Marc replied. "We're finished. We booked an earlier flight home."

"Good. Patrick, how did it go?"

Patrick sighed deeply. "Painfully. The Muranos were floored. Nora Murano sobbed as if her heart would break. I almost broke down and cried with her."

"The Russos were heartbroken, too," Claire said.

"Tell us what they knew and what they didn't know, and whether or not you believe them." Casey didn't want to relive the emotions. She wanted to get to the facts. It was the only way they could help their clients.

Patrick relayed a story that was similar to the one Casey and Claire had experienced. Shock and pain. Reluctant sharing of information and admitting how little they actually knew about the details of the adoption—just the sheer joy of having the precious child they'd always wanted. Same rules and conditions as Gia's parents had been given.

"Were they assigned Minneapolis as their new home?"

"They were," Patrick replied. "And they were told never to visit Bozeman or Manhattan because—"

"Because the anonymous father lived or worked in those places," Casey finished for him.

"Exactly."

"What about Dani's birth? Was she a preemie?"

"Actually, she was a week late in her arrival."

"Interesting. Gia was premature." Casey processed that bit of data. "What about adoption papers?"

Again, Patrick gave them a report that was a mirror image of their own.

"They shared the few documents they did have with me. I took photos."

"Send them to me." Ryan jumped in. "Casey and Claire sent me photos of Gia's papers. I want to compare the two and work with what I've got."

"Will do."

"How did Dani take it when you called her?" Claire asked softly, in a voice that said she already knew the answer to her question.

"She fell apart. I told her only the basics, but I assured her that her parents loved her deeply and that they were waiting to hear from her. They understood why she was in New York, but they plan to fly here to be part of this. They won't venture into Manhattan. They'll fly to Westchester County Airport and go straight to Rye."

"I can't blame them for coming," Casey murmured. "The only thing worse than hearing about this is not being with their daughter to share it. We're going to have to up security, Patrick. I have a feeling that the Muranos and the Russos are going to want to meet, my guess is at the Russos' house. Gia and Dani are being watched. This can only up the danger."

"Already being arranged," Patrick responded. "One of my guys will be meeting the Muranos at the airport and driving them to Rye. No taxis or Ubers. Too much risk."

"Smart move. Also, I'm going to need one or two of your guys glued to Gia and Dani tonight. They're going to the Russos' for dinner."

"I'll take care of it as soon as we hang up."

"What time does your flight get in?"

"Five forty into La Guardia," Marc replied.

"Great. Rush hour."

"Not a problem. I asked the car service for a driver who's heavy on the gas pedal and knows Queens like the back of his hand. I figure the Grand Central Parkway will be a parking lot. It's his job to skirt that. I promised to make it *very* worth his while."

Casey began to laugh. "Only you would think of that. So we'll be seeing you ten minutes after landing time?"

"Very funny. You'll be seeing us a hell of a lot earlier than you would have without my clever tactics."

Claire wasn't feeling their levity. "Marc, did you get the items I need?"

"All taken care of."

With that, Casey glanced from Claire to Ryan to her cell phone. "Anyone have additional questions or info before we hang up? Otherwise, catch that flight, hop into your Batmobile, and come home."

CHAPTER 22

Emma arrived at Lina's apartment at six thirty, wine in hand. She was pissed at herself for not having provided anything from her visit to Rye that was of major importance to the team. She had no intention of letting that happen again.

Subtle she would be. But tonight, she'd find out not only that Lina wasn't in danger but also something about her and her family.

The door flew open before she could knock, and Lina hugged her in the hallway. "It's so good to see you! Come on in."

"It's great to see you, too." Emma grinned, walking in and handing over the bottles of wine. "Red and white, as promised."

"Perfect." Lina put the bottles on her kitchen counter and then scooped up a pile of takeout menus. "We can go through these and decide what we want to eat." She handed the stack to Emma, whose grin widened.

"I see you love cooking as much as I do."

Lina wrinkled her nose, a gesture Emma had seen Dani make. "I'd say that no one in their right mind loves cooking, but actually my mom is an awesome cook and she relishes her time doing it. I'd probably starve to death without her humongous doggie bags. Now let's go into the living room and catch up." She pointed, and Emma followed her lead.

"I love your place." Emma plunked the menus on the coffee table and took in the fuzzy white love seat, butterfly chairs, and bright aqua and hot pink accents. "It's super cool and it's very you." Quickly, she scanned the wall of family photos, looking for a resemblance between Lina and her parents. Same coloring, same petite build as her mother, but nothing else that jumped out at her. She'd try to study the photos more closely later.

Meanwhile, Lina looked puzzled. "I don't understand. You've been here already."

"Nope. That was just Casey and Claire."

"You're right." Lina brightened right up. "Well, then, I'm doubly glad you suggested this. My living room is home base for all my friends who need to chill. Flop down on the fluff-couch. It's the best."

Emma did just that. "This is awesome. No wonder your friends never want to leave."

Lina nodded, settling herself next to Emma so they could pore over the menus together. "I like having my place be the center of things. I guess that's what happens when you're raised in a tight Italian family. Now let's order so you can fill me in on the latest excitement at Forensic Instincts."

* * *

Half an hour later, the coffee table was filled with cartons of Chinese food and a tray of sushi, and the girls were settled on the fluff-couch, glasses of wine in hand, ready to chow down and talk.

"How are things with you?" Emma asked, watching Lina's face. "When we had brunch, you didn't mention your summer plans. Are you getting a chance to chill out, maybe hang out with Brianna and your other friends, or are you working at your mom's boutique?"

"Mostly working at the boutique," Lina replied, looking distracted and giving the briefest answer she could. Clearly, she was eager to end this part of the conversation and to get to the happenings at Forensic Instincts. "I love to keep busy. I'm not good at lying around. So life is good."

Excellent, Emma thought silently. *No signs of worry or danger. The tsunami has yet to crash over Lina's life.*

"So what's going on at FI?" Lina quickly changed the subject, preventing Emma from asking another question. "I know you can't get into details, but anything cool you want to share with me?"

"The cool stuff is what I can't share." Emma would give Lina the update she wanted. But that was it. She was determined to keep this conversation on track. "Let's just say that we don't get much sleep and our lives are crazy."

"Well, I know firsthand how awesome you all are. How's Casey? Claire? Everyone?"

"Busy. Our caseload is way high. Marc's back from his honeymoon and Patrick's back from his family vacation, so they're both frenetically bringing themselves up to speed. Ryan's working on some new techno-gadgets. Hero's being enrolled in an additional training course. All I know about it is that it's cutting-edge, which is good because Hero always needs a challenge. And you know all the latest from Casey and Claire. We're quite the diverse but always loyal family." Emma made the smooth segue. "I'm sure you understand. You said your family is tight."

"We're like this." Lina held up two crossed fingers, evidently content with what she'd learned about FI. "When I was younger, I felt a little smothered and overprotected. My parents have always been very much *there*, my mom being the head of every school committee, my dad interrogating every guy I ever dated. It was overwhelming and embarrassing for a teenager. But now that I'm grown, I get it. It's all about love."

Emma nodded. "My parents were protective, too. They died when I was just a kid. I still miss them."

"You poor thing." Lina reached out to squeeze her hand. "I'm sorry if what I said brought up painful memories."

"Don't be. I'm okay now, especially since I became part of the FI team." Emma inclined her head. "Did you like being an only child, or did you ever wish you had sisters or brothers?"

"I'm a brat," Lina said without a drop of self-censure. "I'd hate sharing my mom and dad with anyone. So it's good that things turned out the way they did. I sometimes wonder if they would have wanted other kids. But my mom's pregnancy was tough. It was high risk, so she was on complete bedrest for four months. It was touch and go, so everyone was holding their breath. I suspect the doctors were pessimistic that I'd make it. I was kind of a miracle baby."

Emma dove into that entrée. "No wonder they're so protective of you. They must have been terrified they'd lose you."

Lina nodded. "They don't discuss it much. I think it's still too painful for them to relive. My mom shared the story with me when I was old enough to understand and not to be freaked out. My dad got all emotional and hugged me for five minutes. I felt very lucky, but also guilty that I caused them so much pain."

"I'm sure their happiness overshadowed their pain and worry." Emma took a sip of her wine. "Did your mom make it anywhere close to full term?"

"She did. I was born a week early—which apparently astounded everyone, since their idea of the best-case scenario was for my mom to carry me seven months tops."

"That's pretty amazing. Are you a winter, spring, summer, or fall baby?"

"Winter. That was another part of the saga. I was born on February third. There was a big snowstorm that day. Of course, being the troublemaker that I am, that's when I decided to make my grand debut. When my mom went into labor, my dad went into command-and-control mode. He called his friend the police chief and got a line of police cars to lead the way. They blasted through the snow ahead of the ambulance. I was born a half hour after the hospital arrival."

"Wow." Emma's eyes widened. "Was the hospital at least close by?"

"Not really. It was Mount Sinai. From what I heard, my dad broke the land speed record. Not to mention fighting the traffic and the snowstorm." Lina grinned. "My dad makes the impossible happen."

"And you certainly know how to make an entrance," Emma teased. She set down her glass and nibbled on a spare rib. She had to come across as interested but not interrogative. The last thing she needed was to arouse Lina's suspicions.

"Was your mom okay afterwards? It must have been a tough recovery."

"Actually, my dad says she was back to herself in no time. I guess she had to rise to the challenge of raising me." Lina gave an impish grin, and the two girls laughed.

"You wanted to hear about the excitement at FI?" Emma teased. "That story rivals it all. Any other over-the-top life events you want to share?"

Lina's eyes lit up. "I just realized you don't know."

"Know what?"

"My dad is running for the US House of Representatives. He'll be the Republican party candidate after next week's primaries, which I know he'll win. How's that for over-the-top events?"

Emma gaped. "Are you serious? That's incredible. Why didn't you ever tell us?"

"Because… I don't know. We were concentrating on Brianna and catching the scumbag who was harassing her. My life was kind of on the back burner. But now that nightmare is resolved, and I'm back in the thick of things on the political front. I'm so proud of my dad I could burst."

"I can only imagine." Emma was processing all this as quickly as she could. Lina's father was a public figure. That could give the team a wide avenue for exploration. "Is he already in politics?"

"Yup. He's the Staten Island representative for the New York State Assembly. He has been for three terms. And he's run his law practice at the same time. He's the smartest, most high-energy person I know." Lina wrinkled her nose again. "People say he's charismatic and handsome. I guess they're right. But he's my dad. I don't view him that way."

Abruptly, Lina sat up straight, her mind clearly coming up with something. "I have a great idea! Next Sunday, after my dad's win, my parents are hosting a huge party at their house. Uncle Neil—Neil Donato, my dad's campaign manager—said I could invite a few of my friends. I'd love it if you guys could come—all of you, including Hero. He's better behaved than most politicians."

Grinning at her own joke, Lina jumped up and dashed into the kitchen. "I have invitations for you to give to the whole team," she said, the decision apparently a done deal to her. "I'll tell my parents to be expecting you. They'll be honored. My dad spoke highly of you the night Brianna came over for dinner. Oh, this will be awesome!"

Emma took the invitations, feeling like a fish out of water. She'd been a street kid most of her life. Lina's lifestyle was completely foreign to her. But she wasn't going to let this chance get away.

"I'm really touched you want to include us," she said. "I have to talk to the team, make sure they're all available. I promise to do that right away and get back to you ASAP."

"That's fine, but no is not an option. Unless someone is on vacation or dealing with an emergency, the whole team will be there. I won't have it any other way. My mom refused to let my dad hire a caterer. She claims they don't know how to cook. In her kitchen, she's the queen. And trust me, once you taste her cooking, you'll agree."

Glancing from the classy calligraphy of the invitation to Lina's decisive gaze, Emma knew this was a done deal. The team would be there—and not only because of Lina's insistence. This could be an opportunity to gather info on Joseph and Donna Brando.

Between this invite and the info Lina had innocently provided, Emma had a lot to share with the FI team.

CHAPTER 23

Ryan was in his lair.

He'd hit the gym at five and then headed straight to the office. Gia and Dani had dropped off their laptops for him to check out. His project had been to find and analyze any spyware in time for the seven thirty–a.m. team meeting that Emma had requested.

Dani's laptop had been first up. Once he'd located the spyware, Ryan reviewed the data from the packet sniffer he had placed onto her computer to see if he could track where the keylogger was sending information. It appeared that the spyware was nothing special—just run-of-the-mill software that was available commercially. Data was being sent to a website where the customer could log in and see the data that had been collected. These companies marketed their digital spy service as well-intentioned: allowing concerned parents to monitor their children, enabling paranoid companies to track errant workers. They strenuously denied having clients with illegal intentions, and their terms of service were crafted carefully by the best lawyers to escape both prosecution and the potential of being shut down. But there were also suspicious and jealous lovers and all forms of pervs watching who knows what.

Ryan decided the quickest path to finding out who had been spying on Dani was to set up his own spyware account. Once he had valid credentials, the trick would be to find and exploit a security weakness in the site where he could elevate his account to admin status. With unfettered access, he could dig in to the logs and find out who was spying on Dani.

It would take him a couple of days to get his answers. Who knows, maybe he could even use the same software to spy on the spy himself.

A wry grin tugged at Ryan's lips. How poetic.

Fifteen minutes later, he wasn't smiling. He'd done a thorough search of Gia's computer and come up empty. Nothing. No spyware. The computer was completely clean. Whoever the person was who was monitoring Dani's every move, her entire online activity, wasn't doing squat to keep tabs on Gia. What the hell did that mean? Was Dani a bigger factor in this surveillance, and did she know more than she realized, more than Gia did?

Ryan swore under his breath. It was good that the two girls were coming in soon. He had questions that needed answers.

* * *

At seven thirty sharp, the entire FI team was gathered around the conference room table. All eyes were on Emma, as she was taking the lead on this meeting.

"Tell us what happened at Lina's last night that has you so worked up," Casey began without preamble.

Emma was practically crackling with electricity. "First of all, did you know that Lina's dad is running for national office?"

"Yes." Casey nodded. "Ryan discovered that yesterday when he was doing his cursory research on Joseph Brando. I take it Lina talked about her father's candidacy."

"She did more than that." Emma slapped the invitations onto the conference table. "She invited us to the victory party they're having after his anticipated win. All of us. She won't take no for an answer."

"That's good." Casey pursed her lips. "I think it's time we met the Brandos. We're going to have to talk to them soon enough anyway. When's the party?"

"This coming Sunday."

"We'll be there. But that's obviously not all you found out. You sounded like you were about to explode when you called."

"I was. I am." Emma looked around the table. "I have a ton of information about Lina's birth—at least what she was told about it, truthful or not." With that, Emma blurted out everything, from the fact that Lina believed she was her parents' biological child to Donna's alleged pregnancy to the snowstorm to the date and place of Lina's birth.

"That's a pretty elaborate story," Patrick said.

"One that's easy enough to check out." Ryan made note of his new assignment.

"You're both right." Marc was tapping his pen thoughtfully on his knee. "Unless Donna Brando had triplets and gave two of them away—which I highly doubt—the story Lina was given was a complete fabrication. You'd think her parents would keep it as mundane as possible, so it wouldn't raise any red flags. Instead, they concocted an elaborate story that's easily confirmed—or disproved. Why?"

Casey recognized the speculative glint in Marc's eyes. "You think they knew the hospital records had been altered and that the existing ones would corroborate their story."

"It would certainly fit. It would also explain why they were determined for Lina to believe she was their biological child. No adoption procedure to explain. No paperwork to present. Just a very emotional, very believable story."

"That suggests the Brandos knew more about this deception than the Russos and the Muranos." Casey shot Ryan a quizzical look.

"Did anything in your research on Joseph Brando raise any red flags? Anything that suggested he might be shady?"

"You mean other than the fact that he's a politician?" Ryan asked dryly. "No. At least not directly."

"What does that mean?"

"It means I did more than a cursory search since last we spoke. Have you ever heard of Angelo Colone?"

"The mob leader?" Marc's brows rose in interest. "Sure."

"Well, he and Joseph Brando grew up in Brooklyn together. They were very tight, right through adulthood—actually right through Angelo's death several months ago. When Joseph started his own law firm, Angelo was his first client. Joseph represented his personal interests and his construction business. My guess? Angelo funded his legal practice."

Now, Casey was leaning forward, her gaze intense. "Are you saying that Joseph Brando has mob ties?"

"Like I said, none that I can find," Ryan replied. "But I am saying that he had access to all kinds of illegal help, even if he didn't get his own hands dirty. Whether or not he used it is still unknown."

"But not for long, knowing you."

"My search engine is busily working. But Marc's theory makes sense from my end, too. I found both Gia's and Dani's filed birth certificates and they're identical to the ones they have. No other records show up in the database of the Department of Health, not in any of the five boroughs. As for triplets? Nada. Which means we're coming up empty on the truth. To get forgeries like that into the system? Only someone with big-time connections could orchestrate that."

"Angelo Colone would match that description."

"Sure would. But even if he was behind this, it doesn't necessarily implicate Brando—although it sure as hell moves him to the top of the suspect list."

"All the more reason for us to go to that party on Sunday," Casey said. "We can get a read on Brando and, if we're lucky, pick up some crumbs of information. So, all of you, get your formal wear out from storage."

Ryan groaned. "Does this mean I have to wear a tie?"

"Yup. The whole nine yards. Suit, dress shirt, tie." Casey's lips twitched. "Maybe Claire will offer to knot your tie for you."

"Only if he doesn't squirm," Claire replied.

The whole team chuckled.

"Anything else?" Casey asked, glancing around the table.

"Yeah." Ryan's humor vanished. "I've been here since dawn working on the girls' laptops. Found and left in place the spyware on Dani's—and set things up so I can hopefully trace it back to the person who installed it. But Gia's? Totally clean. No spyware whatsoever."

"That's weird." Marc frowned. "It suggests that either Dani represents more of a threat than Gia or that whoever did this had more access to Dani's computer."

"He—or whatever thug he's got working for him—was in Gia's townhouse the morning of the fire," Ryan pointed out. "He could have installed the spyware then or talked someone through doing it. So I opt for your first theory. We need more info on Dani."

Casey glanced at her watch. "Gia and Dani are due here soon. We'll have to dig deep into their lists of friends, boyfriends, co-workers, everyone they know. Without saying anything, we'll concentrate more heavily on Dani's list. Maybe that'll give us something to go on."

Claire was gazing into her coffee mug, her expression bleak and faraway. "I'm picking up on a lot of anguish. Gia and Dani have been through the emotional wringer since yesterday. Leaning on them would be a huge mistake. Please. Let's take this slow and gently—for their sake and for the sake of our investigation."

* * *

Claire's assessment was, unfortunately, more than accurate.

Gia and Dani arrived looking like hell. The past day had taken a huge toll on them—Gia's morning visit with her parents, Dani's emotional exchange with her parents followed by working with Patrick to coordinate the arrangements for them to fly in, and finally last night's dinner with the Russos.

The pair sat with the FI team in the small conference room, sipping coffee and relaying information.

"I don't know whose parents are in worse shape," Gia told them in a watery voice. "Actually, I do. Dani's. Mine at least had the chance to meet Dani and to see what a wonderful person she is. They're also more involved, since they live so close by. Dani's poor parents haven't seen their daughter since this all began, and all they know about me is my name and that I'm the twin who just surfaced out of nowhere and uprooted their life." She ran a hand through her hair. "Although this is tearing my parents apart, too. I feel like a horrible daughter—I can't do a thing to ease their pain."

Casey felt a wave of sympathy, for both the girls and their parents. This situation was one big emotional devastation. And there was a whole facet yet to reveal—Lina and all the ramifications that came with that revelation.

"I'm so sorry," she said quietly. "You know we'll do everything we can to ease your way through this."

"We know," Dani replied. Her eyes were puffy from crying, and pain was etched all over her face. "It's just all too much. My parents are in shock. Gia's parents are, too, although they were lovely to me. But they couldn't stop staring, and Mrs. Russo was blinking back tears all night. It was the most difficult evening of my life, and certainly of theirs."

"Your parents will be arriving later today," Patrick said, trying to soothe her. "Then, all of you can get together. It will comfort and strengthen you. You'll see." His jaw tightened. "And this time I'll be heading up the security team. Safety won't be an issue."

He turned to Gia. "You have three weddings this weekend. I'm uneasy about you handling them. It's too risky. Too many people. Too little control. I'd suggest you send Liz Watts, the assistant planner you mentioned, in your place."

"Not a prayer." Gia's response was immediate. "As it is, I had to call on Liz to be my stand-in this past weekend—with me on the other end of the phone for hours. But that was for my parents; they needed me and they needed to meet Dani. But the upcoming weekend? No way. Two of the three weddings are enormous events I've been planning for over a year. The third is smaller, but the clients are even more demanding than the other two sets. There's no way Liz can run the show on these, and there's no way I'd let her. My clients would eat her alive, then they'd hunt me down and shoot me."

Patrick's brows shot up. "That bad?"

"Worse."

"Fine. Then I'll have to double security on you." He turned to Dani. "And I want you in a controlled environment while Gia's away. That means Gia's townhouse or your parents' hotel room."

Dani nodded. "As long as my folks are with me, I'll stay put."

Gia pressed her lips together, anger mixing with pain. "I hate this. I have no control over my life. Neither does Dani. Our lives are in the hands of some lunatic."

"We'll change that. And soon." Casey's words were more than a statement. They were a promise.

Ryan cleared his throat. "We've got another angle to cover." Remembering Claire's words, he kept his delivery nice and easy. Normally, he'd be going at this like a missile. But there was no point in making things worse and impeding his progress. "We need to talk about the spyware I found on your computers." He intentionally used the plural. If he told Gia and Dani the truth now, it would push them closer to the edge and destroy their ability to think clearly.

"So we were being monitored, just like you suspected." Dani sounded wearier than she did shocked. "What were they privy to?"

"Besides seeing everything on your screen? Audio and video feeds."

Gia blanched. "They could hear what we were saying? And worse, watch us?"

"When your computers were on? Yes. Otherwise, no. But I've made that go away," he added hastily. "I put a piece of masking tape over both your microphones and your cameras. That'll frustrate the hell out of your hacker. When you take these babies home, all he'll see is what's on your screen—which will be none of the important stuff. That you'll continue to put only on your Raspberry Pi. The video and audio feeds will be blocked."

Gia and Dani didn't look appeased. They looked green.

"I can't believe he was watching us," Dani said, her mind clearly racing to all kinds of creepy places. "And if he can't see or hear us anymore, won't he know we're onto him?"

"He already knows that," Ryan replied. "He figured it out the first time whoever's keeping eyes on you saw you walk through our front door. And it was confirmed by the absence of data you've been posting. He more than realizes he's been made. This is just a great gotcha to raise his blood pressure."

"I'm glad you're having fun." Gia was angry—angry and scared. "But doesn't taunting him escalate the danger?"

Ryan was stunned by the barb. "Not to my way of thinking, no. Sure, he'll get pissed off. But he's the IT guy, not the big boss. He'll report in and they'll try to figure out another way to keep tabs on you."

"That sounds like escalated danger to me."

"I…" Ryan was in way over his head and sinking deeper. He dealt in facts. Dealing with emotional freak-out was not his thing.

He shot Claire an imploring look.

She picked up on it at once. "Please don't let your imaginations run wild," she said in that calming way of hers. "Ryan just removed your invasion of privacy. That's a huge relief. I know you're freaked out. I don't blame you. But I agree with Ryan that this won't up the danger. This spyware guy is just a pawn. And remember, he was hired only to keep tabs on what you do now that you've found each other. He's not some perv who's stalking and ogling you." Even as she spoke, Claire had the oddest feeling that that wasn't quite right. Something more was going on here. And whatever it was sent a shiver up her spine.

Her reassurances, however, seem to have the desired effect, as both Gia and Dani settled down.

"I'm sorry I snapped," Gia apologized to Ryan. "My nerves are just frayed."

"No sweat. I understand." Ryan shot Claire an I-owe-you-one look. She responded with an I-intend-to-collect look.

"Now that you know about the spyware, what's next?" Dani asked Ryan.

"I'm running traces on the hacker's origin. But I want to cover all bases. Which means we need to make lists of everyone you know. Just in case," he added quickly. "I'm not leaning in the direction of any of them being guilty."

"You want a complete list of everyone we know?" Practical realization struck, and Gia sounded like she'd been asked to boil the ocean.

"That's the drill, yeah. Family, friends, boyfriends—including exes—co-workers, acquaintances, potential enemies."

"Ryan." Gia clearly couldn't wrap her mind around this one. "I've handled more weddings than I can count, most of them with at least one snarky bride, mother-of-the-bride, or wedding party participant. Who knows how many people I've pissed off? Or how many people I've interacted with during the planning stages?"

"I'm not in a much better position," Dani added. "My circle of contacts is smaller than Gia's, but, in addition to all the other vets at my clinic, the techs, and the support staff, I see dozens of pet owners a week, not to mention my veterinary network. I go to conferences, attend meetings, cross paths with so many others in my field. That list alone would be crushing and, most likely, incomplete."

"Good point." Casey could see the agitation re-escalating, and she wasn't about to let it happen. Enough buttons had been pushed already. "Since we've determined that that's the least likely scenario, why don't you both just list the regulars in your lives? That's a strong start. Later today, skim your emails, contact lists, and work files and see if anyone you had negative dealings with jumps out at you. I think that should be sufficient, right, Ryan?"

Ryan got the hint. Casey wasn't asking; she was telling him to put the brakes on.

"Right," he said. He produced two legal-sized notepads, pausing before he passed them over to Gia and Dani. "Can we do the basics now?" He was asking Casey as much as he was asking their clients.

Casey scrutinized Gia and Dani to assess their state of mind. No sign of panic at the suggestion. Just two tired nods.

"Yes, I think that would be fine," she told him. "It shouldn't take more than an hour, maybe less."

It actually took fifty minutes, because that's when Casey called a halt. The girls were starting to grasp at straws, and that would only deplete them and waste time.

"Go home and chew on it," she said. "We'll start with what we've got."

"Just one last question." Marc spoke up. "Is there anyone on this list who you've discussed even a small part of the investigation with?"

"No one." Gia gave an adamant shake of her head. "Except, obviously, my parents."

"Same here." Dani placed her empty coffee mug on the table. "I haven't even told Gabe and he's left me about ten text and phone messages. I don't know what to say to him."

"Just tell him what you told your veterinary practice," Casey replied. "That you're dealing with a family crisis—one you're too upset about to discuss right now. Spend as much time talking with him as you want. Just find a way to do that without divulging info on Gia or the investigation."

A stricken look. "That's the problem. I already told him about my Facebook connection with Gia and how I was leaving Cleveland to fly to New York to meet my look-alike. I even sent him a few photos of Gia and me together."

"That's not a problem. What about afterwards, during the couple of days you were home? You didn't mention the mugging or the fire, did you?"

"No." Dani shook her head. "I kept all that to myself. Especially once I knew we were contacting you. My texts with Gabe were pretty brief. His schedule was jam-packed, and he assumed I was playing catch-up at the clinic. But now it's been a while and he's concerned—so what do I say? I can't give him details about my family crisis."

"Let him know it's a bad situation—one you've been asked to keep confidential," Marc replied. "Stick to the truth without elaborating on what's really going on. After that, talk about other relationship things."

"Okay." Dani nodded.

"Most of all, call him back," Casey said emphatically. "He's clearly worried. Plus, the longer you wait, the harder it will be to dodge questions and explain why you've been ignoring him. Once you tell him what a hard time you're going through with your family, he'll understand if you only send brief texts and don't call for a while. He'll know you're short on time and shorter on emotional strength."

"I'll call him from Mr. Nickels' car on the way back to Gia's place."
Dani pushed back her chair and rose. "After that, I need some time
to prepare myself for seeing my parents and helping them through
the initial trauma." A quick glance at Patrick. "Are we okay on the
updated logistics?"

"Yes." His tone and expression were calm and in control. "Your
parents will land this afternoon and be driven directly to their hotel, where they'll check in and get settled. You'll be waiting there for
them. Afterwards, John will drive you to the Russos'. Gia will already
be there."

"Then let's get this day underway." Gia glanced at her watch.
"I have to go into the office for a while; they're starting to wonder
where I am. I also have a client meeting, but you already know that.
I'll be ready for the evening way ahead of time."

Dani sighed. "I doubt I'll ever be ready."

Gia squeezed her hand. "We'll do this together, just like we did
with my parents. After tonight, we'll just have a bigger, closer family.
And Forensic Instincts will keep us all safe."

Gia's words were a prayer and a plea.

Casey planned to make them a reality.

CHAPTER 24

Gabe sounded pretty frantic when Dani called him back.

"Are you okay?" he demanded over the sound of running water. "I'm freaking out here. All I've gotten from you in days are a few I'll-talk-to-you-later texts. I'm torn between thinking something's very wrong and thinking you're dumping me."

Dani shut her eyes and leaned her head back against the smooth leather of the backseat of the car. She visualized Gabe, setting up his water treadmill and worrying about her. Casey had been right. She'd only screwed things up more by delaying this call. But she'd been such a wreck. She was also a horrible liar. She'd have to follow Marc's advice: the truth, but only bare bones.

"I'm so sorry, Gabe." Her voice rang with genuine regret and equally genuine anguish. "I didn't mean to freak you out. I'm just a mess. My family is going through a real crisis, and I've been with them day and night. I can't seem to focus on anything else. Of course I'm not dumping you. In fact, hearing your voice means more than I can say."

The sound of running water ceased. "What kind of crisis? Is someone ill?"

Here came the hard part. "I . . ." Dani choked back a sob, which—even though it was as real as it gets—she supposed would help her cause. "I can't talk about it. It's very personal and it involves confidences I can't break. Just know that, if I could discuss it, you'd be the one I'd do it with. And when I can, I will."

"Okay." Reluctant acceptance. "How can I help?"

"Just be there when I need to talk. Understand when I can't. And focus on all the feelings we rediscovered when I was in Cleveland."

"That part's easy." Gabe's tone was tender. "Do you want me to fly to New York? I could at least be there for you while you work this through."

Dani swallowed hard. "No, but thanks. It's easier for me to cope with this alone. I promise I'll make it up to you."

"You don't have to make it up to me. Just know that I'm here if you need me—whenever you need me." A pause, during which Dani heard Gabe call out to someone. "I'm sorry, Dani," he said. "My next patient just arrived—a Papillion who's recovering from patella surgery. I've got a back-to-back day and a ton of files to update after that. But can we talk later? Maybe tonight?"

"I'll text you." Dani never thought she'd be relieved to get off the phone with Gabe, but she was immensely so. She couldn't do this anymore, not now. "I'll be with my family. But even if we can't talk, we can text. Please understand. I'm stretched as thin as I can be without breaking."

"You won't break. You're too strong for that. And I do understand. Now go do what you have to. Text me when you can. And remember that I'm thinking of you."

"I'm thinking of you, too," Dani replied quietly.

She disconnected the call and blew out a slow breath.

"You did great," Gia said.

Dani turned her head toward her sister. "It was tough—really tough. But I think I managed to control the situation."

"From my end, it sounded like you did. Was he angry?"

"Gabe is a pretty sensitive guy. So, no, he wasn't angry. I'm sure he has a million questions. But he'll be patient. Hopefully, it won't be long before this whole nightmare is over and I can fill him in."

Gia nodded, seized by an unexpected pang of emptiness. "I've never felt like I was missing something by not having a serious guy in my life. I'm all about my career. But right now, I really envy what you and Gabe have got. Hold on to it."

"I plan to." Dani chewed her lip, visibly hesitant about whether or not she was about to overstep her bounds, and then deciding to go for it. "Open yourself up a little more, Gia. Let people in. Show a teeny bit of the vulnerability that I've seen you show with me and with your parents. The right guy will find you."

A small smile curved Gia's lips. "You mean leave the bulldozer at work?"

"Something like that."

"Thanks for the advice. We've known each other for such a short time, and yet you know me so well. I'm used to running the show and managing people. My family's been the only exception. But it's time I separated personal and professional and opened myself up to some possibilities. I'll work on it."

"I'm glad. Sorry if I overstepped."

"You didn't. You're my twin." Gia still savored the word. If anything could soften her tough exterior, it was finding Dani.

Abruptly, her thoughts shifted. "Let's talk about tonight and about your parents."

* * *

Gabe swore under his breath. Gripping his cell phone, he sank down on the chair next to his water treadmill. How could he have been so stupid? Slipping up like that, telling her he'd visit her in New York? He shouldn't have a clue she'd be in New York. His assumption should be that she'd be home in Minneapolis, right there with her family.

Shit. Shit. Shit.

He dragged a hand through his hair, trying to calm his racing heart. She hadn't picked up on his screw-up. She couldn't have. Because, if she had, she would have said something. Plus, she'd barely been focused. She was too freaked out about her life. And if the realization struck her later, he'd figure out some way to explain it away. She'd believe him. She trusted him. She fucking trusted him. It would be okay.

He'd almost convinced himself by the end of the day when his last recuperating dog had gone home.

He was just going through his files, adding his pets' therapy updates, when his phone rang again. A dark premonition shot through him. What if Dani were calling to demand answers? What if she'd guessed?

The "anonymous" on his caller ID put that fear to rest and raised another.

Reluctantly, he answered. "Hello."

"What the hell is going on there?" the familiar voice demanded. "I haven't heard from you in two fucking days. What are you pulling off her computer? What is she saying? What is she doing? And why am I paying you if you're not doing a goddamned thing?"

Gabe swallowed hard. "You know the situation, Mr. Carp." *Yeah. Mr. Carp, my ass.* "Things have changed. You're the one who told me about the investigators Danielle and her sister are working with. They're good. Very good. Dani and Gia knew their phones and Facebook accounts had been hacked. Once the Forensic Instincts team heard that, the first thing they must have done was to shut down any telling communications on the twins' computers. Which is why I'm only seeing innocuous Google searches and emails to Dani's friends and co-workers. It's only a matter of time before Forensic Instincts blocks the video and audio feeds, after which I won't pick up much of anything."

"Then find another way." There was a level of unleashed fury in Mr. Carp's tone that scared the shit out of Gabe. "I don't care how. You're sleeping with the bitch. Get her to talk to you, to spill her guts. I've got to know where things stand."

"I'm trying."

"Try harder. Otherwise, you're dispensable."

The phone line went dead and Gabe dropped his head into his hands. What had he gotten himself into?

When Al Carp—or whatever the hell his real name was—had first approached him with this job, it had seemed like a gift from the gods, even if Carp did look more like a hitman than a businessman. With cold eyes and an ominous tone, the heavily muscled gorilla told Gabe that he knew all about his preoccupation with Danielle Murano, and that he also knew about Gabe's side jobs in technical support for extra cash. How the gorilla had known all that had been unknown and unexplained. What *was* explained was that Dani was in danger—from the deadbeat who was her biological father—and that Gabe was just the man to ensure her safety.

The allure was too much to resist. Not only would Gabe get to keep tabs on and protect the woman he'd never stopped loving, but he'd be in her life every day—even if she didn't know he was there. He'd be able to watch her, hear her, and reclaim a piece of the past. Plus, he'd be well compensated for something he would have done for free.

He was in before the gorilla finished laying out the terms.

Gabe had gone to the veterinary convention to seek out Dani and to figure out a way to upload the spyware onto her computer. The rest had been a dream come true. Discovering that what they'd had was still simmering beneath the surface and that it was mutual? That Dani wanted him as much as he wanted her?

Gabe had been blown away. It didn't matter that Dani hadn't even remembered that she'd been the one to end things—and at the very worst time. Gabe had planned to propose marriage the very night she'd suggested they take a time-out to grow as individuals rather than as a couple. So how could she know he'd spent six years fantasizing about what should have been? About the life and the family that should have been theirs?

He'd fallen to pieces—pieces he'd never fully reassembled.

Until their reunion.

All Gabe's pain and bitterness had vanished the second he'd felt Dani's body under his. She belonged to him again, and he intended to keep it that way. Just as he intended to keep her safe. He didn't buy the deadbeat dad story, but he did buy the fact that someone was after her.

But the attack in Rockefeller Center? Threats to Dani's life and to his? Gabe hadn't signed up for that. He was in way over his head. And he wasn't an idiot. He now realized that whoever Carp's boss was wasn't trying to protect Dani from some anonymous culprit. *He* was the person who was after Dani. It obviously had something to do with her twin sister. God only knew what. But Gabe was at a total loss about how to keep both Dani and himself safe.

He couldn't tell her the truth. It wouldn't stop the bastard. Plus, if he poured the full story out now, Dani would dump him in a heartbeat. Hell, she'd probably turn him over to the cops. But if he didn't… where was this leading? Which way did he turn?

The walls were closing in and Gabe was starting to suffocate.

CHAPTER 25

The Brandos' home
Todt Hill, Staten Island

It was primary results night, and Joseph was the only composed member of the group that was assembled in the Brandos' living room. Donna was bustling around, nervously bringing in additional platters of antipasto—when no one had finished the first two platters—Lina was pacing around the room, and Neil Donato, Joseph's campaign manager, was eyeing his cell phone, scanning his local updates, and waiting for a definitive call that would finalize this race.

"You're going to burn a hole through that phone, Neil." Joseph bent one knee and crossed his leg over to rest on the other. "We've got a wide lead. It's almost over."

Neil turned to Joseph, brows raised. He was a good six years younger than Joseph, although his craggy features negated that fact. Tall and lean, he was all high energy and crackling ambition. Even his attire spoke volumes about who he was. While Joseph was dressed casually in a golf shirt and jeans, Neil was wearing a suit—his only concession having been that he'd tossed the tie and opened the top buttons of the dress shirt about an hour ago.

"Yeah, the lead is substantial," he agreed. "And luckily, we only have one competitor. But it's not over till it's over."

"Such optimism," Joseph said dryly.

"I am optimistic. Just cautious."

"That's why you're so good at what you do." A grin. "Glad I hired you."

A corner of Neil's mouth lifted and then turned into a full indulgent smile as Lina walked over to him with a plate of antipasto.

"Here, Uncle Neil." Her eyes were twinkling as she handed him the plate. "Please eat something. Otherwise, you'll pass out and Mom will never forgive us."

Neil took the plate and gave Lina's hand an affectionate pat. "Okay. But only because it came from you. Otherwise, I'd stare at my phone until my eyes crossed."

As if on cue, his cell phone's ringtone sounded.

He grabbed the phone, his index finger sliding the screen to accept in one fluid motion, after which the phone was at his ear. "Neil Donato." A pause. "Yes, Ken, of course." Neil walked over and handed the phone to Joseph, a broad smile splitting his normally serious face. "It's your opponent," he said.

Joseph rose from the sofa and took the phone. "Ken, hello." A smile. "Thank you. I appreciate your graciousness. You ran a strong race."

Lina was already jumping up and down, stifling her shriek of joy, when her father handed the phone back to Neil and said, "Ken just conceded the election."

"Congratulations." Neil clapped Joseph on the shoulder. "You're now the official Republican candidate from our district. Every polling platform says you'll run right over our Democratic contender. After that, you're on your way to the United States House of Representatives."

All chaos erupted at that point, with Donna and Lina flinging their arms around Joseph, practically knocking him back down onto the sofa, and Neil popping open a bottle of champagne, which had been nestled hopefully on ice.

Glasses were poured and passed around, and everyone lifted theirs high in the air.

"To Joseph," Neil said. "May he take Congress by storm."

Cheers and smiles greeted Neil's toast, and the clinking sound of glasses was resounding.

"Hard to believe that such a small crowd can be so noisy," Joseph teased. He pulled Donna to his one side and Lina to his other, and his expression transformed to one of grateful tenderness. "Thank you. I'm a lucky man. I love you all—even you, you slave driver," he added, raising his glass to Neil.

"And we love you." Donna gave him a resounding kiss. "You're a fine man, Joseph Brando. You're going to do great things for our country."

"Mom's right." Lina gave her father a huge hug. "And *we're* the lucky ones. We have you." A dubious look. "I'm not sure how I'm going to feel about sharing you with the country."

"You'll get used to it," Neil admonished her with that same indulgent grin.

"Okay, I'll try, but only because I'm such an awesome daughter." Lina leaned around her father to grab her mother's arm. "The party," she reminded her. "We've got to finalize details."

"Now?" Neil stared.

"Did you expect our nonstop Lina to adhere to the dreaded word *wait*?" Joseph asked, completely unsurprised.

"You're right," Neil replied, listening as Lina began sharing specifics with her mother. "I don't know what I was thinking."

Offices of Forensic Instincts

The brownstone was quiet, which suited Ryan just fine. Downstairs in his lair, he needed solitude and mental concentration.

"There is late-breaking confirmation that Joseph Brando was the victor of today's Republican primary and that he's proceeding with his quest for a seat in the United States House of Representatives," Yoda announced.

"Good and bad," Ryan murmured, hunched over his work. "Good because we can go to the victory party and do our thing. Bad because I have to wear a suit. But not a surprise. The guy was leading by a mile."

"I have a vast number of videos showing the proper knotting of a tie," Yoda informed him. "There is one on YouTube that is especially exacting."

"Thanks, Yoda. But I'll leave that honor to Claire. Nothing like the personal touch."

"Very good, Ryan." Yoda fell silent and Ryan resumed his task: tracing Dani's hacker.

When he'd started the process a few days ago, he'd used his spyware account credentials to gain access to the web application. Once he looked "under the hood," he knew what he needed to do. Leveraging an unpatched security flaw, he'd gained access to the security tables and elevated himself to an admin. From there he FTPed a month's worth of log files to a secure drop location and then downloaded them to the FI server.

For the past few hours, he'd been searching the spyware application for the account that was spying on Dani. There was no personally identifiable information except for the user ID and password. But that was all Ryan needed. He searched through the server log files, looking for entries containing the alphanumeric user ID.

And then, just minutes ago, bingo. The log showed the IP address of the computer that had invaded Dani's privacy. Time for a reverse lookup to determine the approximate geographic location.

Cleveland. That certainly rang a bell—and not a welcome one.

Ryan frowned, rummaging around on his desk for the list of people Dani had supplied him with, seeking confirmation of what he remembered. Yup. There it was. Cleveland, Ohio. The city where Dani's boyfriend, Gabe Hayward, lived.

Ryan didn't believe in coincidences. He immediately began searching through the header information in each of Dani's email messages. Sure enough, multiple messages sent by Gabe to Dani showed a match between the IP address of the email and the spyware account.

Shit. Dani's boyfriend was a scumbag—and a criminal. He was being paid by whoever was running the show to do this. The way Dani had talked about him, it was obvious this wasn't a random hookup, it was a relationship. And now she had to be told that this guy was a creeper and a felon.

Well, one thing was for sure. Ryan wasn't going to be the one to do the telling. That would be up to someone worthy of the task.

He picked up his cell and called Claire.

"Hey," she answered. "I'm in lotus position, trying to relax."

"Well, un-relax. I need you."

"A booty call?" He could hear the amusement in her voice.

"That's not why I called, but actually, yeah. I'd love one of those."

"Wouldn't you always?"

"Can't deny it."

"Ever honest." Claire sighed. "Well, it just so happens I'm having trouble unwinding and I could use the help of your unique set of skills. Why don't you come to my place? My bed's a lot more comfortable than your lumpy sofa."

"Not this time, Claire. We need to be here."

A poignant silence, during which time Ryan could actually sense the transformation in Claire—from lover to claircognizant.

"This is about Dani," she said at last, her tone quiet and sober. "You found something. And it's not good."

"Yes. And no, it's not." Ryan blew out a breath. "Just come to the office and straight down to my lair. We've got a problem—a major one."

"I'm on my way."

* * *

Claire walked into the lair and automatically locked the door behind her. But the expression on her face wasn't a sexual invite. It was a pained awareness.

"The person doing the spying—it's someone close to Dani, someone she cares for," she said without preamble.

Ryan nodded. He might never understand Claire's gift, but he no longer minimized it. "Big-time."

"Gabe. Her boyfriend." Claire waited for the confirmation in Ryan's gaze, then sank down onto a chair when it came. "Dammit. When I started calming Dani down about the hacker's intentions, I started getting the creepiest feeling that there was some level of sexual gratification involved in this spying arrangement. Yes, there's money involved. But there's also more. Emotional entanglement, desire... it all flashed through my head while I was assuring Dani it wasn't the case." Claire shook her head, sadness tugging at her heart. "This truly sucks."

"I know." Ryan walked over to the well-worn sofa he kept in the room and dropped down onto it, arms folded behind his head, forehead creased in thought. "If I give you some of their email exchanges, maybe show you a Google Earth photo of the bastard's apartment, can you get a more detailed read on things? Maybe a hint of who Hayward is working for?"

Claire shook her head. "I don't think that will work. I've never experienced the slightest awareness of this guy, even when Dani talked about him. But Dani? That's an entirely different case. The connections I have to her—and to Gia and Lina—they're all quite strong."

"So you think talking to Dani might help trigger something?"

"Hopefully, yes."

"Good."

Something about Ryan's tone made Claire incline her head, gaze intently at him. "You want me to be the one to tell her about Gabe."

"Yeah, I do." Ryan's shoulders lifted in a helpless shrug. "You know I'm no good at this... *stuff*. Emotions... they're not my strong suit. But they are yours. You'll tell her in a way that will minimize the damage."

Claire exhaled sharply. "I'll tell her. I'll catch a train up to Rye tomorrow and talk to her while Gia's at her client meeting."

"Do you want me to go with you?" Ryan was clearly choking on the offer, sincere though it was.

A hint of a smile. "No, hotshot. I can handle this. You just stay close to the phone in case I need any backup with your technological... *stuff*."

"Sure. That I can provide."

"I know you can."

There was a weary silence that hung in the air, until, wordlessly, Claire crossed over and sank down beside Ryan on the couch, letting her head rest on his shoulder.

It was an innocent enough gesture, until Ryan turned his lips into her hair and trailed his knuckles slowly down the side of her neck.

Abruptly, the atmosphere in the room changed, and the heated sexuality that always crackled between them surged to life.

Ryan twisted around and pressed Claire down onto the sofa cushions.

"There's nothing more we can do tonight," he said, unbuttoning her blouse. "At least not for Dani. So can we get to my unique set of skills?"

Claire reached up and tugged his T-shirt over his head. "Promise to help me relax?"

"Eventually, yeah." Ryan unhooked the front clasp of her bra. "But it'll probably take repeat performances and long hours."

"I can wait."

"No, you can't. And neither can I."

CHAPTER 26

Rye, New York

Dani handed Claire a cup of herbal tea and gestured for her to have a seat on one of the tub chairs in Gia's living room.

"You sounded very serious when you called," Dani said, perching at the edge of the sofa with her own cup of tea. "Does this have to do with my parents and our two-family meeting last night? Because Patrick told me he'd let you all know that we're hanging in." A tired sigh. "My mom and dad are amazing. They're being so strong—or at least trying to, for me. They're scared and they're in shock, but they want answers as much as Gia and I do. They hit it off with the Russos, partly because there's now a bond between them and partly because Gia's parents are fine and loving people. The emotional part of this we'll get through. The rest, the scary part… that we can eliminate only with your help."

"That's why I'm here." Claire was frank and to the point. This wasn't news that could be spun in a positive light. It was news that had to be delivered gently but without hedging. There was no room for Dani to try to explain it away to herself. That would waste time and intensify her pain. She had to believe what Claire told her. Only after that could Claire truly comfort her and then lay out FI's plan.

Dani had picked up on Claire's tone. "So I'm not wrong. This is serious. You've found out something." She visibly steeled herself.

"When Ryan first examined your computers, he determined that the spyware was installed only on *your* computer, not Gia's. We didn't know why. Now we do."

"Wait." Dani held up a palm. "Ryan told us—"

"I know what Ryan told you." Claire put her own cup on the coffee table and moved to sit beside Dani, gently placing her hand over Dani's. "He didn't want to frighten you, not until he knew why it was just your computer that was being hacked."

"Am I the primary target? Is that what you're saying?"

"No. I'm saying that the person who installed the spyware was only interested in watching and listening to you. The rest, the communications between you and Gia, the DNA test results, that he could see on either end. If it was on your screen, it was on Gia's. So there was no need to access her computer, as well."

"So besides being a criminal, this guy *is* some kind of pervert?" All the color had drained from Dani's face. "He's not only stalking us for some terrifying end, he's fixated on me?"

Claire squeezed Dani's hand as she spoke. "He is fixated on you, but he's not the terrifying monster you're imagining. And he's not random."

Dani stared. "Are you saying I know this sicko?"

"That's exactly what I'm saying." Claire didn't avert her gaze. "Dani, it's Gabe."

Silence.

"Gabe." Dani repeated the word as if she were tasting a foreign object.

"Yes—Gabe." Claire could feel Dani's white shock transform to searing pain as it singed her fingers. But that wasn't all she picked up on from the physical contact with Dani's hand. For the first time, she could sense Gabe, get a preliminary insight into him. Fear... inner turmoil… conflict. He was experiencing a myriad of emotions even as he did what he'd been hired to do.

"He's in love with you," Claire said, staring off into space. "He has been since you were together in college. He needed to feel close to you. He didn't know you'd reconnect at the conference the way you did. He might have blown off the money he's being paid and made different choices."

"It can't be Gabe." Tears were glistening on Dani's lashes. "He'd never accept a payoff to do something like this to me. You must be wrong."

"I wish I were. But I'm not." Claire got a quick glimpse of an image from the past—a small box nestled in Gabe's jeans pocket with a tiny glistening diamond ring inside. "This isn't about money, not really. Yours and Gabe's breakup—it wasn't mutual. You ended things. He was going to propose to you. But you left him. He's never accepted that. And he's never let go. He signed up for this hacker job to get close to you, but he's in way over his head. He's scared, Dani, for you and for him. He doesn't know what to do or how to get out."

"Oh my God!" Dani sobbed, pulling away her fingers and covering her face with both hands. "Oh my God."

Claire felt the connection snap as Dani's hand left hers. The flashes of Gabe and his motives began to fade. So Claire switched gears, instead supplying Dani with the facts she needed to hear. "I can't explain all the techno details, but Ryan traced the hacker's IP address back to Cleveland. He then used Gabe's emails to you to compare the IP address to the hacker's. It matched. There's no question that it's Gabe."

"I just spoke to him. He was so worried about me."

"That wasn't a lie."

"He even said he'd come to New York to be with me while…" Dani's voice broke off. "How did he know I was in New York?" she realized aloud. "I told him I was with my family. That would mean Minneapolis. How could I have missed that?"

"You're on emotional overload," Claire replied. "Please don't beat yourself up."

"He was going to ask me to marry him? When we were in college?"

Claire nodded. "But you broke things off before he could—at least that's the way he views it."

"That's not what happened." Dani was visibly racking her brain. "We went our separate ways. It was mutual, or at least I thought it was. We needed time and space to evolve as individuals. It never occurred to me..." She swallowed, turning to face Claire. "Does he know the reasons he's doing this? Is he in on the entirety of things— like hurting Gia and me, or worse?"

"My instincts say no. I think he was misled. Things have changed from when he first started this. He now realizes there's danger in- volved. He didn't before. He's a wreck. I think he might even be re- lieved when we confront him."

Dani stared. "You're flying to Cleveland?"

"Marc and I are, yes." Again, Claire spoke gently. "We need in- formation and Gabe needs to be held accountable for what he's done. And before you ask, no, you won't be there. In fact, you won't give Gabe so much as a hint that we're coming or that you know the truth. Just send him your usual texts. No phone calls. You'll have plenty of time to confront him. In the meantime, we'll be there in a few hours."

"He won't be home," Dani said woodenly. "He'll be at work. Do you need the address?"

"We have it. We'll be visiting him there. Given the circumstanc- es, I think he'll clear his schedule." Once again, Claire reached over and squeezed Dani's hand. "I'm so sorry. And for what it's worth, so is Gabe.""Thank you, Claire." Dani rose, as did Claire, and Dani dashed the tears off her face. "I'll be okay. Just find out who's behind this. Please."

Cleveland, Ohio

Gabe's waiting room was conducive to both animals and humans. Twin love seats sat adjacent to each other, upholstered with animal prints. Bowls filled with dog treats sat on the long bench spanning one wall, beside which hung a rack with canine life vests and rehab balls for sale. *Animal Wellness* and other, more mainstream magazines, were splayed on the end tables, and photos of patient success stories lined the walls. The desk was the only mundane item in the room, containing the usual computer, paperwork, and adjacent printer.

From inside the office space, Claire and Marc could hear the motorized hum of the water treadmill and the occasional words of praise, both from the man who had to be Gabe and the young woman who had to be the pet's owner.

"Let's sit," Marc said to Claire, gesturing at one of the love seats. "Marching into that PT room with accusations is only going to cause a riot. Let's wait for the client to leave, and we'll have our face-off before the next one is due."

Claire nodded in agreement, sinking into the pet lovers' settee. "How do we handle it if his next clients show up early?"

"We'll approach the desk and make our presence and our purpose known. Believe me, Gabe will talk. He just needs the proper motivation."

Claire looked a tad bit alarmed. "You're not going to get physical, are you? I think that would be a mistake."

"So do I—unless it becomes necessary. But something tells me it won't. I suspect he'll cave with just a few words. And he'll clear his schedule on the spot." Marc settled himself beside Claire, glancing down at the upholstery. "A pet parade," he muttered. "Abby would love this."

Abby was Marc's niece, the daughter of his older brother, Aidan. She was a four-year-old hellion, and she had both of the implacable Devereaux men wrapped around her little finger.

"I'm sure she would." Claire smiled. "I'm also sure she'd grab some crayons and draw some dog houses and cat beds on the upholstery as accoutrements."

A deep chuckle. "That—or worse."

The humming sound halted, and a conversation between Gabe and the young woman commenced.

"The laser therapy and ultrasound should ease the joint pain," he said. "And she did beautifully on the treadmill today. The limp is much better. Keep her quiet for the rest of the day and off that leg as much as possible."

"Thank you, Gabe," was the reply. "Trixie thanks you, too. Her recovery has sped up rapidly since she started seeing you."

"I'm glad." Gabe shuffled around. "Here. Towel her dry. Then use the blow-dryer to finish the job." The sound of something—presumably an oversized blow-dryer—rolled into the room.

"No problem." The woman was clearly used to the procedure. "While I'm doing that, could you put us in your schedule for Friday? And bill us for today, of course. Just put it on the usual credit card."

"Sure."

The blow-dryer whirred to life just as a lanky, wavy-haired guy with strain written all over his face entered the waiting room.

"That's Gabe," Claire said quietly, stating the obvious but confirming it for Marc.

He nodded, rising to his feet as Gabe glanced quizzically in their direction. "Can I help you?" he asked.

"We need to talk."

The combination of Marc's tone and his formidable presence made Gabe shift nervously. So did the appearance of Claire, who came to stand beside Marc. "Did you want to make an appointment for your pet?"

Marc jerked his thumb in the direction of the room with the treadmill. "I want you to do what that lady just asked you to do. Don't bother setting up her next appointment, just charge her credit card for today. Then I want you to cancel whoever's due in next. You won't be seeing them. In fact, you should cancel all your appointments for the rest of the day, as well as the next several days. Go for the family emergency excuse. It's very effective, wouldn't you say?"

By this time, Gabe had turned sheet white. "Who are you?"

Marc slapped a business card on the desk and stared Gabe down. "Marc Devereaux. And this is Claire Hedgleigh. From Forensic Instincts, which I'm sure you've thoroughly researched. Enough said." A pause as Gabe stared at the card, looking ill. "But just to refresh your memory, our investigative firm represents Danielle Murano. And isn't that reason enough to cancel your appointments?"

"I'll take care of it right away." Sweat trickled down Gabe's face, and his hands were shaking as he made the list of necessary calls.

By that time, the blow-dryer had stopped, and the young woman inside had walked into the waiting room with a beautiful golden retriever who had the slightest limp. She glanced quickly at Marc and Claire, giving them a tentative smile. "I'm sorry, I didn't realize I'd run over on time." She turned to Gabe. "Why don't I give you a call to book our next appointment?"

"I think that would be best." Gabe's tone all but ushered her out, and she took the hint, leading her dog out the door and letting it swing shut behind her.

Claire walked over and flipped the lock, turning the sign that read OPEN to CLOSED. Then she rejoined Marc at the desk, facing Gabe with all of the anger Marc felt, but with a tad of sadness. The guy had looked like hell to begin with. Now he looked like he was going to vomit and wet his pants simultaneously.

"I can't do this anymore," he managed, collapsing in his chair. "I just can't."

"Then don't," Marc replied. "Let's skip the preliminaries and any denials you plan on issuing. We traced the spyware back to your IP address. We know it's you who's been keeping tabs on Dani. Now you're going to tell us the why, along with the who. Who hired you? What's his agenda? And why is he going after Dani and Gia?"

Gabe slumped farther down in his chair, obviously caught between two terrifying alternatives. "He'll kill me," he whispered.

"Not if you talk to us, he won't. We'll protect you."

"And if I talk to you? I'll go to jail and he'll still find a way of getting to me."

"We'll keep you out of jail—but only if you cooperate."

"Why would you do that? What I'm doing is illegal."

"Because our job is to protect Dani and Gia. Not to turn in some part-time hacker. But all that could change if you don't start telling us what we want to know."

"Gabe," Claire added softly. "Do it for Dani. Her life is in danger, and you know it. You didn't before, but you do now. You love her. So help protect her."

Briefly, Gabe shut his eyes. When he opened them, there was resignation written all over his face. "The guy calls himself Al Carp. I'm sure that's an alias."

"What does he look like?" Marc demanded.

"He dresses like he works on Wall Street. But there's something about him—he's scary, really scary, in a way that makes my blood run cold. Thick muscles, cruel features—he looks like a hitman from an old movie. He approached me about a month ago. And he knew all about me—my past relationship with Dani, my side jobs in tech support, everything."

"Then why would you sign on to help him?"

"Because I was an idiot. Because I believed what he told me."

"Which was?"

"That Dani was in danger from her biological father, who was tracking her down. That he meant to hurt her, really hurt her. Carp made the guy sound like some kind of psycho. And I love Dani. I was afraid for her. And, yeah, I was being paid, and well. Plus, I liked the idea of being Dani's knight in shining armor, and of watching her every day. She's all I've thought of for the past six years. Being back in her life was... everything. But now—I don't believe all that crap about Dani's father I was told. I think it's *Carp* who's after Dani and her sister. But I swear, I don't know why. All I know is that I was hired to report back on their activities so he could keep the sisters apart."

"Wait a minute." Marc's mind zoomed in on a previous bit of information Gabe had supplied. "You said that Carp approached you a month ago. But Dani and Gia hadn't even made contact back then. So what made Carp seek you out? And why scrutinize Dani and not Gia? What made Dani a bigger threat—or any threat at all?"

"My guess?" Clearly, Gabe had thought this one through. "Dani told me she'd had a recent job interview in Manhattan. That trip must have raised a red flag to Carp or whoever he's working for."

"That's the reason there was spyware only on Dani's and not Gia's computer," Claire said. "Carp wanted to monitor things to see if Dani took that job and moved to New York."

"Right." Marc's wheels were turning. "This guy Carp probably *is* a hitman. Whoever's running the show, Carp works for him. When was the last time Carp contacted you?"

"Yesterday. He was all over my case, furious at me for not providing information. But I had nothing to report. I'm sure your guy Ryan McKay removed the spyware and covered up the microphone and camera. So I was coming up empty." Gabe swallowed, his Adam's apple going up and down in a sickly fashion. "Carp said I was dispensable. And the truth is, I am." He gazed pitifully up at Marc. "What should I do? How can I help Dani?"

"Fly to New York," Marc said. "Not with us. On a separate flight." Marc slapped a one-way plane ticket on the desk. "No one knows we're here. We made sure of it—false identities. Call Carp and tell him that Dani broke down and told you she was with her sister, and that you're flying there to get a firsthand take on things. That'll please him enough to hold off on killing you. We'll take care of the rest."

"Where will I stay?"

"Exactly where we tell you to."

Gabe sucked in his breath. "Fine. I'll do as you say." A pause. "One more question," he began hesitantly.

"Yes, Dani knows," Claire supplied. "I told her myself this morning."

"God, she must hate me."

"Right now, she's in shock. But yes, she's livid, not to mention feeling totally betrayed. Do you blame her?"

"Of course not."

"You'll have to face her yourself and deal with the fallout." Claire wasn't sugarcoating this. "It's what you deserve."

Gabe gave a bleak nod.

"Tossing you out on your ass isn't an option," Marc surprised Claire by saying. "She can't. It's imperative that your friend Mr. Carp thinks you two are still a couple. He'll be watching you. Don't doubt that for a minute or let your guard down."

"I won't." Gabe turned his palms up. "But how am I going to convince Dani to go through this charade?"

"That's our job. Now call Carp," Marc instructed. "Put him on speakerphone. I want to hear his voice."

"I… Okay." Gabe did as he was told.

"Yeah?" A harsh, threatening voice answered. "And it better be good."

"It is," Gabe assured him.

Marc and Claire listened to the terse exchange between men. Carp was a bastard. But there was no doubt he was pleased as hell with the breakthrough.

"Get details out of her," he demanded. "And call me as soon as you do."

"I will, Mr. Carp."

The phone line went dead.

"We'll have a guy waiting for you at La Guardia," Marc told Gabe. "You'll be going straight to Gia's townhouse. You'll have your reunion there."

CHAPTER 27

Gia's townhouse
Rye, New York
The next afternoon

"Marc just got here," Gia said, handing Dani a glass of wine as her sister stood at the townhouse window, gazing out at nothing in particular. "He parked at the other end of the development and came in through the patio slider. So his visit went undetected." She pressed her lips together, determined to keep her hatred of Gabe in check. Dani didn't need any more negativity piled onto her. "And Patrick's guy will be bringing Gabe back in fifteen."

"I can hardly wait," Dani replied dryly. "As if last night wasn't enough." Gabe had been delivered to the townhouse door fresh from his flight. He'd been broken, pleading, and pathetic. Claire had called hours before that and prepared Dani for the visit. But she couldn't prepare her for the hurt or the furious sense of betrayal that still gnawed at her.

"You okay?" Gia asked, touching her sister's arm.

"Yeah. Great." Dani gave Gia's hand a squeeze to soften her biting reply. "Sorry. I don't mean to be bitchy, especially not to you. I didn't get much sleep last night. And I guess I'm still pretty much a wreck."

"Don't apologize. Finding out what Gabe was doing was a major blow."

Frowning, Gia sipped at her own Pinot Grigio. She was worried about Dani. She'd taken this whole Gabe thing very hard. From what Dani had told her, the initial confrontation had been more of a pained confession and a plea for understanding from Gabe than a knock-down-drag-out fight between two furious lovers.

Like Gia, Dani was stubborn and proud. She'd heard Gabe out, accepted the pretense they'd have to put on, but the real relationship? That she'd ended firmly and finally. There'd be no forgiveness—not for something of this magnitude. Dani had informed Gia that Gabe badly needed a therapist, and she wasn't playing that role. As for pressing charges, that wasn't something she was ready to do, not with the investigation on the line. But later? That decision was up for grabs.

Dani had been stoic. But Gia had heard her weeping far into the night.

And now she had to contend with yet another visit from the scumbag just so Gabe's sicko boss believed that she and Gabe were bonding and that she was spilling her guts to him.

Forensic Instincts had gotten Gabe a room—which he shared with his assigned security detail—at the local inn. They'd instructed him to inform Carp that he'd made these arrangements so that he and Dani could have the privacy he needed to get her talking. He sure as hell couldn't do that at her sister's place.

What a crock of shit. And what a heavy weight for Dani to carry.

"I'll be fine, Gia," Dani said now, turning to give her sister a stoic smile. "But I'm glad Marc is here. Otherwise, this room would be deadly silent. Plus, there's something calming about his presence."

"Glad to hear that," Marc said as he walked into the room. "I'll keep things under control. Meanwhile, I wanted to let you know that the car just arrived. This way you can steel yourself." Marc was clearly trying to ease Dani's way. "Gabe will stay only an hour or so, just enough to keep up the pretense of him meeting your sister. The hard part will come later when you have to go to the inn. But I'll be there, too."

Dani turned to face him. "How much longer does this whole charade have to go on?"

"Hopefully, today will be it. Once you've had your alleged bleeding-heart visit, Gabe can call Carp and relay the story we conjured up. You're cracking under the pressure. Yours and Gia's parents are shattered. Everyone is terrified. All you want is to be safe and to go back to your normal, secure life. You and Gia are twins, so you'll stay in touch, but from your respective cities. Anything more than that—including this investigation—isn't worth the risk. You'll be spending this weekend with Gia and then heading home. Once Gabe reports all that to Carp, he'll be appeased and the immediate danger will be held at bay. Meanwhile, it'll give Ryan enough time to trace the phone number for Carp that Gabe gave us. That's a giant step closer to our answers. It's almost over, Dani. You've got this. And so do we."

Dani nodded. "What happens to Gabe after that?"

"He'll go back to Cleveland to keep up pretenses. But we'll have full-time security on him, not only to keep him from running but to see if Carp shows up in person. We're going to get this guy any way we have to and find out the name of his boss—the son of a bitch who's threatening your lives."

Green Hills Cemetery
Brooklyn, New York

Joseph sat on the edge of the white bench, facing the exquisitely crafted marble mausoleum that bore the name ANGELO COLONE in gold block letters. The structure was extravagant, made entirely of solid white marble with gilded touches and twin marble columns flanking it. The land on which it sat was peaceful and undisturbed— all green manicured lawns and gently sloping hills. It was an idyllic spot for eternal rest, one that bespoke the power and importance of those who resided there.

Angelo was the epitome of that definition.

He'd always been bigger than life, even as a boy with a legion of loyal followers—other kids standing behind him, playing stickball in the street. As a grown man, he kept that legion, expanded upon it, and climbed the ladder in a major organized crime family, a capo with a team of soldiers who did his bidding. Still, while the direction his power had taken him had been dark, his loyalty to and love for his friends and family had been indisputable and unwavering.

Joseph was the living example of that.

A songbird trilled in the tree overhead, and Joseph looked up, smiling as he felt Angelo's presence. He'd planned this particular visit for the past few days, but he'd pictured it in his head since the day Angelo had passed. And now that the initial pandemonium of the primary win had quieted down, with only Donna's and Lina's frantic last-minute party planning as center stage, it was time to make this moment a reality.

Time ticked by as Joseph sat, head bent, paying his respects to the man who'd been his closest friend since childhood and who'd gifted him with his greatest blessings: his family, his career, and now his future.

"Hello, Angelo," he said at last. "You know why I'm here. I've been thinking of you ever since the phone call came, and I wish you could have been there to share it with me." Joseph interlaced his fingers, trying to put his feelings into words. "I've visited you here many times since you left us, and yet, this time seems the most humbling and significant—the culmination of all you've done for me and for my family."

He reached down to open the cooler he'd brought with him, taking out a bottle of Prosecco and two fluted glasses.

"I've celebrated with Donna and Lina, with my campaign team, and with my constituents. But this bottle I saved to share with you. Just the two of us." Joseph held the bottle up as if for Angelo to see. Then, sensing his friend's approval, he placed the Prosecco back down on the bench beside him, removed the foil and eased out the stopper, and filled the two fluted glasses. He placed one glass on the smooth stone in front of the mausoleum and gripped the other in his hand.

"I don't know how you did it, but somehow everything good that's ever happened to me had your hand in it. You've given me all my dreams, including Tuesday night's win—and gifts that are so much more precious. Always know that I'm fulfilling my promise to you, Angelo, and doing all you asked. Jimmy is safe and thriving, and I plan to make sure he always will be. But I can never truly repay you. I wish you were here in the flesh to toast with me—I know how much you believed in my success. I miss you, my friend. But a part of you will always be with me." Joseph lifted his glass. "To you, Angelo. *Grazie, amico mio.*"

* * *

From behind a thick cluster of trees, Jimmy watched and listened.

He shouldn't be anywhere near this cemetery. He'd been expunged years ago. But he loved his brother. He *needed* his brother. And he couldn't stay away. So he'd crept onto the grounds, choosing a hiding place where he could pay his respects and beg for Angelo's strength and guidance.

He hadn't expected Joseph to be here. Joseph would ream the hell out of Jimmy if he saw him.

Still, Jimmy didn't leave. He remained where he was, listening to everything Angelo's dearest friend had to say. As the words sank in, Jimmy squeezed his eyes shut, tears seeping out from beneath his closed lids. *Safe? Thriving?* He was anything but. Day after day, he battled the drowning sensation that threatened to engulf him, drag him under for good.

Joseph could promise Angelo the world, and God help him, he believed what he was saying. But he didn't know what he was talking about. Yeah, Angelo had been shrewd enough to keep those fucking girls under surveillance all these years—just in case. But now that "just in case" had happened? Unless Jimmy could make Gia Russo and Danielle Murano go back to their separate lives, the past would become the present, everything would blow up in his face, and his entire world would come crashing down.

And there was no way he was getting them to back down. Not with that ball-breaking investigative firm on their payroll.

He'd run out of options. He'd have to get rid of them. It would have to be done carefully, in two separate hits, so there were no glaring red flags about twins being knocked off. And the media coverage, especially the photos, would have to be hidden from Lina. She was Angelo's godchild and his namesake. She had to be protected at all costs.

Maybe it was Jimmy's proximity to the mausoleum that made him feel so close to Angelo. Maybe it was his mind playing tricks on him. But he could actually hear his brother's voice clearly in his head: *Finish what you started, Jimmy. Make things right and make me proud.*

Jimmy would do that, no matter what it cost him. He'd make his brother proud and silence the damage he'd done twenty-seven years ago, the night he'd set this nightmare in motion.

The night he'd killed Anthony Ponti and his wife.

CHAPTER 28

Offices of Forensic Instincts
Sunday midday

Hutch was nursing a cup of coffee in Casey's kitchen when she appeared in the doorway, wearing a fitted, cobalt-blue Armani jersey sheath and matching heels.

"What do you think?" she asked, turning from side to side. "Appropriate for the Brandos' social scene?"

Staring, Hutch let out a long, low whistle. "You look… wow. I'd like to forget the promise I made to my boss to come in for a Sunday workday, call your regrets in to Donna Brando, and peel you out of that dress."

Casey laughed. "I take that as a yes."

Hutch studied her with that intense expression of his, not sharing her laughter. "I know you told me that Emma is friends with Angelina Brando, Joseph's daughter, which is why you're attending this victory party. But I'm not stupid. The fact that you didn't ask to bring a plus-one and that the whole FI team is going means this isn't a social appearance for you. If you're investigating the Brandos for the case you're working on, be careful. They're a powerful family, and Joseph Brando represents the interests and estate of Angelo Colone. That hasn't hurt his campaign, so it probably means nothing other than the fact that the two men were childhood friends. But it does mean you should be careful."

Casey blinked in surprise. "I didn't realize you'd done so much research on Joseph Brando. Pretty impressive, given I haven't even told you what we're investigating."

"You never do. That doesn't stop me from being smart."

"Or humble."

A corner of Hutch's mouth lifted. "Yeah, or humble." He rose and went to Casey, threading his fingers through her hair. "Let me know if you need me," he said quietly. "I love you. And I worry."

"Right back at you, SSA Hutchinson," Casey murmured. "And you know I'll come to you if I need to. I've certainly done so in the past. I don't see that changing."

"Good." Hutch drew back, tipped up her chin, and gave her a lingering kiss. "Now go catch the bad guys."

"Oh, I intend to."

* * *

Downstairs in the conference room, the FI team started gathering, ready to hop into the van for the drive to Todt Hill.

"I must say that we all clean up nice," Emma said, twirling around to show off her turquoise and purple swing skirt.

"Agreed." Marc was wearing a deep navy suit with a blue silk tie. "Although Claire has been downstairs for fifteen minutes trying to get Ryan to sit still long enough for her to tie his tie. Evidently, he's come up with some crucial piece of data that he wants to share with us before we leave."

"That sounds important," Casey responded as she entered the room, a shiny, just-brushed Hero at her heels.

Patrick, in a herringbone suit, smiled. "You look lovely, Casey."

"Thanks. So do all of you." She turned to Marc, brows drawn in question. "Any idea what Ryan's come up with?"

"We're about to find out," Claire replied, walking in wearing a pale blue silk pantsuit and an exasperated expression. "The man is impossible. It took me four tries to properly knot that damn tie."

"Sorry, Claire-voyant." Ryan strode into the room, stretching his neck to accustom it to the foreign object around it. "I didn't mean to make your life difficult. But this find is big." He held up a page that contained what looked to be a printout of a tiny article from an old newspaper.

"What is it?" Casey demanded.

"My genius, and a huge find," Ryan replied. "We were getting nowhere with the birth certificates. Whoever falsified them did a good enough job so the real ones were obviously destroyed and gone. Dead end for us. So I've been simultaneously working on another angle. I've been researching every regional archived newspaper I could find, looking for missing triplets. Unfortunately, most of the old NYC papers are long gone, and some weren't even being published in 1990. They were even more historic—like the *Brooklyn Eagle*, which was gone in the 1950s and is now up and running online just like the current newspapers are."

"Ryan, get to the point," Marc said.

"Okay, okay." Ryan rustled the page. "I finally found this tiny clipping in an out-of-print local Bay Ridge paper. The issue was published in March 1990." He paused, then read aloud, "Anthony and Carla Ponti were found shot to death in their Bay Ridge home last night. The killer is still unknown and at large." He looked up, his eyes bright with discovery. "The couple's infant triplets are officially missing and assumed to have been abducted by the killer."

Casey reached over and plucked the page from Ryan's hand. Skimming the short paragraph, she said, "Based on the timing and the circumstances, Anthony and Carla Ponti have to be Lina's, Gia's, and Dani's biological parents. There's no chance of a coincidence here. Did you find anything else?"

"Yeah. That there is absolutely no record of Ponti triplets in the Department of Health database. Their births have literally been erased—which is why I couldn't find anything. Whoever master-minded this did one hell of a job of covering all the bases."

"What about the parents?"

"Carla was a stay-at-home mom. Anthony was a little bit of this and a little bit of that. It looks like he had ties to Angelo Colone."

"What kind of ties?" Casey wasn't letting this go.

Neither was Ryan.

"From what I can piece together, he worked for him. He did col-lections for Colone's construction business. That's about all I could find. Not exactly a prominent figure."

"He could have been skimming," Patrick said. "It would certain-ly explain what got him killed. But even if it was a mob hit, why take the babies? Why not just leave them there?"

"Maybe because things went wrong," Claire answered softly. "Maybe the murder didn't turn out to be just a simple hit. Maybe it became more complicated than that. And maybe Colone capitalized on it by setting in motion a plan that served his needs."

"Is that a supposition or a sensory intuition?" Casey asked.

"More of the latter." Claire frowned. "Colone definitely factored into Lina's life. She's named after him." An intent pause. "She's his goddaughter. As for Gia and Dani…" Claire gave a frustrated shake of her head. "There's too much stimuli pounding at my brain. Now that we're getting closer to the truth, the three girls' energies keep converging in my head. I'm having trouble separating the threads."

"Don't force it," Casey said. "You always tell me that's the worst thing you can do."

"That's true." A hint of a smile curved Claire's lips. "Thanks for reminding me of what I should always remember but don't." Her smile faded. "I'm just so desperate to get to the heart of this. The sense of danger surrounding Dani and Gia is weaving in and out in an odd way. It's as if whoever's after them is waffling in his approach. He's panicking. That's a bad sign. It means he could get impulsive and do something rash."

"You said Dani and Gia." Patrick looked thoughtful. "I notice you didn't mention Lina. Is she in less danger than her sisters?"

A shrug. "I don't know. Maybe. Or maybe her energy is fusing with Gia's and Dani's. I can't be sure."

"Up until now, we've kept Lina in the dark. It's time that changed," Marc stated flatly. "We've got to talk to her—but not until after we confront Joseph. If we go to Lina first, she'll run straight to her parents and we'll lose the element of surprise." A frown. "Still, we can't confront Joseph Brando without being supported by iron-clad facts. He's a lawyer. He'll either clam up or spout some well-rehearsed bullshit at us."

Casey sighed. "You're right. Lina and her parents have to be spoken to. But we do need proof. How do you suggest we get it? Joseph Brando isn't about to offer up a DNA sample."

"We don't need him to," Marc replied. "We need to prove the girls are triplets. That will call Lina's birth certificate into question—along with the claim that she's an only child—and it will disprove the elaborate story Lina told Emma about her birth. All that will force Joseph's hand—to be tested or to tell the truth. We already have Gia's and Dani's DNA analysis. We just need Lina's."

"And you think she's just going to open wide and give us a cheek swab, no questions asked?" Ryan asked wryly.

"Obviously not. We'll have to figure out another way."

"I'll get her DNA sample," Emma said.

Everyone's head snapped around in surprise, and all eyes were on Emma.

"Stop looking so stunned," she responded to their startled expressions. "You keep forgetting how resourceful I am. Pickpockets have deft fingers. Plus, I've done my research. Ryan taught me that skill when we worked Brianna's case."

"Go on," Patrick said.

"As you know, there are other ways to get a DNA sample. One of those ways is through a strand of hair."

"Emma," Marc said patiently. "I'm impressed by your resourcefulness. But I don't think you realize what getting a hair sample means. You can't just pluck a stray hair off Lina's shirt. You—"

"Need the hair root," Emma supplied. "Yes, I know. And I'll get it."

"How?" Now it was Casey who sounded intrigued. "Don't you think she'll notice if you pluck an entire strand of hair out of her head? Trust me, it hurts like hell."

"Uh-huh." Emma grinned like the Cheshire cat. "And how would you know that?"

"Because I've done it myself. If I happen to spot a..." Casey's voice trailed off as realization dawned in her eyes. "You're going to notice an imaginary gray hair in Lina's head and do her the great service of getting rid of it."

Emma tapped her nose in a spot-on gesture. "One trip to the ladies' room—which is guaranteed since we're female—and I'll get the job done. I'll drop the hair right in a paper envelope, seal it, and give it to you to send out for lab analysis. I won't use a Ziploc, since those don't allow the proper airflow. Envelopes are recommended, so an envelope it is. I know a cheek swab is the best way to go, but this method has a high success rate if handled correctly. So, with a modicum of luck, we'll have the proof we need."

Marc's brows rose in a rare show of admiration. "Nice research and smart, creative thinking. You're right—we don't give you enough credit. We keep forgetting we have our own in-house Artful Dodger."

"Terrific plan, Emma," Casey praised. "Now the only problem will be getting the lab work done faster than ASAP without provid-

ing any specifics or raising any red flags. That's going to require pulling some strings and going to the right facility."

"I think I have the answer to that one," Marc replied.

Casey held up a palm. "Please don't suggest Hutch. I can't com-
promise him by asking for FBI resources again, not for something
like this."

Marc arched a brow. "I used to work with Hutch at the BAU, remember? I know the FBI's rules, and I only ask him to break them in
extreme circumstances—like the time when your life was on the line.
Hutch is a close friend—one I introduced to you if you recall. No, I
wasn't even thinking of him. The person I was thinking of is Aidan."

"Aidan." Casey was nodding even as she spoke. The choice was
logical. Marc's brother was responsible for troubleshooting the laby-
rinthine communications infrastructure at Heckman Flax, the larg-
est investment bank in the world. He was also former Marine Special
Ops, with specialized training in communication and intelligence.
Between the two roles, Aidan had a wealth of contacts worldwide
and more resources than Marc could count. If some of those resources seemed outside the box, Marc didn't ask and Aidan didn't
say. But he'd assisted FI on more than one of their cases, most recently orchestrating a life-threatening rescue.

"Will Aidan do it?" Casey asked, skipping over the word *can*,
since they all knew Aidan could do pretty much anything. "And is he
in the country?"

"Yes and yes." Marc's mind was already on the best way to get
Aidan alone long enough to elicit his help. "We're going to see him
in about an hour."

Casey blinked. "He's attending the Brando party?"

"Not happily, but he'll be there representing Heckman Flax.
They're big on the philosophy that a strong technology infrastructure is important for business, particularly *their* business. As a result,
they're big supporters of Joseph's campaign. One of their high-level

execs had to be roped in to be the face of the company. And my lucky brother fit the bill." Marc whipped out his cell. "Give me a second." He tapped the Aidan button and put the phone to his ear.

"Yeah," Aidan answered, seeing his brother's name flash on his screen.

"You sound bored," Marc said. "I guess you're already at the party."

"Good guess. Where are you guys?"

"On our way. Listen, I need you for five minutes as soon as we've said our hellos."

"No problem. I have a picture to give you from Abby, anyway. It's of you, Maddy, and her, and she made you about ten feet tall since she hero-worships you. So you'd better hang it on your fridge tonight and text us a photo of that or I'll be forced to beat the shit out of you."

Marc chuckled. "I'd do it without the threat. Anything for our little princess. So you'll be available?"

"I'll meet you at the bar."

"See you there." He punched off. "Done," he told the team.

"Great." Casey picked up her purse, then squatted down to snap on Hero's leash. "Time to get going. We've got a lot to accomplish in a few short hours. And the clock is ticking."

CHAPTER 29

The iron gates marking the entranceway to the manor were slightly ajar, and there were two security guards flanking either side of them, holding clipboards with lengthy "subject-to-verification" guest lists. Marc pulled the van up to one of the uniformed men, and the entire team proceeded to produce various forms of photo IDs until they'd satisfied the necessary requirements. At that point, the gates swung open, and Marc drove up the endless serpentine driveway until he reached the front of the house.

"Geez," Emma said in amazement. "This place is a palace. I can't believe Lina grew up here and she's not a total spoiled brat."

As she spoke, a uniformed guy in his early twenties came around and assisted them all out of the van. He took Marc's valet key and handed him a coin with the name "Brando" etched on it as a receipt. He flashed them a courteous smile, hopped into the driver's seat, and drove off to park the van.

"It's a good thing they have valet parking," Ryan noted, gazing around and wrapping Hero's leash around his hand. "Otherwise we'd be walking a mile. There are at least fifty cars parked on the outside blacktop, and a ton more around back where those garages are. The grounds are massive. Talk about rich."

Casey was already leading the way to the front door. She'd seen this kind of wealth before, with some of FI's clients. And it didn't impress her.

Claire glanced around but remained silent. She'd grown up in this kind of wealth, and she knew it didn't buy happiness. Her childhood in Grosse Point had been painful, with parents who didn't understand or encourage her gift and who were more than a little relieved when Claire had taken the hint and gone her separate way, relieving them of the burden of explaining their eccentric daughter who didn't fit the mold. It was a childhood that Claire didn't discuss much, not with anyone. But it had definitely left its emotional scars.

The front door was open, and the whole team congregated in the lobby, waiting to be either announced or frisked. Instead, a squealing Lina rushed over to them. She looked exquisite, in a red cap-sleeve bandage dress that must have cost a fortune.

"You're here!" She gave each of them a hug—even those of them she hadn't yet met—and then squatted down to stroke Hero's ears.

"You're such a handsome boy," she praised him. "My aunt and uncle have a golden retriever named Frisbee who's here today. There's a fenced-in portion of the yard for you guys to play in and lots of gourmet dog treats for you to eat. I even hired a doggie sitter to supervise you so we know you'll be safe." She raised her head and gazed quizzically at Casey. "I hope that's okay?"

"Are you kidding?" Casey laughed. "Hero will probably want to move in."

"I'll head out and play ball with them for a while, too," Ryan said. "The exercise will do me good. And besides," he said with a grin, "I'd love an excuse to unknot this tie—even for a half hour."

Lina's smile was infectious. "My dad feels the same way. He'll probably go with you if he can slip out for a bit."

Everybody chuckled.

An attractive woman in a stunning Valentino embroidered-tulle cocktail dress hurried over to greet them. "You must be the wonderful investigative team Lina keeps raving about." Emma recognized her immediately from the photo in Lina's apartment. "I'm Donna Brando," she said. "Welcome to our home."

"Thank you for having us, Mrs. Brando." Casey shook her hand. "I'm Casey Woods. Congratulations on your husband's victory."

"Hopefully, one of many to come." Introductions and handshakes all around, plus a gentle pat for Hero. "And please call me Donna. Mrs. Brando is my mother-in-law."

She gestured toward a wing of the house, one that was jammed with guests, all dressed like something out of a designer catalog, all talking and laughing in full party mode. Uniformed servers were weaving their way through the crowd with hot and cold hors d'oeuvres. And the champagne was flowing.

"Come in and meet Joseph," Donna urged. "He'll be delighted to put faces to the names Lina talks so much about."

"Yes, Dad will be thrilled to meet you." Lina was nodding vigorously. "While you're chatting with him, I'll get Hero settled with the techs and Frisbee. After that, I'll introduce you around. Once you've gotten through the formalities, it'll be party time. You can eat, drink, and hang out with me and my friends. Brianna's here. She can't wait to see you. Oh, and don't be fooled by the sous chefs you'll catch a glimpse of in the kitchen. Mom cooked almost everything herself. So it's all homemade and it's all amazing. If it weren't for Dad's insistence, Mom would be serving on her own, too."

"Okay, enough doting on me." Donna was already maneuvering the team through the house and, presumably, toward her husband. "Joseph is in the living room. This is his day, so let's get you all introduced."

Lina took Hero's leash from Ryan and guided him toward the rear of the house, while Casey and the team followed Donna Brando through the throng of guests.

"Shit, it's like seeing another Gia and Dani," Ryan muttered under his breath to Claire.

"The resemblance alone is almost proof enough," Patrick agreed quietly.

"Visually, yes. Scientifically and legally, no." Marc, ever-pragmatic, watched Lina walk Hero in the opposite direction. Still, his former BAU training kicked in. "But the stance, the facial expressions, even the walk—not to mention the identical features—I doubt we'll be surprised by the DNA results."

"I can't wait to get that hair sample," Emma murmured, tightly gripping her purse. "That'll clinch it."

With a warning glance at her team, Casey put an end to the discussion. Donna was slowing down, then easing into a packed living room. She gestured for them to follow.

"Joseph is over there with his campaign manager, Neil Donato, and a dozen friends and legal colleagues," she said, pointing to a tall, charismatic man who was laughing and making easy conversation with the folks gathered around him. Affable, approachable, and dynamic in his power suit and tie, Joseph Brando commanded attention with his presence alone. And the lawyer-looking man with the sharp dark eyes standing beside Joseph, subtly keeping all the attention on his candidate, had to be Neil Donato.

"The consummate politician and the guy destined to take him to the top," Ryan muttered again. "I see a presidential run in the future."

"Stop, Ryan," Casey told him. "Save your running commentary for the ride home. We're on now."

Ryan nodded and fell silent just as they reached the man of the hour.

"Joseph," Donna said, putting a hand on his sleeve. "I'm sorry to interrupt, but I'd like you to meet the Forensic Instincts team." She indicated each of them with a motion of her hand. "Casey Woods, Marc Devereaux, Ryan McKay, Patrick Lynch, Claire Hedgleigh, and Emma Stirling."

Joseph turned, a smile on his face as he extended his hand to shake theirs. "It's great to meet you all. Your reputation speaks for itself, and Lina thinks the world of you."

Again, handshakes all around.

"Congratulations, Assemblyman," Casey said. "It's a pleasure to meet you, too."

"Joseph," he corrected. "Please, no formalities." He half turned toward Neil. "This is my campaign manager, Neil Donato." A corner of Joseph's mouth lifted. "He's the brains behind the victory."

Neil, who looked about as serious as a heart attack, gave what Casey was sure was a rare chuckle. "I like that introduction, even if it is a gross exaggeration. Nice to meet you all." His brow furrowed as he looked at Marc. "There's another Devereaux here—an Aidan Devereaux from Heckman Flax. I see a strong resemblance between you. Any relation?"

"My older brother," Marc supplied, pleased to have been handed the opportunity he needed. Now he could go say a proverbial hi to his brother without it looking anything but natural.

He scanned the room, pretending not to spot Aidan gazing at him from the bar. "We're both so busy, we rarely see each other. Do you know where he's hiding? I'd like to say hello."

Neil scanned the room, then gestured toward the bar. "He's right there."

"Ah." Marc nodded his thanks. "Would you excuse me for a moment?"

"Of course." It was Joseph who replied. He turned to Casey. "I'd enjoy chatting with you and your team for a few minutes, hearing

more about the workings of Forensic Instincts. I'm fascinated by
your abilities. After that, I'll release you all to go have fun." He lowered his voice. "But first things first. I want to thank you for what you
did for Brianna. She's like a sister to Lina, and she's come back to life
since you caught that animal who was stalking her."

"We were relieved to get that case solved," Casey replied. She
kept it short and sweet since she didn't intend to get into it. All FI's
cases were strictly confidential, even after they were solved—unless the media got wind of them. Then they had murkier waters to
navigate.

And how ironic that Joseph would use the word "sister." A coincidence or a fishing expedition?

It was hard to tell. Joseph's game face was honed to perfection. If
he was aware of—or guilty of—the events that had been taking place,
he wasn't about to show his hand.

Fair enough. Crowd or not, Casey intended to get a handle on
Joseph Brando. And she had a strong feeling he planned to do the
same with them.

Okay, Mr. Congressman. Game on.

* * *

Across the room, Aidan watched his brother approach. The two
men really did look alike—tall, with straight black hair and the
powerful builds of Special Ops. But while Marc had inherited the
shape and color of his eyes from their Asian maternal side, Aidan's
eyes were navy blue and round. He had a high forehead and a pa-
trician nose. And as serious and unreadable as Marc looked, Aidan
looked even more so, making him chillingly intimidating to everyone he faced.

"It's about time you got here," Aidan greeted Marc, sliding a
glass of wine over to him. "It's not Joseph Phelps Insignia, but it's
a decent cab. Oh, and here." He slapped a folded piece of drawing

paper into Marc's hand. "It's yours. And Abby's got real talent, except for her perception of size."

Marc grinned, unfolding the paper. Definitely him, Maddy, and Abby. His adorable niece had drawn a little girl with a mop of dark hair and a party dress, a petite woman with light brown hair and a big smile, and a broad-shouldered man with a sort-of smile and dark eyes, who towered over both females.

"I'd say she got it spot-on," he told Aidan, refolding the paper and slipping it into his pocket. "I'll text you both tonight. My text will include high praise for Abby's skill, loving thanks from Maddy and me, and a big photo of us flanking the drawing on our fridge."

"Good." Aidan took a sip of his Cabernet Sauvignon, propping his elbow on the end of the bar. The party was loud enough so that no one could hear them. "So what do you need?"

"Lab results. Yesterday."

One dark brow rose in amusement. "That long. What are you looking for?"

"Triplet zygosity."

That captured Aidan's attention. "Now that's a new one."

"We like to keep you on your toes." Marc picked up his glass of wine and drank as he surveyed the room. This conversation had to look casual and brotherly. There were way too many eyes in the room.

"Do you have DNA samples for me?" Aidan asked.

"Ryan emailed you the results of a twin zygosity test while we were driving. So you have a baseline and we have proof that two of the girls are identical. I'll have an envelope for you with a DNA sample from the third girl before you leave the party. That'll give us the confirmation we need that we're dealing with identical triplets. And, Aidan, we can't wait days for the results. We need them rushed through."

"Yeah, I got that. But there's a certain amount of analysis time for, you know, things called accuracy and reliability."

"Fine. How soon?"

"I'll get my contacts to work overtime. I'm guessing a day." Aidan took another thoughtful sip of wine, studying his brother. "Just how do you plan on getting me that third DNA sample in the middle of a party?"

"Let me worry about that. Just know that when Emma slips an envelope into your jacket pocket, be careful with it. That's your sample."

Aidan looked amused. "Will I even feel it happen, given that it's Emma the pickpocket supplying it?"

"She'll make sure you know it's there. Just take care of it."

"Done. And, Marc, make that text happen before Abby's bedtime."

"You mean before *your* bedtime," Marc corrected. "Abby tucks you in when she gets her second wind. But not to worry. You'll get your text."

"And you'll get your answers."

* * *

After fifteen minutes of chichat, Casey had the distinct feeling that Joseph was keeping this conversation clean. He hadn't once alluded to knowing about any ongoing cases, nor had he made further reference to sisters and Lina in the same sentence. He seemed genuinely intrigued by FI's different team members' talents, but not in a digging-for-information way. In short, he either had no idea that Lina had identical siblings out there or he was biding his time before he so much as hinted at the situation without implicating himself. Also, it was difficult to keep talking one-on-one, since everyone at the party wanted a piece of Joseph, and Neil was constantly interrupting to bring someone new into the fold.

Still, Casey's instincts were rarely wrong. And they were reinforced at the conclusion of the conversation, when Joseph apologized for the ongoing distractions and concluded with:

"I guess this isn't the best time for a closed group discussion. Donna and I would love to have your team over for dinner one night. Then I could ask all my groupie questions." A broad smile that enveloped the room. "We'll call your office and set something up for next week if that works for you."

Oh, you'll be seeing us a lot sooner than that, Mr. Brando, once we have those test results, Casey thought, even as she answered, "Of course. We'd enjoy that very much."

Not so much after you hear what we have to say.

* * *

Emma was in her glory.

It was so cool hanging out with Lina, Brianna, and the five other friends Lina had invited. One of the guys was so hot that Emma had to remind herself of her mission so she didn't get off track and try to hook up with him. Still, once her job was done, she might find a way to give him her cell number.

In the meantime, she was glad that three of the five friends were male. That eliminated them as contenders for the bathroom. Men had bladders like camels, and Emma always lamented the fact that there were long lines outside every ladies' room in the world and none outside the men's rooms. Men's rooms should be reduced in number. Ladies' rooms should be doubled.

She'd already scouted out the party arena and spotted two bathrooms—a small powder room just inside the front entranceway and a large bathroom in a vestibule off the living room. That one was her target. A powder room attracted a single occupant who just wanted to get in and out. A spacious bathroom invited schmoozing and reapplying makeup, which meant going in pairs—something women were famous for.

Emma didn't want to waste time. That way, in case her first attempt to get Lina in there failed or the bathroom was occupied, she'd get a second chance. She prepped herself, staying close to Lina's side without being obvious. Timing was everything. She needed to accomplish this in a swift, whispered request.

As good luck would have it, two women with freshly applied makeup and perfectly brushed hair emerged from the vestibule bathroom. This was Emma's shot.

She turned quickly to Lina.

"I'm not used to being at such a high-powered party," she murmured in a small voice. "My nerves are so bad I think my makeup is melting and my hair is stuck to my neck. Would you mind coming with me to the ladies' room and helping me get it together?"

"Of course not." Lina, ever kind and generous, agreed at once. "Although you look great. But let's go." She turned to the others with a twinkle in her eye. "Excuse us for a minute. Emma and I are going to get even more beautiful."

"As if that's possible," Liam Banks, the hot MBA student Emma had her eye on, spoke up. He was responding to Lina's words, but his gaze was on Emma.

She smiled at him—a melting, let's-talk-later smile. She was so going to hook up with this guy. But for now, her attention had to be on the major task she'd volunteered for.

Lina led the way to the vestibule and into the bathroom, locking the door behind them.

"Will you redo my makeup?" Emma asked, pulling out her mascara and lip gloss and waiting for Lina's nod. "I'm all thumbs." She almost grinned at the irony of that comment. Her fingers were as deft as they came. "Sorry I'm being so immature," she added, going for a piece of the truth. "But I want to look good for your friends."

"Any friend in particular?" Lina was grinning as she took the makeup Emma handed her and began reapplying a touch of mascara to Emma's lashes. "Like Liam, for instance?"

"Is it that obvious?"

"On both your sides, yes." Lina stood back to admire her handiwork. "He's a great guy. And he's so into you. Go for it. I'll do my part to help it along."

"Thanks." Emma's reply was barely understandable, given that Lina was gliding the lip gloss applicator across her lips. But Lina got it. And she looked very pleased with the opportunity to make this happen.

"Perfect." Lina handed Emma her makeup and nodded her approval. "Now I'll do mine. Then we can brush our hair and get back to fixing you up with Liam."

Emma opened her purse, easing the unused envelope to the top and opening the flap as she removed her brush. She glanced over at Lina, who was staring intently into the mirror as she reapplied a dab of color to her cheeks.

"Uh-oh," Emma said, frowning as she came up behind Lina and inspected her hair.

"What is it?" Lina looked up.

"Nothing serious. Just a pain-in-the-ass gray hair."

"A gray hair?" Lina looked appalled. "Are you sure?" She pivoted around, gazing over her shoulder and squinting as she tried to spy the culprit.

"Yeah, I'm sure. It's way in the back. You won't be able to see it." Emma sighed and rolled her eyes. "It sucks when one of those shows up."

"You've had gray hair before?" Lina asked incredulously, still trying to get over the horror of it all. "You're practically a baby."

"I've had one or two, right in the front, and they stood out enough for me to see even though I'm blonde. Your hair is gorgeous and dark, so it sticks out." Emma moved in for the task at hand. "Let me get rid of it for you."

"Please." Lina looked ready for battle. "I'm mortified."

"If you don't want it to grow back, I'll have to pull it from the root. It'll hurt for a sec, but you won't have to deal with it again."

"I don't care how much it hurts. Please just get rid of it—all of it," Lina pleaded.

"Okay, just stand really still."

Lina didn't budge.

Carefully, Emma separated strands of hair as if she were focusing in on one in particular. That fact worked in her favor, because it gave her even more time to press right up against the scalp and grab hold of the base of the hair shaft. *Here goes*, she thought.

She pulled.

Lina gave a little squeak, but Emma almost shouted with triumph. The tiny bulb at the end of the hair shaft told her she'd accomplished her goal.

"All done," she announced, reaching for her purse while being careful not to touch the hair root. "I'll give you my little mirror. You can turn around and reassure yourself. It was barely visible before, but it's all gone now." Emma realized how irrational that sounded, but she also knew Lina would take the bait. She'd have to convince herself that she was gray-free.

Sure enough, Lina nodded. "Thank you."

The strand was sealed inside the envelope by the time Lina was turning to scrutinize herself. She held up Emma's mirror and used it to search the back of her head on the wide mirror spanning the bathroom wall.

"Death by drowning." Emma used the time to turn on one of the gilded sinks and wash an imaginary hair down the drain.

"It's gone." Lina sagged with relief. "I'm so grateful. I never would have known it was there, but I'm sure every female in that room would have noticed it. Thank you, Emma." She gave her a big hug. "Now I'm doubly determined to make you and Liam happen."

Emma grinned. "Okay, but I'll need something to calm my nerves. How about if I grab a glass of wine and meet you back at the table, fortified and ready for you to work your magic."

Lina grinned back. "I'll get started telling Liam how wonderful you are."

"Do you want anything?"

"Later. I'll be busy matchmaking."

Lina flipped the lock, they stepped out into the vestibule, and Emma gave herself a mental high-five. Phase one complete. On to phase two.

She walked back into the living room, scanned the area, and spotted Aidan chatting with some unknown but important-looking men. Deep in conversation as he was, Emma had the distinct feeling that Aidan was well aware of her presence. He was one scary-amazing guy, that Aidan. And she'd be forever in his debt—his and Marc's. They'd saved her life. Literally.

Pushing aside those terrifying memories, she weaved her way through the crowd until she reached Aidan's side. By that time she was palming the envelope. She slipped it into his pocket, and, with a light tap on his suit jacket to let him know he had what he needed, she gave him a quick smile and continued on her way. She stopped at the bar and ordered a glass of Pinot Grigio.

Diagonally across the room, Casey caught Emma's eye and gave her an imperceptible nod of congratulations. Emma smiled before taking her wine and heading off in the direction of Lina and her friends.

A job well done. Praise from her boss.

Emma had earned a date with Liam.

CHAPTER 30

It was seven forty-five the next night when Aidan called Marc's cell.

"I've got the answers you're looking for," he said. "I'll email them to you now."

Marc had been sitting with Casey at the conference room table, discussing the investigation and their mutual gut instinct that the key answer was just out of their reach. Now, Marc signaled to Casey that it was Aidan on the phone.

"I'm in the office," Marc told his brother. "Casey's with me. Send it to us both."

"Done."

"And thanks—I owe you one."

"I'll hold you to that."

Marc disconnected the call and waited. Casey perched at the edge of her seat, staring at her cell phone.

A few seconds later the email with the lab results popped up.

The DNA test was conclusive. Lina, Gia, and Dani were identical triplets.

Casey drew in a slow breath. "We have our proof. Now we have the Brandos and Lina to deal with, each in different and separate ways. The Brandos come first. Getting information out of them is crucial to the investigation. We owe that to our clients."

"Plus, whatever answers we get will give us more facts to present to Lina when we talk to her."

"You mean when we upend her entire world." A flash of sadness crossed Casey's face before she got back to the business at hand. "I'll run the meeting. But in this case, I want you to be my wingman. You're the best when it comes to intimidation."

"I aim to please." Marc glanced at his watch. "It's still early. We can call the assemblyman and see how soon he can see us."

"It'll be sooner rather than later—and it won't be Brando who'll make it happen." Casey rummaged around in her purse, extracting a business card. "This is Neil Donato's card. He practically shoved it at me when he saw how enthused Brando was during our conversation."

"He probably visualizes us as potential campaign donors."

"Big-time. He hung on to every word of our conversation. I thought he was going to ask for a check from us on the spot."

Marc's grin was wry. "Donato will probably bump some appointments to fit us in."

"Count on it." Casey picked up her cell and dialed the number on the card.

Two upbeat minutes later, Forensic Instincts had an appointment at the future congressman's home for ten a.m. Rush hour would be avoided, and magically, Joseph's other meetings didn't begin until eleven.

"Setup complete," Casey said after hanging up. "Ten o'clock at Joseph's home office. Oh, and I think I'm Neil Donato's new best friend."

"I'm sure you are." Marc tapped his coffee mug thoughtfully. "Brando has no idea what we're really there to talk about, so his guard will be down. We'll get an honest reaction."

Casey nodded, continuing to think things through. "We're only going to discuss the reality that Lina is a triplet. No sisters' names.

No cluing Joseph in on the dangers Lina's sisters are in or how we're investigating those dangers. And certainly no mention of the fact that we know who the three girls' real parents were and what happened to them."

"Very little talking, a whole lot of listening." Marc was well-trained in this science. "If Joseph is guilty, maybe our revelation will shake him up enough to blurt out something incriminating."

"Whether or not that happens, this is going to be an ugly confrontation. We can handle whatever Brando throws at us. But once we hit him with what we know, he'll want to talk to Lina, to tell her his version of the truth. We're going to have to find a way to get to Lina first."

"I already thought of that," Marc replied. "Joseph will want some time to discuss all this with his wife and to decide together how they're going to approach Lina and what to tell her. So we'll beat them to the punch. We'll call Lina before we leave for Todt Hill and ask her to meet us at the brownstone for a late lunch."

"A thank-you get-together for the great time we had on Sunday," Casey agreed. "Good idea, I like it. She'll get here right after we get back from seeing her parents, who, as you just said, will be figuring out what to say to her." A pause. "They might ask us not to talk to Lina until after they do. In which case, we'll lie. We're talking to Lina right away. She's a grown woman with two sisters she deserves to know about."

"Agreed. But remember, Dani and Gia have to be told first." Marc slowed Casey down, saying what had to be said. "The two of them are our clients. Lina is just our friend. I know that sounds hard, but it's true."

"You're right—it does sound hard." Casey struggled, realizing that what Marc was saying was accurate, and unable to combat her emotions enough to be objective. "You're the one who suggested getting Lina here ASAP. So how do you suggest we handle this?"

"Other members of the FI team need to go to Rye while you and I are in Todt Hill," Marc replied. "They need to fill Dani and Gia in, find out what they want Lina to be told, and ask if they want to meet their sister—which I'm sure they will."

"I'll send Claire and Emma," Casey said without hesitation. "They've got a great rapport with the girls. They'll do what has to be done, and we'll have our answers by the time Lina gets here. That'll lay out the course of our conversation."

"Once Lina is ready—and assuming all parties want to meet—Emma and Claire can drive Gia and Dani to the brownstone," Marc added.

"Once Lina is ready," Casey reiterated Marc's words. "She's going to need some time to process what we tell her. Even though it's going to be a shocker for Gia and Dani, it's going to completely upend Lina's life. The poor girl is completely in the dark. Not only is she going to find out she's a triplet, she's going to find out her parents have been lying to her all her life. And if it turns out that those lies were told for any reason other than because the Brandos wanted her to think she was their biological child, Lina is going to go to pieces. I don't blame her. I would, too."

Pausing, Casey picked up her cell and forwarded Aidan's email to the rest of the team. "Last I heard, everyone's in-house, working late tonight. I want them to see the lab results. That'll get them in the conference room fast so we can share our plan."

Sure enough, not three minutes later, the door flew open, and Ryan burst into the room, with Emma and Patrick close behind. Claire entered a few minutes later, wearing her yoga clothes and looking a little out of it.

"At last—a lucky break," Ryan said. "I've been digging into Brando all night—his campaign supporters, his law firm, his personal life—and so far, I've come up empty. Now we've got what we need to get the truth out of him."

"Assuming there's a criminal truth to tell," Patrick reminded him. "He could be innocent of everything except lying to his daughter. We have to tread carefully."

"Great. More diplomacy." Ryan was clearly disgusted.

"Patrick's right." Claire's dazed expression, accompanied by that faraway look in her eyes, said her words were based on more than just opinion. "Taking a confrontational approach with Joseph Brando is a bad idea. He's going to clam up quickly even if we soft-pedal it. We need to find out what he knows in a backdoor way."

"That's easy," Ryan responded, looking at Marc. "We'll get the information *after* you guys leave Brando's house."

"You want me to plant a bug?"

"Damn straight. I'll have one ready to go with you in the morning. And I'll rent myself a nice, unobtrusive gardening truck to park outside the grand manor—close enough to monitor whatever's said inside. Who knows what we'll find out?"

"It might not be what you think," Claire replied.

Casey regarded her soberly. "Judging from your comments, you think Joseph is innocent?"

"No. And yes." Claire rubbed her forehead. "I'm picking up mixed energy when it comes to Lina's father. He's involved in some way. But there's a dark corner of his life that he's both aware of and unaware of. I can't wrap my mind around it. I just know that this situation is complicated." She met Casey's gaze. "And Lina... she has to be brought up to speed—right away. That poor girl. She's so full of life and love, and this is going to shatter her."

"We want to fill her in tomorrow." Casey told Claire what she and Marc had discussed as a plan.

Claire nodded. "Good. Emma and I will go talk to Gia and Dani. They'll be stunned, but by this time, they're pretty much braced for anything. It's Lina I'm worried about. I wish I could be here when you talk to her."

"Me, too," Emma said.

"You'll be here when the three girls meet," Casey replied. "In some ways, that's more important. Emotions are going to run high. Emma, they'll need your friendship, and we'll all need Claire's insights."

"I wish I had something concrete to tell them from my end." Ryan made a sound of disgust and frustration. "Not only have I come up empty on the birth certificates but that Carp guy who's been Gabe's contact trashed his phone—probably as soon as he realized Gabe was with Dani and therefore vulnerable. So far Carp hasn't resurfaced with a new cell number. So I've got nothing."

"Oh, you've got something—and it's huge. But I don't want to share it with the girls," Casey said firmly. "No showing them the article about the Pontis' murders and the missing triplets. We can't drop that bomb on them right now. It would be total emotional overload."

"Yeah, I know. I wasn't even thinking about going there." Ryan began pacing around the conference room. "Actually I was trying to dig deeper into Angelo Colone, to see where he fits into the bigger picture. Because I just have this feeling that he does."

"Your feeling is right," Claire said abruptly. "He has a crucial role in all this."

"*Has*?" Ryan reiterated. "He's dead." A pause. "Although none of the threats to the girls occurred until after his death. Was he in on something with Brando—something Brando has to clean up now?"

Claire shut her eyes, visibly struggling to make sense out of what she was sensing. "All I know is that there's a part of Angelo Colone left behind. I don't know what that something is or if Joseph Brando is directly involved. It's tied to Lina… and maybe to Gia or Dani, as well. I just can't get a firm grip on this. Too many conflicting images in my mind. Somehow, in some way, Colone was there from the start. I just don't know how.""Yeah, well, neither do I." Ryan and uncertainty were not a good combo. "So while I'm monitoring things from the gardening truck, I'll be digging away on all things Angelo Colone, just as I'm digging away on Brando. So far, everything involving Brando's legal representation of Colone—his construction company, his estate—is on the up-and-up. Every damn thing I dig up about their relationship—both business and personal—shows Joseph to be clean as a whistle."

"Either that or it's been scrubbed to look that way," Casey said. "If there were a single hint that Brando has mob ties, he wouldn't be headed for Congress." She considered that for a moment. "Ryan, have you checked out Neil Donato? If anyone had the motive to make Joseph look squeaky clean, it would be him."

"I did an in-depth search on the guy from the start," Ryan supplied. "He looks like a Boy Scout. City College, Fordham Law School—all with honors. Passed the Bar on the first try. Applied for a job at Brando's law firm and was hired as an associate right away. He actually handles a good chunk of the Colone construction company legal work—probably an extra precaution to keep Brando's name from being too closely associated. But there's not the slightest hint of anything dirty going on. Donato appears to be an excellent lawyer, a well-liked, well-organized guy, and, given how put-together and PC he is, the perfect choice for a campaign manager. But not to worry. I never count anyone out. I've got eyes on everyone."

"I know you do." Casey gave a weary sigh. "Go take care of your bug. And let's all get ourselves mentally primed. It's going to be a long, emotional—and hopefully informative—day."

CHAPTER 31

Todt Hill
10:00 a.m.

Joseph Brando himself greeted Casey and Marc at the door. He was wearing a pin-striped, open-necked sports shirt and perfectly creased navy slacks—clearly ready for a day in the campaign trenches.

"Good morning." He gave them that warm, practiced smile of his. "I'm so glad you made the trip. Please, come on in." He stepped aside and waited while they did just that.

"Thank you for seeing us on such short notice," Casey said.

"Of course. I'm delighted that it happened sooner rather than later." He glanced behind them. "It's just the two of you?"

Casey nodded. "Given how busy we are, it's impossible to get our whole team in one place at one time. Your party was the exception."

"Then I'm honored." Joseph was already leading the way down a hall that was in the opposite direction of the living room. "We'll talk in my office. The Nespresso is on and ready, and there's a plate of Donna's addictive cinnamon buns on the coffee table. Unfortunately, she had a morning commitment and couldn't join us. So she made extra pastries to make up for it. We can enjoy and talk at the same time."

"That was thoughtful of her."

They followed him through the hall, turned a few corners, and crossed the threshold of a huge paneled office with rich mahogany furniture, an oriental carpet, twin love seats, and lots of family photos—most of them of Lina. Off to one side of the room was a credenza with the Nespresso machine and a wide variety of coffees and teas. To the other side, nestled between the plush love seats, was a carved mahogany coffee table set with a tray of incredible-smelling pastries, as well as the necessary china and silverware.

Casey wondered just how big a check Joseph was expecting from them.

"Please." He gestured toward one of the love seats. "Sit down and relax. What can I get you?"

There was no point in pretending this was a social call complete with a campaign contribution. Tact was important, but pretense was insulting.

"Actually, much as we appreciate it, what we'd really like to do is talk." For the first time, it was Marc who spoke up. He lowered himself to the sofa cushion, bent one leg at the knee, and crossed it over the other—keeping his tone and expression nondescript.

Nonetheless, Joseph seemed taken aback. His gaze flickered from Marc to Casey, who was perched at the edge of her seat, regarding Joseph with quiet intensity. He was an intuitive man. Clearly, he sensed something was up.

"All right." Joseph went and made himself a cup of espresso—clearly taking a few moments to try to figure out what was going on. He then crossed over and sat on the adjacent love seat. "I'm all ears," he said.

"We need your input on a discovery we just made," Casey began, intentionally presenting the matter as if they wanted to work with him, not against him. "I'm sorry we misled you about the purpose of this meeting. But we had to explain things in person."

"Explain what things?" Joseph set down his cup. "What is this about?"

"It's about Lina."

"Lina?" He stiffened. "Is she all right? I just spoke to her last night."

"She's fine," Casey assured him. Definitely a father's concern—one that wasn't put on. "She's just inadvertently involved in a case we're investigating."

"Involved... Is this about Brianna? I thought that case was closed."

"This isn't about Brianna." Marc took over, just as Casey knew he would. "This is about the fact that your daughter has two biological sisters, and that the three girls are identical triplets."

Joseph physically started. He looked as if he'd been punched in the gut.

More significantly, he looked totally, genuinely shocked.

"What did you just say?"

"I think you heard me," Marc replied.

"Is this some kind of sick joke?" Joseph still hadn't recovered from the initial blow. His posture was rigid, but his voice was trembling.

"We wouldn't joke about something like this, Mr. Brando." Casey purposely avoided calling him Joseph. That easy camaraderie no longer existed. "What Marc just told you is a fact."

"It's anything but." Joseph was regaining his composure—and getting angry in the process. "Lina is an only child."

"No, Assemblyman, she's not. We have DNA evidence to support that. So either your wife gave birth to monozygotic triplets or Lina is adopted and you chose not to tell her. Which is entirely your right," Casey added quickly. "Except that there are questionable circumstances surrounding the adoption. That's where we need your cooperation. We have to sort out the truth."

"I have no idea what you're talking about. Lina is our daughter. That's the only truth there is."

"Your natural daughter?" Casey asked quietly.

"Our daughter in every way." The politician in him provided the non-answer.

"Would you be willing to give us a DNA sample to prove that? If you're so sure we're wrong, that shouldn't be a problem."

"I'll do no such thing." Joseph rose. "And I have nothing further to say. This conversation is over."

Casey came to her feet and angled herself in a way that blocked Marc from view. That gave him the seconds he needed to plant the bug underneath the love seat.

"I notice you didn't ask to see the evidence," she said to Joseph. "Is that because you know what we're saying is true and you're protecting your relationship with Lina?"

Or protecting yourself from admitting to a crime? she thought silently.

"It means I won't address such outrageous claims. They have no merit. I'll show you out."

* * *

Two painfully silent minutes later, Casey and Marc found themselves on the front doorstep, the door slammed in their faces.

"So much for not antagonizing him," Marc muttered as they headed to the van. "Although I don't know how Claire could expect a different outcome. There's no way Brando was going to greet our announcement with grace. Any way you slice it, we just implied he's a liar and possibly a criminal."

"We handled it as diplomatically as we could," Casey said, sliding behind the wheel and putting on her sunglasses. "We gave him more than enough outs and more than enough chances to straighten this out amicably. He wasn't about to make that happen." She turned on the ignition. "On the flip side, the one thing I'm sure of is that he was blown away by our revelation. He had no idea that Gia and Dani exist. To my way of thinking, that exonerates him of orchestrating the violence against them."

"Okay, I'll buy that." Marc shut the passenger door and buckled up. "But he's sure as hell guilty of something. He shut down like a clam as soon as he got over the initial shock. And the DNA test was a no-go. He won't admit Lina's not their natural child, but he knows he can't prove that she is. That smacks of guilt in a situation already rife with illegalities."

"I know." Casey backed up, then shifted into drive and headed up the winding driveway. She flashed her headlights as she pulled away. A short distance down the road, Ryan flashed back. Ensconced in his gardener's truck, he was all plugged in and ready to go. They'd communicate by phone as soon as there was something to say.

"I hope Brando chooses to talk to his wife in the office and not another part of the house," Casey said to Marc, voicing yet another concern that had kept her up last night.

"The odds are in our favor."

A quick sidelong glance. "How can you be so sure?"

"Human nature. Brando is in shock. He'll retreat straight to his sanctuary. Donna isn't home. He's probably calling her right now, telling her to get back ASAP and to come straight to his office. He'll pace around the room, probably chuck his coffee and pour himself a drink. His office is private, away from the servants and the flow of traffic. The only other room that has that advantage is the bedroom. And he won't take the time to drag Donna upstairs. No, they'll have their talk right where I planted Ryan's bug."

Casey digested that with a nod. Marc still thought like an FBI agent with the BAU. Given that she was a behaviorist, she had to respect that. His reasoning here was solid.

"Then we'll have our answer soon enough," she said. "Ryan will call us as soon as he hears their voices. Now it's time to check in with Claire and Emma."

Claire picked up on the first ring.

"Are you finished?" she asked quietly.

"Heading back to the office," Casey replied.

"Then I'll call you back. We need a few more minutes."

"Done." Casey disconnected the call and glanced over at Marc. "That was Claire's intense voice. Gia and Dani have been slammed with one shocker after another. Given their depleted emotional states, I guess this hit them harder than even Claire expected."

"Not really a surprise," Marc replied.

"I'm hoping that once the news settles in and they realize they have another sister, the joy will trump the shock." Casey sighed. "But we'll have to wait and see."

CHAPTER 32

Gia and Dani were sitting on Gia's sofa, still wearing the exact same expressions as they had a half hour ago, when Claire and Emma broke the news to them about Lina. They'd finally started blurting out questions, most of which Claire and Emma had to carefully field.

"What else can we say to make this easier?" Claire asked gently.

"You can tell us why this is happening and who's masterminding it." Gia ran both hands through her hair. "I'm sorry. I didn't mean to snap. I just… Another sister. Triplets. We've all been kept apart for twenty-seven years. Why? *Why?* I can't seem to process this."

"Nor can I," Dani said, her eyes glittering with tears and her voice trembling with emotion. "And not to sound rude, you're being very stingy with your explanations. Is there something you don't want us to know?"

This was the hard part—the part that both Emma and Claire had dreaded. No matter how many scenarios they'd reviewed before coming here, there was no way the girls wouldn't feel they were being kept in the dark.

Because in so many ways they were.

As planned, Claire took the lead on this, hoping that her calm and gentle demeanor would take the stress level down a notch and diffuse the girls' sense of unease.

"We're not intentionally hiding anything from you," she reassured them. "There are just so many open threads to this investigation, and much of what we're looking into is still guesswork. Until we have concrete answers, please, let us do our jobs."

Gia didn't look convinced. "Clearly, you *are* hiding things from us. You just told us we have a third sister—Lina—who lives in New York City and who is as much in the dark about us as we are about her. You haven't told us how or when you even found out she exists, much less how you got her DNA sample without telling her why. You haven't told us her last name or anything about her parents. You haven't told us if her life has been threatened." A frustrated pause. "Actually, Dani is right. You haven't told us much of anything."

"That's why we're here—to answer all your questions," Claire replied. "But initially, we were just more worried about your ability to handle this. You've been through hell already."

"Thank you. But it's up to Dani and me to cope. Please tell us whatever you can."

Emma took over with the initial facts. "We met Lina purely by chance during one of our other investigations," she said. "Obviously, we saw the physical resemblance the minute we met the two of you. But we had no proof and no basis to ask for it. Plus, we didn't want to alert Lina to anything. You're our clients. You had to be told first—once we had something real to tell. We had to play this carefully."

"The DNA confirmation just came in last night," Claire added. "That's why we're here first thing this morning. We not only wanted to tell you about Lina but we wanted to ask if you're okay with us filling her in, as well. And most important of all, we want to know if you want to meet her. That decision is yours."

Gia and Dani both blinked, glancing at each other with the same of-course expression.

"Definitely, yes," Dani said, speaking for them both. "We want to meet our sister right away."

Claire picked up her phone. "I'll call Casey and tell her to speak to Lina immediately. As soon as she gives us the okay…"

"I don't want to wait until then." Gia jumped to her feet. "It'll take Mr. Nickels an hour to get us into the city. If we leave now, we can go in and meet our sister as soon as she's ready. I don't care if we have to circle the block for an hour, waiting for her to process what we just did. I can't just sit here and wait, doing nothing."

"I agree one hundred percent." Dani also stood. "Please tell Casey we're on our way." A pointed pause. "And you can answer the rest of our questions during the ride down."

A half block from the Brando manor
Todt Hill
10:40 a.m.

Ryan was clicking away on his laptop when the muffled sounds of a second person entering Joseph's office came through his headphones. He'd been waiting for this ever since Joseph had returned to his office, slammed the door, and called his wife, practically ordering her home.

Immediately, Ryan stopped what he was doing to listen.

"Joseph, what is it?" Donna asked, clearly alarmed by the urgency of her husband's call.

"Close the door and sit down," Joseph replied. "We have a huge problem."

The sounds that followed indicated that Donna was doing just that.

"You're scaring me," she said. "What problem? What happened?"

"Casey Woods and Marc Devereaux were here this morning. And it wasn't to support my campaign." In a tense, shaken tone, Joseph relayed the entire conversation to his wife.

"What do you mean triplets?" Donna had started weeping halfway through Joseph's revelation. "Lina is an only child. She's our child. Why are they doing this?"

"I don't know. Some investigation they're working on. Does it matter? Clearly, there *are* triplets, and Lina is one of them. We can't pretend that away, not when there's DNA evidence involved."

"Did you see that evidence?"

"They wouldn't have shown it to me. And how could I have demanded to see it? It would be as bad as an admission of guilt."

"If there were triplets, we would have been told." Donna was in a total state of denial.

"Would we?"

"Of course. And we'd know who and where the other two children were."

"Stop it, Donna. You know better. We were never supposed to know about this. Please." Joseph's voice gentled. "I need you to face this with me. We have decisions to make, and we have to make them fast. There's too much at stake to deny the facts."

"Oh, God." Donna broke. She was sobbing so hard it was difficult to understand her words. "Lina. She doesn't know anything about the real circumstances of her birth. How are we going to tell her? This is going to destroy her and our relationship with her."

Joseph made a pained sound. "We can't think about that yet—not until we get at the full truth. Remember, there are criminal actions involved here. We both suspected that from the start."

"I didn't want to know then, and I don't want to know now."

"We don't have that choice anymore. We must find out what we're dealing with."

"How do you suggest we do that? Angelo is gone. We have no other ties to the truth."

"The only person who might know anything is Jimmy. As a kid, he was like a shadow, following Angelo around. And he worshipped the ground his big brother walked on. Maybe, just maybe, Angelo said something to him."

"Do you think so?" Donna had moved on to grasping at anything to make this go away.

"I don't know. Angelo wasn't the type to confide in anyone. I was his closest friend and he said nothing to me about triplets. Maybe because I was involved, maybe for some other reason."

A loud squeak from the couch told Ryan that Joseph was standing up.

"We can talk this to death," Joseph said. "But there's Lina to consider. And Forensic Instincts is moving forward on whatever they're investigating, which could reveal too much. I've got to get whatever answers I can, as fast as I can." A nanosecond of a pause. "I'm calling Jimmy. I want a meeting. Now."

Ryan leaned forward, listening intently. He would only get one end of the conversation. But that was enough for his needs.

Even as he waited, he was typing rapidly into his laptop, seeing what he could dig up on Jimmy Colone, and wondering why he hadn't shown up in any of Ryan's previous searches. Probably because Ryan had been digging into Angelo Colone's mob connections, not his separate personal life. All he'd found on the personal front was that Angelo was a widower of many years, he'd never remarried, and he'd never had kids. So while his public persona was dominant, his private life was seemingly not noteworthy.

Seemingly. Because evidently he had a younger brother who was way under the radar.

Before Ryan could dig up anything of substance, Joseph's voice resumed.

"It's me," he said. "You and I need to talk. Where are you? Fine. Meet me at Angelo's mausoleum in an hour. I'm leaving now." Another pause, during which Joseph had to be disconnecting the call.

"Do you want me to go with you?" Donna asked.

"No. Jimmy will be more apt to open up to me if we're alone." A quick peck on the cheek. "Let me get moving. You sit tight and I'll call you as soon as I'm done."

"Okay." Donna sounded like she was still a mess. "But please, Joseph. Make this go away. For Lina's sake."

It was a ridiculous request and they both knew it.

"I will," Joseph promised anyway.

* * *

Ryan called Casey, simultaneously searching the web to find the location of Angelo's burial site.

"You heard something?" Casey answered from the van, putting Ryan on speakerphone so that Marc could listen.

"Oh, yeah." Ryan told them what had transpired. "Ah," he said aloud. "I've got it."

"Got what?" Marc asked.

"The information on Angelo Colone's mausoleum." He filled them in as quickly as possible. "Where's Patrick?"

"At the office," Casey replied. "He's been on the phone all morning, trying to locate any of his former law enforcement contacts who might remember something about Anthony and Carla Pontis' murders. No luck yet."

"Okay. He can keep making his calls while he drives. I need his eyes and ears at Brando's meeting."

"I agree. Go ahead. Call and give him the cemetery address."

"I'll keep you posted." Ryan ended the call, pressing Patrick's cell number even as he continued typing Jimmy Colone's name into his laptop.

"What do you need, Ryan?" Patrick answered, his tone saying he already knew it would be something crucial.

"I need you to get to Angelo Colone's mausoleum." Ryan rattled off the address. "Evidently, Colone has a younger brother, Jimmy. Joseph Brando is meeting him there in less than an hour to talk about the two other triplets he knows nothing about. I need ears on that conversation."

"I'm on it." Patrick was already on the move. "I'll check in when I have something."

Once again, Ryan disconnected his call and went back to his research. Getting info on the mob was tricky. Backdoor channels were necessary.

Ryan bypassed the obstacles quickly and efficiently.

Not much on Jimmy Colone. He was seven years younger than Angelo, and as Ryan's info revealed, he'd been a schoolyard fighter and a "potential" drug user, all, of course, with no formal charges and no proof.

Ryan skimmed that data and dug deeper.

Abruptly, he sat up straight. Jimmy had disappeared off the grid, off the map, and was totally invisible since he was a kid of eighteen. Which was exactly twenty-seven years ago.

He'd vanished a month after Anthony and Carla Ponti were murdered.

CHAPTER 33

Offices of Forensic Instincts
10:50 a.m.

The twenty-five-minute drive from Todt Hill to Tribeca gave Casey and Marc enough time to accept delivery for the deli platters Casey had ordered for their light lunch and arrange everything in FI's modern kitchenette.

A short time later, the doorbell rang.

Hero picked up his head and woofed.

"I've got it, boy," Casey said, heading straight for the front door. She'd already disengaged the Hirsch pad by the time Yoda announced: "Angelina Brando has arrived."

"Thanks, Yoda." Casey opened the door, her chest constricting when she saw the happy, beaming young woman standing there.

"Hi," Lina said, giving Casey a warm hug. "This was such a great idea. Lunch with the team. I can't wait."

"We're so glad you're here. Unfortunately, so are only Marc, Hero, and I. Everyone else will be arriving shortly. Why don't the few of us sit in the small conference room and talk? The food's all set up and ready to eat when the whole crew shows up." *If you have any appetite at all once we've talked.*

"Sure." As always, Lina was open and trusting. It would never occur to her that this would be anything but a social gathering.

Casey felt the heavy weight of responsibility settle on her shoulders. It was up to her to keep this wonderful young woman in one emotional piece.

"Hey, Lina." Marc was already in the conference room, and he rose, giving Lina one of his rare smiles. He stuck out his hand, but in usual Lina fashion, she bypassed it and gave him the same big hug she'd given Casey.

"Hiya, Marc. Thanks for inviting me."

"It's always good to see you." Marc walked over to the credenza. "What's your pleasure?"

Lina grinned. "It's too early for wine, or I'd have some to celebrate everything from my dad's victory to this get-together. But I'll settle for a Diet Coke."

Marc fished one out of the fridge, poured it in a glass, and added some ice. He then brought over the glass and handed it to Lina.

"There you go." He glanced at Casey. "Bottled water?"

"Please."

Marc got two, wishing it were later in the day and he could offer Lina that wine she'd mentioned. She'd sure as hell need it in a few minutes.

Lina settled herself on one of the settees, looking surprised when Casey sat down beside her. Given the fact that all the tub chairs were unoccupied, as was the second settee, it seemed odd that Casey would choose to station herself close beside Lina.

Casey didn't wait for her to ask about the mother-hen action.

"We need to talk to you about something important," she said. "It's pretty complicated and it's pretty overwhelming. It's going to be tough to absorb. But I'm counting on you to be strong. And you can count on us to be right here by your side."

Lina's eyes widened. "Is everyone okay? No one's sick, are they?"

"Nothing like that." Casey sensed Marc lowering himself into the tub chair closest to her, a tangible statement of his support for Casey and for Lina. Bless Marc for always being her right hand.

"I think it best that we not be interrupted," Casey continued, gesturing at Lina's purse.

"Okay." Lina pulled out her cell phone and turned it off. Her glow had dimmed and she was starting to look a little scared.

"I'm honestly not sure where to start. So I'll just start with the most important part, the part that's absolute, indisputable fact." Casey drew a deep, preparatory breath. She'd never had the chance to buffer this life-altering news with Gia and Dani, who'd already made peace with it when they came to Forensic Instincts. This time she did. She wasn't going to blow it.

"This revelation is going to be a shocker, but in some ways, it's really a wonderful one." Casey took Lina's hand between hers. "You're not an only child, Lina. You have two sisters."

"I have... *what*?" Lina's glass crashed to the floor, sending water and shards of glass everywhere.

"Two sisters. You're identical triplets."

"I don't know what you're talking about." Lina looked as confused as she did thrown. "I'm an only child. I don't have any siblings, much less identical sisters. I have no idea where you got your information. But it's wrong."

"It's not wrong," Casey told her gently. "It's right. You've been misled."

"By whom, my parents?" Lina shook her head adamantly. "They'd never do that to me." She snatched her hand away from Casey's and fumbled for her purse. It was clear she was about to bolt. "I don't know why you're doing this..."

"We're telling you the truth, Lina," Marc inserted in that calm, quiet voice that both soothed and made people believe. "We know this is hurting you, and we're very upset about that. We're on your side, whether or not you believe it. But what Casey just told you is hard-core fact. You have our word."

Lina released her death grip on her purse and just stared at Marc. "I don't understand," she whispered. "This is impossible. I'm twenty-seven years old. How can I have sisters I never knew about? How can I be a triplet? My parents only had…" Her voice trailed off. "You're saying that's all a lie?"

"We don't know where the lies begin and how comprehensive they are," Casey replied. "Not yet. What we do know is that you and your sisters have been separated since infancy. None of you knew about the others."

Tears glistened on Lina's lashes, although doubt still clouded her expression. Her face was the color of snow. "How did you find this out?"

"Through DNA evidence. We'll show the lab results to you after we've talked."

"I want to see them now."

"Okay." Casey signaled to Marc, who reached over to the end table and picked up a thin manila folder. Opening it, he pulled out the page they'd printed before Lina arrived and handed it to her.

Lina stared at it, reading and rereading the contents. "This is just a bunch of medical terms and percentages. There are no names. How do I know I'm one of these"—she squinted at the words—"monozygotic triplets?"

"Because we submitted your DNA sample to the lab to compare to the results your two sisters just got. Again, you have our word. You're one of the triplets."

"My DNA sample?" Lina lowered the page to her lap. "I didn't give you a cheek swab. You don't have my DNA."

"We didn't ask you for a cheek swab because we didn't want to upset you unnecessarily. We wanted to be one hundred percent certain of the truth before we approached you with it." Casey was feeling sicker by the minute. "Cheeks swabs are only one way to obtain DNA. A hair follicle can also be used."

Lina gasped. "Emma," she managed. "When she pulled that gray hair out of my head… it was all part of your agenda?"

"It wasn't an agenda. It was a search for the truth."

"Why? *Why*?" Lina started to cry. "I was perfectly happy with my life. Why would you do this to me? You're supposed to be my friends."

"We *are* your friends." Time to peel back another layer. "This all started with an investigation initiated by your two sisters. Whoever's trying to keep you three apart is threatening them. Their lives could be in danger. And if that's the case, yours could be, too."

Lina's eyes widened through her tears. "Danger? What kind of danger? From whom?"

"That's what we're trying to find out."

"Oh, God." More tears. Then a question. "They came to you together? I thought you said none of us knew about the others."

"You didn't. The two of them just learned about each other a few weeks ago, and it was by pure chance."

"Do they know about me?"

"As of an hour ago, yes. Claire and Emma told them. They're as stunned as you are. But they really want to meet you—if you're up for it."

"They're local?"

"One of them lives near the city, yes. The other flew in so she could be here." Casey continued to keep the details impersonal, offering Lina only as much as she could, and wanted to, handle.

Sure enough, Lina's mind shifted to the ugly part of this truth, and she stiffened. "Did my parents have triplets? Or are they not even my parents? Is everything a lie? Did the other two… Did my sisters' parents know?"

"Neither set of parents knew that triplets were involved. They adopted their daughters in good faith and raised them with the knowledge that they were adopted. They were as stunned as their daughters were to find out the rest."

The tears were now flowing down Lina's cheeks. "My parents told me stories about my birth. They said I was theirs. And that I was their one and only." She lowered her head and covered her face with her hands. "Either way, they're lying to me. Either they had two other babies that they farmed out or I was also adopted and they made the rest up. Oh, God."

This time, Casey just laid a hand on Lina's arm. "We spoke to your father this morning. In fact, we just came from Todt Hill."

Lina's head came up. "What did he say?"

"Not much." Casey refused to be less than honest. "He shut us down, refused to provide a DNA sample, and threw us out."

As Casey spoke, Lina searched her face. "You think he was lying."

"Not completely. I think he was stunned by the news that you were a triplet. But I think he knows a lot more about the circumstances of twenty-seven years ago than he's willing to say."

"So he isn't my natural father." Lina stated the fact in a wooden tone. "At the same time, he also isn't involved in trying to hurt my... sisters. That's what you're saying."

Casey gave an uneasy nod. "That's my gut instinct, yes. But even if I'm right—"

"That doesn't mean he wasn't involved in something suspicious surrounding my birth."

"Exactly."

For a long moment, Lina said nothing, just gazed down at her lap, grappling with an overwhelming and incomprehensible reality. Then she raised her head.

"I want to meet my sisters."

Green Hills Cemetery
Brooklyn, New York
11:40 a.m.

Joseph was already seated on the bench at Angelo's mausoleum when he heard Jimmy's footsteps. He glanced up, seeing his own grim expression mirrored on Jimmy's. Clearly, Angelo's brother realized something serious was up.

"Sit down," Joseph said.

Jimmy complied. "What is this about?"

Rather than answering the question, Joseph replied, "Let me remind you that Angelo asked me to look out for you all these years. I gave him my solemn promise that I would. And I've kept that promise. I've provided you with everything Angelo requested. In addition, since his death, it's been on my shoulders and my shoulders alone to keep you safe. I've done that, as well."

Jimmy shifted in his seat. "And you know how grateful I am."

"I don't want your gratitude. I want the truth."

"What truth is it you're looking for?"

"The truth about Lina." Joseph angled his head to face Jimmy. "I've just had a bomb dropped on me. I need to know if it's for real. Angelo's dead. Which means you're the only one I can turn to for answers. Whatever you know, I need to know, too."

"All right." Jimmy was now visibly unnerved.

That reaction wasn't lost on Joseph.

"Two investigators from Forensic Instincts just visited my home," he stated flatly. "According to them, they have evidence that Lina has two identical sisters. Needless to say, I was stunned since this is the first I'm hearing about it. You were still around when Lina was born. And you were glued to Angelo's side, so I doubt something went down without you knowing about it. Tell me what that something was. Is what they're saying true? Is Lina one of three?"

A prolonged silence.

"Answer me," Joseph commanded.

"Yes," was the reluctant response.

"Dear God." Joseph wiped a palm over his face, his hand shaking as he did. "Why wasn't I told?"

More silence.

"I'm not going to ask again. This is my daughter we're talking about."

"Angelo was your best friend," Jimmy replied, desperately trying to diffuse the situation. "You knew him. So you had to know that strings were pulled to make this adoption happen—and that some of those strings were illegal."

"Stop sidestepping my question. Of course I realized that Angelo took illegal actions to make Lina ours—actions that he never divulged to me because, as always, he didn't want to make me complicit. Plus, in this case, I was emotionally involved. So, yes, he kept me in the dark. But triplets? That's a whole different level of deception. Specifics—*now*."

Jimmy blew out a slow breath. "I don't know a whole lot. I know that Angelo wanted to make things as easy for you as possible. No complications, no worries, no guilt—not when he knew he could make you and Donna so happy."

"Go on."

"Someone brought infant triplets to Angelo. I don't know who or why. All he told me was that he knew how much you and Donna wanted a baby, so he was going to take care of things so that you got one of the babies and the other two were adopted out."

Joseph's eyes narrowed. "You're right. Angelo knew that Donna and I were desperate for a child. We would have been thrilled to take all three babies. So why split them up? If Angelo didn't want them to be a package deal, it means there's a lot more to this story—like the whos and the whys you're not providing."

"I'm not providing them because I never knew them." Jimmy was staring off into space. "You know how Angelo was. He kept things to himself. He always had his reasons and I never questioned them. So, yeah, I'm sure there was a reason he split up the kids and never told you the truth. But I have no idea what it was. You asked me if Lina was a triplet. The answer is yes. The rest died with Angelo."

Joseph dropped his head into his hands. "God help me. What am I going to do? How can I possibly explain this to Lina?"

"Why does she have to know?"

Joseph's head came up, his expression both pained and furious. "Because if Donna and I don't tell her, Forensic Instincts will. This has something to do with an investigation they're conducting. I have no clue what. What I do know is that they're thorough. They'll interview anyone even remotely connected to their case. Not to mention that Lina has become friendly with them. There's no way they'd keep this from her." Joseph came to his feet. "I've got to go." He turned. "If you think of anything else—and I mean *anything* else—you'd better come to me with it, and fast."

Jimmy stared after Joseph's retreating figure, his heart thudding in his chest.

Then, he said a silent prayer to Angelo, stood up, and left before he could be spotted.

Brooklyn Bridge
11:50 a.m.

Patrick leaned on his horn again, his teeth clenched in frustration. Bumper-to-bumper traffic. Covering the full span of the bridge. And thanks to the fender bender that had caused the tie-up, there were few signs of a reprieve.

For the third time, he punched up Ryan's number.

"I'm not going to make it," he said as soon as Ryan answered the phone. "The tow truck just showed up. It's going to take time to clear up this mess and get traffic moving again."

"Shit." Ryan stopped working. "How far away are you?"

"Five minutes, once things open up."

"Then stick it out. Brando and Jimmy Colone have a lot to discuss. If you get lucky, they might still be there."

"Doubtful. But I'll let you know."

Offices of Forensic Instincts
11:55 a.m.

Claire punched the entry code into the Hirsch pad, and Emma opened the door, holding it ajar so that Gia and Dani could follow them in. Both girls were eager and unnerved. And the delayed go-ahead call that Claire had received from Casey—resulting in John Nickels having to circle the block five times—had only escalated their already heightened emotions.

"Was she waffling about whether or not she wants to meet us?" Dani asked, glancing around as if, by doing so, she could spot Lina.

"Quite the contrary," Claire replied, determined to convey Casey's message that Lina was adamant about meeting her sisters. "She's anticipating this meeting as much as you are. It just took a while for her to digest everything that was thrown at her." A pause. "I didn't mention it on the ride in, but I think if you know this you'll better understand. Lina had no idea she was adopted. She was raised to believe the Brandos were her natural parents. So she has even more to take in than you did."

"Wow." Gia's brows rose as she absorbed this new and vital piece of information. "That's more than I could have withstood. At least Dani's and my parents were honest with us from the start. The poor girl."

"That definitely would have broken me," Dani agreed. "Although I guess I can comprehend the Brandos' logic. They probably felt that keeping Lina in the dark would make her feel more theirs or more loved. Instead, it's backfiring. It's causing her inexplicable pain." Dani gave an empathetic sigh. "You're right, Claire. This is worse than anything Gia and I went through."

Claire gave a sad nod, simultaneously gesturing toward the small meeting room across the hall from Emma's desk.

"You both have a seat and let Emma and me pave the way," she said. "I want Lina to know you're here and that this meeting is about to happen. Then, I'll come and get you."

* * *

Lina was seated on the settee, her back ramrod straight, with a glass of wine sitting, untouched, on the side table next to her, when Claire and Emma walked in. Her head shot up, her body went rigid, and she stared past them, searching the empty doorway.

"Where are they?" she asked.

"In the waiting room," Claire replied. "We wanted to check on you first—to make sure you were okay and to let you know that all of us have arrived." Claire placed a gentle emphasis on the words *all of us.*

"I'm hanging in there—thanks." Lina's dazed and haunted look contradicted her claim. "I really want to meet my sisters."

Claire exchanged glances with Casey, and Casey gave an affirming nod. Lina might be hanging on by a thread, but she was as ready as she'd ever be.

"And they really want to meet you," Emma assured her, having intercepted the look between her teammates.

With that, Claire turned and retraced her steps. "I'll show them in."

"Thank you." Lina continued to stare at the empty doorway after Claire had exited. She took a quick sip of wine to fortify herself and then set down her glass, interlacing her fingers tightly in her lap.

"It's going to be okay, Lina," Emma told her. "Better than okay. I promise."

Lina gave her a thin smile. "Thank you—all of you—for your moral support."

Approaching footsteps interrupted them, echoing through the hall, and then Claire reappeared in the doorway.

This time she wasn't alone.

CHAPTER 34

Lina gasped, her hand flying to her mouth as she gazed, unblinking, at the two mirror images of herself. Prepped as she'd been, there was no real preparation for this.

Dani and Gia were nearly as shaken as she. Tears filled their eyes as they got their first glimpse of their sister.

"Oh my God," Lina breathed, rising to her feet. "You're… We're… really identical. I… Oh my God."

Gia crossed over to her first. "Hi, Lina, I'm Gia," she managed, her eyes bright with unshed tears as she studied every detail of her sister's face. "I can't believe this," she added in a choked whisper. "It's like déjà vu all over again."

Lina's lips were quivering, as she visibly struggled for—and failed to attain—control. Tears began streaming down her cheeks, and wordlessly, she gave Gia a tight hug. "I can't believe this is real," she wept. "But it is. You're my sister." She gazed past Gia, her stare locking with Dani's. "And so are you."

Wordlessly, Dani nodded, coming over to join the two of them, also weeping as she joined in the hug.

For a long moment, the three girls just stood there, crying and alternately hugging each other—finding each other after twenty-seven years.

The FI team remained respectfully silent, although tears were gliding down everyone's cheeks, and Marc's eyes were suspiciously damp. Claire had unobtrusively slipped into a tub chair, recognizing that this moment belonged to Gia, Dani, and Lina.

Joy pervaded the room, and the ugliness of the past weeks was held at bay.

But the danger hovered close by, threatening to eclipse that joy.

Green Hills Cemetery
Brooklyn, New York
12:20 p.m.

"I'm finally here," Patrick announced into his cell phone. "They're gone."

"Shit. Shit. Shit." Ryan slammed his fist against the truck's wall. "Is there anyone around to question? Someone who might have seen them?"

"Not a soul. I combed the grounds. I didn't see a single visitor. And the mausoleums are placed so far apart that I doubt anyone would have noticed other visitors anyway." Patrick blew out a disgusted breath. "We'll have to find Jimmy Colone another way. This is a dead end."

"Oh, we'll find him." Ryan was furiously typing again. "I'm working every lead I can find. He's the key to all this. And he's not getting away."

Todt Hill
12:25 p.m.

Joseph pulled into the driveway and jumped out of the car, simultaneously trying Lina's cell phone for the umpteenth time.

And like all the previous times, it went straight to voice mail.

"Dammit," he muttered, striding into the house and heading straight upstairs to the master bedroom, where he knew he'd find Donna.

She was sitting on the edge of their bed, holding a photo of Lina, and sobbing aloud as her fingers traced the lines of their daughter's face. Hearing Joseph enter the room, she looked up, a trace of hope glittering in her eyes. Seeing the anguish written all over her husband's face, her trace of hope vanished.

"What did he say?" she asked in a quavering voice.

"Nothing good." Joseph relayed the conversation to his wife, desperately trying to soften his words when he had no strength to do so.

By the time he fell silent, Donna had gone deadly still. "So it's true," she whispered. "Lina is a triplet. And with Angelo gone, we have no way of knowing how or why this happened." She swallowed her tears, seeking and finding a mother's strength. "We have to tell Lina."

Joseph dragged a hand through his hair. "I've been trying to call her since I left the cemetery. All I get is voice mail. I'm trying not to think the worst, but..."

"She knows, Joseph." Donna spoke with absolute certainty. "God help us, but she knows."

"You can't be sure of that." Joseph was grasping at straws and he knew it. "She could be in a class or she could be with a guy or she could be—"

"She could be, but she's not." Donna reached for her purse. "We've got to find her, to talk to her. It's the only chance we have of preserving our family—if there's any chance at all."

A hard nod. "I'll drive."

12:40 p.m.
Brandos' block
Todt Hill

Ryan had been sitting in the back of the landscaping truck, pounding away on his laptop, when, fifteen minutes ago, Joseph's car had come roaring around the corner and turned into his driveway. Quickly, Ryan had squatted down low, staying that way as the assemblyman jumped out of the car and strode into the house.

Tightly coiled, Ryan had poised himself to listen to whatever Joseph told his wife. But nothing came. Not a sound from Joseph's office. In fact, you could hear a pin drop. Which meant that Donna wasn't in there, and now, neither was Joseph.

Ryan had sworn under his breath. Obviously, Lina's parents were talking behind different closed doors. And there was no way in hell that he could get inside the manor to catch that all-important discussion.

He was racking his brain for a creative solution when the front door flew open again, and Joseph and Donna both exited the manor, climbed into Joseph's car, and took off.

Where the hell were they going?

Scrambling into the front seat, Ryan turned over the ignition, eased the truck away from the curb, and as per what he'd learned from Marc and Patrick, followed close—but not too close—behind the Brandos' car.

It was his turn to do the tailing.

Offices of Forensic Instincts
12:45 p.m.

The initial emotional wave had passed, and Gia, Dani, and Lina had already begun forming the unique bond that identical triplets shared. They'd talked, laughed, and even nibbled at some of the lunch Casey had ordered, celebrating their union with the FI team.

But now was the time for questions, answers, and a search for the truth—a truth that, with the aid of Forensic Instincts, would free the girls from danger and put whoever was after them behind bars.

With Gia's and Dani's consent, Casey opened her mouth to bring Lina up to speed.

Her cell phone vibrated—once, twice, then repeatedly, showing no signs of going silent.

Quickly, Casey glanced at the phone display, saw that the call was from Ryan, and rose. This had to be important or he wouldn't be calling. He knew what was going on at this end.

"I really have to take this," she told the girls. "It'll be quick. Then I'll pick up where I left off."

She walked off into a corner of the room, keeping her back to the group.

"Yes, Ryan," she said quietly into the mouthpiece.

"Sorry to interrupt," he said without prelude. "But this couldn't wait."

"Go on."

He ran through the events that had occurred since he'd spoken to them in the van. "I'm in the truck, following Joseph and Donna Brando. Obviously, Joseph's already talked to Jimmy. I have no idea what was said or what Brando now knows. But there's something *you* should know. Jimmy Colone disappeared a month after the Pontis' murders and the triplets' kidnapping. That can't be a coincidence."

"Disappeared?"

"As in fell off the face of the earth. There's no record of him being anywhere, doing anything since he was eighteen. No credit cards. No phone records. No job. No addresses. Nothing."

Casey's heart was pounding. "You're thinking he did the hit and Angelo arranged his disappearance to protect him."

"Makes sense, doesn't it?"

"On all fronts, yes. It would explain why the triplets were separated. Angelo was afraid that keeping them together would alert law enforcement to the coincidental timing of a double homicide and the adoption of the victims' three missing babies. He was probably terrified that an investigation would lead them to Jimmy. So he split them up and organized three separate adoptions."

"Which worked—until now," Ryan said. "Gia and Dani found each other and Jimmy is freaking out. His big brother's not around to protect him, there's no statute of limitations on murder, and he's fighting for survival."

Casey's fingers tightened on the phone. "Plus he now realizes that Lina's about to learn the truth. Everything's unraveling. That's going to push him closer to doing something drastic." She sucked in her breath. "Ryan, we've *got* to find Jimmy Colone."

"Let's see where the Brandos are headed," Ryan replied. "Maybe they're going back to confront him together. If they do, I'll be all over it."

"Call Patrick. He's obviously still on the road. Tell him where you are and in what direction you're headed. He'll be armed. And he'll catch up with you. Call me when he does."

* * *

Casey disconnected the call, took a second to clear her head, and then rejoined the group. Time to fill Lina in on everything and to see what Lina might know without realizing that she did. And to that end, time for Casey to reverse her earlier decision not to tell the girls who FI believed their natural parents were, as well as how they'd died. Everything tied to Jimmy Colone, and he was now FI's number one suspect.

"I'll start from the beginning," Casey told Lina. "First come the facts that led Gia and Dani to hire us, and then the events that followed."

Lina listened intently to every word Casey said, until she was up to speed on everything Gia and Dani already knew. She was clearly distraught but equally puzzled by some of the nuances of the story.

"Why hasn't anyone come after me?" she asked. "I've had no threats on my life, not even a menacing letter or phone call. Is it because I didn't find Gia and Dani the way they found each other?" A pained pause. "Or is it because you think my father is somehow involved in this and I'm being protected?"

"Probably both." Casey leaned forward, her gaze fixed on Lina. "Tell us everything you can about Angelo Colone."

Rather than looking surprised, Lina sighed. "Once you said you believed my dad knew more than he was saying, I assumed this would somehow involve Uncle Angelo. I'm not sure what to tell you. I was his goddaughter, I'm named after him, and I loved him very much. But I was also aware of his mob connections. They just never affected me in any way. My only exposure to him was family dinners, birthday parties, lots of presents, hugs, and laughter. The rest..." She shrugged. "I was never privy to it. Nor did I want to be." Her eyes widened. "Do you think his death incited whoever's doing this to try to hurt Gia and Dani?"

"It's increasing his anxiety," Claire responded in that quiet, far-away voice that said she was speaking from sensory perception. "But it's not why he's going after Gia and Dani. Their finding each other triggered that. And whatever act caused you three to be separated is what's driving him."

"You sound as if you know what that act was." Perceptive as always, Lina made her assessment while studying Casey's body language.

"I believe we do," Casey said, sparing Claire from having to hedge. "We think this all ties into a double homicide that happened a month after you were born."

At this point, all three girls were sitting up straight, staring at Casey as they waited for answers.

"We don't have hard-core evidence, but the coincidence of those murders is too great to ignore." Casey took out a copy of the tiny article Ryan had produced and leaned forward to hand it to the girls. "The couple that was killed were Anthony and Carla Ponti. All signs point to the fact that they were your biological parents."

Three audible gasps as, with a trembling hand, Lina took the article, and the three girls huddled together, poring over every word.

"The Pontis were shot to death in their home in Bay Ridge, Queens, and their infant triplets were kidnapped from the crime scene," Lina read aloud. "No suspects have been identified, no murder weapon has been found, and there were no witnesses on the scene." Her voice cracked. "Our parents," she whispered.

"There's no other explanation." Dani pressed her hands to her face, the realization as crushing as Casey had known it would be.

Gia was practically vibrating with shock. "What else do you know?" she demanded.

"We know that Anthony Ponti worked for Angelo Colone's construction company," Casey replied. "He made collections for him."

The implication sank in.

"You think it was a mob hit," Lina said. "You think that Unc... that Angelo Colone had the Pontis killed and had us kidnapped."

"But why take us?" Gia spoke up before Casey could respond. "I get the mob hit. Anthony Ponti probably helped himself to some extra cash that he wasn't entitled to. So he and his wife were killed. But why take three infants? Why not just leave us in our cribs? We weren't exactly what you'd call witnesses. Plus, three babies would be a huge burden for an escaping killer to juggle. It doesn't make sense."

"My guess?" Casey replied. "We know that Angelo and Lina's father were best friends. If the Brandos were desperate for a child, Joseph might very well have shared that fact with Angelo."

"After which Angelo provided them with one?" Lina looked ill. "I was a commodity that was exchanged out of goodwill and friendship?" Bitterness laced her tone. "Given how tight the two of them were, why wouldn't Angelo just have turned over all three of us? My parents could have struck gold three times over."

Casey hurt deeply for Lina's pain. But she pushed on, because it had to be done. "That's not the way Angelo wanted it. He wanted to split the three of you up. So he made careful plans for three separate adoptions—adoptions that would keep you three from ever finding each other."

"Why go to all that trouble?"

"My opinion? Angelo was protecting his hitman."

Again, all three girls startled.

"You *know* who killed the Pontis?" Dani asked, turning up her palms. "Why are Gia and I first hearing about this?"

"Because we only figured it out three minutes ago," Casey replied. "That phone call I just took from Ryan fit the pieces together." She sidestepped the oncoming questions to ask Lina one of her own. "What do you know about Angelo's brother, Jimmy?"

Lina stared. "Not much. Is that who killed our... parents?"

"It looks that way. So please, try to think of anything—*anything*—Angelo might have said about his brother."

Frowning, Lina racked her brain. "I know Angelo was all about family, and Jimmy was the only blood tie he had. I know he had a soft spot in his heart for Jimmy—he'd tell us how smart he was, how successful he'd be. And I know that Jimmy moved away when I was an infant, so I never met him."

"So Angelo spoke of him in the present tense—like he was alive and thriving somewhere other than New York?"

"I guess so, yes." Lina gave a definitive shake of her head. "This doesn't make sense. The way Angelo talked—he was super-protective of Jimmy. Why would he put him in danger by making him a hitman?"

"He didn't." It was Claire who answered the question, a spark of awareness in her faraway gaze. She was connecting with Jimmy via his high level of panic—both then and now. "Jimmy did this on his own, a way to impress his big brother. It all went wrong. Only Anthony was supposed to be killed. The shot that killed Carla was meant for him. Jimmy freaked out, just like he's freaking out now.

That recurring emotion—that's what I'm sensing. His world was falling apart then. It's falling apart again now."

"The mob has rules," Marc murmured. "No women, no children."

Claire nodded. "Having broken those rules, all Jimmy could think about was Angelo's reaction. He'd be livid. So he tried to make amends. Rather than abandoning three orphaned infants, he took the three of you and brought you to Angelo. After that…" The veil over Claire's eyes lifted. "You know the rest."

At that moment, Casey's cell phone vibrated again, Ryan's number flashing on her screen. She gave a quick glance at her watch, surprised to see that almost forty minutes had passed since his last call.

This time she answered right where she was. "What's happening?"

"Patrick and I are both on the move together. I'm right behind him. The Brandos just left Lina's apartment. They're clearly trying to find her. And as a quick heads-up, it looks like they're headed for Tribeca."

"Then we'll be ready," Casey replied. "Thanks. When you get here, you and Patrick stay put outside the building. I'll handle this."

She hung up and turned to Lina. "Your parents are on their way here."

CHAPTER 35

"No." Lina jumped up, looking around as if to seek sanctuary. "I can't face them. I *won't* face them. Not yet. Not until it's on *my* terms. Please, Casey, don't do this to me."

"I have no intentions of it." Casey exuded calm and control in an effort to tamper Lina's rising hysteria. "You, Dani, and Gia will stay here with the team. I'll go out there and speak to your parents." She paused, then gestured at Lina's purse. "Check your messages."

"Why?"

"Because I want to see what we're dealing with."

On trembling legs, Lina rose, going over and opening her purse. She pulled out her phone and checked. "I have a half-dozen texts and a ton of voice mails from them," she reported woodenly. She scanned the texts. "They're all the same, either begging or demanding that I call them." She handed the cell to Casey. "You can listen to the voice messages. I'm not."

Casey nodded, taking the phone and running through the process quickly, listening to each message. "They're pretty much the same as the texts, just increasingly desperate." She looked at Lina. "No matter what happens, I do believe they love you."

Lina dragged a hand through her hair. "I don't know how you can love someone and keep a secret like this. Maybe I'm too upset to even consider their side of things. But that's the way it is. I need to regroup. Then I'll talk to them."

Another nod. "Obviously, they realize you've spoken with us. So I have to tell them we gave you the truth about being a triplet. Otherwise, they'll know I'm lying and all hell will break loose. And with your permission, I'd like carte blanche about what else I say. Maybe the right provocation will trip them up and make them give something away."

Without hesitation, Lina agreed. "Go ahead. I don't care what you tell them. I'll be having it out with them soon enough. But in the meantime, just keep them away from me, and from Gia and Dani." Without realizing it, Lina turned to her sisters for comfort. And also without realizing it, each of them offered it—Dani with a hug and Gia with a supportive stroke of her shoulder and soothing words.

The moments that followed were tense.

Finally, the front doorbell sounded—a prolonged ring that meant one of the Brandos was leaning on it.

"My facial recognition database says that Joseph and Donna Brando are here," Yoda supplied. "They are highly agitated, judging from their vital signs."

"I'm sure they are," Casey answered, already rising and heading out. "Thanks, Yoda."

She went straight to the front door, punched the entry code into the Hirsch pad, and let the Brandos in.

"Where's our daughter?" Joseph marched past Casey and planted himself in the hallway, gazing rapidly around. His wife followed suit, her eyes swollen and red from crying.

"I have no idea," Casey replied. "Why don't you call her and ask—or isn't she speaking to you?"

Joseph's eyes narrowed in anger. "Don't play me, Ms. Woods. Donna and I have left a dozen messages. We've also checked in with her friends and stopped off at her apartment. She's nowhere to be found. Which leads me to believe you've filled her in on your theory."

Casey folded her arms across her chest. "It's not a theory. It's a fact. And, yes, we told her. It was necessary to the investigation we're conducting. And frankly, she has the right to know."

"It was *our* right to tell her," Donna shot back. "She's *our* daughter."

"Donna." Joseph silenced his wife before she could say anything else incriminating. She'd just admitted that there was something Lina should be told, which was all but admitting that FI's accusations were true.

Casey seemed neither surprised nor disturbed by the admission. "It's not necessary to censor your wife's words, Mr. Brando. As Marc and I told you earlier, we have concrete DNA evidence. We also have proof that all three girls' birth records were forged. So, whether or not you discuss the truth, we have it."

Joseph bristled. "I'll repeat my question. Where is our daughter? You obviously communicated with her either by phone or in person to tell her your theory." He wasn't going to back down about using that word.

"We met with her earlier," Casey said, her own stare telling him that she wasn't intimidated. "We relayed the facts. She was very upset. My guess is that she needs some time and space to absorb the enormity of what she learned."

"Is she all right?" Donna asked, her motherly concern outweighing her discretion. "You say she was upset. How upset? She must have been emotionally crushed."

"Lina is a strong young woman," Casey replied, feeling a twinge of sympathy for Donna Brando. It was unclear how much she knew about Angelo's involvement in the adoption. But either way, she loved Lina. And Lina loved her. Deception or not, she'd raised and nurtured Lina from infancy to adulthood. She was the only mother

Lina had ever known. "Lina will come through this, Mrs. Brando. She has a great support system."

"A great support…" Donna caught on to that before Joseph did. "You're not referring to her friends, are you?"

"No. I'm not."

Donna swallowed hard. "You're talking about the other two girls you claim are her sisters. Does that mean she's met them?"

"A short while ago, yes. She could very well be with them right now. They have a lot to share and to catch up on."

Donna had begun to cry. "Can you tell us about them?" She shot her husband a look that said *I'm doing this.* "Whether or not your claim about them being triplets is true, I need to know."

"And *I* need to know about this supposed investigation you're conducting that led you to Lina in the first place," Joseph said.

"Our investigations are confidential—as are the identities of the other parties involved." Casey gestured toward a nearby anteroom. "But in this case, interviewing you is critical. So let's talk." A quick glance at Joseph. "We're not the enemy, Mr. Brando. We're actually protecting your daughter from possible danger."

"Danger?" He looked alarmed, which was exactly the reaction Casey was hoping for. Like his wife, he loved Lina. "What danger?"

Donna was already halfway to the anteroom. "Joseph, let's hear what Ms. Woods has to say. If Lina is in danger, we need to know how and why."

The three of them sat down in the leather chairs. Casey didn't insult them by offering them refreshment. This wasn't a social call.

"What do you know about a man named Anthony Ponti and his wife, Carla?" Casey purposely didn't give them time to think. The first reaction was usually the real one.

Both the Brandos looked blank.

"Who?" Joseph asked.

Casey repeated the names.

Again, blank.

"We have no idea. Tell us who they are and why you're asking," Joseph said.

"They *were* a young couple who lived in Brooklyn. They were shot and killed in their own home. The killer was never found."

"That's horrible," Donna said. "But what does it have to do with Lina?"

Casey sidestepped the question. "Anthony worked for your friend, Angelo Colone. He handled collections for Colone's construction company." A pause, during which time Casey angled her head in Joseph's direction. "You do represent that company, correct?"

For the first time, Joseph shifted in his seat. "My firm does, yes. Neil is the attorney of record. I handle Angelo's estate and I handled his personal affairs. I doubt you'll be surprised to hear that he and I were childhood friends."

"I'm also not surprised to hear you separated yourself from his questionable businesses. Any hint of impropriety, either then or especially now that your career goals are so much loftier, would put an end to your political future."

Joseph's eyes narrowed. "Are you threatening me, Ms. Woods?"

"I'm reminding you that being forthcoming is in your best interests."

"If Joseph won't, I will," Donna surprised her by saying. "But please, tell us where you're headed with this story about the murdered couple. Are you suggesting that Angelo had something to do with their deaths?"

"Donna." Joseph cut her off again. "Let's listen, not ask questions."

For the moment, Donna complied.

"Since you and Angelo grew up together, I assume you knew Jimmy Colone, as well."

"Of course I did," Joseph replied. Casey could see the pulse at his neck beat a little faster. "He was Angelo's kid brother. He followed us around, always trying to please Angelo. And Angelo was always protective of him. Jimmy took off when he was a teenager. There's nothing else to say."

"So you have no idea where he is?"

"None. Why would I?"

"Interesting about his disappearance," Casey said thoughtfully. "He vanished a month after the Pontis were killed. That was twenty-seven years ago. Oh, and I neglected to mention one key point. The Pontis had triplets. Three identical baby girls. They were kidnapped from the murder scene."

"Oh dear God." Donna swayed in her seat. "Are you saying those are the triplets… that Lina…"

"Donna," Joseph snapped, although his own face had gone sheet white.

"I'm only stating the facts," Casey replied. "And the final fact is that, as of a few weeks ago, physical threats have been made against two of the triplets. I have no reason to believe that Lina won't be next. Unless you can think of a reason why she'd be spared?"

"Joseph…" Donna began, staring at her husband.

"We're leaving." Joseph came to his feet. "We have to find our daughter, to make sure she's safe."

"Very well." Casey rose, too, closing with a bomb that had just occurred to her. "If that's the way you want to play it, fine. But let me leave you with one parting thought, Mr. Brando. I'd follow your wife's lead on this one. Because for twenty-seven years, there's been a killer out there, and an unsolved murder case that I'm sure the NYPD would be glad to close. The girls want closure, as well. So, with their testimony, the tampered birth records we've uncovered, and the DNA evidence we have, I'm sure we can get a court order to exhume the Pontis' bodies."

Donna gasped, but this time, Casey ignored it, determined to drive home her point.

"One test would prove, beyond the shadow of a doubt, that Anthony and Carla Ponti were the girls' natural parents. At which point, the girls would be well within their rights to reopen the case. So think about it while you're searching for Lina. Cooperate and you're merely a man who was so desperate to adopt a baby that he didn't ask questions about the paperwork involved. Fight us and you could be found complicit in a double homicide."

CHAPTER 36

Park Slope, Brooklyn, New York
2:05 p.m.

Jimmy sat down heavily on the edge of his bed, wiping the perspiration off his face, taking deep breaths to steady his nerves.

His whole life was about to be obliterated—again. And this time, it would be forever.

He reminded himself that he was a survivor and that, thanks to Angelo's guidance, he'd learned to do what had to be done. He wasn't eighteen anymore. He was far older, more mature, and definitely prepared. He'd been making provisions for years now, just in case. He'd set up that offshore account in the Cayman Islands. He'd been stashing large amounts of cash in his home safe. And his passport had been ready and waiting for this one-way trip to Montenegro.

After his telltale meeting with Joseph today, he'd set the wheels in motion. He'd withdrawn the maximum amount of money from his local bank account and wired the rest to his Cayman Islands account. He'd emptied his home safe of the stacks of cash, his passport, and the antique pistol Angelo had passed down to him from their father— the very pistol that had killed the Pontis and started this snowballing nightmare. He probably should have dumped the weapon a long time ago. But he couldn't. Partly because he was terrified that the cops would find it and partly because it was a gift from Angelo. And now—it was just as well that he'd kept it, just in case he needed it again.

He'd chartered a plane from New Jersey's Teterboro Airport to Podgorica Airport, Montenegro—a country that had no extradition policy with the US. The flight plan was filed and the jet was ready to go. And his bags were packed and loaded in the trunk of his car—all but the duffel that contained the items from his safe. That bag was right by his side, where it would remain.

So, yeah, this time he was ready. He'd followed Angelo's advice to a tee. His big brother might be gone, but he'd coached Jimmy carefully, reminding him all these years that, given the nature of his crime, he might someday have to truly vanish at a moment's notice. The escape plan was well thought out, even though both brothers hoped and prayed that it would never have to be implemented. But as they both knew, life happens.

Well, life had just happened. And it was time to go.

For the umpteenth time, Jimmy cursed himself for the events of twenty-seven years ago. Why the hell had he taken it upon himself to make that hit? Angelo had already arranged for one of his mob soldiers to do it. But Jimmy had jumped the gun, confident that he could do it faster, better, determined—yet again—to prove himself to Angelo. Instead of coming out the hero, he'd screwed everything up. Rather than making Angelo proud, he'd showed up at his doorstep like a whimpering child, freaked out to the max and juggling three squalling infants in his arms. As if, by giving them to Angelo to shape their lives rather than leaving them for the cops to find, he'd be making up for blowing away their mother.

What an asshole he'd been.

He'd poured out the whole story to his brother. And, shit, had Angelo been ripping pissed—especially about the babies he now had to deal with.

"Why didn't you leave them there?" he'd snapped. "You'd fucked up enough already. What do I look like, a goddamned wet nurse? What am I supposed to do with them?"

But in the end, Angelo had calmed down, and he'd known just what to do. He'd called on one of the young lawyers on his payroll to play the part of Constantin Farro, adoption lawyer. The attorney had drawn up the necessary papers, made the necessary visits, and once the job was done, gotten a fat payment in exchange for fading into the woodwork. Angelo had used his far-reaching connections to doctor records, forge birth certificates, and—most of all—to make provisions for Jimmy's disappearance.

Fulfilling Joseph's and Donna's dream had been the one thing that had quieted Angelo's rage. He knew how badly they wanted a child, how long and hard they'd tried to have one, and how heartbroken they were at the lack of results. This was Angelo's chance to give them one. And he'd made that happen, too. He'd also carefully chosen the other two couples—the Russos and the Muranos-- because they were so desperate to adopt a child that they were willing to accept all conditions without question. Still, in the event that, over time, they "forgot" the rules, he'd put long-term surveillance into place to ensure there were no violations.

It had all come together. And it would have stayed that way if two of those fucking triplets hadn't found each other.

Jimmy rose from the bed. The time for reflection was over. It was time. He had to leave his cushy life behind and run.

He'd just grabbed his duffel bag when his cell phone rang.

His iPhone screen told him it was Joseph.

Jimmy couldn't ignore him. The risk was too great. Given the precarious state of affairs right now, Joseph would track him down like a hunted deer if he blew him off. And Jimmy had no idea how much more Joseph had learned.

He had to answer and find out.

"Hey." Jimmy wondered if Joseph could hear his heart pounding right through the phone.

"I'm headed home," Joseph replied in a voice as hard as stone. "Meet me at the gazebo. Leave now."

"Why? What's going on?"

"We'll discuss it when you get there."

Click.

Office of Forensic Instincts
2:15 p.m.

The tension that filled the brownstone was palpable.

So much had happened during the minutes since the Brandos had taken off that everyone's head was spinning.

The door had barely shut behind Joseph and Donna when Casey called Patrick, striding back to the sitting room as she did.

She collided with Lina, who'd been hovering in the hallway, listening. This time, instead of looking devastated, she looked furious.

Casey held up one finger as she spoke to Patrick, who was parked directly across from the brownstone.

"The Brandos just left," she told him, crossing the threshold to the room where everyone waited. "They claimed they were leaving to search for Lina. My gut tells me they're headed to meet Jimmy. Follow them." She met Marc's gaze and tipped her head toward the door, giving him a tacit signal. "Marc's coming with you, just in case there's trouble."

Marc was out the door before she hung up.

Casey turned to Lina. "I'm sorry for what you overheard," she said simply.

"You have nothing to be sorry about. My parents do." Lina's chin was set in an uncompromising line. "I'm confronting them—now," she announced. "I know what I said a few minutes ago, but the conversation you just had changed everything. My father's hiding something major. I might not be his natural child, but I know him well. I'm also as stubborn as he is. So whatever information he's hiding, I'm getting it out of him." Her gaze met Gia's and Dani's. "I'm catching the next ferry to Todt Hill. I'll wait for my parents there."

"Wait." Casey grabbed her arm. "Let me find John Nickels. He's probably close by, waiting to give Gia and Dani a ride home. I'd rather you not go to your parents' place alone, not when I can't predict Jimmy Colone's next move."

"I'm not worried."

"Well, I am."

Quickly, Casey called John and explained.

"I'm a few blocks away having a cup of coffee," he said. "I'll get the car and be there."

Gia's and Dani's anxious gazes were on Lina, and they both stood up and went to her.

"What can we do?" Gia asked.

"Just send good vibes my way." A weak smile touched Lina's lips. "And be here when I come back. I'm bringing answers. This charade is ending today."

"Please be careful," Dani said. "This Jimmy Colone is dangerous."

"Not to me." Lina sounded almost guilty as she spoke. "That's why I haven't been touched. Angelo's loyalty to me and my family must have extended to his brother, as well. So I'm being spared while the two of you have been through hell. I'm so sorry."

Casey's cell phone rang.

"I'm back and in my lair," Ryan reported. "Patrick called to let me know that he and Marc have the Brandos covered. So I'm down here digging up info on Jimmy Colone. I'm getting somewhere. Tell the girls to hang tight."

Casey had barely hung up when John Nickels called to say he was right outside the building.

Lina hugged both her sisters and took off.

Claire stared after her, her brows drawn and a flicker of apprehension in her eyes.

"What is it?" Casey asked.

"I'm not sure that Lina's really free of danger," Claire replied. "We're missing something, something besides Jimmy's frantic state. A plan, a deception—both." Claire massaged her temples. "I'm uneasy—no, I'm worried."

"Should we be doing something more?" Casey asked.

A tentative shrug. "Other than that one time I experienced an emotional connection, I've never felt in touch with Jimmy Colone. Maybe it's because he's cast in a strange web of shadows. Maybe it's because I never had a personal item of his to hold or touch. But he keeps fading in and out of my awareness. Sometimes I can almost grab on to the feeling, and then it dissipates. He's there, and then he's not. It's frustrating. But I am deeply connected with the girls. So that apprehensive feeling that I have... let's just say I'm glad Marc and Patrick will be following the Brandos and that John will be with Lina. Because something's not right."

Brooklyn Bridge
2:20 p.m.

Donna stared out the passenger seat window of their car, watching the water below and feeling as if her entire world was crumbling around her.

"Why didn't you tell Casey Woods the truth?" she blurted out.

"You know the answer to that." Joseph was driving home on autopilot, as tormented as his wife about the current crisis. "I'd be admitting to being complicit in events I knew nothing about."

"What about those you did? You knew Lina wasn't our natural child. You knew Angelo made arrangements for us to have her. You knew questionable strings were pulled to make that happen. You knew—and so did I." Donna dabbed at her eyes with a tissue. "But at the time, we didn't care. We didn't ask a single question. And now... dear God, we're paying the dearest of prices. Worse, so is Lina."

Joseph's hands tightened on the wheel. "When Angelo brought Lina to us, we had no idea what Jimmy had done or that she was one of three triplets. So, yes, we leaped at the chance of having a child. Do you remember the depth of your depression before then? You wouldn't even leave the house except to go to those support group meetings with other women desperate for a child. I was terrified I'd lose you, that's how bad you were."

"I remember. I also remember that that's how we managed to invent that story about my high risk pregnancy confining me to bedrest for a huge chunk of my term."

"It worked. And because of it and thanks to Angelo, we got Lina. And given the circumstances, we were desperate to protect her."

"So we lied." Donna wasn't putting on blinders anymore. "We told her she was our natural child. We invented a beautiful lie about her birth."

"Okay, fine," Joseph snapped. "We looked the other way. We latched onto our opportunity. We brought Lina up believing she was our biological child. We're not the first set of parents to do that, and it's a choice, not an illegality. So that's the extent of our guilt. But confessing to the adoption would bring us under investigation for a double homicide. I can't allow that—not for my political future, but mostly not for Lina."

"That's out of our hands now, Joseph, and you know it. Casey Woods says she has DNA evidence, and I believe her. So the investigation Forensic Instincts is conducting will bring the truth to light."

Joseph pressed down on the gas pedal. "The only way to extricate ourselves from the allegations of murder and kidnapping is to get Jimmy to admit the truth. And he's about to—if I have to beat it out of him."

Three cars behind them, Patrick turned onto the BQE and followed as they headed for the Verrazano Bridge to Staten Island.

CHAPTER 37

The Brando house
2:50 p.m.

"I don't want you going in alone," John Nickels told Lina as they pulled into her parents' driveway.

Lina turned to him, a resolute expression on her face.

"I appreciate that, Mr. Nickels," she said. "But these are *my* parents, and I'm handling this on my own. They're certainly not going to hurt me. If anything, they've gone to extremes to protect me. So I'm not in danger. You can wait out here if it makes you feel better. But I *am* going in alone."

John looked uneasy, but he didn't argue. He'd stay put and keep his eyes wide open. Any sign of trouble, he'd be all over it.

Lina got out of the passenger side and leaned in the car window. "I truly appreciate your concern, Mr. Nickels. But I'll be fine. And thank you for getting me here."

With that, she turned and marched up to the front door.

2:55 p.m.

Marc and Patrick waited until Joseph's car turned into the driveway before parking the van in a quiet alcove diagonally across the street. An average vehicle in this neighborhood would be too ho-hum to give a second glance to.

"Brando must be meeting Jimmy here," Marc said, double-checking to make sure his pistol was loaded and ready. "We'd better start prowling around, in case our target got here first."

As Patrick reached for his gun, his cell phone rang.

"Yeah, John." His brows went up. "Already? That's not good. I'll explain later. Just stay where you are. I'll call if I need you." He hung up and turned to Marc. "Lina's here. John dropped her off right before we drove up. He's parked in the driveway. No need for concealment, since he's her driver. And he's on standby, just in case."

"That still doesn't make me happy," Marc replied, already out of the van. "None of us know what Lina is walking into."

"We'd better change that now."

Office of Forensic Instincts
3:05 p.m.

Ryan's eyes narrowed on his computer screen. He was getting really pissed.

Much as he'd try to dig into Jimmy Colone's background, all he could find was what he'd already told Casey. Nothing further about his personal life, no family photos—not even of him and Angelo—nothing. It was as if he were deliberately being kept under the radar. It didn't take a genius to figure out that Angelo had found the right members of the press to separate Jimmy from him and from the mob. But the extent to which he'd gone was beyond extreme. And Ryan's hands were somewhat tied, since Jimmy had disappeared over twenty-seven years ago, when there were no social media avenues to explore. He'd hit a fucking dead end.

Or had he?

Ryan sat up straight, his mind going a mile a minute. Angelo Colone had grown up in Brooklyn. The odds were that whatever high school he'd attended, Jimmy had attended, too.

Based on Joseph Brando's age, Ryan quickly figured out the years that Angelo would be in grades nine through twelve. Then, as quickly as his fingers could fly across the keyboard, Ryan hacked into the New York City Board of Education office.

Brooklyn High School. That was Angelo's high school alma mater. He'd graduated in 1982.

That meant Jimmy would have graduated in 1989.

No more hacking necessary. Ryan logged into e-yearbook.com and called up the 1980 Brooklyn High School edition. Exactly what he needed appeared. Pages of all the graduates, their nicknames, career goals, and photos.

He scanned through the pages until he got to the C's. Several pages to get to Colone. But there he was—James "Jimmy" Colone. Baseball player with the goal of becoming a lawyer.

Ryan blinked. The kid looked familiar—too familiar.

An eerie feeling crawled up his spine.

"Yoda, I need you to run this photo through your facial recognition software," he said. "But first, morph him into a forty-five-year-old. The guy would be twenty-seven years older now than he was then."

"Facial recognition software search underway," Yoda replied. A short while later, he announced, "Facial recognition complete after age enhancement applied. Photos printing now."

Ryan hung over the printer until the photos came through. He took one look at them and then raced for the stairs, taking them two at a time.

He burst into the room where the rest of his teammates, and Gia and Dani, were waiting for news of any kind.

"Casey." He shoved the photos at her. "I know where Jimmy Colone disappeared to. Photo one is a graduation picture. Photo two is Jimmy Colone today—sans his broken nose and a few other cosmetic tweaks."

Casey's gaze darted from one picture to the other. Then she raised her head, her expression utterly stunned.

"My God," she breathed. "Jimmy Colone is Neil Donato."

CHAPTER 38

The Brando gazebo
3:05 p.m.

Joseph arrived at the white lattice structure to find his campaign manager already waiting for him. He was standing, feet planted, clearly ignoring the bench, and poised and ready for whatever confrontation Joseph had in mind. Oddly, he exuded an air of calm that Joseph hadn't expected.

Then again, he had no idea how much Joseph knew.

"I assume this isn't about the campaign," Neil began as Joseph stalked up to him.

"No. It's not."

"Then it's about Lina." An irritated sigh. "I told you everything."

"That's a crock of shit." Joseph's eyes were blazing. "What you told me is that you had no clue where the triplets came from. I'll refresh your memory. They came from their natural parents, Anthony and Carla Ponti, the couple you shot to death in Brooklyn twenty-seven years ago."

Neil's head jerked back in surprise, but Joseph didn't wait for a denial.

"You brought those babies to Angelo, and he split them up and turned the world upside down to protect you. *You*, you son of a bitch.

You. My long-term legal associate, my family friend, my campaign manager. I gave you your first job, took you under my wing, and made you a part of my family."

"What do you want, Joseph?" Neil demanded, abandoning all pretense. "I love your family. I kept you all out of this, not just because Angelo wanted it that way but because *I* did."

"You did this to save your own ass. It's why you had to vanish so quickly, not because Angelo was keeping you away from the mob the way he told me but because he was keeping you out of jail. What do I want? I want you to look me in the eye and admit the truth. I want you to provide the authorities with a full confession. I want you to flush yourself down the toilet and exonerate me of any wrongdoing."

"Now who's saving his own ass?" Neil shot back. "Plus, you're crazy. You want me to look you in the eye and admit that everything you just said is true? Fine, consider it done. I killed the Pontis and took their three kids. But you're insane if you think I'm turning myself in. Prison? After all these years? No fucking way."

"Fine. Then I'll do it." Joseph reached into his pocket and pulled out his iPhone. "The voice recorder app—a wonderful tool." He tapped the icon and played a few sentences back to Neil. "I'll be playing this for the cops and the FBI—who I'm calling right now." He opened the phone app to press 9-1-1.

Neil's composure snapped.

"Give me that!" He lunged forward, grabbing for the cell phone.

Joseph held it out of reach and punched Neil in the gut.

Neil recovered quickly, groping in his pocket and pulling out a gun. With a shaking hand, he pointed it at Joseph.

"Don't make me do this, Joseph," he said. "Just give me that cell phone and let me walk away. You'll never see me again."

Joseph went still, his stunned gaze fixed on the weapon.

"You're not going to shoot me, Jimmy," he said at last, purposely using Neil's real name. "You're no more of a killer now than you were twenty-seven years ago. You screwed it up then and you'll screw it up now."

Neil's lips thinned. "Don't call my bluff."

"I'll take my chances." With lighting speed, Joseph pressed 9-1-1, yelling out, "Help... a gunman is at my home..."

"Goddamn you!" Neil used the barrel of his gun to knock the phone to the floor, where it rattled just out of reach.

Joseph went after it. As he bent down to retrieve it, he spotted Lina in the distance, making her way through the thick grove of trees and approaching the gazebo.

He tried to call out to warn her, but Neil brought the butt of the gun down on his head, striking him as hard as he could.

Joseph crumpled to the ground, blood oozing from his head.

* * *

Through the tree branches, Lina could make out her father and her uncle Neil in the gazebo. She'd known her parents were home; her father's car was in the garage. Her mother was in the master bath crying, but Lina had purposely avoided her. It was her father she wanted to have it out with. Her mother would be too emotional to provide the hard-core answers she needed.

She'd searched the whole house, with no sign of her father. So she'd resorted to combing the grounds.

As she neared the gazebo, her heart leapt. Her father was lying on the floor, a pool of blood oozing from his head. And Neil was straightening to his feet, a gun clutched in his hand.

Lina broke into a run. "Dad!" she screamed, oblivious to the fact that she was placing herself in danger. "Oh my God, Dad."

She raced past Neil, kneeling down to check her father's pulse, to see if he was alive.

Thank God she felt the steady thud beneath her fingers.

"You did this." She twisted around to look up at Neil, her eyes glazed with non-comprehension. "Why? *Why?*" Out of the corner of her eye, she spotted her father's phone. She crawled over to snatch it up. "I'm calling an ambulance."

"The hell you are." Neil kicked the phone away, simultaneously grabbing Lina's arm and yanking her to her feet. He turned her around, locking her back against his chest and pressing the barrel of the gun to her temple.

"He'll bleed to death," she said on a sob. "Please..."

"Calm down, Lina." Neil locked an arm around her waist. "I didn't shoot him. I just knocked him out. The problem is, he called 9-1-1. Which means the police are on their way. So you're going to help me get out of here."

"Or what? You'll kill me?" Lina's chest was pounding as she desperately tried to sort this out. Why was Neil doing this? What was his part in this nightmare? "I've known you all my life. You're like family. Why would you do this?"

"No time for a Q and A," Neil replied, dragging her across the gazebo and down the steps. "We're getting out of here. I've got a plane to catch."

"Sorry, but we'll be canceling your reservations." Patrick's voice came from behind them, and Neil whipped around, clutching Lina tightly against him as he watched Patrick step out from a thicket of trees. Patrick's pistol was aimed at Neil, despite the fact that he didn't have a clean shot. "The only place you're going is to prison... Jimmy."

"Jimmy?" Lina lurched against him in shock. "You're Jimmy Colone?"

Neil stared at Patrick, his silence answering Lina's question.

Quickly, he turned his gun on Patrick, gesturing at Patrick's pistol. "I'd drop that if I were you. Or I'll blow your head off. And you won't touch me—not with Lina as my human shield."

Patrick hesitated for effect. Then he nodded. "Fine. Just take it easy." He bent, dropping his weapon to the grass and straightening to a standing position.

Neil's eyes narrowed. "Now that was a little too simple." He waved the pistol at Patrick's suit jacket. "Open that. Slowly and completely. We'll get to your pockets next. I want to see if you have any surprise weapons hidden."

Patrick complied, pulling open the sides of his jacket and spreading them wide.

Neil's concentration was on Patrick, which was just enough of a distraction for Lina to act.

She lifted her foot and slammed the heel of her Jimmy Choo into the arch of Neil's foot.

"Shit!" he howled, his grip on her going slack as he doubled over.

Lina wrenched herself free just as a shot rang out, piercing Patrick's jacket and striking Neil in the shoulder.

Neil cried out and jerked backwards, dropping his pistol and clutching his arm, as Marc stepped out from behind Patrick, where he'd been crouched low, waiting to strike.

Lina acted instantly. She picked up the gun before Neil could recover and raced over to hand it to Patrick. "My father..." she managed as Marc pushed Neil down, pinning him to the ground.

Sirens sounded in the distance, growing closer to the manor.

"Stay put." Patrick ran up the steps and over to Joseph's limp body. He checked his vitals and, without touching it, studied the head wound. The bleeding had already slowed down and the wound looked to be shallow.

"He'll be fine, Lina. I called for an ambulance the minute I saw him go down. The paramedics will be showing up any minute. Both they and the police know where we are on the property. I made sure of that." He returned to Lina's side and placed a paternal hand on her quaking shoulder. "It's over, honey."

"I love him," she whispered. "No matter what, he's my father. He's a good man. He's flawed, but..." She covered her face with her hands, sobbing as the emotional tidal wave finally struck.

"He *is* a good man," Patrick replied as the police cars raced around to the back of the house. "He's also a good father. Good parents will do anything to protect their children. And that's what he was trying to do—protect you. And now you've returned the favor, Lina. You protected him. You're a wonderful daughter. He'll tell you so himself the minute he wakes up."

"That might be sooner than you think," Marc said, tipping his head in Joseph's direction. The assemblyman was shifting around, groaning as he tried to pick up his head.

"Dad!" Lina blew by everyone to reach her father, taking his hand and gripping it in hers.

Joseph blinked, his unfocused gaze finding his daughter. "Lina," he murmured. "Thank God. He didn't hurt you." A pained pause. "So... sorry. So much... to explain."

"Later, Dad. We'll get through this. It's time for us to heal."

EPILOGUE

Casey glanced at her watch. The girls would be here any minute.

Gia had called from the train, telling Emma that she and Lina were taking Dani to the airport to fly home to a veterinary practice that was straining at the seams without her. The head partners had been more than understanding—but enough was enough. So Dani was Minneapolis bound, and her sisters were seeing her off. The three of them wanted to stop by and see the FI team first.

Glancing at the notes she'd typed into her iPad during the team's last debriefing session, Casey felt a deep sense of satisfaction.

The wheels of justice were already turning.

Jimmy Colone had had the bullet removed from his shoulder and was now in custody. The charges were extensive: a double homicide, three kidnappings, and a slew of ancillary crimes—not to mention what he'd done at the Brandos' gazebo the other day. As a result, he wouldn't be seeing the light of day for years, if ever. Al Carp—real name Alberto Costa—was in custody, as well. Ryan had easily found his contact information in Jimmy's phone, Gabe had identified him for the police, and the guy was talking a mile a minute to save his own ass by describing what Jimmy had hired him to do.

As for Gabe, it looked like he'd be facing a minimum sentence—most of which would be converted into community service—along with some intensive counseling.

Joseph Brando had been lucky. His injuries had been only a concussion and a nasty head wound that the hospital staff had stitched up in no time. He'd been released the next day and was home healing with Donna.

After a long, hard discussion, the entire Forensic Instincts team had agreed that Joseph Brando was primarily a victim. There was no reason to reveal details that might destroy his political career. He'd have his hands full anyway, between the reopening of the Pontis' murder case and the fact that Brando's campaign manager, Neil Donato, was, in fact, Jimmy Colone, brother of reputed mob leader Angelo Colone, and killer/kidnapper. But Casey had no doubt that Joseph and his team of lawyers would find a way to prove that he was completely ignorant of Neil's identity—due to the natural aging process and some damned fine plastic surgery—and that he was genuinely horrified by the reality of where his precious Lina had come from. That last crucial part was, of course, very true and very tragic.

The country's sympathy would be immediately evoked, especially after hearing how the Brandos had suffered and prayed for the miracle of a child, and their abounding joy in finally adopting one.

Consequently, the FI team would let things play out on their own and reveal nothing about the pieces of truth that would be omitted, that being Joseph's knowing Neil's real identity and watching out for him because Angelo had asked him to. The press would, of course, have a field day speculating, based on Joseph's lifetime friendship with Angelo, but there was only smoke with no discernable fire. And Casey and the team knew that, even though that fire did exist, the fact was that Joseph had been protecting Angelo's little brother from a life in the mob, not harboring a killer.

In her gut, Casey believed that this story would die down and Joseph's congressional goals would be fulfilled. But that was in the hands of the voters.

All in all, the total outcome of this investigation was positive.

Casey's thoughts were interrupted by the ringing of the front doorbell.

"Gia Russo, Danielle Murano, and Angelina Brando have arrived," Yoda announced.

"Thanks, Yoda. I'll show them in."

She opened the door to see three smiling, if exhausted, young women, juggling Dani's luggage and already planning their next get-together, this time in Dani's home city of Minneapolis. Lina was urging Dani to rethink her decision about pursuing that coveted veterinary position in New York. Dani wasn't flat-out dismissing the idea. And Gia was carrying a huge pastry box, which she immediately thrust at Casey.

"This came from my best dessert vendor," she said. "They bake a blackout cake—as Lina would say—to die for. Brides give up the idea of a white wedding cake the minute they taste this. In this case, I had them make it as a sheet cake so the whole team could enjoy it."

"There's no real way we can ever thank you all for what you've done for us," Dani added.

"But chocolate is always a good start." Lina grinned.

"Wow, thank you so much—and come on in." Casey was delighted to see the transition that was already occurring. All three girls were coming back to themselves—right down to Lina's natural exuberance. And they were already bonding as sisters.

It was truly a pleasure to behold.

Upstairs in the conference room, the entire team awaited, all of them greeting Gia, Dani, and Lina as the friends they'd become. Emma didn't lose a minute before getting plates, napkins, and utensils and then taking it upon herself to slice and serve the cake.

There were choruses of oohs and aahs as everyone tasted pieces of chocolate heaven.

"If I ever get married, I want this baker," Emma said, savoring the bite she'd just taken.

"I'll make a note of that," Gia assured her. "Blackout cake it will be. I'm planning a birthday party for my uncle. This is his cake of choice, too."

"Speaking of which, how are your parents?" Patrick asked. "All three sets."

"Mine are weak with relief that the danger's been eliminated," Dani replied. "They're meeting me at LaGuardia, and we're flying back to Minneapolis together. There's an enormous sense of relief that this whole thing is over, on every level."

"Same with my parents," Gia said. "All they want is for things to go back to normal and to not have to worry about my life being in jeopardy."

Lina stared down at her cake. "It's a little more complicated at my end, as you would expect. The process is slow."

"How's your father doing?" Claire asked gently.

"Physically, he's much better. Emotionally, he's still pretty shaken. Neil's—Jimmy's—betrayal hit him like a ton of bricks." Lina paused and looked up. "It's no secret to anyone in this room that my father knew who Neil was. But Angelo was his best friend. He took him at his word when he said he was making Jimmy disappear to protect him from being affiliated with the mob. He had no idea about the murders or the kidnappings." She sighed. "Between that and making peace with me about lying all these years... it's been tough."

"But down deep, you know your parents love you," Casey said. "And that will get you through this."

Lina nodded. "The Russos and the Muranos have been awesome. They're not only treating me like family, they're completely sympathetic to my parents' situation. They feel that, just as they are victims, so are my parents. There are no bad feelings at all."

"That's as it should be," Dani said. "Given how close your family was to Neil Donato, this is even harder for them than it is for our parents." She looped an arm around Lina's shoulders. "It's all going to work out."

"Without question," Gia agreed. "We're one big extended family now." She glanced at the grandfather clock in the corner. "And now we'd better run, or Dani will be chasing the plane down the runway. I'm sorry to cut this short."

"No problem." Casey put down her plate and went to hug each of the girls in turn. "But you'd better include us in your plans the next time Dani's in town."

"Promise."

The girls hugged every member of the FI team, said their good-byes, and followed Casey to the door. With additional promises to keep in touch, they gathered up Dani's luggage and headed out.

Casey retraced her steps, returning to the conference room to see Marc, Ryan, and Patrick wolfing down their second huge chunks of cake with no signs of slowing down.

"We're saving a piece for Hutch," Marc said between mouthfuls. "He's coming over right after work to celebrate with us. That should polish this baby off.'"

Emma and Claire rolled their eyes.

"It's a guy thing," Emma said wisely. "I might rethink that future wedding. I'll forget the husband and just opt for the blackout cake."

"Heaven forbid, what if one of us wanted a second piece of cake?" Claire asked.

"You'd be SOL," Ryan stated flatly. "When it comes to food, men rule."

"Wrong." Casey marched over, sliced off half the cake, and transferred it to a serving plate, which she brought over and stored in the mini-fridge. "When it comes to Forensic Instincts, *I* rule. And that half a cake has *FI women* written all over it."

Marc's brows rose in amusement. "In other words, case closed."

✱✱✱✱✱

ACKNOWLEDGEMENTS

My thanks to the following people who were instrumental in my creating *A Face to Die For*:

Retired FBI Supervisor Konrad Motyka
Angela Bell, FBI Office of Public Affairs
Paul Sedlacek, DVM
Vito Milano

We hope you enjoyed this book from Bonnie Meadow Publishing.

Connect with us on BonnieMeadowPublishing.com for more information on our new releases!

Other ways to keep in touch with Andrea Kane:

andreakane.com

facebook.com/AuthorAndreaKane/

@andrea_kane

goodreads.com/AKane

DISCARDED BY FREEPORT MEMORIAL LIBRARY